politically inspired

EDITED BY:
Stephen Elliott

ASSISTANT EDITOR:
Gabriel Kram

ASSOCIATE EDITORS:
Elizabeth Brooks
Harriet Clark
Anna Rimoch
Jenny Zhang

A portion of the proceeds from the sales of this book will go to Oxfam America's humanitarian response in Iraq. Oxfam America seeks lasting solutions to poverty, hunger, and social injustice around the world. Oxfam's humanitarian work in Iraq includes the delivery of clean water and safe sanitation as well as support for vulnerable and displaced children. Oxfam America relies on private donations and does not seek or accept U.S. government funding. For more information, we invite you to visit us at www.oxfamamerica.org. The ideas and opinions expressed in this book belong to the individual authors and do not reflect the views of Oxfam America.

MacAdam/Cage
155 Sansome Street, Suite 550
San Francisco, CA 94104
www.macadamcage.com

Library of Congress Cataloging-in-Publication Data

Politically inspired / edited by Stephen Elliott.
p. cm.
Includes bibliographical references.
ISBN 1-931561-58-3 (alk. paper) — ISBN 1-931561-45-1 (pbk. : alk. paper)
1. Political fiction, American. 2. United States—Politics and government—Fiction. 3. Current events—Fiction. I. Elliott, Stephen, 1971—

PS648.P6P65 2003
813.008'0358—dc22

2003017623

Manufactured in the United States of America.
10 9 8 7 6 5 4 3 2 1

Cover design by Gabriel Kram.
Book design by Dorothy Carico Smith.

politically inspired

EDITED BY:
Stephen Elliott

ASSISTANT EDITOR:
Gabriel Kram

ASSOCIATE EDITORS:
Elizabeth Brooks
Harriet Clark
Anna Rimoch
Jenny Zhang

MacAdam/Cage

Due to Heightened Security
Please Register at
www.politicallyinspired.org
Prior to Reading This Book

introduction

There was a time when I could separate politics from writing, or rather, separate my political writing from my fiction. Political writing was something I did when the urge hit me, a special project, like spending the summer in Gaza or touring in the Ralph Nader Campaign Van through the Deep South. I'm the opposite of many writers in that I make my living writing fiction and dabble in nonfiction. My fiction has been where I explore deep personal issues, my nonfiction where I connect with the world.

September 11th changed that. Our buildings were collapsing, and with them our freedom. People who questioned the government were labeled traitors. The Vice President was in hiding. American citizens were being held indefinitely without probable cause. Our civil liberties were eroding. Businesses like Halliburton and Bechtel were influencing our foreign policy and people would die. Our Attorney General didn't dance. He threw sheets over statues that were merely naked.

In the days that followed September 11th, I felt the way everyone else felt, dazed. I was unable to write anything. In October 2001 the Patriot Act went into effect. Plans were mounting for an attack on Afghanistan. I wasn't sure how I felt about all of it, but I couldn't think of anything else. As mountains were bombed into rock piles I began to feel that fiction was irrelevant.

Of course, fiction is always relevant. Fiction can illuminate and explore in ways that nonfiction can't. Because fiction can zoom in on individual fears and desires, illustrate different perspectives. Fiction can go further than nonfiction because it can test conclusions and follow events far ahead to their logical or illogical end. Fiction can teach. To quote Picasso, "Art is a lie that makes us realize the truth."

I started writing a weekly series of fiction based on political events. Some of it was published in *Adbusters*, *The Chicago Reader*, *Watchword*, and *The Sun*. The rest was syndicated through Alternet. I organized political fiction readings with Lydia Lunch and Michelle Tea. Then Elizabeth Tallent said I should put together an anthology. She said I'd meet interesting people.

I knew Elizabeth was right. She's my mentor. She's always right. I thought there was a movement here. OK, I'm a fiction writer, but I can still participate. I don't have to be blind, and I knew if I was obsessing over the issues of our time then other fiction writers were too. The world was coming in, the dam had burst, we couldn't hide. I thought we could do this, create an anthology of fiction representative of the new world we are living in, and it would matter and fiction would be relevant and we would raise money for a good cause, humanitarian aid in Iraq. It meant putting a lot of time into something and not getting paid for it. But many times I've gotten paid lots of money without working hard, like the time I broke into my boss's e-mail and discovered that he was putting nonemployees on the payroll and setting up people for phony sexual harassment suits. I got six months' severance for that, but that's another story. The point is, sometimes you get paid without working and sometimes you work without getting paid.

I organized a crew of student volunteers, and we began poring through manuscripts. The students, Gabriel, Harriet, Anna, Jenny, and Elizabeth, did so much work and were so inspiring. I would come out of our meetings buzzing with their energy, youthfulness, and hope. I was surprised by their toughness. We received hundreds of submissions. The students kept nixing things I wanted to publish. When Gabriel didn't like the cover I was going to use, he showed up two days later with a better one he had designed himself. Such initiative! For me, working with them was the greatest part of making this anthology. They were strong where I was soft. They made this book what it is. Anne Ursu heard about what we were doing and kindly offered her services. She was like the fifth Beatle, except there were seven of us. It was Anne who, along with contributing a great story, put me in touch either directly or indirectly with Charles Baxter, Stewart O'Nan, and Jim Shepard. She also gave fantastic editorial advice and wrote me kind letters when I was feeling frustrated. We gave ourselves two months to gather and edit the stories for this book. MacAdam/Cage agreed to put the book out immediately, which enabled us to do this in six months instead of the year or two it might usually take.

The result is a book of original, previously unpublished fiction by a diverse group of new and established writers from as far away as Sudan,

Paris, Gaza, Lebanon and China. An anthology is only as good as its authors. I often wanted to weep, both from the quality of the stories we were getting and the generosity of authors submitting their work.

When I originally told David Poindexter I was going to do this we were both drunk and neither of us believed it. But people got involved right away and I learned one of the most important lessons of my life: that if you do something good you will quickly be surrounded by good people who will help you.

We sincerely hope you enjoy reading the book as much as we enjoyed putting it together. With much love,

—Stephen Elliott, June 2003

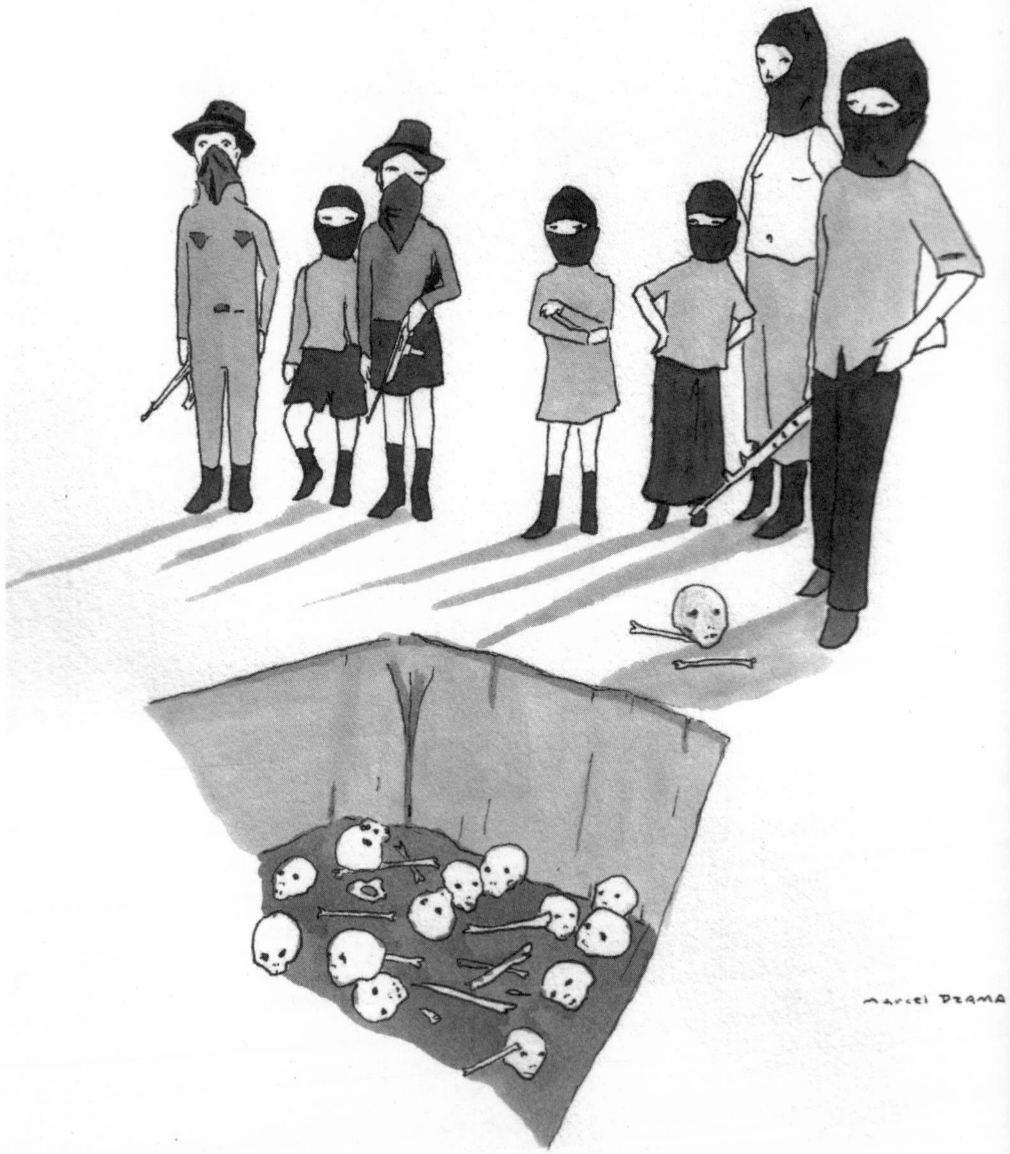
marcel DZAMA

table of contents

i. the politics of children

ii. the politics of culture

iii. the politics of fear

iv. the politics of desire

v. the politics of destruction

vi. the politics of war

the politics of children

the president's new clothes

by anne ursu

He is always up several minutes before his daily wake-up call. Sometimes he sets his alarm just to make sure, but he rarely needs it; he has an internal chronometer so exact that the pantywaists at NASA would be in awe. Every morning, he gets out of bed, stretches, washes his face, brushes his teeth, then does a few jumping jacks for good measure. If there's enough time, he showers; but he's careful—he'd hate to miss that call. Each day, when the phone rings at four A.M. sharp, he's ready. He picks it up on the first ring and says, bright as day, "Good morning, Sleepyhead!"

Sleepyhead—Marie her name really is, nice girl, father always been loyal, oil man, gave a pile of money in '99—says, "Good morning, Mr. President. It's four A.M."

"That late? I've been up for hours!" he says, every time. And she laughs, every time.

So, on this morning, he is not at all surprised when his eyes open on their own. Ten minutes to four, he thinks. Perfect. He yawns, and rubs his hands over his eyes, and stretches a bit in the bed, careful, as always, not to disturb the First Lady, who likes to sleep until six. (Lazybones!)

It takes him several moments to notice that anything is amiss. It is not until he sits up in bed that he notices there is something wrong with the light in the room—rather, that there is light in the room, filtering in through the curtains. The sun is up. He gasps slightly, and turns to where his clock should be.

And that's when he falls out of the bed.

No wonder; it's not his bed at all, but a child's bed, a—what's-it-called—a "twin." Huh. He is, in fact, in a child's room, a ten-by-ten study in boyhood clutter. His bedspread and sheets are printed with the image of a comic book character, the one with the movie…Spider-man. His walls are covered with posters—another Spider-man, a muscle-bound Batman, a basketball player mid-dunk, a pitcher in the stretch. Trophies line one shelf, toys another—action figures, games, piles of comics, Lego robots. There's a little basketball hoop on the door. On the nightstand is a Nerf ball and a plastic baseball clock that reads 7:03.

"Ah," the President thinks to himself calmly, standing up. "I am dreaming. I have not overslept at all, but in fact I am still asleep in my bed in the Presidential bedroom, with the First Lady by my side. This is a very vivid dream."

It is a very vivid dream. That is unusual. The President's dreams tend to be mundane: he oversleeps; he's late for a meeting; there's an exam in Colonial History and he hasn't done any of the reading. But this is something quite out of the ordinary. In this dream, it is as if he has awoken from slumber to find himself in a strange boy's strange room. The dream-room is nothing like his rooms were in the Texas houses. All his toys were kept in closets, his trophies in a case. He did not have posters taped to his walls, and he certainly did not have sheets with superheroes printed on them; Mother disdained comics—she thought they kept boys from reading real books, and he could only read them in secret.

And there is something else. In this very vivid dream, he has shrunk quite a bit. When he stands he finds that he only goes up half as high as he should. His legs are little hairless twigs, his arms are matchsticks, and instead of the blue silk monogrammed pajamas that Laura got him after the election, he is wearing nubby poly-blend Spider-man long johns. In this very vivid, very unusual dream, the President is a child, a Spider-man-crazed child who sleeps until 7:00, and this is his bedroom.

A sense of foreboding fills the President. He does not like this dream. He does not like it one bit. He would like it to end. He would like it to end soon.

Surely it will end soon, surely it is almost 4:00, surely it is time for his internal alarm to go off, surely soon Sleepyhead will call and he will tease her and she will laugh her sweet little laugh, with just the most delicate twang in her voice, music to his ears, that's Texas talking, surely she will call and laugh and twang like Texas and the dream will end, and then he can, surely, begin his day—he would surely like the dream to end soon, surely he would—because he cannot escape the feeling that something is terribly wrong.

A pint-size pit forms in his pint-size stomach. His pint-size heart begins to burn. His pint-size lungs constrict pint-sizedly. And then he does the only thing his pint-size brain can think of:

He pinches himself.

Twenty minutes later, the President of the United States is sitting cross-legged on the shaggy bright green rug of this strange room in his Spider-man jammies, with his head in his hands. He looks up once in a while to watch the baseball clock announce the minutes as they pass in an all-too-real way.

A knock interrupts the silence. The door, on which is taped several glossy magazine pictures of baseball players, opens a crack.

"Kyle?" a woman's voice sings. "Kyyyy-le?... Wake up, Sleepyhead!"

The President stands up. "Don't come in!" he shouts quickly. His voice is high, squeaky, flat.

"Okay, honey," the voice says indulgently. "But hurry, you'll be late for school!"

The President quickly puts the pieces together. Whatever they say about him, he is not a dumb man. He may not be much for book-learning, but he can tell a boobie bird from a titmouse. There's a woman outside the door who thinks the President is her son. And, judging by the situation, he might well be.

In a single bound, the President leaps into the bed and crawls under the covers. "I can't go to school!" he squeaks.

And with that, the door swings open, and a pale, fortyish woman with red hair and a soft blue sweater strides in. The President is reminded uncomfortably of Maureen Dowd. He pulls the covers up tight.

"Honey?" she says. "Are you okay? What's wrong?"

The President has to think fast—something has gone terribly terribly wrong: he is roughly ten years old, he is named Kyle, and no matter how much he pinches himself, he does not wake up. It is a national emergency, an international crisis, and he cannot go to school today.

"I don't feel good…Mom…," he says meekly.

The woman sits down on the bed. She puts her hand on his head; the hand is soft and as it passes over his face he catches a whiff of lavender. He wills his temperature up.

The President used to be very good at faking illness in his formative years. A weak look, a soft sigh, a hand on the stomach. It's all in the presentation. Keep it simple. Stay on message. Once in fifth grade he stayed out a whole week because of the World Series. Mom never caught on; of course it wouldn't occur to her that her boy would fake and lie his way out of school. Of course, Jeb never did it; Jeb *liked* school.

"I hurt all over," the President says. "My sto—tummy."

"You're all sweaty!" the woman says. "And so pale! Poor baby." She strokes his hair. "There's a flu going around. You rest today." She sighs heavily. "I better call the store."

"The store?" he says dumbly.

She smiles gently. "Someone's got to watch over my sick boy."

"Oh!" That hadn't occurred to him. The mother works—this is a concept he understands more in theory than in practice. Mom didn't work, of course, and even then they always had a girl to watch over them. Laura quit her job as soon as they were married, of course; he found himself a nice old-fashioned gal. (A looker, too!)

"It's okay. I can stay by myself."

"Always thinking of your mother," she smiles. "Don't worry. It will be fine. I better make the calls, you rest up and I'll come check on you later, okay? Holler if you need anything?"

"Thanks...Mom," he says weakly. He can't help it; he's a little touched. He is filled with compassion. Compassion fills him. This woman, this hard-working woman, taking such good care of her sick boy. She is nothing like Maureen Dowd; Maureen Dowd does not smell of lavender. This woman is gentle, loving, feminine. A mother. Sure, she can have a job if she wants, something to get her out of the house, work at a store selling clothes or handbags, earn herself a little pocket money and work with other nice gals, work hard, gossip a bit; but when the family calls, she is there to answer. Mom. What a beautiful thing. A beautiful concept. Motherhood. The binds that tie. He can use her in a speech sometime. That's it, he should give a speech. He could even invite her to the White House. He should have a whole forum on motherhood—that'd make Rove happy—with awards and parades. He should declare a day, a day to honor mothers everywhere, he should call it Mothers' Day—

Ah, shit.

No matter. He can't have any parades or days or mothers while he is like this. The first priority is to let the White House know that the President is all right. There is no need to panic. Something has happened, something very strange, something smelling of witchcraft or…something, but he, the President, is still fully functional and able to lead the country. Stay calm. Do not panic. America is Strong. The Country still has its Leader. The Body still has its Head; the Head is just…Smaller.

He knows he has to get to a phone, pronto and lickety-split, but he has to be careful; Kyle's mother might find it a little strange for him to be placing calls to the White House. So he sits on the bed and waits.

The President is not very good at waiting. That is why it is good that he is President; you don't have to wait much when you are President. People tend to do things when you want them to. He just can't sit still; he's never been able to. (He can't watch an entire movie to save his life, though Rove leaked that he sat through all of that movie about the black kid.) That never served him well in school, but it's certainly done wonders for Washington; this President's White House is a model of efficiency, punctuality. His meetings never run long. If you can't do it in fifteen minutes, it's not worth doing.

Now, the President sits on the small, hard bed, waiting impatiently, sighing heavily, listening to Kyle's mother on the phone as she calls into school, then work. She says something about making up her hours later, and the President is impressed with her dedication to her store job. She calls someone else, Kyle's father probably. "A stomach flu…" he hears. "Nothing to worry about…he's definitely not well, though…hope he's better tomorrow…well, they didn't fire me..."

The President finds himself rocking a little bit. He'd like to throw a few hoops with that Nerf ball, but Mom might hear. Why couldn't he have landed in the body of a kid who was old enough to stay home by himself?

He pulls at his short little left eyebrow and squints at the posters around him. The basketball poster blares "Minnesota Timberwolves," but he doesn't recognize the player. The President knew all the Rockets once upon a time, but basketball was never really his thing. Baseball, now, there's his game. He starts working on the other eyebrow and looks at the pitcher. A young guy, the President doesn't know him, in a Twins uniform. (Oh, great—he's in Minnesota. His new parents probably voted for *Dukakis*.) Righty. Good stance on the guy. He's got a look in his eye, too, a pitcher's look. His first name is Kyle. Heh! That's cute. Kyle!

The President stands up on the bed and stares straight ahead. He brings his matchstick arms together, tiny fist in palm, sets, kicks his spindly leg up, and throws, a perfect strike! Right down the middle! The crowd cheers! *Like to see John Kerry do that, huh? Might muss his hair.*

"Ky????"

The President starts, then flops back on the bed just as the woman appears in the doorway with a tray. "Mom?" he says weakly.

"How's my baby?"

"Um….I dunno…"

"Oh my poor boy," she says. "I called school, it's just fine. You don't worry about a thing, okay?"

"I won't," he says bravely.

"I brought you a hot water bottle," she says, placing the tray in front of him. "And some ginger ale. You can drink it after you have your Pepto."

"I hate Pepto!" the President exclaims.

"I know, I know," she says soothingly. "But it makes you better, huh?" The President watches as she pours some of the sickly thick pink liquid into a big spoon—the President hates Pepto; Laura makes him take it all the time. Pepto *Dismal* he calls it—"Open wide," Kyle's mother says. The President closes his eyes and opens his mouth. He swallows and smacks his lips—*blech!*—then reaches quickly for the ginger ale. "That's my boy," she smiles. "Look, I'm going to be working at the computer, okay? You call down if you need anything."

That, there—he thinks, gulping down the ginger ale—is his chance.

A few minutes later, the President is creeping on his child's feet down the narrow hallway of the house. His room, no, Kyle's room, is right across the hallway from the staircase. On one end of the hall is a bathroom, which is good to know, as the Presidential bladder has just gotten quite a bit smaller. Next to his room is a bigger bedroom; the parent's room, clearly, although it doesn't even have a bathroom attached. And at the end of the hallway, in a room with the television, he finds what he needs—a phone.

His first call is to Rove's cell phone, but not before having to think for a few moments about the number; he's not used to dialing on his own. Turd Blossom/Boy Genius picks it up on the first ring.

"Yeah?"

"Turd?" the President says hurriedly. "It's Dubya. Look, I'm all right—"

"Eh?"

"I'm just fine. I'm in Minnesota. Something's happened, but—"

"Who's this?"

"Turd, it's Dubya! There's been…an incident, but—"

"Hey, kid," Rove says in a low voice, "Why don't you fuck the hell off?"

And he hangs up.

Well.

The President is slightly taken aback. He is not used to being hung up on. Turd Blossom's going to feel bad about that one later. Some boy genius. Turd Boy's more like it.

Heh. That's a good one. Turd Blossom and Boy Genius makes Turd Boy!

Next he tries Card. Then the Vice President/Big Time. Then his secretary. He can't get past hello any time. When he gets back, he's going to talk to them all about hanging up on people. It's important to be cautious, but this is absurd. Finally, he calls Laura—she's in Boston for a conference and may not have the news yet, but she will know her husband.

"Firstie?" he says plaintively. "It's me."

"Excuse me?" she says softly. That's his Firstie. Always polite. Turd Boy could learn a thing or two…

"It's Bushie—something's happened—"

"Who is this?"

"Firstie, it's me. You've got to listen—"

"How did you get this number?"

There's a rustling on the phone, then a man's voice—threatening, forceful. It's Laura's lead agent, Mama Bear. "Hello? Kid? If you call this number again we'll put you where the sun don't shine."

And then, *click.*

Frankly, the President is not amused. Frankly, his feelings are a little hurt. Frankly, he expects more. If a member of his staff—if his wife, his Firstie!—woke up in the body of a ten-year-old boy, he would surely at least stay on the phone with them long enough to hear about it. And shouldn't they be paying attention? It is midmorning in Washington, the President is mysteriously gone…

…or is he?

Perhaps the President is right where he is supposed to be…or at least his body is. It hadn't occurred to him to wonder about the fate of little Kyle, but perhaps the boy has somehow become him. Or something. Perhaps he and Kyle have…switched. It happened in that kids movie, the one the twins used to love—they had it on video—the one starring that girl who grew up to make the Hannibal Lecter movie. (Rove says she's a lesbian, but the President doesn't believe him; she was in Disney movies, for the love of God.)

That's exactly what's happened, the President knows it in his heart. It doesn't even occur to him to wonder how this happened—the President is not interested in "causality"; he's more of an action man. What is important is that it has happened. The President of the United States has switched bodies with a little boy, no one will take his calls, and now a Minnesota ten-year-old with action figures, comic-book sheets, and toy robots is running the free world.

A few minutes later, the President has moved his base of operations into the small, dark TV room. He has set himself up on the couch with the Spider-man comforter, a pillow, his ginger ale, and the hot water bottle, and he is monitoring the state of the nation as best he can.

"Honey—what are you watching?" He didn't even notice his mother appear in the doorway. She's looking at him with a strange kind of bewilderment, and he wonders if he is seeming too healthy.

"Fox," he says, fixing his face in a pained expression.

"Fox News?"

"Uh-huh," he nods.

She's staring at him. "Why on earth?"

"I…I want to stay informed, Mom."

She blinks a couple times. "Can't you watch another channel?"

"Why…?"

"Well, sweetie…" She seems about to say something, and then shakes her head. "Your dad's on the phone."

The President sits up straight and gasps, "He is?!"

"Yes. He wants to see how you are."

"Oh!" Oh, *that* dad.

He has no idea what Kyle's father says to him; all he can think about is what his own will think when he finds out about this. 41 never switched bodies with a ten-year-old when he was in office; he stayed right where he was supposed to be—that's what Bushes do, son, we fulfill our commitments. I'm disappointed in you, son.

Well, perhaps it won't come to that. Sooner or later, someone will figure out that the President is not himself. Then someone will take his call and they can get this sorted out, and he can go back to the business of running America. He just needs to wait. They'll notice soon enough.

Three days later, the President of the United States is sitting in a small desk in a fifth-grade classroom at F. Scott Fitzgerald Elementary School. He has already embarrassed himself once by sitting in the wrong desk; seating in the fifth grade at Fitzgerald is assigned, like the Cabinet.

He couldn't call in sick another day; Kyle's mother—Jane—was threatening to take him to the doctor, and anyway he was getting weary of saltines and ginger ale. Kyle's father—Michael—stayed home with him yesterday because Jane wanted to go back to work or something. The President was a little taken aback—41 never stayed home with him a day in his life. Michael is some kind of small-business owner—just like the President's father was. Small businesses are what make this country great.

The President has tried to keep abreast of things the best he could; he insisted on keeping the news on in the background all day yesterday while he and Michael played video games. But whatever crisis is occurring in the White House, word has not leaked to the press, and the country is proceeding as if everything were normal. This is probably for the best.

So, the President is in elementary school. He's not worried. He is very adaptable. He adapts. He always has. He's been lucky. Blessed, really. Like when he was running for Congress and people saw him as a playboy, then the woman-of-his-dreams waltzed into his life and he married her up in the blink of an eye. Or when Poppy was trying to get the nomination in '88 and the religious right said he was too moderate—the President happened to find Jesus just then and was appointed the liaison to the Christian Coalition. Timing. Luck. Blessing. Destiny? Life has always brought him just what he needs when he needs it. Everything always works out for him. He adapts.

Anyway, if there is a crisis, news will reach him soon enough. Perhaps there will be an assembly. The principal will solemnly address the school: *Children, I have terrible news. Oh, children, the President of the United States has undergone a body-switching. Like in that one movie. Investigators are working day and night to find the location of the real President, but until they do, all we can do is pray for him. And pray for America.*

And the children will gasp as one, some will cry, some will faint, but then, then the President will stand up, right there in the middle of the gymnasium, and say, *Never fear, children! Your President is Right Here!*

And the children, the beautiful children, will all stand and applaud and cheer. And he will say, *You children, you are what makes America strong. You are America's future—*

"Kyle!"

"Huh?"

He is no longer in the gym with the throngs of cheering children, but back in fifth grade and Mrs. Anderson is staring at him suspiciously.

"Kyle…are you paying attention?"

"Yes." He does not like her tone.

"Well, can you name the three branches of government?"

The President grins. "Congressional, Judicial, and Executive."

The teacher nods. "Good, Kyle."

The President smirks. People are always underestimating him. His teachers always did. This one, too, doesn't like Kyle, he can tell. She dresses like a liberal, all baggy sweaters and slacks. Poor Kyle. The President knows what it's like; people were always underestimating him, too; just because his dad was famous and great, they always assumed he was just trading on his name. What's he supposed to do, not run for office just because he has the same name as his dad? It's not his fault that his dad worked hard and made a lot of money and did great things. The President had to be twice as good as everyone else just to prove himself. He sighs audibly and the teacher glares at him.

"Are we boring you, Kyle?"

"No," says the President. He sighs again.

The morning consists of a civics lesson, and then some geography. The President already knows all this stuff—the state capitals! really!—so he spends the time studying his classmates; there are 32 of them, which seems like a lot of kids for one class. No matter; by the end of the morning, the President has learned the names of almost every one of them; it's easy since Mrs. Anderson just calls on students, just like that, even if they don't have their hands raised.

Gym class comes in the nick of time. He cannot sit still a moment longer, plus he hasn't gotten any exercise in days. If the President's not careful, young Kyle will start looking like he switched bodies with Clinton.

As he's filing into the gym, one of the boys, Jimmy—the troublemaker, he got his name written on the board already today—pokes him in the arm.

"Where you been?"

"Sick," the President says.

"Sucks."

"Yup."

Two girls from the class—Emily and Laura—run past them, holding hands and laughing. Jimmy punches him and points to the giggling pair.

"They're *lesbians*," snickers Jimmy.

Really?—the President's eyes go wide. And then he realizes—

Oh! Those girls are probably not really lesbians. They're just girls. But in elementary school, you call girls who hold hands "lesbians." That's just what you do. You call them "lesbians," because they're holding hands and it's funny, and no one yells at you for it, you don't get hate mail from lesbians and lesbian-type groups who can't take a joke, and you don't have to worry about how to appease them without angering the religious right, you don't have to send a message that you value their contributions to America without in any way condoning their lifestyle choice. You can just call the girls "lesbians."

It's so wonderful! *Lesbians!* The President starts laughing. He can't help himself. *Lesbians!* He laughs so hard tears run down his cheeks. He laughs and laughs, he can barely stay upright, he laughs so hard he begins to wheeze a little, and Jimmy smacks him on the shoulder and hisses, *"Retard."*

Gym class today is Capture the Flag. The President knows the game well; they still play it at the Ranch. You have to thin out the ranks of the enemy forces before you can go in for the kill. Go for the fat kids first, then the girls. The President surgically singles out the slow, the weak. His team cheers, his friends slap him on the back. And then it's time: Jimmy nods to him. The President nods back. Jimmy darts across enemy lines, past Maggie, past Ben, past Timmy and Tom. He heads for the group of prisoners, and just as the line guards turn to follow him, the President goes in. By the time the enemy realizes what is happening, it's too late. He's got the flag in his hands, he runs straight for the line; Kyle's body is lithe, his feet are fleet, he sails and flies and there is nothing anyone can do. Behind him, the liberated prisoners leap to their feet and roar. The President dives across the line, and his teammates surround him, cheering, slapping him on the back. He looks to Jimmy, who grins at him. The President grins back and raises the flag triumphantly in the air.

After lunch—hot dogs and Tater Tots (not bad!)—the President is greeted with a rather unpleasant surprise: the weekly spelling test. The President cannot help it; he has a flash of nervousness. The President was never very good at these in elementary school; he never got the stars and stickers of his classmates. *Needs improvement. Study harder. You need to focus.*

Notes were sent home. Talks were had. Goals were set. Improve, study, focus. I'm disappointed in you, George. His mother made him learn 25 new words every Saturday before he could play baseball. She'd write out the flashcards for him: *skirmish, crave, pertinent,* and would test him on them until he got them all right. Twenty-five out of twenty-five. *Tranquil, authentic, infuriate, empathize.* He was often late to practice and he protested to his father once that Bar's rules were *unjust, excessive, perverse,* and his father told him never to complain about his mother again.

But Kyle's spelling test is easy, and the President smiles a little as he writes down each word: *citizen, buffalo, museum, emergency.* He gets every word right, and today there will be no notes sent home. 1/2 times 1/2 is 1/4, 1/4 times 1/3 is 1/12. There's recess, then drama, then group reading, then test review, then—school's out! The President is caught in the inexorable rush of students toward the door—"Goodbye Lew," he waves. "Goodbye Maggie, bye Emily and Laura! Bye Henry, bye Harry, bye Helen! Bye John, bye Jean, bye Jack and Jackie! Bye Melanie! Bye Mike! Bye Betsy—"

"Hey, Ky," shouts Jimmy from the throng of boys gathering on the schoolyard. "Aren't you gonna play?"

"Can't," says the President. "Gotta watch the news."

Jimmy stares at him. The President just shrugs and turns away; he's got to get home. It's been fun, really, but he's got to check on his country.

Michael's in the kitchen working at the computer when the President gets home. The President wasn't expecting this. He turns and beams when he sees his son, "Hey, kiddo! You're home early."

"Yup. Homework," the President lies.

"Oh! Good for you! Finish up and we'll play some catch later."

"Really? You've got time?"

"Sure."

"Cool!" The President grabs a handful of pretzels from the cupboard and is about to head out of the kitchen when he stops suddenly. "Oh, and Dad?"

"Yeah?"

". . . I got a perfect score on my spelling test."

Michael smiles. "Kiddo, I'm so proud of you!"

A few minutes later, the President is settled down in front of the television, munching on pretzels (which he is just now able to eat again after the Incident) and looking for some sign of governmental destabilization. There's not much. The Dow is up. The NASDAQ is down. The Yankees lost. And then, suddenly, the President sees himself on the television, crossing the White House lawn, hand in hand with the First Lady.

But it's not him at all.

The pretzel falls out of the President's mouth. In front of his eyes, Kyle Johnson is strolling—no, *strutting*—up to Marine One, waving to the press. And, just before he steps into the helicopter—the President's helicopter—Kyle whispers something to his wife, and the two stop and wave. And then Kyle Johnson, ten-year-old Kyle Johnson, grabs the First Lady, dips her, and kisses her.

The President lets out a little muffled yelp.

"What's wrong, Kyle?" Michael appears in the doorway.

"I can't believe this guy!" the President yells, pointing to the television.

Michael looks at the screen. Kyle and the First Lady are still locked in a kiss. He shakes his head.

"I know," he says.

Over the next few days the President leaves repeated messages for Kyle with his secretary—but Kyle won't return his calls. Little shit. Every day, the President leaves school as soon as the day is over, while his friends stay to run around on the playground. Jimmy may call him names, but the President has no time for games. He has to get home, get to the television, get to Brit Hume and Bill O'Reilly, Greta Van Susteren, Hannity and that commie Colmes. He has to monitor world events, to keep his eye on the state of the country, to see if Kyle is still pitching woo to his wife.

And something is happening; Rummy has given a press conference: Iran is put on notice. He says they are destabilizing the region. He says they are harboring terrorists. He says they are a brutal regime that needs to be dealt with. He says they are an immediate threat to American security.

The President watches, wide-eyed. It's a time of crisis—and how on earth can the government run without its leader? Decisions need to be made, and without him, who is going to make them?

He spends his evenings in front of the television. He jumps every time the phone rings—did they realize? Did they find him? Do they need their President back? He does his homework to the dulcet tones of Bill O'Reilly *(Tonight, our Talking Points. The President declares National Snickers Day. Will the pansy-ass liberals cry tooth decay?)* he studies his spelling—*serious, collection, mirror*—and reads the crawl at the bottom of the screen waiting for some sign that his country is calling for him to come back and lead her.

There is no sign, and the President grows impatient. He learns nothing. Nothing happens, and nothing comes. The President cannot do nothing. He needs something to do. He doodles all over his fifth-grade reader, then an idea occurs to him. Of course. He goes into Kyle's room, brings the stepstool over to the closet, climbs up, reaches to the top shelf, and finds what he is looking for.

It is a treasure. A beautiful treasure. He carefully cradles the shoebox in his hands as he climbs down from the stepstool, and with two hands, he carries it into the den. There are hundreds of baseball cards in this box, all unsorted. How on earth does Kyle expect to keep track of them?

The President has always loved baseball cards. He loves the way they smell, the way they feel in your hands. He loves running his finger down the columns of stats and reading the stories they tell. The President had hundreds of cards when he was a boy, and he could name every one of them without having to look. He can still see them when he closes his eyes, the '56 Yogi Berra (.272 batting average, 27 home runs, 108 RBI), a '55 Stan Musial (.330, 35, 126), the Whitey Ford rookie card—

When he was a kid he wanted to play ball; every kid did. But he wanted to longer than most. And then he got to Yale and it turned out he was only a junkball pitcher, and not a very good one at that. He tried out for the freshman team, and then he stopped trying. He would be the first of his family not to play a varsity sport at Yale. His father's name appeared in trophy cases all around the campus, his face looked sternly down from pictures of legendary championship teams, and all Junior could do was start an intramural stickball league.

When the President became managing general partner of the Rangers, he had baseball cards printed up with his picture on them. It started as a joke, but the cards caught on. People loved the cards. Fans would come up to him during the games and ask for one; he was the First Son, he was an owner—kind of—of their baseball team, and he was a Texan—he had the flags on his boots to prove it.

The fans loved him, and he them. There was no politics, no fundraising, no partisanship—just baseball. Balls and strikes, bats and gloves. That was the happiest period of his life, to tell the truth. He could never admit this, of course—the Presidency was something he was called to do, it was like his destiny. He never really chose it; it was chosen for him. But being a partner on a baseball team, that was just pure joy. He had his own box seat just off the dugout. He could walk through the dugout, the locker room, and backslap players. He could stand on the field with Nolan Ryan and talk pitching grips. He got a stadium built, that beautiful stadium, a shrine to baseball.

Things got bad for him very quickly; there was the Harken mess, then the '92 debacle, and suddenly it was time for him to begin his career in public service. But there is a part of him, still, that is in that dark green seat in the ballpark that he built with the sun streaming down on his arms, eating a hot dog, watching a game.

"Hey, sport." The President looks up from his shoebox to find Kyle's dad has appeared in the doorway. "What are you doing?"

"I'm trying to organize these cards," the President says.

"Want help?"

"Yeah!"

Michael crouches down while the President goes over his system; year, then team, then alphabetical. "This is such a great collection!" he says, he can't help himself. "A Derek Jeter rookie card!"

Michael smiles and fingers a card. "I love these things," he says. "Every one tells a story."

"That's just what I think!" the President says.

"Kyle…um…" Michael nods to the television. "Can we turn this off?"

The President looks at the screen, where O'Reilly is interviewing Wolfowitz about Iran, and then back at Kyle's father. Truth is he hadn't been paying attention for some time. He shrugs. "Okay."

They work for a few minutes, father and son, looking at cards and reading the stories the numbers tell. If you put as much attention to your schoolwork as you do to those baseball statistics, his mother used to say—

"Hey, look," his father says. "You've got a Lohse rookie card!"

"I do?" The President runs his finger along the back. Kyle Lohse, Twins pitcher, is Kyle Johnson's favorite player, and is it any wonder? Look at those stats!

"You know, son…," his father says suddenly, "you're everything to your mother and me. You know that, right?"

"Uh-huh."

"Well, it's just…you might have noticed…business…if things are tough, we'll make it through."

The President blinks at Michael. He scratches his nose. "I know, Dad!" Everything always works out. Life throws you a curve, and you adapt. Lemon to lemonade. Raw deal to rawhide. There's no need to worry.

Kyle's uncle and aunt come over for dinner. There's some talk of politics; Uncle John says, "Can you believe they put Iran on notice? We'll invade just before the election, I'm sure."

Everyone lets out a pained laugh, but the President is confused. Does Iran even have elections? Rummy wants to bring democracy to the Middle East. He wants people to be free. Rummy sends him reports all the time about the terrible things some of these guys do. He would never have known Saddam Hussein had gassed his own people if Rummy hadn't told him. That's what happens. Rummy, Condi, Wolfowitz give him the information and he makes the decisions, because he is President and that is his burden to bear.

"So, Kyle, how's school?" Aunt Suzy asks. She has a sweet smile, quite a bit like his Laura.

"Kyle's been doing really well on his spelling," Michael says. "He's really improved."

"Good for you!" she says, then turns to the table. "Jack's announced he wants to be a lawyer today, just like his dad."

"He's got it in him," says Jane.

"What about you, Kyle?" asks Suzy. "What do you want to be when you grow up?"

He knows this one. "I want to be President," he says, matter-of-factly.

"You do, Kyle?" Michael and Jane exchange a surprised look.

"Yes!" he says, a little offended.

"Well, that's terrific," says Aunt Suzy. "Why?"

"Why?"

"Yes, why? Why do you want to be President." She smiles at him. All the adults around the table swivel their heads and wait for his answer.

He blinks. He gulps. Words he was once given float through his head...*principles*...*leadership*...*strong*...and then they float right out again. "I just do," he says.

Uncle John laughs quietly and mutters something to Jane about the "real president" which the President cannot quite hear. Michael, though, is looking at him curiously. "Hey, kiddo...I thought you wanted to be in the Big Leagues?"

"I did?" the President says.

"Yeah! All your life!"

The President thinks for a moment. "What position?"

"A pitcher."

"Oh!" he sits back in his chair. "Really?" His father nods. "Cool!"

At gym on Monday they start their baseball unit. The gym teacher—Skip, the President calls him—is doing the pitching, so the President doesn't get to try out Kyle's pitching arm. But the President is captain, and he gets to pick the team. Jimmy is his first choice; this is both a smart move and a political one—Jimmy is one of the best athletes in the class, and he also has seemed a little hostile toward the President for not staying to play after school, but what can the President do, he has obligations—then Benny Boy, then Maggie/Maggles, who is very good for a girl. When there's only eight kids left, Skip assigns them to teams on his own so no one will have to be the last one picked, like some sort of welfare for fat kids.

The other team bats first. The President plays shortstop, and Jack lines the ball right at him. Most ten-year-olds would have gotten out of the way, but the President reaches his hands up and the rubber ball lands in them perfectly. His team cheers. Then Betsy hits a pop-up that Skip plays cleanly. With two outs, Tom hits a ball that sails over the head of the President, past the first tier of outfielders, and bounces right in front of the dead weights behind them. The ball rolls back and three girls chase it off into the sunset, but not before the Tom Cat has exuberantly crossed home for the game's first run.

Maggie is first to bat on the President's team—she's skinny and quick, a prototypical lead-off hitter. She smacks the ball right over the head of the first baseman, a base hit, good, good, she did her job. There's probably no stealing when you're playing with a rubber baseball, but otherwise he'd send her. Then Jimmy hits a ball to Jack, who misplays it ("E-6!" the President shouts gleefully). Maggie makes it to third and Jimmy lands safely on first.

Then it's the President's turn. He saunters up to the plate and looks Skip right in the eye. Skip launches the ball, and the President swings the aluminum bat, his body pivots, his eyes see the ball at the moment of contact with the bat—THWAP!—and the ball goes flying, out past the first outfielders, the second outfielders, the third! Maggles scores, Jimbo scores, the President scores!

By the time there's one out in the inning, the score is 6-1. Even Dawn gets a hit—lumpy, pasty, Twinkie-fingered Dawn is planted at first base. Emily/the Em-ster launches a shallow high fly, and the President watches with horror as Dawn begins to run, run as if her life depended on it. "Go back!" he screams. "Go back!"

But she doesn't go back. Melanie catches the ball in right field and alertly throws to Tom, who steps on first base.

Double play.

The team runs off the field, and as Dawn passes him, she shrugs and giggles. The President has not been this angry since Gore.

"Tag up!" he screams. "Tag up! You moron!"

Dawn's face twists up. Her cheeks burn red. The President just shakes his head. "Lesbian," he mutters.

On Monday night, Kyle Johnson addresses America. Mom and Dad watch in the kitchen, while the President sits at the table and sulks.

"He looks pathetic," says Mom. "All puffed up."

"Yeah," mutters the President, doodling on his workbook. Fat is what he looks. What's Kyle doing? Are those Skittles on the desk in front of him?

"God, he's even worse with the teleprompter than usual!" says Mom.

"Yeah!" sulks the President. Stupid Kyle thinks he's so smart and so cool. Stupid. Is that cheese dust on his chin? "Mom, does he look fat to you?"

"Huh?"

". . . the Iranian regime poses an im-me-di-ate threat to America's people. . ." "We've heard that before," mutters Mom.

"Yeah!" sulks the President.

". . . The regime is providing an environment in which those who wish us harm can fl-fl-flourish..."

"So is Pakistan," says Mom. "And Saudi Arabia. But you don't see us calling them out."

"Yeah!" sulks the President.

". . . We know that key Iraqi officials have fled into this country. Some of these officials possess knowledge of how to create weapons of mass destruction. They may even have the weapons themselves. . ."

"Oh, that's what happened to the weapons," says Mom.

"Yeah!" sulks the President.

". . . To the Iranian regime: America has put you on notice. You cannot continue to fight against freedom. To the Iranian people: One way or another, soon you will be free..."

"I can't watch this anymore," says Dad.

"Me neither," sulks the President.

On Tuesday at recess, Jimmy holds court on the brewing international crisis. "Iran did 9/11," Jimbo says. "We should nuke 'em."

"That's stupid," says the President. Jimmy sounds like Wolfowitz.

"You're stupid," says Jimmy.

"Am not!" says the President. "You can't just *nuke* people."

"You would know," Jimmy says. "You're always running home to watch the *news.*"

The President sighs heavily. Jimmy will never understand. There is a big difference between nuking people and liberating them. This is why ten-year-olds are not in charge of foreign policy.

"Jimmy. . .," says the President, but Jimmy has tossed him the football and shouted, "Smear the queer! Kyle's the queer!" The boys come running. The President could throw the ball away, but that's not the kind of guy he is. He holds on and accepts his beating.

It is three weeks since the President woke up inside the body of Kyle Johnson, and it is now getting close to summer. In a few weeks, the President will go to baseball camp. The small classrooms of F. Scott Fitzgerald Elementary School slowly cook the students trapped inside. Schools should be air-conditioned, the President thinks. It should be a law. As the day draws to a close, he fans himself with his spelling test (*achieve, deceive, believe*)—nine out of ten he got—and waits for the clock to tick the minutes by. He'll make himself a glass of lemonade, he'll start sorting the '01 baseball cards by team, while he monitors the news to see what Kyle has done to the country now, and if he's still excessively snacking.

And then the bell rings: salvation. The President picks up his backpack and begins to run out of the classroom, but Mrs. Anderson stops him. "Kyle, may I talk to you?" she says.

"Yeah, sure," he says, standing in the doorway, bouncing a little.

"Kyle...I just wanted to commend you on all the good work you've done lately. You've really been working hard, I can tell."

The President exhales. "Thanks, Mrs. Anderson!"

"It shows real maturity to make a change in yourself," she says solemnly. "I'm proud of you."

He grins, ear to ear. "Thanks, Mrs. A!"

"Mrs. A!" She giggles girlishly. "I like that! Well, anyway, keep up the good work."

The President walks through the schoolyard, still smiling a little to himself. He is about to head out the gate when he sees the boys at the end of the block heading off with their baseball gloves.

"Hey, Ky, you wanna play?" shouts Benny Boy.

"Nah," shouts Jimmy. "He's got to go watch the *news*."

The President stops. He looks at Jimmy. He looks at the Tom Cat, the Johninator, the Jackal, Benny Boy, and Bubblehead. The boys stare at him uncertainly. Jimmy throws the dirty, veined baseball up and down in the air pointedly. The sun streams down and the ball seems to glow.

"Come on," the President says, running toward them. "Let's play ball."

da bomb

by k. kvashay-boyle

First house I ever egged was the duplex of Lisa's big crush. We nailed the wrong side. The delicate crunch of crushed shell, the wet slap, the sailing, blurred arc of the oblong ball, the threat of night and the insistent thrill buzzing in our two silent, pounding throats—all of it tickled some dark underside of ourselves that either had nothing at all or exactly everything to do with Evan Torrance and the place where that fifth-grade heartthrob throbbed inside our fifth-grade minds. This was love. We stood side by side in the dark, in front of his house, and what we were was hardcore, incognito, teenyboppers prematurely precocious, worldly in the ways of *Seventeen Magazine*, *Cosmo*, and *Sassy*, and, eggs in hand, finally and irrevocably we were submerged in some hoodlum realm: teenageland. What we wanted was blood. Eggs splattered on the painted trim, the paneled siding. But what hatched against the face of that house? Our fumbling desire, and nothing more. What hatched, what was crushed, was deep inside of us. I know that now. It was invisible, untouchable, elusive. A secret.

"Feel it," Lisa had said, first as we gripped the smooth firmness of the unbroken shell and felt our palms heat it up, and then later, after we scattered rushing to the farthest patch of bushes—duck and cover, shut up, hold still—after we stopped panting, stopped clutching at our giggles, and decided to creep back up to the house. Feel it I did, and it was slimy. Wet. Ruined.

"You smell that?" I said. "It's the sulfur, right?" Lisa said she smelled it, yes, sure she did, and probably she was thinking of Evan too as we left, slowly, freezing at each echoey twig snap. The periodic table loomed in my mind. Science class. Evan Torrance. The night was like an uncooked cake, doughy scent, sticky skin. It was magic.

The next day what my mother said, as Randa's bags settled like some rouge element in the narrow office space, was that Randa would stay with us awhile. Just that. Awhile. A guest. Randa would be staying, with her squawking baby, in the room closest to our front door. The room sure to be disturbed by my sneaking out. I still felt the thrill of bombardment jitter my pulse, my limbs, my brains, and even after climbing silently back into bed sleep hadn't come last night, leaving me both cranky with the morning's chores and supercharged with residual excitement. What my mother said was that Randa was the wife of Omar Hassan and that Siri had made arrangements for as long as she could, and that what I had to do was mind Randa. It was very important. Make her feel at home. Siri was my mother's closest friend, and as I saw my vampire books, my boom box, and my art supplies stacked in the hallway to make room for Randa's bags, the bags that would overtake our space like mold, sprout from the countertops, thrive in the closets and drawers, escalate over the dryer, I knew there wasn't a thing I could do about it. I absently slammed the vacuum around the coffee table. Siri was also a Hassan, married to Omar's oldest brother.

"The ones who cause the trouble are her in-laws, so what can Siri do? Her hands are tied." My mother told me all this, yes, but there was one thing I knew for sure: Omar had a new American wife now. It was a scandal. A disgrace. Such a shame. My mother and Siri held counsel over this matter many times, and I could hear them whispering all the way down the length of the hall and into the front room.

"No retribution? It's shameful," they said.

"In this country maybe," they said. "Some compensation."

I knew that Omar was not handsome and Randa was not beautiful. They did not keep secret candies hidden like coins in the folds of their sleeves, they did not indulge the kids when prayer was over—no, their faces were stern, unbending, severe. I moved on to the recycling, pulled out the blue bin, felt the clank of aluminum collapsing underfoot in a satisfying progression of crippling stomps. Randa, with her gnarled teeth and her heavy chestnut smell, was exactly what I would never become. I did not want to mind her. I wanted to listen to the Top One Hundred Countdown on my boombox. I wanted to sneak out at night. I wanted to draw long hair. I wanted to see blood get sucked.

* *

First beer I guzzled was a stolen one. Obviously. From the center pouch of my hooded sweatshirt came the inaugural Bud Lite, furtively sipped when I was fourteen and ready for the promised land of an accelerated life. After school Lisa and I would take the bus, and sometimes she would stay over at my house. But the best was when I got to stay at hers. Her parents were big on cookouts and pool parties. They were sloppy and prim in some elusive way to which I was never fully accustomed. Lisa branded them a couple of retards, major A-holes, but they weren't really. Sodas were in an adjacent tub, floating slick in soupy, reconstituted ice. The cold heavy cans tugged the strained front of my sweatshirt, bulked up my midsection, and I felt as clever as some savvy sitcom girl, I felt like I was Angela Chase and this was *My So-Called Life*. While the illicit thrill of the take was exciting, the reward was less stellar.

"Oh gross," said Lisa, twisting her face into a disaster. "It's like some raunchy old guy's breath, oh man that's some nasty-*nast*." After the first fizzy chug, she threw back her head and laughed recklessly. "Hey, how many did you snag, anyway?"

"Well, I *am* a major klepto, right? You knew that?"

From the billow of my mother's skirts came all sorts of treasure: Tootsie Pops, Kleenex, gum—and now, from mine, came two more contraband cans, salaciously beaded with sweat. Lisa let loose a gleeful shriek and slapped my knee.

Drunk felt like laughing underwater.

Lisa barfed, discreetly, in the bougainvillea.

Omar had six brothers. I knew them from our Mosque; I knew them—I'd known them—all my life. The Hassans, one more impossible than the next, starting with Siri's husband and ending with Omar. When Omar first brought his new American wife to services, I was fourteen, and I watched as every woman smacked disapprovingly at her teeth, and in their guts more than a few husbands felt the jab of an elbow. I remember the day for the impression Anne Marie Hassan's proudly bulging stomach made on me, but also because it was the first time I was called Assam's girlfriend. Assam was obnoxious—or not simply obnoxious, but obnoxious and amorous both. He leered, he winked, he smelled like cheap cologne. His mother, Siri, was an *Auntie* to my family, confidante and adviser to my mother, and what could I say? I was not Assam's girlfriend. Not only was I not Assam's girlfriend, but I wasn't even really his friend. I did not like Assam. I didn't like the way he told the kids at school that his name was *Awesome*, I didn't like his lame crew of basketball players, his stupid jock-core haircut. We were both freshmen at Verdugo, both in American History together, and I didn't like that either. I didn't like how Siri called up my mother to ask after Assam's lost assignments, didn't like how our moms acted like we were buddies, didn't like his swagger, and at Mosque I especially didn't like being associated with ugly Omar and his bad new wife.

"Traitors," people called them, "sellouts."

I was fourteen, it had been years since Randa stayed with us, and though she still stopped by for tea, I barely ever saw her or her daughter. Randa was living in an apartment on Vermont that my mother helped her find, with a dirty pool in the back and a market on the corner—plus the Islamic Center of Los Feliz was within walking distance, so she wasn't there the day Anne Marie Hassan converted; she hadn't been to our Mosque since she lived with us and we drove her over ourselves, everyone crammed into our tiny hatchback and her baby wailing all the way. Still, when Anne Marie stalked in with Omar, it was clear that Randa was on every woman's mind, Assam's mom's as much as mine. Or more. I watched Assam surreptitiously that morning as I knelt in the rear of the Mosque with my mother. He was somewhere near the middle, next to his brother, a kid to whom I'd given my outgrown paperback thrillers, and his father, who was flinty and solemn. When Anne Marie walked in I saw Assam duck his head.

What I hated most about Assam was that he liked me. From his overloud jokes to his tripping me in the hallway, it was painfully obvious and everything about him was weird and uncool. He would, for instance, play the same trick on every new kid who came through school, the same trick he must have learned when he was twelve: whenever anyone asked about his dad, he would get one of his varsity cronies to answer for him while he ducked his head in mock mortification: "Oh, his dad? He died. Didn't you know that?" That was fine for him to do, but I obviously did not want to be associated with it. I wanted to date, sure, wanted a boyfriend to make out with, a guy to hold my hand in the halls, a clear objective to my art projects. Evan Torrance had long since moved, but in his place sprung up a revered procession of tall-dark-and-handsomes, skater boys, and punk-rock-dreams-come-true, all of them posing dangerously while Assam whaled raspberries with a fist under his armpit. I wanted a lean and hungry look, Catherine and Heathcliff, black T-shirts stretched across sinewy angular boys. Assam, as he so aptly put it, wanted to feel me up. I saw him as if he were air, heard him like the aphasiac, ignored him entirely. If you ask me, the arrangement suited both of us just fine. School was a locker room. He was a meathead. And then there was the time Mr. Van Dynwk, with a casual trick of the alphabet, paired me off with him.

We had to give debates in American History. Everything about giving debates was intolerable. It was not freehand drawing, collage, or color scale. E, F, G. Assam Hassan. Nalia Javid. We had to practice out loud with our partners, give each other tips, and do rewrites. My idea was to do the contested election of John Quincy Adams in 1824. Assam could say that political dynasties keep the government focused, and I would say that the lack of the popular vote proves nepotism. I'd win, easy.

"Yo, you oughta write mine for me, Nalia. You got mad skills."

"Great," I said, "thanks, but the assignment is what should I change."

"Well, here's my idea: we could do *men are superior to women* and you could argue it, and then *women are superior* and that would be me. Huh?"

"Assam, I care about my grade in this class, okay? You might not, but I do."

"What," he paused, grinning, "you some kind of—*master debater* or something, Nalia, is that it? That why you so up on it?"

When he gave his speech it was on me. Not American History. Not the assignment. And no one even cared. They just laughed. Because he's so funny. So wacky. It was the first time I saw the crude charisma of privilege win in an environment that was supposed to be based on merit, supposed to be fair, academic, not *The Lord of the Flies*, but ever after, when I saw frat boys and jocks, CEOs and politicians, I saw Assam's sneer, the tottering of unsure confidence and unearned acclaim. I wanted to punch his ugly face.

"Group five," called Mr. Van Dynwk, and up sauntered Assam, no fear of the podium, no creased notes, nothing. He clicked a wink at me as if we'd planned this.

"Nalia is the type of girl who would care about my man John Adams, and that's a point right there," he said. I realized immediately what he was doing. He flashed me his most winning smile. I wanted escape. Give me a medical emergency, a fire drill, an earthquake. One of his friends hooted in support, and Mr. Van Dynwk frowned at his grade sheet. My face pumped red and the humiliation was incalculable, mounting in potential with each sentence out of Assam's mouth. "My partner Nalia is the type who upholds the values of womanhood, no, the ah, well, how should I put it? The—ah—*superiority* of womanhood, right? Right? The qualities, and the seriousness, the, uh, *appeal*, and don't you pay any attention to her if she argues for the masculine. It's just her way of being *fair*." I wanted to bolt, stand up and run. I wanted to just take the F, wanted to shield my face, wanted revenge, invisibility, disownership.

The girls snickered, the boys glanced my way. People started laughing. I was sitting next to Jessica Glazer. Her speech had been on how isolationism had nearly brought down the western democracies.

"What a chump," she said, under her breath. Askance, she squinted at me. "Wow, though, he really does like you, you know? It's so obvious."

"The main thing I want to debate here is that—"

He went first, trashed our collective grade, warmed up the crowd, and then it was my turn. What could I do? I had my speech prepared. I had done my homework, written it in advance, typed it up and practiced it out loud. "In 1824," I said, untangling my voice, catching my breath, "the election was stolen in a backroom deal, and our president was a known fraud." I held my own, I knew I had to do it, and at least my rhetoric was decent, at least I'd outlined my points. "My first proposal," I said, and as I forced myself on, therefores and thuses stuck on like Band-Aids, I started to warm up, to get through it. After my second tenet I paused to let the point sink in.

"Damn, dude," Assam said to his friend, fully audible from the second row, "that chick's da *bomb*."

"Awww," groaned some girl in the back, "you two should totally hook up."

I lost my place. I could feel the dampness of my bra. *Keep going, keep going*, I thought. I looked up. I held my breath. *You're making it worse*, I thought. I clutched at the paper as if it would parachute open and brace my fall. It was the kind of silence deaf people hear when they die. Of all the faces in the crowd, only one was smiling at me.

* *

Up to this point there were no whites at our Mosque, there were no Germans or Puritans, no French, Poles, or blue-eyed blondes. Those first shocked ones came only a few at a time, but by senior year there were fifty white faces fresh from the Balkans, whole zombie families huddled in the back rows. While at the Mosque we were all both, while we discussed to which varying degrees we were both, they were neither Desi nor American. They were alien. Foreign. Displaced. After the first few were taken in, Anne Marie Hassan's crispy yellow hair didn't scream out of our throng so obviously. While she still tugged at her blouse, and seemed to bend awkwardly when we prayed, Anne Marie didn't have the same desperate, pinched look, and at least she spoke English. She ate curry. She was married to a Pakistani and on the dotted line she signed *Hassan*. Lisa had a tense dog named Rerun, whose zigzagged tail proved he'd been hit twice by a car, and whose pedigree was the L.A. County Pound. If we laughed too loudly, or if I stood up suddenly, Rerun would startle and cower. Those new people were like that, too, and anyone could tell. But they were not Puritan, or Hassidic, or Orthodox. No, they were Muslims. Like us. Like me.

"Some people are more vulnerable than others," my mother said when she caught me looking at a Nordic woman washing for prayers one afternoon. Siri nodded grimly.

"Not like I can help that," I said, because those people made me feel weird in some way I couldn't yet identify. All I knew was that I wanted them to leave.

"Oh, oh—everything is circumstance, Miss ABCD." Siri could have looked long and hard, she could have lifted her finger to scold, but all she did was sigh. "Yes, yes," she said. "Circumstance."

I stared at the woman as she unfastened her shoes, and someone walked up to her, gave her a soda. ABCD: *American-Born Confused Desi*. ABCD: me. I looked down at my feet. Most kids at our Mosque were born here and they all acted as if none of it mattered to them, to us, though it did, and we were duplicitous despite ourselves. Because what were we—if not Americans, if not Indians, then what?

At first it was just a few tall, apologetic strangers who didn't wear saris or *shalwar khamiz*, who ruefully didn't know Urdu or English, towering skittishly over everyone and sporting severe, ruined faces like burned pots. I saw their helplessness, the hardened defenseless gaze, and I felt no pity. I was not like them. I felt nothing but embarrassment. I was ABCD. American.

The refugees appeared and almost immediately my mother began to receive women around the kitchen table, hot-palated women with whom we shared our penchant for *tikka masala*, red chilies, and sweet coconut milk, women now armed with questions about mildness, cream, and inoffensive seasoning. "Spaghetti?" they asked. "Peanut butter?" No one knew what these white people would like to eat, and families with spare rooms had as many as four wrecked Bosnians at a time. I was called downstairs to speculate, and when she was with me, Lisa's opinion on the matter was cherished.

"I don't know," Lisa said, "chicken, I guess? Or maybe potatoes?" The women looked at each other, they waited. "But with cheese," Lisa said, and then they nodded.

"Of course," they said, "with *cheese*."

That was the year my first love letter came. It was not from Jared, Matt, Gio, or Adrian. I knew that much. It was signed *Your Secret Admirer*, and caused Siri to smile knowingly at me as she poured hot chai into our good blue china. I didn't show it to anyone, not even Lisa. The tone, the vulnerability, it filled me with shame, contempt, anxiety, and worse. It had been surreptitiously slipped into my backpack either during fifth period or in hallway as I was walking between classes. I studied the blocky handwriting, the weird syntax, and deep inside of me tensed a small tight coil of revulsion. Finally I hid the note between the pages of *The Crucible*. I stuck the book on the bottom of a big pile. I put my radio on top. *Now while the dark about our loves is strewn,/Light of my dark, blood of my heart, O come!* Gross.

Homecoming was in April. Fire and Ice, 1995. I knew the note's timing was no coincidence, but too bad because Lisa and I had already made a pact. Homecoming was conformist and lame. We were going to rent movies and dye our hair instead. I wanted mine burgundy and she was finally going to go platinum. It was going to be awesome. But as it turned out, poor Assam the basketball star had no date to Homecoming, and my mother immediately began receiving mysterious telephone calls.

"Tell Siri to stop trying," I said. "He has to find his own date and no matter what, okay? It's not going to be me."

"It could be worse," said my mother. "He's very wealthy, you know."

"Oh please, *amee*, save it. He's repulsive."

"*Na-hi*, Nalia. A nice Indian boy like that? It's not so bad as you think."

My So-Called Life reruns were Wednesdays at three-thirty. I flung my backpack against the couch and blipped on the television. I waited for Angela and Jordan to nearly kiss, for rumor to escalate to crisis, angst to love, but when the screen burst into color what I saw was rubble. Every channel the same. The news crews were there, the cameras were broadcasting live. A firefighter stumbled, covered in ash, clutching a bloodied ragdoll to his chest. The Murrah Federal Building in Oklahoma City lay splayed open, structural ribs dangling uselessly like cracked bone in a vivisected chest. At first I sat frozen. I saw the crushed cars, the sooty debris, and I thought, Oh my god no. What crazy Muslim did this?

The building was gouged. They said it was a car bomb. You could see office furniture. There were rescue workers, people with dirty, blood-speckled faces, people hobbling arm in arm, people crying, but underneath the rubble there were people buried alive. And dead.

I felt it in my throat. I stood up to get water. Only then did I notice the frantic pace of our answering machine light. I called my dad at work. I walked through the house and turned on every light.

"When *amee* gets home, you just stay there," he said.

"Yeah, okay, dad, but what about you? You'll be here soon, right?"

"Get yourself a glass of milk, Nalia, something to eat. You stay where you are and I will be there when I can."

The counterterrorism expert said that the Middle Eastern connection was unclear at the moment. The next day I stayed home from school. I wasn't sick. I wasn't playing hookie. My mother made me.

I missed a vocab quiz.

On CBS they said it was most likely a Middle East terrorist. They said the modus operandi is similar, that they have used this approach. All the firefighters were filthy, and digging. I flipped channels. A specialist in a gray suit and a grave face said there was very clear evidence of the involvement of fundamentalist Islamic terrorist groups. I flipped channels and saw tearful mothers, then wallet-size stills of glossy department-store baby shots.

I skipped dinner to watch television and no one stopped me.

Witnesses had seen two dark-skinned men flee immediately after the explosion. They were looking for the suspects: Middle Eastern males, twenty-five to twenty-eight years old, six feet tall, athletic build, dark hair. They caught one. His name was Abraham Ahmed. His luggage was suspicious. He was being questioned.

Assam's uncle was a computer programmer in Oklahoma City. He was a middle brother. Turns out, unlike a typical Hassan, he was no troublemaker. He was decent—hardworking, Siri told my mother, and my mother told me. Responsible and a family man.

In Oklahoma City, the green lawn of Abraham Ahmed may have been neatly clipped or it may have been a rolling lush tangle of crabgrass and dandelions. A white picket fence may have delineated its borders, it might have been a plain sidewalk, maybe a nice hedge. Whatever the case may have been, Abraham Ahmed's front lawn was now trashed. Angry neighbors had strewn glass bottles and rotten scraps across his doorstep, dog shit and eggs. While he was being detained, Ahmed's wife and two daughters stayed home, alone, with locked doors. People strategically poured weed-killer, they shouted things from their passing cars, I knew it because Siri told my mother, and my mother told me.

"One tragedy to the next," she said.

Assam's uncle was in charge of taking the three women in. He had to drive there and pick them up. They would be easy to follow. "Siri is worried for him, oh, what if he's found out, what if the people go to their home next? Who knows where it will end?" My mother sat beside me, transfixed by the screen, and I watched her envelop the news as if she could reinterpret it, undo it, make it some other way. She held the phone in one hand and mine in the other.

I thought about Assam's father. I thought about Omar Hassan and his old abandoned family; his new, American one. I felt my mom's firm grip and there was the footage: one hundred and fifty dead, and counting. Together, we watched the daycare center, we watched the fire trucks and ambulances. The news said this was done in an attempt to inflict as many casualties as possible, the news said that that was a Middle Eastern trait and something that has been, generally, not carried out on this soil until we were rudely awakened to it in 1993. The news was on all night long.

* *

"You remember Athia? Randa's daughter?" A week later my mother looked up from the calculator and a little machine buzzed, congesting the roll of white paper with taxed figures and debts owed. "Tonight they need you to babysit. Eight o'clock." The stack of W-2 forms and receipts towered like scrap at the recycling center and it was clear there would be no extraneous accommodation from her, not for days. Reading glasses balanced on her nose, desk besieged by sharpened pencils, her glaze of concentration had long since descended. The television still flickered beside her, CNN's relief coverage flashing mute destruction. "Your father will drive you. It's okay?"

Randa had a spare room, and a Bosnian woman. My dad dropped me off at ten to eight and the whole place smelled like Randa's chestnuts, except that room. Athia was in second grade, hyper as a puppy and too big to happily relocate to her mother's bed.

"That," she informed me, "used to be *my* room." I peeked in at the cloth sacks, the neatly folded towel, and the single, sad magazine page the woman had tacked to the wall: an aqueduct surrounded by some fake-looking sagebrush. "My bed," said Athia, pointing from the doorway. "My desk, my shelf, my light." For a second I flirted with telling Athia that when she was small she took up the space in my house, but instead I just told her that it was nice to share. "Yes," she agreed and then, smiling up at me, pointed like a sultan to the cupboard above the refrigerator. "Let's share the Oreos," she said. "Want to?"

When Lisa called, *America's Story* was balanced on my knees, my binder was open to the review sheet, and on TV someone in black and white was about to bite the dust. She said my mom gave her the number. "Hey, when are you done? Come to my house after. You totally should."

"Yeah okay," I said, "We should check stuff out tonight, look around. I'm really in the mood, you know?"

I stared at the television and I thought about the things my mother made me do, the chores and obligations. Siri's smug matchmaking. I wanted to slip into Randa's room, I wanted to see what her life was like, but Athia was in there, asleep. I had investigated the pantry, opened up the rickety chest of drawers the TV sat upon. They told me nothing.

Randa dropped me off around ten. Lisa's house loomed impassively in the blank dark. I slipped around back and tapped gently as a cat against the window. Lisa's face appeared and then we were out in the night, charging down the street, feeling free and unmoored. We were reckless and wild, sure, but looking back on it I realize the burst of liberation was typical, it was our shtick, and so when Lisa lobbed the first roll my way and said, "Which house?" it was a surprise to realize that I was ready with an answer as natural as arithmetic, world history, and English lit, as natural as flipping a light switch to light up a room. I didn't say "this one," or "that one over there." I didn't point or flip a coin. "Assam's," I said.

We really did a job. Strewn from every branch, the streamers of toilet paper looked like the weeping-willow boughs of some new tree. We spat on the doormat, stuck gum to the key-lock. I had an old tube of lipstick and we drew on the windows: UGLY STUPID ASSHOLE. On the off-chance of confrontation, we'd shoved the rolls of toilet paper down our shirts so that they were snug there, ticking against the skin like some secret apparatus. We worked silently, of course. We tossed, flung, pitched the rolls. We hurled dirt clods, chucked two eggs at the mailbox, trampled the flowers out front. I didn't have to say it, Lisa knew. This was hate. We were avengers, heartbreakers. The black torrent of the night transformed us into warriors, it engulfed our other selves. Reject admiration, crush what's weak, blame who you can. No cars drove past, no police stopped us. I reached into my back pocket and took out the enormous cotton bra I'd lifted from Randa's closet. It looked so lonely stretched out there across the front door, caught like some ridiculous web between the knob and the frame. Siri would think it vandals, racists. My mother would hear about it on the phone. And eventually, in a true way, I would come to regret it. But right there, standing with Lisa in the night, feeling the rage bubble over in my gut? I loved every second of it. I lifted my arm, and crickets chirping, stars twinkling, enemies asleep, I let loose with everything I had.

where eric fell

by zz packer

1.

That one boy bad as can be was always after all them little ones. Oh they pushed that poor child out the window, let him go, I suppose. Threw him down fourteen floors, them two boys shaking him for Jolly Ranchers and Apple Stix and Lord knows what not. Over where that red brick building meets the yellow bricked building at the corner. Dropped on a bald patch of earth. About the size of a baby blanket.

2.

I tell you what happened. We were all here in the Viceroy catching up. Avery Whitcomb over there was folding his paper in half and fourths and such, circling and checking the *Chicago Tribune* with a pencil like a racing form. July Henry had just turned around on his stool and ordered him some Newports. Robley Wilson was staring straight at the television with no sound on. Marvetta had just walked in. I tell you that gal was once a good-looking woman, but now ain't a one hardly pay her no mind. Lost a front tooth or someone knocked it out, eyes gone all muddy and heavy-lidded. The time we fount out about the boy, about that time or just before, Marvetta done notice ain't nan one of us move to buy her a drink so she say, "All right, niggas. I see how y'all gone be."

She done through with them drugs but on any given day them eyelids barely made from half mast. I remember a time when she would *dress,* the way people here in the Ida B. Wells used to dress before they lost all they sense, before the drugs come in. I mean Marvetta would dress, but around the time the boy fell, a year or two before, she'd put a stop to them little red or yellow numbers that made you think of the hood and ass of a Corvette.

Taint the boy's mama, but she's a aunt or some kinda kin, supposed to be looking after him. Marvetta come into the Viceroy and talk your ear off about some no-good hood-thug boyfriend or other, try to get you feeling sorry about her kids, all the while sidling up for a few dollars. She had a habit of taking the long nail of her pinky finger and worrying her scalp, working from back to front. By the time she finished, her hair was sticking up all over like the spikes of one of them palmettos you see down in Florida.

Oh Marvetta. Time that boy fell or just before, she done scratch her head then scratch her head some more. I turn my eyes from it. I don't want to see no raggedy woman's dandruff. Probably by the time she call up for a drink again is when we all heard the screaming. Went to the door, try to see what it was. High-yella girl, she say, They done kilt him! They done kilt shorty!

Shorty. That's they new word, how they talk. Talking about 'shorty' for the youngins, you heard such a mess? Go out and call a slim young gal shorty, too, and don't matter how short or tall they be rising. Lordamercy, Avery and Robley and just about everybody in the Viceroy went to the door, just to peek, cause if it was some driveby or bullets whizzing they'd put a bullet in a old man same as a new one, sure as I'm born. So we peeking 'round the corner, and that high-yella girl coming at us in some flip-flops, but everything flopping and hanging out, and her face all twisted up and tears running down, she say, "They killed little shorty," and by the time she get to the door of the Viceroy, ain't nobody thinking bout her titties, swear to god, old Avery just hold her and try to calm her down, but she been running and her eyes all red we done thought whoever done got kilt was kin of hers. "Want some pop?' Avery say, and can't no one tell wheter she done shook no or nod yes but Robley went in and brought it to her, and I tell you I notice he done got himself a Budweiser in the mix, and Marvetta just sitting there right up in the Viceroy, just she could just feel it, she just knew she shouldn't be where she was.

Ordinarily, Marvetta would a been the first one out there, head all snaked around the corner, yelling out the street, "Who done got shot?" But I tell you, sure as I'm born, she set up there on that little stool and just stare right in front of her.

After word on the street came out and said two boys dropped another little boy fourteen stories, Lord, I don't know. I tried to search my heart to see what black folks had come to. Folks didn't do stuff like this back in Mississippi, back in Chicago before the drug foolishness. Didn't even look at Marvetta. I knew she had something to do with it. Let them other mens chew her out.

Well I made up my mind. The least I could do was pay my respects, find out that boy's Christian name. Didn't take me long to find the mama. When something happens here, you just follow the trail, people everywhere, yellow tape, po-lease cars. You could see the mama and tell who she was. Someone try to take her somewhere, cover her with they coat, and I went hat in hand to the mother of that young man and I say, "Pardon me. I know you grieving. But I just came to let you know you don't have to go through it alone."

She sniffed up, told me his name, like I was a reporter coming to write it down. She say Eric. Eric Morse.

I ain't never heard a no boys throwing another boy out no window. Over some candy. Wanting the one boy to turn on his Christian mother and steal some candy for 'em. Now you know that ain't right. I trembled, and I ain't ashamed to say that I did. You get old, you see things. You all right with crying.

3.

I remember, back in the day. It was like a year ago or something when I seen Eric for the first time. Everybody else had gone I-don't-know-where, and him at first I thought he was a little slow in the head, you know, because everybody rolling, and I stop and catch my breath and look out at the same time because sometimes them driveby dudes'll do reduxes. That's when I seen him. Little dude was across the street pushing the crosswalk button! Know what I'm saying? Them crosswalk machines ain't even hooked up to nothing! You can push that button all you want, but it don't make no difference. So I'm all, "Shorty! Get over here!" But the cars on kept whizzing by, and little shorty *would not move*. That was Eric for you. I didn't know little man's name at the time, but now, it's like, Eric this, Eric that. So, back to what happened last I saw him. I'm like, "Shorty! Shor-TAY!" It was a driveby, and he pushing the street signal! Finally, some cars stop and little dude run on over to where I'd run when I caught my breath, but I was bout to wait for him. I just kept on.

4.

You can't see something that happen that fast, that happen—blip—just like that. No offense. I was coming away from the Jewel grocery, wasn't even looking in that direction. I was seeing this brother across the street, walking with this ol limp-haired white girl. No offense, but that burns me. To see some good-looking brother with some white girl, usually fat. I'm like, you can't find no sisters? Don't matter, he wasn't that good-looking no way. So anyhow, before I can even tell the brother and that bitch where to get off, I hear screaming. I mean real screaming.

After the screaming, it got quiet, but you could tell something had happened. Usually somebody screaming, you cock your head a little, try to figure out who it is and what's going on, but after a while you just ignore it, you know? Specially if you don't hear no followup. But this screaming, then that silence? You don't be hearing silence like that in The Wells except for maybe the day there's a funeral, and even then it be three hours before the go on and break the silence, talking about, "I'm get revenge on they asses." Silence like that, I just knew somebody had died. You can tell a whole lot by listening. Knew it wasn't they fault, knew it was a goddamn shame, and ain't nobody even said nothing. See, my mama say I'm psychic, but I ain't even gone play and pretend like I knew who it happen to. I heard it was someboy name Eric. Didn't know him, but I did know them bad boys that done it. Someone should a whupped they asses long ago.

I'm like, they done killed this little boy before he done got to see something. Just think, he done live in here all his life, see the same old brick, same old parking spaces, same old bad kids and no-count fools trying to get high or doped up. I keep thinking, this so sad, this so sad, and when I heard about them services, I called up Tamara and said, let's go, and she talking about, "ain't no dudes *our age* gone be there," and I'm like, "forget you, then, ol' superficial ho." Now she's my girl, too, but I was mad. Here this boy done had his head split and she talking about *some dudes our age*. Usually we fall out, I call her back, but I was too mad. Next day I got dressed, black dress I got from the Marshall's on Magnificent Mile, done wore it to five funerals that year alone. I get there, worrying, I don't know why. Thinking, I don't know him, somebody gone see that I didn't even know him, or somebody gone ask, "How you know Eric?" But finally I stop worrying, they so many people there that I barely got inside them doors. They let you go up to the casket, which you know had to be closed, but they got his picture up there, big nine-by-eleven. He was so cute. In a little suit, all his little white teeth like Chiclets. I don't know why, but I closed my eyes and kept wondering if he'd ever seen a deer. It made me break down. I stood there and cried, thinking, he ain't never seen no deer. I stayed there for I-don't-know-how long, and finally, somebody come put they arm around me, and usher me away, so the line could keep moving.

5.

I was on the couch, watching cartoons because that's what was on. Not like I'm into Bugs Bunny or nothing. The cartoons, they just *on*. Not no Saturday neither. My uncle, Doc, had sat down next to me, and everytime Bugs say, "What's up Doc?" Uncle Doc just laugh his ass off, like it's all about him. Mama was over at church, but it wasn't Sunday, so it must have been Wednesday night prayer meeting. One time I done told her she gone to pray her brains out. So, I'm just watching TV, can't enjoy it cause Doc's all, "You still being all you can be?" Motherfucker couldn't say "Army" like a normal person. He elbowing me, and I yank up my face like, *Give a nigger a break.*

He knew I quit doing the Guard thing long ago, knew that I done got sick and tired of going to redneck Rand Toole in Nowhere, Illinois, every fucking month, but he's all, "You still doing more before four A.M. than most people do all day? You still 'Semper Fi, Do or Die?'"

I'm like, "That's the Marines, black."

"Same difference," he say.

But on he go, talking about some cousin who was in the Army, some cousin I ain't never heard of, and how that cousin had joined the Army about two months ago in San Antone and how Uncle Doc wanted to know—what *he* wanted to know—was about the weapons, but all this cousin would talk about was the *mosquitoes* in *San Antone*, and— I'ma tell the truth. I wasn't listened after that, he just carry on a whole conversation by himself, laughing Har, Har, occasionally like he's some white politician.

I'm wishing I had a remote to turn him off when there was this screaming, I mean, this was something else, even for The Wells. Then I got this bad feeling, like psychokinetic. Bad, man, bad. I could feel it on every inch of skin. Somehow, *somehow,* I knew Johnny was behind it. I don't know how, but I knew.

I was looking out the window, Bugs Bunny in the backgound because we can't find no remote, and then there's some crying and I don't know what all. I guess the scream was the girl who done saw him fall, they say she just flipped, worser than the mama, and she wasn't even related.

You know the rest. They discover it was two boys that done it, and one of them, sure enough, was Johnny. Roman come over and tell me about Johnny and Tyrone, throwing that boy out the fucking window. I didn't even bother waiting for the police to bring Johnny's ass home. Knew it would be years before that boy come home.

Wish I could say I went to Mrs. Morse to pay my respects, apologize for my brother, but I didn't. I took the El to my mom's church over on Indiana and 44th. Didn't want to go, cause I ain't set foot in that church for five years. But I had to tell her. Had to.

6.

I was there. I done told it so many times, I know it like a poem. Told the police on Johnny and Tyrone, the ones that done it, told my mama, she shaking, voice shaking, asking me to tell it one more time, then stop me before I get to the end, send me out the room. We all cry at the funeral, like we supposed to, and they have the wake at my Aunt Carlene's so it ain't in the projects, but when I go to pee, I bump into Mama outside the door, and she led me to the room where there's all the coats, and sit me down on the bed so I'm almost falling off, and she standing this time, and she say, Leonard, go on. Tell me what happened. Again.

I say, but I done told you, and she say, but there's something missing. There's something missing! And I say, I told you mama. And she get tears in her voice, all over again, but I done heard the tears so much they get boring to me, so I say, they had pushed him out, but he was still hanging onto Johnny's wrists with his hands, and they kept saying, Is you gone tell? Is you gone tell? And he keep saying, I'm gone tell on you! And I'm talking to them, saying, He won't tell, I promise, swear to God, now bring him back inside, but Eric was shaking his head, and Tyrone was hammering his fists where Eric was holding on, and I kept trying to grab Eric's forearms but he kept saying It hurts! And Tyrone would push me back when I kept trying to grab Eric and the one time, the last time, he pushed me down. I got up. I could see him biting where Eric was holding onto Johnny's wrists, and Eric was screaming, I'm gone tell! I'm gone tell! and that's when I saw it: He only had one hand holding on, and Tyrone kept on pushing me back like he didn't want me to be on his team for kickball, and by then I'm thinking, he only got one hand holding on, and Tyrone won't let me get at him, and that's when I see Johnny at the window, and he ain't holding on to Eric no more, but I don't got time to go to the window, I don't got time for nothing but to run down them stairs, so that's what I do, I run down the stairs, Mama, I run down them stairs cause if I run down them stairs fast enough, I knew I could be there for him, I knew I could catch him.

proper dress

by joan wilking

Last Wednesday, during third period, Mrs. Ridley handed the burqas out to the boys.

"I whipped these up," she said.

The neatly folded stack looked like a pile of matching bedspreads. When Angela asked, Mrs. Ridley said it was because that was exactly what they were.

"We bought these on a trek through India. Years ago. Packed them away and forgot all about them until last week."

She picked one up and let it fall open. The fabric was heavy cotton; red, blue and yellow-ochre paisley bordered by dark green lotus flowers. A hole had been cut, a little bit off-center, and replaced with a patch of something dark blue and stretchy.

Mrs. Ridley poked at the patch.

"A pair of my old pantyhose," she said. "Don't worry. I tested it out. It's pretty see-through. At least enough so you won't be bumping into things."

Three of the boys looked at each other and shrugged, but Kevin, as usual, hadn't been paying attention.

"Burqa?" he said and looked down at his Birkenstocks and socks. "I didn't know they made tablecloths."

The other boys all laughed. Mrs. Ridley didn't. She ignored him. She always ignored Kevin. Then she handed one to each of the four boys. Tom held his up and pressed the fabric to his nose.

"Phew-eee," he said. "Smells like incense, incense mixed with cat pee."

"Patchouli," Mrs. Ridley said. "Mr. R loved the smell of it, so I used to douse myself with the stuff, way back when. That smell never goes away, the perfume equivalent of plutonium."

The boys all laughed at that. Michael tried his on. It took a minute for him to get the eyes right.

"I can see, but it's like looking through a screen."

Mrs. Ridley picked up a ruler and whacked Michael on the thigh.

"What was that for?"

Mrs. Ridley whacked him again and turned to the other boys. Jake and Mark took a step back. Kevin was still inspecting the converted bedspread hanging from his hand.

"When you're wearing your burqas you don't speak unless spoken to," she said.

The boys all laughed again.

That was last week; they aren't laughing now.

Caroline Crowley has been the hardest on them. I always thought she had a mean streak. She's constantly looking for infractions. At first Angela, Melanie, and I tried to tell her to go easy, but after Kevin threw the tantrum on Friday all of us started to get the point. If you let one get away with it, the rest will follow, so we're starting to make the boys toe the line.

Surprising how quickly they all started to look alike. After Mrs. Ridley made them take off their shoes, and wear only black socks and blue jeans, they kind of disappeared as Kevin, Michael, Jake, and Mark. Melanie's the one who came up with the nickname. We all started calling them the Burqa Boys and the name stuck.

There are only eight of us in ELP. That's short for Extended Learning Program, the smart kids. That's us. Third period Mrs. Ridley plays mind games with us.

She's set up a hot plate at the back of the room. While we work on brainteasers the Burqa Boys prepare snacks. Tuesday she had us bring in dirty underwear, and made them wash it out, and dry it with Caroline's blow-dryer. The boys really didn't like that. When Mike muttered something about the detergent doing a number on his hands Angela gave him a good crack with her math book. That shut him up and they all went back to scrubbing away.

Jake's developed quite a cough. Melanie suggested he go down to the nurse, but Mrs. Ridley said, "No. Have a woman examine him? Sacrilege."

So Jake's been hacking away and sniffling. A couple of times I caught him uncovering his hand when he tried to blow his nose on a corner of the cloth, and I had to whap him on the wrist. In the trough in front of the chalkboard I found a long wooden ruler that works really well. It gives me enough reach so that if one of them tries to hit back they can't get to me before I'm well out of the way.

Angela says she admires my technique.

You've got quite an arm on you, Janine, is what Mrs. Ridley says every time I take a swipe at one of them.

By yesterday we thought we had them pretty well tamed. When third period started, they filed in and only one of them made any noise. Caroline took care of that. She's rigged up a pencil with a dressmaker's pin taped to the tip of it. They all sat nice and quiet in the back of the room after that while we did our math drills. Then we started on vocabulary, test prep for the SATs. That's when Michael lost it. He stood up and ripped the burqa off.

"That's it." He was shouting. "I'm dropping out. I'm dropping out of ELP. Enough of this bullshit."

Blasphemy.

Caroline's the one who poured the lighter fluid, while Melanie and Angela hit him with the books and the ruler.

"Go ahead, Janine," Mrs. Ridley said. "You light the match."

balancing genius

by peter rock

Can you imagine an artist who works with a tractor and chains, who drags broken machines and wrecked vehicles across the ice, balances them against twisted jungle gyms from abandoned playgrounds—who leaves a rusted junkyard on a lake frozen thick and calls it art when the thaw sets in and the jagged pieces tip and settle and slice down, gone into the black water, disappeared from that winter horizon?

Some people didn't see this as art. They called it pollution. Brian can imagine it, though, and he would not call it that. Now he stands in his living room, the furniture clustered in the middle of the floor, and holds an insulated mug of hot water. This is his drink of choice while he watches his son draw on the walls.

Jeremy cannot reach high; he is six years old. He sighs and gasps and whistles, these sounds soft behind the scratch and skitter of the charcoal. He is working on a tangled landscape of people and machines, all fit together and atop each other, thick. He reaches into the bag of briquettes when he wears one out. He's in pajamas, and is barefoot. The palms of his hands are blackened, and a dark line marks one side of his face, where he's scratched an itch.

Seven months ago, Brian found her. Angela. He found her in the classifieds; so few in child care dealt with special-needs cases, and she had come right away, as soon as he had checked her references. That first day, she leaned down to say hello to Jeremy and her heavy black braid swung off her shoulder and caught him in the side of the head. Jeremy stepped back, bewildered. That was the last moment of awkwardness between them.

From the covered bed of her yellow pickup, she brought the tools she'd need, the rolls of butcher paper that she spread across the hardwood floor.

The boards are still marked where Jeremy's tremors ran the paint beyond the edges. She started him with watercolors, then acrylics. She had him paint with his fingers, then with splintered sticks that she snapped from bare bushes. She never gave him a brush.

Jeremy watched her; he followed her instructions as if that had never been a problem. She hardly ever spoke to Brian, outside of making the arrangements. She never told him where she was from. He remembers one day when a rainsquall rose up and the water came thick from the sky, impossible to see through; Jeremy was distracted, delighted, pressed against the window, and she turned and said that it reminded her of another thunderstorm, a time when she was out in a cabin with a lover. *We took off our clothes, and went out and stood on the wooden porch, handing a bar of soap back and forth. I've never felt so clean, all that crashing hard water.*

She always spoke in a very low voice to Jeremy, so it was impossible for Brian to hear what she told him. It was only possible to see the colors he chose, his drawings some hint at her words. Sometimes, Brian leaned above the two of them—closer to Jeremy's sweet scent that is like milk, yet is not milk—and Angela would glance up, her expression a warning, as if Brian's presence threatened to break a spell. Her black eyes forced him back.

Yet sometimes she let pieces of her past show. Standing before Jeremy's scribbled, overlapping machines and people, she had once stepped back and whispered, *It looks like a war*. And then she said that her lover (a current lover? the same one from the rain? the braider of her hair?) had fought in 1991, had been lost for two days in a storm, flat in the desert, breathing sand, sharpened silt. The man had dreamed of water, ice water, until the sky finally cleared.

Now Brian steps to the window, squints through Jeremy's jagged lines on the glass. Outside: the bare, rainy street. Angela not arriving. No one. Not even the people marching with their banners stretched taut between them, protestors of the new war (is the lover there now, fighting again, nostrils choked with sand? is he in some other country, or no country at all, in a bare cell surrounded by cold water?) Angela has not been with them, these protestors. Brian wonders what she thinks, which side she would take.

He remembers how, before, early one morning like this one, she arrived with a bag of cheeseburgers, saying *Jesus I'm hung over*; she unwrapped one and held it out so Jeremy could take a bite. On his way to work that morning, Brian had stopped at a drive-through and bought himself a cheeseburger. He'd eaten it, hot and greasy, as he sat at his desk. He is an accountant. At night, when he closes his eyes, he sees rows of numbers, scrolling and scrolling, the same way the white lines of highways stripe truck drivers' dreams. Merle Haggard has a song about that, called "White Line Fever," that Brian long believed was about cocaine; when he found out the truth, he almost felt he owed Merle an apology, for thinking the worst. No one can be blamed for traveling.

Brian never uses a calculator. The numbers come easily to him, not that that means anything. It sickens him, the frequency with which people assume that Jeremy must also have some special facility with numbers, or memory, or music—as if every handicap has its balancing genius.

Jeremy can only reach so high. There is a line of horizon and then—beyond the length of his extended arms—nothing but white. He was responsive, he changed around Angela, and some of that change remains as he hums and circles, even now that Angela is gone. It is one of the only words, that name, that can make Jeremy take notice. Brian says it now, to check, to remind the boy. There is a pause, a peek at the window, a glance to the empty driveway, and then the drawing resumes. Brian stands in his suit and tie, his polished shoes, watching and waiting, the water in his mug lukewarm and half gone. On the walls stretch one-armed people, cars with feet, tractors with human heads, spirals of smoke hissing out of every last thing. Thick, dark strokes mark fields that could be grass or sharp wire, and the drawing continues across the windowpanes, overlapping and changing the world out there—peopling and confusing and fascinating it so that walking through the door, outside, is a disappointment.

Still, Brian stares out the window. Thirsty, he sips at his water. The last visitors, two weeks back, came in a group, men and women. He mistook them for protestors; he told them he had his own battles he was fighting. But he was wrong—these people were parents. It turned out that Angela had plenty of special-needs children she'd worked with, whose paintings she had encouraged and collected. Brian recognized the names of these people as her references, parents who had spoken so well of her and now had turned. These other parents told him that Angela was not actually her name; they brought a newspaper article about an art show in a gallery in New York City. What she had done was pass off their children's paintings as those of the sole survivors of tragic fires. She claimed she'd found patients in psychiatric hospitals, people who could not speak, whom violence had shocked beyond language.

All that was fine with Brian. It didn't change a thing. What she said was not a lie, exactly, and he believed that she'd given more than she'd taken. He exasperated them, the other parents said. They walked away as he waved and wished them well.

Brian is grateful to these people for providing him Angela's real name, a name he cannot pronounce. The thawing ice had also been her artwork; he has read about it, seen photographs, and now he feels as if he is down in the cold water, looking up at the broken hole he's fallen through. Now that he has her real name, he has written to her. If only time can be turned back slightly, he'll rise with the rusted machinery, the broken playground and totaled cars—up from the lake's murky bottom, slicing through the water and slowly into the thin sky, the ice lifting and hardening beneath. She will return to see these walls, to see Jeremy and to see him, and she will say where they came from, and who they will be.

jumping jacks

by doug dorst

The skyline of a city you've never visited blazes night-vision green on your TV screen, and the audio track is all thumps and sirens, pippitypops and batterclangs, and you are reminded of the hiss and spit of sixteen flaming fuses on a pack of jumping jacks on that day twenty years ago when you and your best friend, Bunk, burned six acres of forest to the hot black ground.

Jumping jacks. You buy them on Mott Street from a toothless grocer who natters on about *fun-fun* and *bang-bang* beneath a canopy of decapitated poultry. You decide this man is a fool. Jumping jacks may look like firecrackers, but they don't *bang-bang*. This man knows not what he sells.

Tear open the red paper wrapping, and a fine peppery dust darkens those candy-cane swirls. The fuses are woven in a gorgeous lace of potential energy. Don't you see it? Can't you feel it?

It is a drought-stricken September after a rainless August and a dust-dry July. You and Bunk walk along the trail, kicking through brittle, crackling leaves. Bunk stops, and in his hand suddenly is one of the red paper packages. He unwraps it and says, *Check this out*, and snaps a flame from his fifty-cent Bic and lights it and tosses it into the air, where it becomes a sparkly gunpowder butterfly—eight jacks per wing on a thorax of fuse—and all this before you can say, *Wait*.

The sound? It's a cartoon sound: when a man is startled and his derby hat spins off his head. *Fweeee!* Math lesson: *fweeee* times sixteen equals the shit you're in. But for a moment it equals glory: the fireworks spray spark trails of red and purple and gold and blue as they sizzle and wheel and whirl and spit and squeal. It is a chaos of motion and sound and color that to you (a thirteen-year-old suburban Goodboy) is epiphany, is rapture, is revelation, is power and light. And then it is sixteen spinning fire-sticks MIRVing through the sere orange air.

And then it is sixteen small fires igniting around you. You try to stamp them out; you dance from fire to fire, but flames keep springing back up in the places you've just leapt away from. The air turns autumn-smoke gray. At first the smoke teases you with chestnut-cart sweetness, but then it turns to black choking guilt, and panic rises in your throat and nose. Bunk is standing still. *Let it burn,* he says, and you quit trying to stamp out all those fires, because you believe he knows something you don't. It's a moment of self-doubt masquerading as trust in someone else. And then the flames spread, feeding on the forest, chain-igniting, now waist-high, now chest-high, now head-high, now high-high, and you snap back into yourself, knowing that this is fucked up, something is deeply fucked up and about to get a million times more fucked up, and you are a party to all this fucking up, you've fucked up, you're a fuck-up, boy howdy you have really fucked things up this time.

Let it burn, Bunk says again, and the deadness in his voice scares you. His mesmerized stare at the flames licking, crackling, devouring—that scares you, too. You don't understand the hypnotic allure of destruction. You understood that initial rush, that flood of wonder and adrenaline, but not this flat-eyed stare when everything around you is heat and blaze. Destruction scares you shitless, and you run home, alone. You change clothes. You hide your singed-hairless forearms under long sleeves.

The aftermath? You were not caught, Bunk was not caught, no houses burned, and the woods came back strong and true: first as lush, bright green life springing from the scorched ground, then as trees thicker and straighter than before. This, you think twenty years later, was exactly the wrong lesson for you to have learned. Where were the consequences? Where were the fucking *consequences*?

Today, when skylines burn in night-green, when the president's *faits* are *accompli,* when smoke rises from spent casings and molten steel and charred skin and newspaper ink and your neighbor's *good morning,* you imagine yourself there again, standing in the woods while the trees are igniting, desperately turning to Bunk and finding him lock-limbed in a fire-gasm, already transformed into someone you don't know.

It is Bunk's crackly, dead-leaf voice that now rasps in your ear: *We lit that place on* fire, *man. We burned that motherfucker* down.

the politics of culture

innocent

by charles baxter

"You were driving?" she asks. She has a faint German accent—that of someone who was brought to this country as a child or teenager.

"Yes. On I-94."

"In Michigan? Close to—?"

"Well, it was the center of the state. West of Jackson, closer really to Adrian, but past that too, I think. Farm country, most of it. Fields and billboards."

"And what vehicle were you driving…?"

"Our minivan. I had some things to take up to the Twin Cities, not all of them my own. They included some of the household ornaments—they were very delicate, breakable—belonging to a friend of mine who had moved there. I mean, I had errands of my own, but I was carting these objects up there for her. For my friend. As a favor."

"You were heading west, then. You were westbound."

"Yes, I was."

"You were alone? In this…minivan?"

"Yes. I was listening to some music. Rock music, I think. REM? A group like that. I don't remember exactly. Rock music keeps you awake. More alert."

"You were on a schedule? Of sorts?"

"Yes, I was supposed to meet with my friend's friend the next day, and this friend of my friend was going to store these objects that I was taking up there in, I don't know, his garage. Basement. I don't remember exactly where he was going to store them. It doesn't matter."

"Was there much traffic? On the freeway?"

"No."

"The usual?"

"Yes. The usual midsummer traffic."

"Did you have a phone in the car?"

"Yes." There is a long pause. I lean back in my chair. "It belonged to my wife. I don't believe I had ever used it."

"Never?"

"Well, maybe once. Or twice. It was an old-time cell phone. In a bag. You had to plug it into the cigarette lighter to power it."

"Yes, I remember those," she says. "So what happened then?"

"Well, I was driving in the minivan, with this music on, a CD, minding my own business, you might say, and looking at this more or less featureless Michigan landscape, passing under various overpasses and not particularly noticing them or the support posts, you know, the steel and concrete that hold them up."

"*Not* noticing them."

"That's right. I *wasn't* noticing them. Because you don't, until or unless you're a civil engineer or you have a particular interest in bridge design."

"So you're telling me," she says, "that you *weren't* noticing the bridges, although they were there."

"That's right."

"So what were you noticing?"

"Not much. I wasn't noticing very much. You fade out, you know, glaze over, when you're on a freeway that you've driven on many times, what my uncle used to call the 'stupor-highway.' Ha-ha."

"But then you noticed something."

"Yes," I say.

"Well, what?"

"I was in the right lane, the slow lane. And in the left lane, the lane for passing and faster traffic, there was this Oldsmobile, and inside it, a woman, smoking a cigarette. I saw her pass me and I saw the woman's hair, which was brown, and her face looked strange."

"How?"

"I knew you would ask me that. But I can't tell you. I can't tell you *how* her face looked strange, only that it did."

"What was her age?"

"Early forties, probably. The Oldsmobile was fairly old, very used-car in its appearance. And she passed me, this woman. And then just after she had passed me, I noticed that she was veering off onto the shoulder, the shoulder of the freeway, and I thought: why is she veering off onto the shoulder?"

"Yes?"

"Anyway, then the car veered off farther, and I saw…I saw that she was now driving on the median, this green grassy area between the lanes of traffic heading east and the lanes of traffic heading west. And she was driving on the grass now, on this bright sunny summer day. And I thought, uh oh, she's fallen asleep. But, no, if she had fallen asleep, probably the car would have slowed down. And her car wasn't doing that. It was speeding up. And then I saw that the car was heading toward this bridge that crossed over the freeway ahead of us, and there was a support post for the bridge in the central grassy median, and she was heading toward the support pillar, and she was accelerating."

"And you…?"

"I started to say, aloud, in the minivan, oh no oh no oh no oh no."

"And what happened then?"

"She accelerated ahead and her car, this Oldsmobile, without slowing down, struck the support post. There weren't any protecting barrels around the concrete, which, you know, they sometimes have, to slow down a car or cushion an impact. They didn't have those barrels there, surrounding the post. Maybe they were saving money on the state budget. Anyway, her car hit this support post at about sixty miles or seventy an hour, and of course I had never seen anything like that in real life, and the speed of the impact caused the Oldsmobile to rise up somehow and then to fall backwards, upside down, on the shoulder of the opposite lanes, the ones heading east."

"Okay," she says. "What did you do then?"

"I pulled over on the shoulder."

"Did you call anyone? The emergency numbers? 911?"

"No."

"Did you go over to her car? To help her?"

"No. I don't know CPR. I don't know any of that emergency stuff."

"What did you do?"

"I waited," I say. "And then I slowly pulled out into traffic and drove away."

"You continued heading west."

"That's right."

"Why?"

"Because…because what could one do? I couldn't revive her. I don't know how. And for those moments I forgot that I had a phone in the car, and that I could've called some emergency number, for a rescue. Jaws of life, and all that."

"You could have stayed to give a report to the officer at the scene," she suggests.

"I figured that others could do that."

"You didn't want to stay."

"That's right. How do I explain this? If I stayed, I would have had to see her, I would have had to see her wrecked bloody body inside that wrecked bloody Oldsmobile, this woman with brown hair who had been smoking a minute or two before, and whose face looked strange, and I couldn't do that. I couldn't stay to look at her inside the wreckage. I didn't want to gawk."

"You were afraid."

"Yes, I was afraid. You know, some people can look at something horrible, at the horrors, but I can't. I know myself. I can't look at them."

"Why can't you?" she asks me.

"Because…because if I look at them…I know I'll go crazy."

"How do you know that?"

"Oh, I know my thresholds. The one for craziness is quite low. You show me those things, I can't cope with them, I'll lose it."

"So you continued driving. Although you were the major witness."

"Yes," I say. "I have never ever described myself as a courageous person."

"What about cowardice? Have you ever described yourself using that word?"

"I don't remember," I say, "whether I have, or not." I wait. "Besides, I had a schedule," I tell her. "I had to meet with my friend's friend the next day to drop off these objects in the van, these objects I was taking up to the Twin Cities."

"Oh," she says, with an edge of irony, "so that explains it."

"I didn't say that that explains it," I say. "I'm only telling you what I thought."

"So you drove on," she says. "At what point did you call the Highway

Patrol to tell them?"

"I never did that," I say.

"Have you ever read Camus' *The Fall,*" she asks me, "the one with Clamence, who tells the story? How he sees someone jump into a canal in Amsterdam and does not save him?"

"Spare me your literary allusions," I say. "And yes, of course I've read that book."

"You don't think it applies?"

"No," I say, "I don't think it applies."

"Why not?" she asks me.

"Because Clamence is guilty and I'm not."

"You aren't?"

"No," I say. "I'm innocent."

"Oh," she says, "Innocent. Yes. But. I don't think you're innocent at all. Not if you leave the scene. Not if you don't care about consequences."

"Who are you to judge?" I ask.

"Just someone who listens," she says. "But there is something. Something that I'm pretty sure of. In this way…in this way that you witness this woman's death and this wreckage, and you don't want to look at shocking horrible things, and you're afraid you'll go crazy if you see it up close, to help her, and you sort of drive away, and you have this excuse, this excuse that you have your friend's things in your car, your minivan. And you know what I think it is?"

"Go ahead," I say. "Tell me."

"It's very American," she says in her faint accent. "This innocence. It's very up-to-date."

9/11 l.a. bookstore

by michelle tea

That morning I lay in bed, unable to fall back asleep from all the sugary pink wine, feeling sort of jittery-sick, restless and exhausted. The phone rang. It rang and it rang and it rang. When it seemed that it would ring forever I figured it was Erika with a really good celebrity sighting, like Ellen Degeneres or Cher. I pulled the Yellow Pages over and sat on it like a stool, not wanting my bare ass to touch the carpet. *Put on the TV, turn it on.* Erika was breathless. What? I grumped. I'm So Tired. *Something fucked-up happened in New York, like the Empire State Building got blown up, I don't know, will you turn on the TV?* I looked at the TV. Its curved gray screen mirrored the gray of the studio, warped it like a fish-eye security mirror in a convenience store. I looked sideshowesque, the small bloat of my tiny booze-belly poofed out, my face drawn and haggard. I'd untangled the dreads from my long blue hair last night at the table, and now it frizzed out around my head, badly damaged and full of static. I looked like Krusty the Clown. Listen I Have To Go Back To Bed, I said. I'm Sick. I Feel Awful. I'll Turn It On Later. *But something's happening,* she insisted. It'll Still Be Happening In Like, An Hour. Come On, I Didn't Go To Bed Till Four. *I know.* I hung up. I swam back into the bed. Through the narrow strips of blinds I could see a movement that I knew was the Rottweiler getting into his stalking position. I rolled over. The phone rang again. It was Fortune, Erika's first girlfriend. They had been teenage speed freaks in love with each other. They dropped out of high school and shacked up in Fortune's basement bedroom, a cramped space filled up with bed and cigarette smoke, and they would get high and crash there, get high and crash and fuck and never go to school, all of this more or less okayed by Fortune's parents, a hippie couple on their own drug-propelled love affair, smoking pot all day and necking in the upstairs hot tub. On the telephone Fortune was crying, but Fortune often cried. She was horribly romantic and had terrible taste in boys, would get knocked up regularly by coked-up pro skateboarders and phone us in tears with new tales of abuse. *I just want to make sure you're okay,* she said, with a little hiccup on the 'kay.' *That Erika is okay and little Deborah, you're all okay?* Fortune's voice was rich and watery and full of tears, with a California twang. Yeah Fortune, We're Fine. Erika's At Work, I'm Sleeping. *Oh she found a job? Oh, good,* she hiccupped. Was There An Earthquake Or Something? Are *You* All Right? *No,* she said, and a fresh gust of sobs rattled the receiver. *Me and my mother were supposed to have breakfast at Windows on the World next week. I can't believe it. I can't believe it...*The Empire State Building? I asked. I could feel a vein in each of my temples, a single vein in the tender corners by my hairline, pulsing. I needed to lie back down. *No, the World Trade Center,* she cried. *I love you guys, both of you guys. Go back to sleep and have Erika call me.* I crawled back to bed and then the phone rang again, my little sister. She sounded somber and reverent, like she was putting a call in from a funeral, but Audrey often sounded somber and reverent. She was born a day after our mother's birthday, and like my mother collected news of deaths and tragedies, impossibly sad stories she would share with me when she phoned. Our mother was a nurse, she hung out with the sick and dying so it made sense that she would be such a font of morbid information, but my sister was young and gorgeous, a casting assistant, both the Wahlberg brothers had hit on her in the past week, and Alyssa Milano had said something bitchy to one of the Hilton sisters during a recent audition—Audrey was full of these stories, but also these dark anecdotes, the ones she hushed her voice for, like the sister of a friend who had worked as a nurse and kept a hidden morphine habit, stealing the drug from the hospital and shooting it up in her home, alone, where she overdosed and died. Now Audrey had her dresser, a beautiful work of hand-carved wood. Wow, I'd said. *No one knew,* she whispered. *She hid it from everyone. You don't do morphine, do you?* No, I was happy to tell her, I Have Never Done Morphine. *You don't shoot drugs?* No, I was also pleased to assure her, I Don't Shoot Drugs. *Swear to god?* Swear To God. *You don't believe in god, though,* she said suspiciously. It's True, I Don't. Swear On Erika's Life. Swear On Deborah. I Don't Shoot Drugs. Shooting drugs was desperate and unnecessary. Everything worth doing could be smoked, snorted and swallowed. Audrey returned to the tale of the dead nurse. This morning it was different. *Oh Michelle you've got to get up,* she said. *Really. You won't believe what's happening. They took planes out of the sky, they did emergency landings, and if the planes don't land they're going to shoot them out of the sky.* Oh My God, I said. I imagined a plane being shot out of the sky. *People are jumping from the World Trade Center, they're jumping out of the windows. I can't get through to New York, I've been calling people all morning. It's an attack.* I imagined jumping out of a window. The window of a skyscraper. I knew once I turned the television on it would be on for a long time. I just wanted to lie back in bed just a little longer, just drink some water and eat an aspirin maybe, and just lie until my headache subsided. *I just want you to know that I love you,* Audrey said. *I love you so much and I'm glad you're in Los Angeles and we can be close. I want you and Erika to come over to my house today.* I Gotta Work, I said. *No,* Audrey said, *You won't work today. Nothing is open except the In and Out. Just come over.* Erika's Working, I said. *She'll come home, I bet. They're closing everything. There could be more attacks.* This just seemed way too sci-fi and dramatic. It was irritating. Well, I said bitchily, Shit Like This Was Bound To Happen. It's Like We're All The Kids Of Mafia Guys And We're Inside When Our House Gets Firebombed. *Yeah,* Audrey said. *Just turn on the TV.*

In the kitchen I killed cockroaches with my bare hands. I'd become immune to it. Every morning they were there, scuttling across the counter, and the only thing to kill them with were glasses that would shatter, so I'd begun bringing my hands down onto them with a slap so hard it pulverized them, it juiced them, and my hand would go warm and sting and tingle, the vibration felt up to my shoulder. I'd turn on the faucet and rinse them from my palm. Big ones, the baby ones we called tweedlebugs, I smacked them all to death. Do You Hear This? I'd holler into the room where Erika lay sleeping, back during the golden age of unemployment. I Am Killing Roaches! I would scream. With My Bare Hands! I needed a witness for this. To both my bravery and the mundane horror of this life in LA, in this apartment. *I'm sorry,* Erika said, and she meant it. She hated the bugs worse than anyone. *You're not gross, the bug is gross,* she would comfort me. Our studio housed bugs we had never known existed, bugs from deep in the jungles of Costa Rica, that somehow came to be inside our apartment, slithering beneath the kitchen sink or lumbering across the scabby rug, alarming Deborah. One looks like a feather, it has a million wispy legs that float its slinky body above the linoleum. It is almost beautiful, except it is so horrifying it makes our throats close and our eyes water. It is an alien bug from another planet. When we killed it, its legs shriveled up and it turned into just another stain on the kitchen floor. Beetles fat as tanks waddled out from a crack in the wall, a sturdy-looking beetle, it looked plastic, a fake beetle, a gag beetle you would scare a co-worker with, a robot manufactured to look like a bug, plodding toward you by remote control. We screamed. If we killed it we would hear its body crunch. We couldn't hear that. It was too much. Our arms rolled with goose bumps at the idea. Deborah hissed and dashed into the bathroom. She has learned how to jump into the empty bathroom window, we caught her there staring wistfully at the alley below. We feared she was planning a suicide, like a disillusioned starlet hurling herself off the Hollywood sign. I grabbed a juice glass we bought at the dollar store, and caught the formidable beetle. I released it outdoors, where it no doubt worked its way inside and back to its family within our walls. I scrubbed and scrubbed the glass in the sink, to show Erika, Watch, I said, and I coated it in antibacterial dishwashing liquid. It took ten minutes to rinse the suds from it, but still Erika refused to drink from the glass ever again.

Eventually I get out of bed. I go into the kitchen and smack some roaches, I dump the half-empty champagne glasses, thick with dead fruit flies, down the drain, I make coffee. I take a shower. Outside the bathroom window is the freeway, which the East Coast calamity has not impacted. The cars whiz by. Sometimes there is a crash, and our apartment building and the apartment building next door empties and everyone crowds around the edge of our dead-end street and tries to peer over the concrete wall into the freeway below. The crashes freak Deborah out, but there is nothing we can do to protect her from life's harsh realities. As I shower, Deborah leaps into the sink and licks the drips from the faucet. She's stopped drinking from her bowl and now will only hydrate herself this way, meowing at the sink's porcelain bowl until we turn the water on for her. I put on Erika's favorite dress, the one she likes best on me. A dense polyester thing that stinks up my armpits the second I zip myself into it, orange polyester shot with white, like a Creamsicle, with plastic gold buttons angling down each side of the torso, a weird mock-turtleneck top and box pleats. I look like a waitress on *Star Trek*. Erika loves it. I boil pasta and crush cloves of raw garlic onto the slippery noodles, bring it all into the bedroom even though we had sworn not to do that, not to eat food in the bedroom for fear that the roaches will follow, and climb through our hair as we sleep. I settle onto the crumpled futon with my pasta and coffee and watch the television. Deborah comes and curls on my lap. I watch the planes hit the buildings again and again, eating my brunch. I watch the people jumping from the buildings. I can barely see them because our TV is so staticky. I'd get up and swat the antenna but I don't want to disturb Deborah who is purring on my polyester skirt. People are running through the streets, being chased by huge rolling clouds of debris, like a monster movie. It looks like the debris stirred up from the pounding footsteps of a giant lizard. I think about the people in the airplanes and cry at how scared they must have been. The ones who called on the cell phones, I cry at that too, and I cry at the stewardesses, the thought of them. My hangover is powerful, I am all exposed nerves, I just sit on the futon and cry. Anthony calls from Boston. He got to work in the financial district after the first plane hit. Everyone was gathered in the lobby watching it live on giant televisions. Then the second plane hit and everyone screamed. Everyone ran back into the streets and down into subways before something attacked Boston. Anthony sounds shaky. We hang up and I go back to the TV, the same crash again and again and then the next one, again and again. I imagine what it felt like to steer the plane into the building, how the plane entered it as if it were water, a liquid column, smooth. Then the blooming fire, the orange bursting out into the sky. Again and again they ran it until it looked beautiful. I turned the sound off. It was a ballet, it was stop-motion photography of a milk drop, or a bullet coring an apple. Ellen called. Her voice warbled timidly. *I don't think I'm going to stay open today,* she said simply. *It doesn't seem respectful. To sell things.* I sort of loved Ellen. For being such an uptight hippie, for opening a junkyard of books on that slick strip of commerce. For crying all the time. *It's a day for us to be with other people,* she said. I hung up. I was thrilled to not have to go into work. Erika came home shortly, sniffing at the air as she opened the door. *Is that garlic?*

Audrey picked us up in her zippy little Honda Accord that made creaking birdlike noises as it drove. We pulled into the In and Out that had remained open all day. A giant American flag was draped over the bushes across the street. The first one. Erika noted mournfully that the In and Out workers were making more money per hour than she was, with benefits. Perhaps it was time to investigate the fast food industry. *Erika, I can see you being a producer,* Audrey said robustly. Audrey was wicked optimistic. She was convinced that if we could just stick it out a little bit here in Los Angeles Erika would find a job producing films, I would write a screenplay, and we would be rich. Audrey had written herself into this fantasy too, she would be the head of a stable casting boutique and her visionary casting impulses would win her awards, make her the talk of the business, a hero to women for casting actresses with real bodies, actresses with integrity. To cast doubt on her plans for me and Erika was to call her own ambitions into question, so I kept quiet and picked at my French fries. I didn't know how Erika would manage to leap from unemployable in the service sector to producer of million-dollar films, but I loved Audrey for seeing Erika's potential. I saw it too, this capability, a certain bossiness that merged with a deep charm, a flirtatious charm. Had she been born into a family of privilege and had ingrained within her a sense of life's possibilities, if she could identify and then believe in all the options that were out there, then yes, Erika would be a fucking awesome producer. But Erika, like me, was not raised with this sense of entitlement, with a belief in possibility, and so we both sniffed out jobs that paid single digits an hour, and every one we scored felt like a huge scam, like we had tricked our new employers into thinking we were someone else, college graduates perhaps, clean people, people with rich wardrobes who did not kill roaches with bare hands. I watched Erika bristle at Audrey's sunny suggestion. There was also the part about Erika being an extremely masculine woman, and those stunning qualities she possessed, the subtle flirting, the winsome charm, the bossiness, they were to die for in a man but in a mannish women, freakish. It made people uncomfortable. Especially male people. At Audrey's house we would no doubt be subjected to more life directions from Audrey's meddling roommate, Alicia, who had a lot of energy and was constantly on the hustle for careers. Like my sister, Alicia was generous, and while she was out there hustling for herself she'd kindly hustle some for you as well. It made me anxious to hear them list the many opportunities Los Angeles had to offer. Did they just think we were losers? If it was so easy why were we making six, seven, eight bucks an hour? What was wrong with us? Audrey pulled her tweeting car into the North Hollywood driveway and we all lumbered out, balancing armfuls of In and Out, the greasy steam opening our pores like a trash facial. Inside we went to watch New York fall apart. Audrey had cable and I saw how blue the sky was, how the flames leapt out from the building like solar flares. The people jumping from the towers were people, not pixels. We sat and watched and watched. *It's too much,* someone would say, and walk into the kitchen. Alicia's husband was a chef for a five-star restaurant on Melrose. He was a mute man and when he talked you could hear that he was from Boston, specifically Dorchester; he had the thuggish inflection of boys from that town. But he didn't talk much. He cooked. He was whipping up some giant end-of-the-world feast for us to eat in front of CNN. Finally we shut it off. Everyone had agreed that it was too much, it had been on for hours and the stations were just milking it, it was sick, there was nothing new to show but they wanted to keep us there, staring. Someone lifted the remote and it was gone. I felt let down. Secretly I'd wanted to keep watching. I was hooked. The commentators kept promising that the surrounding buildings were going to fall and I wanted to see it happen. I knew there was something really wrong with wanting to keep watching. There was this detached fascination that I wanted the reality of the images to wear away, burn it down so I would finally and truly *feel* whatever it felt like to *feel* what had happened. Surely this alarmed car-crash-style interest was not what I was supposed to be feeling. I was supposed to be feeling something a few layers down, something authentic. I had a hard time matching the land on the television with the New York that I knew. It was like watching *Blade Runner* and looking for Los Angeles. It was like a horror movie, or an asteroid-hits-Earth film. Rachael in Boston will e-mail me later, *I keep waiting for Bruce Willis to pop up and save us.* The television now rested on a film about a plucky lady alcoholic who gets sent to rehab and eventually comes to understand that she really *is* an alcoholic, and then she finds love, real, nonalcoholic love, and dumps her British partyman boyfriend to be with her new recovery soul mate. When it was finally very late I was scared to leave Audrey, because she has problems with anxiety and I knew she would sit up all night long in front of CNN watching the buildings burn and having panic attacks. Which is exactly what she did.

The next day I had to go back to work. When I went to work I'd leave by the back door. Out the little area where the homeless kids sometimes hung out, a sort of yard I guess but it was in constant shade from the building, it was cracked pavement with lots of dead leaves and some little shoots coming up through the rocky gaps. There was a bike out there, and a junky motorcycle, and some weights. Once I sat out there and smoked a cigarette but that was it. It was just an experiment. I'd been experimenting with the idea of private spaces, places I could go if I needed to be alone, if Erika and I had a fight or if I felt trapped and claustrophobic, if I needed to pretend I was alone in the world, free like that, nothing but me. There really wasn't anyplace to go. The crappy back alley with empty booze bottles fallen over against the wall. Once I saw a dead palmetto bug there, all stretched out in rigor mortis, and I thanked the baby Jesus we hadn't found one of those in our studio. Yet. There was a front fire escape that hung over the entrance. I sat and smoked there a few times and felt like a strange woman-statue blessing the front of the building. It was a bad place to go to cry, on display like that, looking out at the lit-up *Lion King* billboard, the Capitol Records building that was promoting a new Pink Floyd record by keeping a giant inflatable pig on its roof. I tried the back fire escape but the fire escape thing was generally bad because of earthquakes. Once I cried in the basement laundry room, but that was a jumpy place as anyone could come in at any time—Freedom's owners, the Tommys, the Think Pink! girl. And then what would I say.

To get to work I left through the back. On the little side street I would sometimes pass the scariest homeless man in the world. In San Francisco there were homeless people everywhere and they were very harmless. They were often aggressively sweet and you wanted to give some change if you had any in your pocket, and sometimes they would give things to you, like the pigeon guy on 16th Street who passed out sheets of his writings and would let the street birds march all over him, cooing and pecking at the seeds he sprinkled across his body. Once he even gave me pot. And Leo, the guy around the corner from where I used to live, he would look at you and place a finger to his lips and say *Ssshhhh,* very solemnly, and if you saw him and beat him to it, if you looked at him and went *Ssssh* he would start giggling uncontrollably and it was the cutest thing you'd ever seen and you just wanted to move him onto your couch. Plus he wore pink feather boas. Many things I had purchased from Leo's grimy market on the corner of 15th and Mission—a rabbit fur coat, black platform shoes, ceramic doves. The homeless people in San Francisco were sadsacks, they'd been fucked by the system, had drug problems and continued to get fined by the cops for being broke. There were fewer homeless people in Los Angeles, or at least in my new neighborhood, but the ones I saw seemed scary. It seemed there were many more murderers in Los Angeles, and I think this scariest homeless man who I would pass en route to the bookstore was perhaps the man who had killed the Black Dahlia back in the '50s. He was covered in dirt and his blue eyes burned out from the grime like gas flames. He stared. It was a stare more menacing than the neighbor's Rottweiler, it was the stare of a vacant human, an empty person, someone whose insides had been vacuumed away by something terrible. He was a large, strong-looking man and his hair curled out wildly from his head. He looked like Charles Manson. That was it, really, he looked like an extra-dirty Charles Manson. He was probably the nicest person in the world, a bit shell-shocked and grimy from sleeping over by the freeway, but sweet as the sweetest hippie homeless guy back home, and because he had the misfortune of resembling a famous serial killer I had decided he was pure evil and wanted to kill me. After briskly passing this guy I turned the corner and walked the long stretch of Scientology, picking a couple of the small yellow orchids they'd planted along the sidewalk. I watched the Scientologists dash in and out of the compound. I especially enjoyed the maids, who wore real, old-fashioned maid uniforms, black and white with little aprons and nursing shoes. I longed to get a job at the Scientology Celebrity Center and clean the rooms of visiting Scientology celebrities while dressed in such a sharp, retro uniform, but they would never hire me. I glared at them. Way up on the hill in front of me the Hollywood sign sat wearily on the dead, dry grass, looking like a wavering mirage in the smog. I crossed the street and walked over to the bookstore. Ellen was already there. Every day I had to tell a customer that Ellen was not a Scientologist, that our store was not a Scientologist bookstore, though we did keep a lot of dictionaries on hand for new Scientologists to purchase. Don't ask me why. They love dictionaries. Customers would remain skeptical. Really, I'd insist. She's Just An Old Hippie. Ellen had written a poem about New York City and was hanging it in the window. My project that day would not be the regular Sisyphean task of finding space on the shelves for more books, but to find books that contained pictures of the New York City skyline, the old one, with the twin towers. She left to tend to a migraine and the husband's esophagus, and I began culling photography books from the cramped art section. Joey stopped by briefly, to throw a copy of Frank Zappa's "Sheik Your Booty" and The Clash's "Rock the Casbah" in the record window. She's Not Going To Think That's Funny, I told him. She'll Take It Out. *Yeah, well.* I loved Joey. If Los Angeles had been filled with nothing but Joeys I could have lived there, happily, forever. The more I worked with him the more he revealed. He was intensely new age, belonged to a private mystical cult. He made fun of customers to their faces without them realizing it, a talent I wanted to acquire. He had a thick, knotty scar running up his torso from his big New York City drug overdose. *Someone was in here this morning and I heard them say 'sand nigger,'* he said. You're Kidding. What Did You Do? *I kicked him out.* Joey was having a domestic crisis—his one working-class roommate wanted to hang a flag out the window, out of respect for the fallen firefighters. The other roommates, upper-middle-class academics, were horrified. Joey thought they could compromise by hanging some sort of peace flag. Oh God, I said. Flags. The flags had popped up quickly, were suddenly everywhere. In our laundry room, where I had recently gone to sob, there was a computer printout flag pinned to the corkboard amidst all the color flyers for the Ibiza-style foam dance parties Tommy Teeth promoted. Then came GOD BLESS THE U.S.A., each letter its own sheet of paper, taped across the wall. All the stores on the strip had hung paper flags in the window; Ellen, bless her heart, thought we would instead install a bunch of these New York City skyline books in the front window. Not to sell, of course—that would be tacky. Just as a memorial. She arranged them nicely beside her poem, and also a book of photography opened to a photo of a bombed-out home in Palestine, and an Italo Calvino short story about the irony of war. The Nostradamus books were selling well, as were our copies of the Koran, and anything about Islam. But business was slow. I liked business being slow as it gave me more time to slack off and read. The little gray-haired lady who was head of the strip's neighborhood group came in, all hustle-bustle. She always ignored me, so I hated her. I wasn't used to this new Los Angeles bookstore person thing. In San Francisco it was totally cool to work in a bookstore. You would starve to death because they only paid seven dollars an hour, but you would die cool. Here in Los Angeles you were not cool. You were a stupid counterperson making little more than minimum wage in a town where people made millions of dollars a day. There was something seriously wrong with you. You were completely invisible. Even Ellen was like that. I found a copy of my book stashed in the gay and lesbian shelves at the back of the store. Oh, I exclaimed, sort of happy. I Wrote This. It was like I'd forgotten I'd existed, so delighted I was by finding myself on the musty shelves. Ellen peered over. *Oh really? Wow.* Went back to sorting jazz records. Clearly, if the book had been any good I would not be working in the bookstore. I crammed it back onto the shelf.

The neighborhood group lady came in with a stack of flyers promoting the neighborhood candlelight vigil that would take place right there on the strip, that evening. You could see she was all jazzed up about the terrorist attack. Before this she only organized meetings where local tenants and local business owners screamed at each other about things like permit parking. Ellen was convinced that permit parking would kill the bookstore. It would go under. All the businesses would. It would be an apocalypse. The husband would come into the store and rail against it, pounding his fist on the counter. If he was a customer I would have thrown him out, but he was king. *Michelle wrote a book,* Ellen told him, as if I had a quaint little hobby, like quilting or building miniature ships. *Oh yeah?* he asked, squinting at me. Oh, yeah, I sighed. *Well, I wrote a letter to the journal about permit parking, and they printed it as an essay,* he gloated. That's great, I said. *It's very controversial. People are talking about it.* I Bet They Are, I said. It's A Real Hot Topic. Now the divisive permit parking issue could be shelved and the neighborhood brought together as Americans, candleburning, flagwaving Americans. *Are you coming to the vigil?* The neighborhood lady actually spoke to me. This really *was* bringing people together. I'm Afraid I Have To Work Tonight, I told her. *Well it'll all be happening right outside the store!* she chirped. Around six o'clock she came back in to drop off some candles. White candles with red, white, and blue mylar ribbons tied in a bow around the base. The sky was darkening and people were beginning to cluster along the curb. First there were only a few and then there was like a hundred. People having drinks at the restaurants brought their pints out onto the street and hoisted them into the air like it was New Orleans and a great parade was passing us by. Someone on the corner had made a poster board sign that said HONK FOR AMERICA and cars were zooming by honking. When they honked, everyone cheered. The neighborhood lady dashed up and down the strip, weaving through the crowds, handing out candles. Outside the bookstore Ellen had set one burning in a glass Coke bottle on top of the quarter paperback cart. *Michelle keep an eye on that candle?* she asked. *Make sure it doesn't fall over and catch the books on fire?* The store was empty. Ellen and her husband had gotten good seats outside the Italian restaurant, but kept checking in to make sure the store wasn't being looted. I lingered outside by the candle. Things were getting crazy. A guy dressed like Uncle Sam was dashing up and down the gutter, pumping his arms in the air, inciting the crowds to cheer and they did, they went nuts. Everyone seemed drunk. A young kid, good-looking, no shirt on, had a large cloth flag and he held it over his head and ran around the block with it fluttering in the wind above his rippled torso. They loved it. Then a Boy Scout troop showed up and stood across the street where it was mellower and sang patriotic songs. That stretch of sidewalk is owned by the Scientologists, a group of whom were standing on the corner holding a large flag and waving to cars. They began shooting dirty looks at the Boy Scouts. A few rebel Scouts broke loose from their troop and climbed on top of the bus shelter by the Scientologists and started chanting *USA! USA!* and the crowd just started to shit themselves, they went buck wild, because what is fucking cuter and more *real* than a gang of little boys chanting *USA!* from atop a Los Angeles bus shelter. Then a fire truck cruised by. Fuck the Boy Scouts. Firemen! The real heroes! People started to cry. The fire truck honked its damagingly loud horn and more drinks were lifted into the air. People were waving flags. People asked me where they could get candles. A Little Gray Lady, I told them. A blonde girl walked by on a cell phone. *Yeah, it's really awesome you should come down, it's awesome*…Tommy Hairdo strutted down the street, his pristine spikes bobbing high above the average head. *We were up on the roof,* he said, *you should see it from up there! You should come up with us, drink some beers.* Can't, I said, nodding my head back toward the bookstore. I'm Working. *Oh,* he said, looking down quickly, as if I said, Sorry, I Can't, I Have Uterine Cancer. What was with these people? They seemed embarrassed by my lack of shame at having this job. It's just Tommy Hairdo, It's Not The World, I scolded myself. But it *was* the world. It was this world, Los Angeles.

The same pickup truck kept circling the block until finally the topless boy with the flag hopped on the back and a roar went up around the crowd. Others jumped into the street and climbed aboard. Now it really was a parade! They clustered there in the bed of the pickup, the boy in the middle with his fluttering flag, a few other guys clutching beers in one hand, keeping flag boy steady with the other. *It looks like Les Miserables,* a passing fag commented. Ellen came by to ask if I wanted to take the candle and march down the block. I'm Okay, I assured her. She looked around the empty store. *Go have a look. There's nothing to do here.* I made it as far as the bar and grill, where the crowd grew thicker and yeastier and my arm was burned by someone's cigarette. I turned and marched back to the bookstore. Too Overwhelming, I said. They left. A tall, loud man, red-faced and robust burst in the glass doors. *How much is that book!* he crowed. *That book in the window, with the twin towers! How much for that?* It's Not For Sale, I told him. It's A Memorial. *Oh,* he deflated. His lower lip sagged down in a pout. *But I want it,* he whined. I shrugged. I Just Work Here, I said. *No, really,* he pushed. *I wanted to buy it, and then walk around and have everyone out there sign it, to commemorate the evening.* You're Kidding, I said. Where was Joey? Joey would love this. Like A Yearbook? *Exactly!* he brightened. *Like a souvenir.* Talk To The Boss, Man, I said. I Can't Help You. He squinted his beady bloodshot eyes at me. *You just could have had a really great sale,* he snapped and pushed back out into the throng.

That's what's wrong with this country, a voice shot out of nowhere. I craned my head around. There was a longhair crouched down in the sci-fi stack, sitting on the floor by a pile of *Star Trek* paperbacks. Long hair and oversized eyeglasses. *They think it's a goddamn sporting event out there,* he grumbled. *This is precisely why everyone hates us.* Yes, I agreed. I shook my head up and down. I wanted to tell him he could pocket a few of the *Star Trek* books and I'd look the other way, but I wasn't sure how he'd take it, so I just gave him a lot of room instead.

dade county, november 2000

by jim shepard

Felton was a fundraiser for a university major enough to go to the Rose Bowl every so often. He worked in what they called the Development Office. He wouldn't have thought it was his kind of job. He didn't even go to the door when repairmen or Girl Scouts came around. When the doorbell rang, he ducked into other rooms. If Lori was home, she got it. Sometimes she had to come all the way downstairs. She rolled her eyes about it.

He was the youngest guy in his office and enjoyed milking his boyishness. People in Development usually looked like they were headed for the cocktail party after the regatta, but for crunching numbers or processing paper, he wore skateboarding shirts with obscure logos. They hung on him like tents.

He was upbeat. He was cheery. He had good skin. He looked like someone who took kids kayaking.

Twenty-somethings in coffee shops argued whether they were in the Midwest or the western part of the East. It was that kind of place. In town, it was not really safe and not really dangerous. Bikes disappeared from garages and the occasional jogger was mugged but you always found cars and houses unlocked anyway.

He liked to say that he had the lowest horizon of anyone he knew, and that he didn't give a thought to Thursday, let alone the upcoming year. He claimed not to judge but somewhere inside believed people preoccupied with the future were nervous, fussy, and nerdy. Leif Erickson hadn't worried about the future.

"Leif Erickson?" Lori said. "The actor?"

"The explorer," he explained. "The Viking guy."

"Yeah. Well," she said. "Next time the doorbell rings, you get it, Magellan."

Things dragged for Development the week after Reunions. They called the end of June Counting the Pile. A new capital campaign didn't kick off until the fall, because as the higher-ups liked to say, at this point they didn't have the meat: they hadn't identified which exhilarating big-ticket items were going to make them need the money in the first place. July 2nd he had a big address—his first—welcoming everyone to the 41st Annual Alumni Golf Tournament, which was enough of a big deal that Alumni Relations ran a lottery to fill the two hundred and forty slots. But that was about it for serious responsibilities until August. He went in late and came home early and hung out at home, playing with the kids and annoying his wife, who was trying to run a consulting business from the study. Sebastian, who was four, insisted on an undersized wooden bat and a real softball instead of the various Nerf or wiffle things they had lying around. He got good wood on it periodically, and since they faced the house, it sounded like a rifle shot on the shingles. When Sebastian pitched, Felton took measured swings but still followed through on the ball, counting on his bat control to keep his kid from being skulled. There'd been a few close calls.

Bradford, the eight-year-old, wanted to be a BMX racer, and spent the month trying to ride his bike down the six-foot-high woodpile beside the garage. He wore shoulder pads he found at a tag sale. Felton would lob the ball up to Seb, while from the back of the house they'd hear a spectacular clatter and crash.

His kids reminded him of himself. They were the kind of kids other parents liked to see around their kids.

He'd had a little deck built off the study. He sat there in the early evening of July 1st in a stew of vague expectations, watching the boys play a game he'd invented called *Evel Knievel: Triumph and Tragedy.* The game involved a ramp made of two pieces of firewood and a toboggan. Seb stood in for the buses. He kept his arms at his side. Brad got a good riding start and usually cleared his brother by three or four feet. Their father sipped his beer and provided color commentary. He'd finished his talk a few days earlier, and liked the way it had come out.

A gray van turtled around their cul-de-sac before disappearing. You couldn't see in its windows. The boys segued to an incomprehensible game involving spinning the front wheel of the overturned bike and throwing clumped and dried grass through the spokes. It did a poor job of holding his attention. He stood and wandered off the deck to the end of the property.

The back was forested. In the summers it was a real jungle. It was dense enough that soccer balls shanked into there were lost until the fall. There was an overgrown evergreen hedge on the property line, and the hedge ended where the slope dropped off to a creek. When he found himself over there, sometimes he crouched beside the hedge and spied on his neighbor. For the summer she'd begun a program of topless aerobics on her balcony after she got home from work. She didn't play music. She sang to herself, huffing the lyrics.

He heard the boys go into the house, their arguing enclosed and more distant. His neighbor was not on the balcony, but he hung around anyway. He supported PBS and subscribed to the local symphony, but if left to his own devices in a hotel room was just as likely to settle in front of the porn channel with some Cheetos from the mini-bar.

It got darker. Bugs cheeped. Lori at this point always appreciated help with the kids' baths, and mosquitoes were humming around, but he dawdled on the way back. A spider like a bluish button sat in midair between two branches.

It felt significant that his neighbor hadn't been working out. He had the gift of finding special meaning in everything that happened. He crouched when he was almost to his lawn, and raked loamy dirt from under the pine needles and leaf debris. It looked like brownie mix on his fingers. He touched some to his tongue.

The gray van coasted around the cul-de-sac again and pulled up his driveway. Two black guys and a white guy got out. They looked about his age. They headed to the back door and he lost sight of them because of the angle.

His molars were gritty and he spat and made exaggerated movements with his tongue. He stayed in the bushes, trying to see into his house. He had a good view of the living room but there was no one in it.

The leaves above him shook with a breeze. He thought he heard Lori's voice but nothing after that.

Not leaving the bushes produced a luxurious, cosseted feeling. He knew what was expected of people in situations like this. It was time to barge on in there and see what was going on. See what they wanted. Who were they, anyway? His stomach registered a flutter of anxiety.

It was the first stage of a daydream he'd had since he was a teenager:

some lucky girl would get to watch him enact his love through the reckless disregard of his own safety.

Brad passed through the living room with the look of someone investigating something. He saw his dad standing like a doofus out in the back and gave him a look before disappearing through the doorway to the kitchen. There was an exclamation from one of the boys, it sounded like. A skating and a jarring sound and the wobbly oscillation of what sounded like a pot lid on the floor. There was a shriek. He stepped forward. He listened. He lowered his head and turned to listen more intently. Lori shouted his name. It was time to go into the house. He folded his arms, and took three more steps forward. He was well out onto the lawn, now. He leaned to see around the front.

This was what cowards did. This was what the most timid creatures on earth did. He huffed out a breath and started walking, and climbed onto his deck. "What can I do for you?" he'd say. He'd be amused at how simple the story would turn out. He slid open the door to the study and heard the back door shut at the same time. Car doors. He passed through the study and the living room and heard the van's engine, and by the time he got the back door open, it was out of the cul-de-sac and down the street.

Blueberries from a Tupperware pint were scattered across the kitchen floor. The TV and DVD player were gone. He took the stairs three at a time calling Lori's name. The little rolltop desk in their bedroom had been ransacked. There was a shirt on the floor in Seb's room. Felton was panicking aloud as he stumbled back down the stairs. God was part of the subject.

His skull cooled. He squatted on the kitchen floor and held his cheeks. He stood, and dropped down again, like someone doing knee bends.

He grabbed his car keys and flung open the back door and scrambled into the Taurus, cracking his head on the sill. He was already despairing as he accelerated out of the driveway: which way to turn? How far to go in any one direction before he gave up? Wasn't he better off calling the police?

At the end of his street he turned in the direction of the main road out of town and almost sideswiped a bicyclist. It was a mile down a pretty steep hill and he whomped along, bouncing on his shocks. He skidded around a curve when he reached the bottom and then had to stand on the brakes and fishtail to a stop, because Lori was standing on the grass beside the stop sign, with the boys crying and hanging on her like mailbags.

There was no relief in her expression, and little panic. Her eyes were terrible.

"Are you all right?" he called.

They stayed huddled where they were, as if trapped on pack ice.

He tumbled out of the car. A pickup behind him had to slow down and nose around him to pass.

"Where were you?" Lori asked.

"Where was I?" he asked in return. It was a good question.

He tried to put his arms around her and Seb but she led the boys to the car.

Who was to say what was possible and what wasn't? The impulse to lie was overwhelming but arrived unaccompanied by specific lies. Her eyes were malevolent with fierceness. It was like he'd lifted a balsa effigy of himself into a typhoon.

She slapped away his hand and strapped her still-wailing younger son into his car seat. He searched his feet for a lie he could use and then recoiled. Every so often he was given a glimpse of himself that was demoralizing for purposes of orientation.

"Where were you?" she asked. She got into the car. He got into the driver's seat.

"What happened?" he asked.

"Where were you?" she asked. "Brad said he saw you right outside."

"I *saw* you, Dad," Brad cried.

"I was right out in the back," Felton said.

"Start the car," Lori said.

"But what *happened*?" Felton said.

"*Start the car*," Lori said. "Get us home."

"Do that much," she said, after he started the car and turned in the nearest driveway.

She looked shattered and repulsed as they drove back up the hill, like she'd had to watch one of her parents eat the other. He was terrified.

"What happened?" he asked again. "Will somebody tell me what happened?"

"Three guys," Brad said.

"Three guys," Seb echoed from his seat. His pronunciation was compromised by thumb-sucking. His cheeks were streaked with tears.

"They just came in the house," Brad said. He was rubbing his arm as if to warm himself up. "One guy had Mom downstairs and his hand on her mouth. Two other guys were getting all our stuff."

"They got our stuff," Seb said.

They pulled into their driveway.

"One of the guys hit me," Brad said. "He bent my arm."

"Are you all right?" Felton asked.

"They were arguing about kidnapping and yelling at each other and the guy driving just stopped and threw us out of the car," Brad said.

"I'm gonna *shoot* 'em," Seb said. He held his fist forward as proof.

"Is your arm all right?" Felton asked. Once back in the garage he threw the Taurus into Park and swiveled in his seat to check. Brad held his arm up. It looked unmarked.

Lori was already around to Seb's door and unhooking him from his safety seat. She hefted him out and carried him into the house. Felton opened Brad's door. Brad looked at him before getting out.

In the kitchen Lori had the phone to her ear. Seb was on her hip.

Brad was wandering around inside the garage with his hands on his head. It hurt Felton's chest to see him that way and he went over and roped him in with one arm, hauling him up like a baby and swinging him around. He carried him into the house. Brad seemed to appreciate it but was still looking away.

Lori had hung up the phone and taken Seb upstairs. He heard the water running in the tub.

He dumped Brad onto the couch and walked to the bottom of the stairs. He asked if she wanted help. She didn't answer.

Brad was still on the couch, looking at where the TV had been.

Felton walked through the downstairs. He surveyed every room. He returned to the kitchen and collected a notepad and Magic Marker from near the phone and began a list. Brad was still sitting there on the couch.

"You okay?" Felton asked.

"Yeah," Brad said.

Speaker wire snaked up from the baseboard, going nowhere. The speakers, the subwoofer, the PowerBook, the MP3. A row of DVDs. They'd taken the receiver and left the turntable. The speakers were Infiniti, the subwoofer was Polk. Lori kept the operating manuals somewhere, which would help with the insurance. Some glassware had been pulled out of the breakfront. He could hear splashing upstairs, but no talk.

There was a knock at the back door. Brad jumped.

Felton hustled over to it. A tall young policeman was standing there, trying to unsnap a little notebook from its carrying case.

He introduced himself as Officer Rowe. Brad whimpered.

Officer Rowe explained that they'd had a report of a home invasion. He asked if Felton could tell him what happened. Felton called Lori.

She came downstairs and sat on the couch next to her son and took his hand. She mentioned as if for everyone's general information that Seb was finished with his bath. Felton went upstairs. Seb was using a cup to dump water onto the bathroom floor. Felton mopped it all up with a bath sponge and then pulled him out of the bath and toweled him off. He drained the tub and shook out the bath toys. He could hear Lori talking below. He dried Seb's hair and found his comb and bundled him up the way he liked and brought him back downstairs. They sat at the kitchen table and Seb said he wanted to comb his hair himself. Felton oversaw his progress. The policeman and Lori seemed to have finished talking.

He asked what Felton could tell him. He turned a page in his notebook.

"I was out back," Felton told him. "I saw them heading toward the house. I didn't know what it was about."

"I'm combin' my *hair*," Seb said in a low voice. "No knots in my hair."

"I stayed where I was," Felton said. "I didn't go in to find out."

Officer Rowe nodded and blinked. He wrote something down.

"I froze," Felton said. "I stood there. I got going toward the end, but then it was too late."

Lori and Brad looked like they were watching TV. The cable wire dangled out across the empty media table.

He added whatever he could think of that might be helpful. Two black guys and one white. About his age or maybe younger. The white guy had a blue warmup with a logo. Maybe the Magic. They'd all been wearing big shorts. But he probably had all this already, from everybody else.

Officer Rowe wrote some of it on his little pad. When he stopped, he cleared his throat and said that anything could help.

A bird outside was making a repetitive, two-note call. Officer Rowe asked what Brad had noticed and Brad gave an impressively detailed rendition of one guy's tattoo.

"Why would they let us go?" Lori said. "Wouldn't they worry we'd identify them?"

Officer Rowe said they probably weren't from around there. He asked if anyone had noticed the license plate. No one had.

Even Seb was quiet. He was looking up at the ends of his hair, held away from his head by the comb.

Officer Rowe asked them to get together a list of what was missing. And to call if they thought of anything else. He told them he'd be in touch. He asked if they were all right.

Lori started crying. Felton got up and knelt in front of her. She put her arm out to keep him away but kept her hand on his shoulder. Officer Rowe looked embarrassed, and said goodbye, and left.

"I'm so *sad*," Lori said after he was gone. "I'm so sad."

Seb combed his hair and chose to say nothing about what his mother was doing. Brad was still looking at the wall with a bleary kind of misery.

She got to her feet with a blundering impetuousness, like a startled Labrador retriever.

He asked where she was going. She said she was really, really tired, and left him to put the kids to bed. But when he did so, she helped him, clearly worried about how they were doing. They seemed okay. Brad asked him to leave the hall light on.

He tidied up downstairs and locked the doors and turned off the lights. Then he trooped back upstairs and brushed his teeth and got undressed and got into bed.

He was beating around a fact the way children hoped that tapping a box would let them know what was inside. He did a lot of mental writhing. In college, his girlfriend before Lori had been a Classics major from Santa Clara who'd broken up with him on their junior year abroad at the beginning of an eight-hour bus trip in Greece. "Your two muses are Narcissism and her sister, Entitlement," she'd said.

"Oh, how poetic," he'd said. Then he'd tried, in his snottiest voice, "I thought it was Narcissus." She'd just given him a withering look.

He hadn't been able to muster anything further as a comeback. It had been their last exchange on the trip. There'd been no other available seats on the bus, so they'd had to sit shoulder to shoulder in silence for the next seven hours.

What was the morning going to be like? How were they going to get through the week?

Lori for the foreseeable future was going to look at him the way she had at the bottom of the street.

The dressers and the rolltop desk in the bedroom waited on him with a malign indifference. I *knew* you were like that, he imagined God saying.

"I chickened out, is what I did," he said to himself, lying there in the dark. "I was a chicken." He remembered the feeling from grammar school. There was no response from Lori.

Why *had* they been let go? If they hadn't been let go, he'd still be in crisis mode. Lori would still have no idea what he'd done. He would be her hope. He imagined others' sympathy. He envisioned his panic, and his resolution.

He was beginning to glimpse the way in which his narcissism locked him into an ongoing contemplation of a tiresomely unpleasant person.

He stopped processing somewhere in the middle of the night while mesmerically repeating Shirley Ellis's "The Name Game." He woke midmorning on his back with his mouth open and his arms spread. Lori passed through the room carrying a load of folded laundry and towels.

"If your speech or whatever isn't finished you better get up," she said from the bathroom.

"All I have to do is pick out a tie," he answered, looking up at the ceiling.

She put away some shirts in his dresser and left the room.

While he brushed his teeth he tried to focus. He listened for the boys. He felt like he was hungover. How many people with a single stroke had blown up their lives?

His talk was at one at the main clubhouse, near the first tee. It followed lunch on the first day, an odd kind of halfway-along welcome. The head of Alumni Relations would address the group at a fancy dinner later that night.

On the way to the clubhouse he thought he should drop off the list of what was stolen at the police station and make himself available.

Bad images of himself tympanied around his head. He went from room to room killing time and squinting.

He got dressed. Once the family had cleared out of the kitchen he made coffee. He drank it at the kitchen table. The paper was on the counter but he left it alone. He couldn't hear the kids, inside or outside.

Lori was in the basement switching and folding more laundry. He finished his coffee and rinsed his mug and called goodbye down the stairs. The boys were sitting on the grass in the back and he waved as he left the house. He walked into campus looking forward with his head down, like someone in a driving rain. He had his speech in a manila folder. He passed the spot where he'd found Lori and the kids.

The police station was in the back of the town hall. No one looked busy but no one made any time for him. Finally Officer Rowe passed from one room to another and must have mentioned him to someone. A woman in a uniform appeared and asked if she could help. He said he'd been the one who'd had the break-in on Torrey Road, and he'd brought a list of what was missing. The woman held out her hand. A man poked his head out of his office to look at him.

He gave her the list. She thanked him and asked if he was leaving town. He said he wasn't, and she said that a patrolman would be in touch.

The golf course was a five-minute walk. When he got there, hundreds of golfers were standing around their tables in large groups. Razzing and ribbing, he thought wearily. They'd rolled a walnut podium with the school's seal into the dining room. He'd have his back to the windows but the sun was coming from the other direction. The golf pro settled everyone down and into their seats while he waited.

There was a fair amount of place-setting noise: coffee cups, silverware. He looked out over the faces. Golfers. Everybody looked genial and impatient. One guy had his putter with him at the table. A smattering offered up encouraging smiles.

The golf pro introduced him as both a young comer and the King of the Bunkers. Felton didn't know why he'd said the latter and didn't think the golf pro had ever seen him play. He'd been chosen to give the talk partially because he'd played golf in college. People in the office brought him rules questions every so often like he was the President of the USGA.

"I want to begin by welcoming you all to the 41st Annual Alumni Golf Tournament," he said. The golfers cheered and applauded.

"My job is to welcome you—and I've done that—" he said. There were some chuckles. "And to give you a short history of the tournament itself. And to talk a little bit about the lottery system." There was a lot of good-natured noise at the mention of the lottery, which was considered controversial. The noise was good-natured because everyone present had benefited from the system.

"So. The history," he said.

There was some coughing, and shuffling of feet.

"There is no history," he said.

"The lottery system," he said. He looked closely at his notes. He felt constituted by a solid block of despair. "Due to the overwhelming popularity of the tournament, and the limited number of spaces available," he read, "in an effort to make the selection process as fair as possible, all entries were chosen by lot from completed applications."

He looked up from the podium. Some of the faces were getting a little beady-eyed. His boss, who was in the tournament, was peering up at him with malice. "Each of you happy few, you band of brothers, was pulled out of a hat by our very own Short Hills Professional, Rich Morey."

He made a gesture toward the golf pro, waiting with his arms folded by the side of the room.

"Out of a hat," he repeated. He was tearing up. He wiped his eyes on his sleeve.

There was a paragraph headed ASSIGNMENTS TO PAIRINGS. He skipped it. There was another headed ALL PLAY WILL BE AT SCRATCH. He skipped that, too. There was a final one headed SO BEST OF LUCK TO ALL. He put his finger on it to hold his place.

"I want to talk today about something that maybe constitutes the opposite of Leadership Studies." He looked around the room. "Isn't that what they call it now? Leadership Studies?"

No one answered. His boss's brows were knitted and he was attempting to signal in some way.

"I was thinking: what's the *opposite* of leaders? Does anybody know? What's the opposite of leaders?"

"I'm going extemporaneous, here," he said. "Anybody know?"

The guy with the putter looked at him.

"Not followers," Felton said. He blinked and twisted his face to get a hold of himself. "Not followers… 'Cause even following takes some…*something*. Know what I mean? Any of you five-handicappers out there know what I mean?"

People were shifting in their seats and starting to talk in low voices. Mutiny was imminent.

"Because let me ask you something: what about those people who can't do that? Or, correction: who *don't* even do that?"

The serving staff had come out of the kitchen to listen. They were ringing the room unobtrusively.

"I *love* my wife," he said, his eyes overflowing with self-pity. "I don't think she'll ever love me again."

People were now standing and heading toward him. "You have to *hold* your reward with *clean hands*," he called to them. "You have to *hold* your *reward* with *clean* hands."

The golf pro and someone else had his arms and were not ungently pulling him from the podium. The clean hands point seemed important and he was reluctant to relinquish the spotlight. They looked at him like they'd all started with the same wishes and ended with the same knowledge. There was a minor struggle of wills, during which he displayed a certain valor. Finally they pried off his hands, and the podium rocked a little when he let it go. It saddened him. He expressed to those listening his desire to go home. He worried about the unknown, and he was aware that his thoughtlessness made the unknown bigger than it was for most people.

He swung at someone, for the heck of it, and found himself immediately pinned to the floor, someone's knees on his arms. Everyone holding him was much more energetic at this point. Everyone underestimated his chances of surviving this, he thought. Since, strictly speaking, he didn't have any. Over the heads of the guys holding him down he could hear others say that they'd called the police. Someone else said that he'd called the wife.

Was this as bad as it got? Was this all the cosmos was dishing out? He struggled to get up, without the slightest hint of success, but even so he could feel the stubbornness of his self-regard waiting there to lift his spirits, the way he'd seen his boys rehoist a collapsed tent after a rain. "What're you doing?" he'd called out to them, stupidly, and his older boy had said, "You *know* what we're doing," and his younger had said, "Don't look at us."

mr. mxyzptlk's opus

by ben greenman

This story begins, like so many have lately, in a bar. I'm writing you this letter on a placemat, the edges of which are scalloped for the sake of elegance. Even once I'm sobered up, even when I emerge from the drab light of the bar into the equally drab light of the early morning, there's no guarantee I'll be able to read most of what I've written, thanks to my penchant for tiny print and the fact that most of the text has been covered with a kudzu of doodles. Right now, I'm finishing up a complex doodle that includes a flower, an airplane, and a puckish self-portrait that's loosely based on a Claeissens. There's the imp from the Fifth Dimension who bedeviled Superman. There's the man who cannot stand.

This morning, I woke up tangled in a mess of sheets with my shoes still on. Worse: I was wearing my hat, or at least had worn it into bed. It was a few inches from my head, turned on its crown like a tipped-over turtle. Whenever I have seen a turtle in that position, I have thought of it as praying, belly open to the heavens, flippers extended in helplessness and urgency. Once I used turtles as the inspiration for a bit of mischief—I took the world's fastest men and made them the world's slowest men, after which I entered them in footraces against various turtles. At the same time, I changed the laws here in the city so that the mayoral race was not determined by popular vote, but rather by foot speed. The courts tried to throw out the results; the newly elected turtle mayor was so angry that he called a press conference and spent the whole time snapping at the microphones set up in front of him. The whole mess delighted me, but then Superman, with the help of a strategically placed billboard, tricked me into saying my name backwards and I was returned to the Fifth Dimension. All the mischief I had perpetrated disappeared. Does that seem fair? I speak my own name in reverse and all my work reverses itself as well? It is said that the power to create is also the power to destroy, but I would prefer a less literal demonstration of the principle.

The barmaid just came by to ask me if I'd like another. I tapped two fingers on the lip of the glass to signal yes. Now I'm doodling a bunch of balloons. You loved balloons. You said "Anything that crashes back to earth gently is a godsend." Remember? And what of things that crash to earth ungently? What of a tower? What of a man?

Remember this? Nice fall day, little while back, we woke up calm, turned toward each other in bed, started the day right. Over my shoulder, you spotted the clock. "Shit," you said. "I have to get to work." You were hanging a show of some new artist you told me was a "second-rate Wolfgang Lettl."

"Who's that?" I said. You were washing your face a second time, because you were still groggy. Your hair was pulled back. You looked beautiful. I was propped up in bed, pretending to read the newspaper, instead watching you in the mirror.

"Lettl? He's a second-rate Magritte."

"So does that make this painter third-rate or fourth-rate? I've lost track."

"You know," you said, breezing over to give me a kiss, "I left my slide rule at the gallery. I'll run some calculations when I get there and call you back."

That's the whole memory. It may strike you as trivial, and I suppose you're right. There's no grand narrative arc in a scene of lovers waking up, trading a bit of banter, parting for the day. The significance doesn't reside in that story, but rather the fact that less than a year later, that story and all stories like it swiftly exited from existence. Ten months later, you didn't say you'd call me. You couldn't.

I blame myself. This is what I tell them all. I blame myself. You should have seen me, I tell them. "Can you describe yourself before the incident?" they say. One of them even gave me a pad of paper and a pencil and asked me to draw myself. I got as far as the purple bowler, the wide collar, the upturned nose, and then I turned the pencil into a dandelion and blew the head away with one emphatic outbreath.

This story may amuse you (you liked anything that involved flowers) but it sweetens a bitter truth: these days, I can only describe myself to myself, and that's too much to bear. My drink has arrived, gin and tonic, a double.

Waitresses love me, especially since I'm going through a "keep the change" phase.

Where was I? Oh, yes: describing myself to myself. For starters, try to fathom a lifetime of mischief. I'm sure I asked you this when we started dating. Now I'm asking again. Try to imagine thirty years of plaguing Superman with the kind of practical jokes that would have been a scream back in the Fifth Dimension but which in Metropolis only got me collared. "Criminal mischief," the judge said after the first arrest, and put me in jail for the weekend. I levitated to eight feet in the middle of the cell and—poof!—vanished in a plume of smoke. Loose again, I made grass grow out of the tops of people's heads, turned fire hydrants into soda fountains, gave dogs the power to speak, until Superman came along and sent me packing. In those days, the abruptness of the expulsion from Earth, the way in which my return to the Fifth Dimension undid all the mischief I had so carefully choreographed, drove me to distraction. I determined to return as soon as I could, and within a few months, I was back, dimming people's sunglasses until they turned black, letting apple trees come to life and hurl their fruit at passersby, causing every phone number dialed to miss its target by a single digit.

For almost three decades, I tipped and twirled the world, turned it on its ear. Then one day Superman put me back in the Fifth Dimension and I didn't feel a thing. No rage. No desire for revenge. Nothing. That's when I decided to retire. The decision wasn't as abrupt as it may seem: in my recent visits to the Earth, I had spent less time devising new forms of mischief, and more time visiting museums. I have always loved human art; we don't have much of it at all where I come from, as every man fancies himself an artist and as a result no man earns the right to the distinction. While one might assume from my own work that my tastes would tend toward pop art and Surrealism, I actually prefer the Flemish landscapes of the late sixteenth century. The scope impresses me, as well as the water, the rivers that wind through the mountainous terrain. I'm not an art historian, so I can't do much more than tell you that I love those rivers, that although they don't really resemble living rivers, they produce the same emotions in me, a feeling at once infinitesimal and infinite, both of being dwarfed by and of participating in the sublime. And then there are the habitations clustered in the middle distance, the little villages hanging halfway up a mountain, just waiting to be disarranged. I have thought of some of my best ideas while staring into the frame of a Coninxloo or a Bol.

At any rate, I had read that a small museum downtown was hanging its collection of van Orley, who has always struck me as a bit too early, though what I probably mean by that is a bit too decorative. Still, Flemish is Flemish. When I got to the museum, it was just before closing time, and there were as many people as paintings: five. Two women huddled around a portrait of Charles V. Two men sentinelled a study for the Job altarpiece. "Such turbulence," one man said.

"And there are wings, too," I said. "Maybe van Orley invented the airplane."

The second man laughed, though I saw then that it wasn't a man. It was a woman, a thin tall woman with a severe haircut and a black suitcoat. It was you. We stood there for a while. You introduced yourself, then introduced me to Paul. Paul shook my hand, and I wasn't worried about him anymore. "Would the two of you like to get lunch?" I said.

"I think Paul has somewhere to be, but I'll grab a bite," you said.

At lunch, you proved better than me at almost everything. Better at putting a new acquaintance at ease. Better at laughing brightly at jokes that weren't necessarily funny. Better at relating the particulars of your life up until then—though, to be fair, you were not yet thirty, and so your life had spanned only a tiny fraction of mine. Because Paul had demonstrated such politeness, I did him a courtesy by asking you if you were involved with him. "Oh, no," you said. "Paul's gay. Isn't it obvious? Anyway, I'm just a single egg frying in a pan."

"Are you saying you want breakfast later on?" I said. You laughed and looked right at me, and it shamed me. I had seen it all, or at least most of it. But the thought of a beautiful young woman looking into my eyes and finding herself not only reflected there, but also somehow completed—that left me dumb. A month later, after we moved into that roomy one-bedroom, they had trouble bringing your couch up the stairs.

When you asked me what I had done with myself all the years before I met you, I answered the only way I knew how: honestly. I told you that I had been in the business of creating mischief. Later I saw that you must have taken me for some kind of intelligence operative, or maybe even a common criminal, but you didn't ask any other questions, and that furnished yet more proof of your perfection. As for that mischief, I renounced it entirely, and we went on, newly paired, suddenly possible. We made friends, we took trips, we stayed too long in restaurants: the young art dealer, the old mischief-maker.

Mischief, mischief, mischief. The word has started to break apart on me. Mis chief. I doodle an Indian maiden. That's her: Miss Chief. She has a feather that squirts water at you when you try to smell it. I must have said "water" out loud. The waitress just brought me a glass. But water calls for sterner stuff. Time to deaccession another Alexander Hamilton from my collection. Do you know about gin? Soon after its introduction into Britain in the early eighteenth century, it flowed like water through the lower classes. The rich both demonized it as the source of the nation's moral rot and depended upon it financially as a result of taxes. Consumption peaked in the early seventeen-forties, when an average Londoner drank more than two gallons per person per year. This strikes me as amateurish. Since you've been gone I must have tripled that in only twice the time.

Gone. It's not a word I understand very well. For me, gone has always referred to a temporary condition, to something that is about to come back. When Superman banished me, I only had to wait a few months to return, until the border between the earth and the Fifth Dimension relaxed, so no matter how angry I felt, my departure always had a comic air about it. That's why I laughed when I first came home that day. Unlike so much else in my life, I remember it perfectly: I shook off a light morning rain from the umbrella, removed my boots in the hall, and entered to find a note on the table. "Can't do it any longer. Can't explain, can't apologize, can't discuss. Please don't call me." I chuckled. "Poof!" I said. But the hours passed, and then day gave way to night. By midnight the comedy had drained away.

When you left I went down to the corner and then around the bend. The only response to a mad world is madness. Was that Cèline? That was also when I returned to painting. I had begun just a few months before I met you, anticipating my retirement, and while the canvases had only failure on them from the start, every once in a while a corner would come to life. I recall one in particular, a pastiche of the Garden of Delights. Most of it was boilerplate, but one section stood out as if illuminated. In it, a rabbit with wings drove a train toward a tunnel whose edge bore a Latin inscription. I can't retrieve the translation precisely, but it followed these rough contours:

"Here he lies without a multitude of brethren." Near him a bird with human arms held a mirror that reflected the inscription. I was trying, in my own clumsy way, to explain my relationship to the earthly world. For years, each time I visited here I came through a kind of tunnel. Each time, I could only return to those like me (the rabbit with wings is no doubt a close cousin of the bird with human arms) by speaking my name backwards, in mirror image (it is what the linguists in our land call "logos reversus," though a simple translation cannot communicate the rich cultural history behind the phrase). When I think on the painting now, I see another dimension to its meaning, one I could not have understood at the time: I passed through a lifetime of darkness to find a mate, and then I lost her.

By now my cramped block print has completely covered the placemat. I doodle a computer over the word "compute" and a movie screen over the word "movie." Then I doodle the fatal crescent shape of California. California, California. Damn California to hell. Weeks after you left the apartment I discovered through a mutual friend that you had booked a trip to Los Angeles, perhaps to buy art, perhaps to visit relatives. I will never know for certain, but I do know that my heart turned instantly to black ice. I assumed that the motive was a man, that the trip would include weeks in another lover's arms. So I came out of retirement for one final act of mischief.

I should sober up enough to explain myself clearly, or at the very least let nine drinks do what eight cannot. I put the idea in his head. Whose head? Atta's head. Atta boy: that was what I said—the actual words I spoke—after I saw his eyes shift from sandstone to quartz, from dull and mean to brilliantly cruel. I saw the plan bloom inside him. This isn't to say he was innocent before. The seed requires fertile soil, and the sour ocean of a sick mind refuses no river. I struggle for a beautiful metaphor in the hopes that I can earn pity through grace. I fail. What I mean to say is that I ordered only a hijacking. Take the plane, I urged him, in silence, in mischief. Take it somewhere else. I knew you would be aboard. I wanted you to feel pure fear, and for that fear to ripen into a desire for me. Instead, I set it all in motion; my dead heart threw off a final spark and caused a conflagration. This isn't by way of apology. I am beyond apology. For days, for weeks, I have come to bars, sometimes this one, sometimes the one down the street, and thought this through, suffered not only for what I have done but for what I have been unable to do. It would take a single word, a single familiar word, to erase the hell this world has become and redraw what the world was: not perfect but without that one atrocity, all things in their rightful places. All things but one, that is. If I unmake what I have made, you will still be on that plane, will still be heading West, will still be moving away from me. Once, years ago, after a particularly satisfying episode of mischief involving a swordfish and a typewriter, Superman landed in front of me and asked a question that was more devastating than any violent blow he could have delivered. "What do you want?" he said. What, indeed? I only knew what I did not want. Now I could answer his question, definitively, with the confidence of a dead man, could stand, take off my hat, and say without a doubt that I want you, that I want a world where I can hold you once again, feel the full length of your body alongside mine, where I can push the hair away from your ear and tell you that we should see a movie, go to dinner, go to bed, that we should travel, that I love you so much that I can no longer keep my hold on my own existence, that I slip down the incline, away from my desires, toward the broad lake at the bottom of the hill, the lake that means annihilation by a single word, by the word that will, when I finally capitulate to my duty and my sorrow, escape my mouth like a bird from a cage, like a soul from a dying body, like a seed from the head of a dandelion:

KLTPZYXM

the winning side

by alicia erian

Dean made me a sign that said CHARGE THEM OR DISCHARGE THEM, then we drove down to the detention center in Sunset Park and marched for twenty minutes. Afterward, there were a bunch of speeches by local politicians, a couple of union leaders, and a Pakistani woman whose husband had been held for three months. Then we got in the car and drove home. We passed our upstairs neighbor, Mr. Roback, in the hall, and he looked at our signs suspiciously. "How's the weather out there?" he asked, and I told him it was fine.

In our apartment, Dean wanted to know if I was going to protest with him again the following week. I told him no. "Why not?" he asked.

"My back hurts," I said. "I have a bad back."

He thought about this for a second, then took the signs and put them in the closet. We weren't sure what we were going to do for the rest of the day. Our marriage was in trouble, and we didn't like spending too much time together.

We made lunch and turned on the television. It was hard to know how long all of this was going to last. How long we were going to have to stick it out. Our marriage counselor advised that if we didn't know what to do at any given moment, the answer simply hadn't arrived yet.

After lunch, we went to see a movie. We got to the theater early so we could pick good seats. We thought we had them, but when the theater went dark, a chair-kicker slid in behind me. I let the first couple of kicks go, then turned around and gave her a look. When that didn't work, I turned around again and asked if she would please stop. She thought this was pretty funny. I heard her laughing with her friend.

There wasn't really anything I could do at that point. I tried to get past it, but I was too mad. I thought about moving to a new seat, but I knew that would only make the girl laugh harder. Finally, I leaned over and asked Dean if we could go. He said I was free to leave, but that he was staying. Then he went back to watching the movie. I thought Dean should've yelled at the girl on my behalf, but that wasn't really his style. Often I had nightmares about having to protect him from large, muscled men.

Outside, it was still daylight. I stood on the sidewalk for a couple of minutes, thinking about the detainees. I knew they didn't have windows in their cells, and that they couldn't talk to their families very much. I thought about the Pakistani woman who had spoken at the rally earlier, and how she'd mispronounced a lot of words. I kept looking around to see if anyone else had noticed, but they hadn't. Then I felt ashamed for paying attention to the wrong things.

I looked up and down the street, trying to figure out which way to go. I had it in my head that whatever I ended up doing that afternoon should be more interesting than a movie. When I couldn't think of anything, I went back to the apartment. As I was walking up the stairs, I ran into Mr. Roback again. He was a stocky older man who had difficulty getting along with the woman above him. She was in her twenties and played her stereo at a high volume. Instead of asking her to turn it down, though, he would open his window whenever she left the building and call her a bitch or a cunt. I always wanted to dislike him for this, but then, whenever I saw him in the hallway, he was very kind to me. He would warn me about the weather or stare warmly at my breasts. I found it hard to resist, being on the receiving end of what little good he had inside him.

"What were those signs I saw you with earlier?" he asked me now. He wore loose greenish pants and big black shoes.

I pretended confusion, even though I knew what he was talking about. "Oh," I said finally. "Those were protest signs."

"Protesting what?" he asked.

"Protesting the holding of Pakistani and Arab nationals in the Brooklyn Detention Center without charges."

Mr. Roback thought about this for a moment, then said, "I think they should deport them all."

I nodded, sort of expecting this, but also feeling kind of disappointed. "Well," I said, "you have a nice day."

"We have to keep the city safe," Mr. Roback said.

"I agree," I told him.

"This city has suffered enough."

"Yes," I said.

When Dean came home that night, we made dinner, then put on the television. I didn't ask him how the rest of the movie had gone, and he didn't ask me what I had done with the rest of my afternoon. All in all, it had been a terrible day, I thought. The answer still hadn't arrived.

The following Saturday, there was a knock at our door. I opened it to find Mr. Roback standing there, holding a protest sign. It read DEPORT THEM ALL in heavy black Magic Marker. "Hi," he said.

"Hi," I said.

"May I ride with you to the protest?"

Dean came to the door to see who it was. He looked at Mr. Roback's sign, then said, "Can we help you?"

"I was just wondering if I could ride with you to the protest."

"I don't think so," Dean said.

"Oh," Mr. Roback said. "Well, I guess I could take the subway."

"Mr. Roback?" I said. "Could you wait here for a moment?"

"All right," he said.

I shut the door and turned to Dean. "You can't let him go on the subway with that sign," I whispered.

"Sure, I can," Dean said. "I'd love to see him go on the subway with that sign."

"He's a crazy old man," I said. "He'll get the shit kicked out of him."

Dean shrugged.

There was a knock at the door then, and Mr. Roback called, "I'll just take the subway!"

"Wait just a second, Mr. Roback!" I said. I asked Dean one more time to drive him, but he said no fucking way. Then he turned and went in the bedroom.

I opened the door. "Mr. Roback?" I said. "How about taking a cab?"

He shook his head. "Too expensive."

"Well," I said, "I'm afraid my husband isn't comfortable driving you."

"The subway it is, then," he said, and he started walking down the stairs.

"Mr. Roback," I said.

He stopped and turned around. "Yes?"

"I'll go with you," I said, and I went and got my coat.

On the train, he kept his sign facing outward, so everyone could read it. "Yo, fuck you," a young dark-skinned man said before getting off the train, and he spit on the sign.

"Pig," Mr. Roback muttered, and he asked me for tissue.

I tried my best to look put-upon for the duration of the ride. I tried to seem like I didn't really want to be there, like I was a paid nurse or something. Even so, people didn't seem to be buying it. No one was as vocal as the young man, but they definitely weren't looking upon us fondly. Occasionally, though, someone would wink or give us the thumbs-up, and I found myself feeling relieved. Mr. Roback loved it, too, and gave the thumbs-up right back.

Dean was already at the detention center when we arrived, marching around in an oval with the other protesters. Mr. Roback tried to fall in step beside him, but Dean hissed, "Get away from me with that fucking sign, man!"

Mr. Roback looked hurt. I suggested that instead of marching, we just stand off to one side, but he shook his head and said, "I came here to march."

Finally he found a small gap to slip into. In response to his sign, the protesters seemed to increase the volume of their chants—"No justice, no peace!" and "What do we want? Justice! When do we want it? Now!"—leading Mr. Roback to cover one of his ears with his free hand.

We stood together during the speeches that followed, and when the chants started again, Mr. Roback handed me his sign so that he could cover both of his ears. I wanted to chant, too, since I liked the idea of the detainees being able to hear us, but in deference to Mr. Roback, I kept quiet.

After the protest, I asked Dean if we could at least ride home with him, and he said no. "But my back hurts," I said, even though it didn't. I had neither marched nor carried a sign.

"Forget it," Dean said, walking away from us. "I can't believe you'd embarrass me like this."

Mr. Roback and I stood on the sidewalk and watched Dean drive off. "That son of a bitch," Mr. Roback said.

We headed toward the subway. Sometimes Mr. Roback held his sign up in the air, sometimes he brought it down. When he had it up, he got a lot of honks from passing cars, which startled him, but which he also seemed to feel were marks of approval. Probably they were. "You see?" he said to me. "This is the winning side. You and I are on the winning side. Not those other people."

When we got home, he invited me up to his apartment for tea. I didn't really want to go. I was tired of pretending that his views didn't bother me. But the thought of having to eat and watch TV with Dean wasn't too appealing, either, so I said okay.

"Shh," Mr. Roback said as we walked past my front door, and I followed his example of a tiptoe.

Mr. Roback had been in his apartment so long that it had never been refurbished. There were pink mosaic tiles in the bathroom by the front door, and the kitchen cupboards were birch instead of white formica, like ours. The floors were still wooden, but scuffed and scratched beyond belief. The walls bore the stains of water damage and the occasional dead bug. Even so, you could tell that the place was generally clean. There was a shine to the stovetop and sink basin. No dust coated the photographs lining the living room walls.

"You were in the service?" I asked, noting a photo of Mr. Roback in some kind of uniform.

"Yes," he said, putting on the kettle. "For a time."

I nodded. "You were very handsome," I said, then immediately regretted it.

"Well," he said, "thank you. You're a very handsome young woman yourself."

"Thank you," I mumbled.

"Do you like Lipton tea?" he asked.

"Yes," I said.

"Lipton is the best," he said, and he pulled two mugs from the cupboard above the sink.

I sat with him at a small square table, and while we waited for the water to boil, the stereo upstairs came on very loudly.

"Goddamnit," Mr. Roback muttered. He went and got a broom and banged the handle against the ceiling. "You fucking cunt!" he yelled. "You fucking pussy of a cunt of a whore! Stop that fucking noise! You cock-sucker!"

The stereo didn't stop, but Mr. Roback went and put his broom away. "This is what I have to contend with," he said when he returned. He seemed very depressed. "You can't understand how the sound bothers me. It's very hard to listen to. Very loud for me."

I nodded. The kettle, which was silent and electric, started boiling, and Mr. Roback filled my mug. After filling his own, he returned the kettle to the counter and sat down. We watched our tea bags steep for a bit while the stereo blared overhead.

"Sometimes," Mr. Roback said, "I can hear you and your husband, too."

I looked at him. In the five years of fighting Dean and I had done since we'd moved to this apartment, no one had ever said anything, though I knew they could hear us. The fact was, you could hear people talking at regular volume whenever you walked by their doors. "Well," I said, "we do fight a lot. It's true."

Mr. Roback removed his tea bag from his mug and set it on a small saucer at the center of the table. "And then," he said, "sometimes, there's thumping with the fighting. Like people are falling down."

I didn't say anything.

"Hitting women is for the weak."

It was true that Dean and I sometimes got a little physical with each other. Only I gave as good as I got. And often enough, I was the one who gave first. It was our greatest shame, mine and Dean's. We had made an agreement before entering counseling that we would never bring it up. When the therapist asked us one day if there had ever been any violence between us, we shook our heads and said no.

"I could do some serious damage to that bitch upstairs," Mr. Roback said. "But I wouldn't. Because she's a woman."

I nodded.

"That's what you call control," he said. "Your husband doesn't seem to have any control."

I nodded again. I should've told him the truth—that I didn't have any control, either—but I couldn't seem to manage it. Instead, I preferred to listen to this new version of things.

"You haven't had sex in a long time," Mr. Roback said. "You used to have it more, when you first moved in, but then you stopped."

I finished my tea and said, "I should go."

"You used to make these little yells," he said. "I'd hear you, and I'd want to help you for a second, then I'd realize you were happy."

"I'm sorry we're so loud," I said, standing. "I'm glad you told me so that we can be quieter."

"Why do you have to go?" he asked, looking up.

I thought for a second, then said, "Dean will worry about me."

"He will?" Mr. Roback asked. He stood, too.

"Yes," I said.

"I don't think he's worried about you. I think he's worried about those ragheads at the detention center."

I didn't say anything.

"He wouldn't even give you a ride home."

"I have to go," I said.

"Well," Mr. Roback said, "okay."

"Thank you for the tea," I said.

"You're welcome," he said, and he went to the front door and let me out.

Back in the apartment, Dean yelled at me for ruining his day. "Shh," I told him. "I'm sorry, okay? Just don't yell."

He kept going, though, on and on about how I had embarrassed him, how the protest was important, how I'd made a mockery of it by bringing Mr. Roback. I got fed up then and started yelling, too. I yelled that all he cared about were ragheads, and then we entered into a brand-new fight about what a racist I was deep down.

Finally I put my coat on and left. I walked down the stairs and out the front door of the building. As soon as I reached the street, I heard Mr. Roback's window go up. "Did he hit you? I'll fucking kill him if he laid a hand on you!"

I walked for a long time, until it got dark. I stopped in a used book store up in the Heights, then had a cheap taco on Court Street. Later, I went to a movie. The same one I had tried to see the week before, only now there was no one kicking my seat. Now I could sit back and watch the whole thing all the way through. It wasn't very good, but I didn't care. It was quiet, with only the occasional muffled explosion from the thriller next door.

the politics of fear

THE K CHRONICLES
BY KEITH KNIGHT
IF YOU BUY DRUGS...
SPLOOSH
THE BLOOD OF SEPT. 11TH IS ON YOUR HANDS!!!...
NOT REALLY, FOLKS..
BUT THAT'S THE GIST OF AN EMBARRASSINGLY STUPID ANTI-DRUG CAMPAIGN THAT HAS TAKEN TO AMERICA'S AIRWAVES RECENTLY...
BUT HEY.. WHO KNOWS? MAYBE IT WILL SCARE ENOUGH PEOPLE INTO GROWING AND MAKING THEIR OWN DRUGS...
IT'S CHEAPER, MORE FUN & MUCH MORE SATISFYING..
ANYWAY.. I'VE BEGUN TO APPLY SIMILAR SCARE TACTICS AROUND THE OL' HOUSEHOLD TO KEEP MY ROOMMATES IN CHECK...
If you don't replace the Toilet paper..
-The TERRORISTS Have WON...
If you don't Take out The Trash--
MariaH Carey makes another movie..
If you don't do your dishes--
God kills a kitten..
I NOW HAVE THE POPULATION OF MY FLAT PARANOID AND UNDER MY CONTROL...
Whatcho guys doin' Tonite?
Locking ourselves in our rooms & being quiet...
That's what I like to hear...
WHO SEZ YOU CAN'T LEARN ANYTHING FROM G.W...
STOP
WRITE!! P.O. BOX 591794 San Francisco CA 94159-1794
send $15 for 120 pages of comix or a stamp for catalogue.
keeflix@hotmail.com
www.kchronicles.com

should i be scared?

by amanda eyre ward

I first heard about cipro at the potluck. "Thank God, I've got cipro," said Maria. "My doctor prescribed it for a urinary tract infection, and I still have half the pills."

"Cipro?" I said, my mouth full of artichoke dip.

"Honey," said Maria, "where have you been?"

It was a cold, clear night in Austin, Texas. After the disgusting heat of summer, the cool was a balm on my arms. Maria wore a giant sweater, knit loosely from rough, rusty-colored wool. She stood next to the barbecue, holding her hands in front of the hot coals. In the kitchen, my husband and his scientist friends made an elaborate marinade.

"Anthrax," whispered Maria. She had just begun dating my husband's thesis advisor, and cast a glamorous glow over departmental potlucks.

"Excuse me?" I said. I took a large sip of wine, which had come from a cardboard box.

"Ciprofloxacin," clarified Maria, hissing over the syllables, "it's the anthrax vaccine. A super antibiotic. If we're dropped on, by, like, a crop duster, cipro is what you'll need. And," she lowered her voice again, "there isn't enough for everyone."

Maria wore scarves around her neck. She had high leather boots and a good haircut. She worked in a steel building downtown, for a company that made very expensive software. She had described her job to me once: "It's an output management solution, and I market it. It connects the world." She said the last with a roll of her brown eyes. She held a large wine glass with her hands wrapped around the bowl. Her fingers were long, her nails painted. We had no idea why she wanted to spend her evenings with us. We wore Birkenstocks.

I was a scientist's wife. This title pleased me. I also worked at Ceramic City, where people could bring their own wine and paint pottery. My title at Ceramic City was "color consultant." This title did not please me. In short, I did not own high leather boots. I had sneakers, sandals, and a dyeable pair of pumps from my wedding day.

"Oh," I said, to Maria, regarding the cipro. It was times like this that I felt lucky to have a scientist for a husband. I could ask him later for details, and he would not laugh at me. If he did not know the answer, he would make something up.

"Hey ladies!" said a dark figure emerging from the kitchen. It was my husband's thesis advisor. "Is that fire ready for some birds?"

Maria smiled charmingly. The light from the coals made her look a little scary when she turned to me.

"Get some for yourself," she said in a quiet voice. "I'm serious," she said, and then she turned her face up to meet her lover's lips.

My husband explained in the dark of our bedroom that ingesting expensive antibiotics for no reason was a bad course of action. We had pulled the covers over our heads and invited the cat into the warm cave. My husband called the cat "spelunker," saying, "What do you think, little spelunker? Do you think we should let the terrorists make us afraid? Do you think we should buy canned goods and a six-day supply of water?" (The last was in reference to my actions of the previous day, when I had arrived home with twenty-eight cans of Progresso soup and three gallons of water.)

This was the beginning of the War on Terrorism. Two weeks before, my husband and I had discussed what fishing rod he should buy with his jar of quarters. We had discussed what to eat for dinner, and if we were drinking too much beer. We had talked about having a baby, mowing the lawn, and what sort of dog we should adopt. (My husband was partial to poodles, and I liked little dogs that could sit in your lap or in your purse. If you carried a purse.) In the end, we had decided that we wanted a baby more than a dog or a fishing rod, and we had thrown away my birth control pills and made love slowly with the moon casting a lovely light over my husband's skin.

Things had changed so quickly and forcefully that it seemed to me that my husband hadn't quite accepted the fact that we were in danger. I lay in bed in the mornings now, hearing helicopters and listening to the morning news.

"Your dad is making fun of me," I told the cat, under the covers, next to my husband, whose skin was warm. I began to cry a little, and my husband said he was sorry.

The next morning, from behind my desk at Ceramic City, I called Dr. Fern. The first time the nurse answered, I hung up. I was alone in Ceramic City, but I did not know what to say to the nurse. Was I being crazy? I wanted to think so. My mother, who lived in New York and had gone to three funerals for her friends' sons, told me that it was unpatriotic to want some cipro for myself. When I told her that I was afraid to get out of bed, she said, "That's just how the terrorists want you to feel." She sounded disappointed in me.

I called Dr. Fern again. This time, when the nurse answered, I said that I would like to make an appointment.

"Issue?" said the nurse.

"Excuse me?" I said. A man peeked into the window of Ceramic City. I thought, Fuck.

"What is the issue," said the nurse, "that you need to see the doctor about?"

"Uh, I'd like to get a prescription," I said.

"For?"

"For ciproflaxin," I said. The peeking man came inside, and began to wander around, picking up Personalized Pottery and inspecting it.

"Beg pardon?" said the nurse. Was she instructed not to use full sentences?

"In case of an anthrax attack on America," I said, "I would like to have my own supply of antibiotics." The man put down a blue bowl painted with fish. He stared at me.

"Oh my," said the nurse.

"Well, so," I said. I put my hand over the mouthpiece. "Can I be of assistance?" I asked the man.

"My wife's birthday is Tuesday," he said.

"One moment, please," I said. The nurse told me that she would have to consult the doctor and get back to me. She took my phone number. When I hung up the phone, the man had put down the bowl.

"Should I be scared?" he asked me.

The pert nurse called me later that afternoon and explained in no uncertain terms that the doctor would not give me the drugs I had requested. She added that it was against every tenet of the medical establishment to prescribe drugs when a patient was not ill. I hung up the phone, instead of saying, "You self-important bitch." At home that evening, I cried again.

My husband watched me skeptically. We were eating Freebird Burritos, sitting on our front porch and peeling off aluminum foil in small, metal rings. "We're not going to get anthrax," said my husband. He made a sound that I would classify as an incredulous snort.

"I know!" I said. I bit into my burrito, which I had ordered with extra guacamole. Extras were a dollar, and usually I refrained, but I had the feeling that I should live life to the fullest, and make a celebration of every day.

"And I want you to stop watching so much television," said my husband. He had been talking, it seemed, for some time. I nodded, and he turned his head toward me, looking at me as if I were a scientific mystery. "Oh, honey," he said, and he folded me in his arms. I breathed in the smell of his shirt, which was the smell of a campfire.

Nonetheless, I did watch television that night, after my husband had fallen asleep. I sat in the front room in my pajamas, watching bombs and food rations fall. I drank a warm glass of milk and watched dirty children rip open bags of Pop-Tarts and jam them in their mouths.

The next day, I saw an advertisement for cipro on the back page of the *Austin Chronicle*. There it was, sandwiched between a massage therapist and a Spanish tutor: CIPRO AVAILABLE 1-800-CIPRONOW. Ceramic City was empty again, and I picked up the phone.

When I got home that evening, my husband was making linguine with clams. There was an open bottle of wine on the table, and two wine glasses. My husband had gone to some trouble: cloth napkins, the whole nine yards. In the kitchen, he was stirring dinner and leafing through his fishing catalog. I came into the kitchen and put my arms around his waist. "I'm your apron,"

I said.

"Look at this," said my husband, pointing to the catalog. "A baby-size fishing rod. I can take our little boy out in the canoe."

"Little girl," I said. This was a long-standing issue between us. My husband came from a family of four boys, and I had three sisters. I had dreamed my whole life of the things I would teach my daughter. What did I want with a son?

"Whatever," said my husband. "Either way. But the change jar is now officially for the baby. For a little fishing rod, and maybe a little life-vest."

My husband came home each night and took the change from his pants pocket and dropped it into a large water jug. He claimed that he had done this since he was six years old, and the first time the jug had filled (right before I met him) he had bought a canoe. The canoe! He loved it ferociously. He had named the canoe after me, written my name in White-Out on the side. One night, when I was reading and he was asleep, he spoke. "You're the best," he said, his arms around my waist, squeezing. I checked: he was in dreamland, speaking from that place. "You're the best," he repeated, "you're the best, best, best canoe in the world."

As we ate the linguine, which was delicious, I explained that the cipro we needed to stay alive for a week would cost $300. My husband explained that we did not have any money. I sadly explained that we had his change jar. He sadly agreed, closing his fishing catalogue (which he had been reading at the table). We finished the wine and sat on the kitchen floor, counting the change, which added up to one hundred seventy-two dollars and sixteen cents. When I tried to seduce my husband that night, underneath the covers, whispering about a little one, he turned away from me.

The man at 1-800-CIPRONOW had told me to meet him in the alley between San Antonio and Sixth. I drove there the next morning, a plastic bag full of change in the passenger seat. "You'll be glad," I told my husband. "You'll thank me later." I saw him shut his eyes, willing away the sunlit afternoon in the canoe, his small boy casting with a titanium rod. The flashing fish, which the boy would hold and then release.

The CIPRONOW man was Hispanic. He wore tight Wrangler jeans and a T-shirt with an American flag. Over the phone, he had explained that the cipro was his mother's prescription, that she needed money more than the drugs.

I had tried to buy drugs twice before. Once was in the Bahamas, on Spring Break. A handsome Bahamian man had pulled up to me in a Cadillac. I had given him a roll of dollars, anticipating the excitement of my sorority sisters when I showed up with a bag of pot, and he had told me to wait and driven away. I am embarrassed to admit that I waited, standing by that dusty road, for two hours.

The second time was in Manhattan, with a boyfriend who had told the cabbie to take us to "a bad area." (We were from the suburbs.) We wandered around for a while, huddled into our L.L. Bean parkas, and then, in the middle of the bad area, I saw a well-lit Gap store. We returned home without drugs. My boyfriend, however, got some Christmas tree boxer shorts for half-price.

So here I was, much too old for subterfuge, meeting a man in an alley with a bag of small change. At times, it is better not to dwell on the twists and turns of your life's path.

The man, whose flag shirt, upon closer inspection, was not very clean, was unhappy about splitting up the prescription. "What you need," he said, "is the full thirty pills. Three times a day for ten days. That's what you need."

"I'm sorry," I said, gesturing to the bag in my passenger seat. "This is all I have."

"All you have," said the man, and he laughed. I blinked. "No deal," said the man, putting his hands on his hips and shaking his head.

"Well, fuck," I said. The change bag and I drove away.

That evening, as my husband grilled hamburgers in the backyard, I thought about how to get another hundred dollars. "I already gave you everything I had," my husband said, dramatically. "You can't live your life this way," he said, among other comments that amounted to same.

"I can sell something," I said.

"Oh really?" said my husband. He put his hands on his hips, and the spatula stuck out awkwardly. "Really?" he said. "What do you have to sell?"

I did not answer. The damn fact was that I had nothing to sell. My books, maybe, or my bod. Unhappily, neither would likely bring a hundred dollars. I did not sleep that night. I lay awake, and dreamed about dying horribly, with lots of gasping. Worse, I dreamed of life without my husband, our house, our canoe. I dreamed of living in a cave, with no access to the sunlight, and no food.

The next day, anthrax was found in a letter mailed to NBC news. "Now tell me I'm crazy," I said to my husband, who had brought me a tuna sandwich at Ceramic City.

"I never said you were crazy," he said, wiping his lip with a napkin, "I'm just trying to say that we can't live this way. If we're going to die, well..." He lifted his hands up, a gesture of acceptance.

"I can't," I said. "I can't just wait. Can you understand? I have to be ready."

My husband shook his head, his eyes full of sadness for me.

We had been here before. According to my therapist, Maureen, my extremely fucked-up childhood left me unwilling to accept peace in my life. My husband's childhood of denial, however, made him a prime candidate for not admitting any sort of problem until it was too late. Way too late. Which is why his father drank himself into a coma before anyone admitted he had issues. Which is why I was going to take the cipro matters into my own hands.

The CIPRONOW man said he would take a canoe and a hundred seventy-two dollars and sixteen cents. God knows why he wanted a canoe. Perhaps he had realized that the tide was turning: the government was in negotiations to buy a zillion tablets of discount cipro, and the terrorists were hatching smallpox. The cipro market was at peak performance. Maybe he liked to fish, I don't know.

I gave the CIPRONOW man our address. He arrived with a Ziploc bag of pills and a trailer for the canoe. I invited him inside for a beer, and he accepted. I gave him a Shiner. "This is a beautiful home," he said. He looked around, nodding. I saw it through his eyes: the books, lined up in a row on the bookcase my husband had built for me, the votive candles on the mantel. The cat—my cat—curled up in a circle on the floor. The large glass windows, which could shatter with little provocation. The CIPRONOW man sipped his beer, and then looked down at his American flag shirt.

* *

My mother called at dinnertime. She had seen Hal Kensington at the Yacht Club Christmas party, and he was not doing well. "He's obsessed with where James was on the plane," said my mother.

"Where was he?"

"Hal thinks he was bumped to first class, next to one of the terrorists. James called his girlfriend and told her he was going to order a free Scotch, even though it was morning."

"I hope he did," I said.

"So do I," said my mother. After a minute, she said, "James was the captain of the hockey team at Princeton."

"I know," I said.

I did not tell her that I was alone at home, drinking and staring at my unpatriotic bag of pills.

My husband did not come home from the lab until late that night. I was still awake, watching television. My husband climbed into bed: his smooth skin, his thin eyelids, his mind full of numbers, his buttocks, warm against my stomach. He turned off the television, but he did not reach for me.

I had left the bag of cipro pills on the kitchen table. Also, I had left a note: "I hope you will understand that this is for us." When I woke up in the morning, my husband was freshly showered and drinking coffee in the kitchen. The morning paper was still rolled, bound by a rubber band. I went to the coffeepot and filled a china mug.

On the table, my note was gone, and in its place was a box of condoms.

We sat opposite each other, the bag of pills and the box of condoms between us. The smell of coffee filled the kitchen. The sun cast a buttery light, and the hairs on my husband's forearm looked like gold.

the patriot actor

by stephen elliott

> *"Any right of privacy possessed by library and bookstore patrons in such information is necessarily and* inherently limited *since, by the nature of these transactions, the patron is reposing that information in the library or bookstore and assumes the risk that the entity may disclose it to another."*
>
> —Assistant Attorney General
> Daniel J. Bryant

I'm talking to Apple Computer when I first hear it. My phone clicks, then a wave of static crushes through the receiver, then passes. I was talking about my printer, about how my computer wasn't printing. "Did you hear that?" I ask the technician on the other end.

"I didn't hear anything," he says. Then he tells me to insert my reinstall disc, hold down the C key, and reboot. "We're going to start from scratch."

When the Patriot Act was signed by President George W. Bush a year and six months ago on October 26, 2001, I read the entire text as posted on the *New York Times* website. There was a photograph of Attorney General John Ashcroft, standing in front of a curtain that had been draped across a naked statue. He looked like an angry, unforgiving father to me. Sixty-six Congressmembers voted against the Patriot Act; 357 voted for it. It passed the Senate overwhelmingly. The government was going to listen in and watch anyone they wanted. I had just broken up with my girlfriend at the time. My father was calling constantly, insisting on giving me his opinion of the current crisis. The administration asked me to take a cut in pay from the university where I teach. They said they wanted to bring in some new talent. I realized that I wasn't anybody's best friend. And it felt as if nobody was listening to me. And why would they? There were bombs destroying entire mountains in the Middle East.

"When you shaved my head it really fucked me up," I say to my father. I'm lying on my wooden floor, my head against the end of my mattress. I'm staring at the pigeons outside perched on the roof of the chocolate factory.

"I didn't shave your head. I gave you a haircut. Why are we talking about this? That was twenty years ago."

"You were hitting me while I was sleeping. I woke up and you were punching me and then you dragged me into the kitchen and shaved my head. I looked like a mental patient. You told the pharmacy on Pratt and California not to sell me any razor blades, so I went to the Walgreen's."

"This isn't like you to rehash all of this old shit. I was an imperfect parent. Look, I said I was sorry. What more do you want? Isn't that enough?"

"No," I say. "It isn't." When my father hangs up the phone I whisper into the headset. "Did you hear that? Are you listening?"

When Sami Al-Arian was arrested for supporting Islamic Jihad I sent twenty dollars to the Department of Engineering at the University of Florida where he teaches. I checked out *Fahrenheit 451*, *The Bomb*, and the *Journal of Irreproducible Results* from the San Francisco Public Library, where I was informed by a sign that the federal government has access to my library records. I joined the Free Palestine mailing list and hung no-war posters from my windows. I went to rallies sponsored by Global Exchange and cheered for Medea Benjamin as she brushed her straight golden hair from in front of her eyes and told the crowd "Regime change begins at home." When the Workers World Party asked me if I wanted to volunteer I said yes.

On February 16, 2003, at the Civic Center they estimate two hundred thousand people show up to protest the impending war. I help build the stage. The volunteers organize behind the shell and then break to pass out flyers. The flyers state that when war starts people should walk off the job and meet at Fifth and Powell in a giant uprising.

Five days after the protest the *San Francisco Chronicle* runs an article using aerial photography to prove there were only sixty-five thousand marchers at the protest. I tape the newspaper photographs to the wall of my apartment, the people, tiny dots filling up the streets, the airplanes watching, documenting the evidence. Soon it comes out that it wasn't just the newspapers. The police had spies in the crowd with tape recorders; they were filming everything. They want to use the film in court to prove an officer's innocence. The officer has been accused of brutality. The ACLU is demanding the police department destroy the tapes. The Chief of Police resigns. Everything is starting to make sense.

"Hello? Hello?" I've wrapped the telephone cord around my ankles and my knees, up over my waist. I'm wrapped in it like a present. "Are you there?" The clear phone cord cuts into my skin. The dial tone vanished hours ago and I speak into an empty line. The cleaning vans wash the streets; I hear their slow beeps as the sweepers drive by. In the darkness I can make out the headlights of cars driving to the top of Twin Peaks and then disappearing behind the back of the hills. "Hello?"

"I'm here."

I catch my breath. I feel my chest swell and a wave of nausea pass through my throat. I roll on my side, facing the wall.

"I knew it," I say. "I knew you were listening."

"Umm-hmm. I can't talk," he says. "My partner's asleep. You should be too. Meet me in Dolores Park tomorrow, the bench on 20th Street, near the statue and the tracks."

"What time?" The phone clicks twice. The dial tone returns. "Thank you."

I don't go to work. It's a wet, dewy day. I lay newspapers over the bench. I sit and I watch as people bring their dogs out to run in the grass. It's too cold and gray for sunbathers, just the dog owners, throwing their tennis balls out, the dogs scampering after them and returning, a repetition of a menial task.

A man with a potbelly and a long beard sits down next to me. He bites on his lip and mutters things to himself and makes cradles from his whiskers. He stands, scratching his stomach. "Don't forget. Don't. Don't forget. Look out," he says. "Wouldn't do that." He looks me dead in the face. "I was the first person to smoke pot with Bob Dylan." Then he walks away.

As night falls it gets colder, then colder still. A man down the hill hangs a chain across the washroom doors. I wrap my arms around my chest and lie down on the bench. I start to shiver. I drift in and out of sleep. He's not going to come. The day is over. The clouds clear back toward the ocean. The stars come out.

I sit up when I feel the pressure of someone's leg against the bench. It's a long, thin man in a gray suit. He's smoking a cigarette and smiling at me. His legs are like sticks.

"You came." I wonder if I am sleeping. He doesn't answer, just exhales a plume of smoke. "How long have you been here? How long was I gone for?"

"Not long," he says. "Maybe twenty minutes."

I rub my fists in my eyes. He pushes his hand against my forehead, then wipes his hand on his slacks.

"You've been listening. I hear the clicks on the phone."

He shrugs his shoulders. "It's my job."

"So you know everything?"

He finishes his cigarette and flicks it toward the Muni tracks. "I know that you're trying to get attention. I know that you didn't read those books you took out of the library. I know that you want to get caught and I know that there are laws against intentionally misleading the government. Those are the things I know."

I nod my head vigorously. "Yes. Yes." I keep nodding. "It's true. I've been so lonely. It's overwhelming."

He swings one long leg over the other. His jacket falls open and I see the gun there, the polished metal against his belt. "We're at war, Paul. Do you understand that?"

"I do. I do." I slowly, carefully, duck my head toward his lap. I lie against his leg, looking out into the empty park. I can make out homeless people camping under the trees. "I know all about the war."

"Do you love your country?" he asks. "You need to be ready to make some sacrifices. Those sacrifices might include the loss of certain freedoms. Things like privacy don't seem all that important when Saddam's bottle-necking our oil supply and American citizens are building dirty bombs. Now do they?"

"No," I say. I realize I'm crying. "I don't care about privacy at all."

I feel the soft skin of his palm covering my cheek. His pant leg soaking from my tears beneath me. I wonder if I am still sleeping and where it all went wrong.

"O.K., Paul, O.K. I know you didn't mean it." His hand runs back and forth over my face until his two fingers are pinching shut my nose. "O.K. Paul. Relax. Close your eyes. The government is here. Uncle Sam is going to keep you safe."

the great rushdie

by stewart o'nan

It has cured me of my irrational terror of helicopters, that is one thing I can say. Now all my nightmares take place in airports, racing down endless corridors for flights I've missed. Heathrow, D'Orly, JFK. He only trusts a few. I wait as he waits, board as he boards, thrill to the same in-flight film.

Sometimes he will drink a brandy, tipping the plastic glass so it touches the bridge of his nose. Sometimes just a Coke. He is not, as I expected, a vegetarian, and I have seen him swap his dessert with his seatmate for an extra piece of cheese. At times, sitting there in first class with my fake beard tickling my neck, the ludicrous spectacles pinching my nose, I will be tempted to raise a finger like him and order myself a Scotch whiskey. Just the word conjures mystery, barrels tucked under rain-beaten, lichened castles, craggy old men with alchemists' powers. But that is not the way of the *yassassin*.

Strangely, his cigarettes hold no such temptation. Dunhills in the maroon packet. The amount of money he lavishes on these! And the pleasure he takes, early mornings, standing out on the balcony of the Royal Copenhagen, a puff drifting across the Ostend, the fag-end flicked off to fall through the treetops. How many high-powered sights have I spied through just to find him killing himself? Later, when we are at the reading, Oosmun will slip into the room and fish the crumpled packet from the trash and the next day mail it to his hosts, a token of our vigilance.

I do not always like it, this intimidation. Or perhaps, as Oosmun continually implies, after these seven years away from our country, I have begun to take on Western ideas, to reason as a Westerner. And while I insist it is not true, I insist in a lavish suite overlooking the Hamptbahnhof, Oosmun tuned to the French Open, watching the pert Martina Hingis demolish all comers.

I personally have not read the book of our enemy. Or I lie: I have begun it twice yet could not interest myself enough to finish. It is long and erudite, and its pleasures are the mind's. I prefer the soul's nourishment (all right, the heart's, since we are being honest) and have a predilection for the work of Leo Tolstoy. In the last seven years I have spent most of my time sitting or flying, and I have read much to understand the West. *Winesburg, Ohio, The Catcher in the Rye. The Great Gatsby* by your Fitzgerald I find interesting, and not a few times I have compared myself to his Nick. For he is my Gatsby, isn't he, wandering the empty mansion that is the world with his useless fame, and I, I live in a rented room I cannot afford, my eye on him always, admiring his old notions of innocence. One day, I am sure, I will find him drifting in some metaphorical swimming pool, a scarf of blood trailing out behind, and I will be sorry and despise myself and this horrible world.

How have I become this cynical man, you ask?

I have been trained to dispatch our enemies in the one-hundred-and-eleven ways, the same as my father, and his father before him. My mother's father was a holy man, his house full of books, but a son must be like his father, and so at nine I began the lifelong training that made the other boys worship and run from me. Until I fulfilled my holy destiny, I would have no woman, no family.

(As he does. That first year, I watched through infrared binoculars the loud bouts he struck up with his soon-to-be ex-wife, a Socialist with a weakness for tea cakes and expensive wine. But I shall not linger on such things, only note that you can see the effect on him; occasionally after dinner with the department chair there will be a comely graduate student who rides a motorcycle and has a deep appreciation of Thomas Pynchon, and you can see him sigh as he turns down the offer of coffee in her apartment, mutter as he clumps up the front steps of the hotel.)

I should say now that I will never fulfill that destiny, or only when he dies from some other hand (or by his own, as I sometimes fear, late at night when only the hotel laundry is alive, the corridors littered with room service trays, scuffed shoes and laundry hung from doorknobs). No, to kill him would be the greatest failure, one I would pay for with my life. The thing is to be here, near him to let the world know that we have not forgotten nor will ever forgive his impudence.

We are not alone, Oosmun and I. We do not move unremarked upon.

Tonight, the Mossad are here in London, the CIA, Scotland Yard.

(That word again! A place he has visited only once since I have been with him—the University of Edinburgh. While he read to a lively, polite crowd, I walked about town. Such quaint pubs and dreary architecture, pigeons pecking chips. I could barely understand the woman at the tobacconist's. I purchased a pack of his Dunhills for Oosmun to leave on his pillow and sauntered through the park. While strollers marked me, they evinced none of the scorn I feel here, or the ugly dismissal projected by even the lowliest of New Yorkers.)

No, we are among colleagues all the time—attendants, I might say, much like Gatsby's minions. (Like gaudy moths, F. says, drawn something something to his fluttering flame.) We circle him, pay tribute to his mystery, his singular genius. But finally I am the one left with him. After the reading, the signing, the late dinner with his British editor. Oosmun has finished his prowling, the paid bodyguards are off the clock. Then it is just him at his toilet and I at my window, my heating grate, my fire escape. I have my headphones on, my starlight scope balanced on the rail.

Whoa-whoa, IIIIIIIII, I heard him singing one night in Palo Alto, California, *should have known better with a girl like you.*

And then in Ottawa: *Baby I need your lovin'. Got, to have all your lo-o-vin'.*

He uses Plax and Crest and Listerine, swishes and rinses and spits. And in a gesture I first found absurd but now find genuinely endearing, he combs what's left of his crown of hair before he gets into bed. And then, like me, he reads. Not much, just a few pages. Contemporaries mostly, sometimes volumes his hosts have inscribed to him. He feels obliged, I imagine (and he is conscientious; never has Oosmun found one of these presents left behind in the bathroom or tucked in a drawer with the ever-present Bible). I have often hoped to see the familiar yellow-and-green cover of *The Great Gatsby* raised before his pillowed head, but after seven years one's optimism wanes.

Yes, one changes.

I will admit that. How to deny it, now, in the very dead of night? And deny to whom? Oosmun has already bowed to the East and is sleeping, while I sit here, listening to him turn the pages. And then he closes the book and holds it to his stomach as if he will begin again shortly, but he is asleep, the bedside light still on. How I would like to spirit myself into his room now, take today's book from his limp hands and replace it with my tired copy of Fitzgerald's and click the light off for him. Come dawn, would he understand it is me, come padding across the great lawn to my cottage and burble nervously about his true desires, the humbling terrors of love?

I wait, silent, and soon he rouses, pushes the novel onto the nighstand and finds the knob, twists it.

This is the time I have been prepared for, the long waiting for morning. My grandfather watched over the Shah's son, his rheumy breathing weak behind a watered-silk canopy, the same son whose SAVAK arrested and then executed my father by a method known as the Rhinoceros, which I have studied and once, unfortunately, witnessed. Now I watch the window giving back the taillights of the road below, listen to his soft snoring (he's had three glasses of Australian wine, served by a Mossad operative with startling eyes and a disarming overbite).

In Scotland the hills go on for whole countries, nothing but sheep and crumbling stone walls, fallen shearing pens. In the pubs, old men in unraveling tweed jackets smoke and sip whiskey all day, dodder home to their families.

I know he dreams of escape, of shedding the life that has been chosen for him. But what choice does a man have? The hand of fate is heavy on us all, isn't that the lesson Nick learns? The world doesn't care about our dreams, punishes our dearest conceits.

Tomorrow we are off to New York again, across that valley of ashes from West Egg. Our tickets have been bought and paid for, our hotel room even now being readied for our arrival, fitted with equipment. He will read from his new novel, the sales of which are disappointing, a matter of no concern to him. He sleeps. I watch, wait. The clock and the world circle. Flight time is six hours, five with a brisk tailwind. In first class the drinks are free. And so to the fresh green breast of the new world we are borne back ceaselessly, something something something.

DUCT SOUP

written by Sparrow
illustrated by Andrew Nielsen

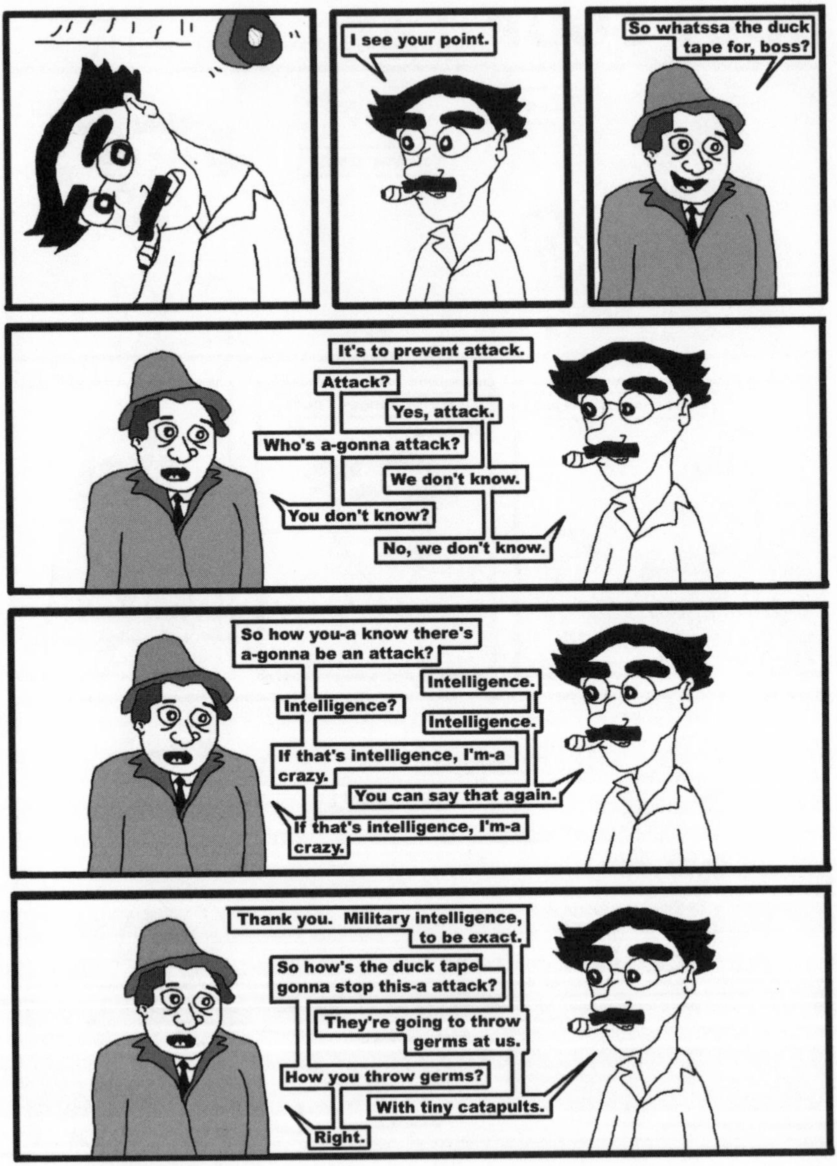
I see your point.
So whatssa the duck tape for, boss?
It's to prevent attack.
Attack?
Yes, attack.
Who's a-gonna attack?
We don't know.
You don't know?
No, we don't know.
So how you-a know there's a-gonna be an attack?
Intelligence.
Intelligence?
Intelligence.
If that's intelligence, I'm-a crazy.
You can say that again.
If that's intelligence, I'm-a crazy.
Thank you. Military intelligence, to be exact.
So how's the duck tape gonna stop this-a attack?
They're going to throw germs at us.
How you throw germs?
With tiny catapults.
Right.

So then the germs come through our windows and murder us.
What germs?
Smallpox.
Smallpox?
Why not big pox?
Shh! Don't give them any ideas!
Who?
The attackers!
Who are they?
We don't know.
Right.
So how's the duck tape gonna stop this-a attack?
You cover your windows with the tape, the germs can't get in.
So then how you gonna breathe?
Breathe! Breathing is highly overvalued! I'm an American! If my government tells me to stop breathing, I immediately respond!
Boss, you-a crazy!
We'll see who's crazy, when I'VE stopped breathing and YOU have smallpox!
© Sparrow and Andrew Nielsen

the politics of desire

end-of-the-world sex

by tsaurah litzky

My friend Carrie tells me that since the disaster her Dom won't let her out of bed. The minute he gets home from work he grabs her. It was like a second honeymoon at first, she says, but now she is exhausted, worn out. Her Jezebel is always sore and aching. I tell her she is free to experiment with my collection of lubes. Lately I haven't had much use for them. She says thanks but she had better get her own.

I am yearning for some end-of-the-world sex, but so far I have had no luck. The art dealer I picked up at the New Museum a week after the disaster had toreador hips. He looked like he could maneuver well in tight places but when we went back to his apartment he only wanted to do sixty-nine. I was bloated, swollen with sorrow and rage, all my juices bottled up inside me. What I wanted was to be pierced, penetrated and drained. I told him I have some wonderful lube with me. I got it in Amsterdam on the Street of Earthly Sorrows. He looked at me as if I had just told him I had an acrylic womb. "No way!" he says. "I know all about those lubes, they are full of estrogens. I've heard they can give a man breasts." I'm astounded at his ignorance. "You must be kidding," I say, "very funny, ha, ha, ha." I didn't tell him that I think hermaphrodites are hot. If he had breasts it would make him really exciting to me, a lover for the new millennium. Instead I put my jacket back on and went out the door.

When I got home, I stripped, fell into bed and slept. I dreamed of men with breasts and hermaphrodite sex. I mated with a hermaphrodite with many sets of arms like a Hindu God and two cocks, one between his legs and one growing from the center of his forehead. Eight, ten, twelve sets of hands caressed me while I held his two purple cocks in my hands and pulled at them rhythmically as if they were teats.

There is a homeless man who lives in a three-sided packing crate house underneath the BQE overpass. I always see him when I am coming and going to the "A" train. He is heavy-set and beneath his tattered sweaters it looks like he has breasts. Maybe he is a hermaphrodite. He often has his prick out and is stroking it with filthy hands. Everyone passes by, pretending not to notice. Since the bombing I can't stop myself from glancing over. His tool is uncut, huge, the size of my forearm, he could spawn dynasties, propagate thousands. When I look over at his terrible, fleshy baton, I become excited. A warm, liquid lava bubbles between my legs. I wonder if this is my end-of-the-world sex.

The headlines become more bizarre, more sensational. Mayor Guiliani announces they have not found any bodies for five days but they are finding more and more body parts. Scam artists try to sell families of the victims dirt from the site, Taliban infiltrating our high schools. Gas mask sales soar. The Mayor says we should get back to normal, eat in our restaurants, take in movies, Broadway shows. When I go to teach my evening classes at a university in Greenwich Village, despite his urging, the restaurants are empty. The once-bustling streets nearly deserted.

At night I keep having hermaphrodite dreams. One night there are two hermaphrodites in the dream. They both have long blond hair, obese, fleshy tits and gray, squiggly cocks like silver corkscrews. One lies beneath me, one on top. I writhe frenzied, sandwiched between breasts and cocks. I come again and again and when I wake up in the morning the sheets are wet, soaking. First I wonder if this means I will meet hermaphrodite twins, then I wonder if this new obsession is a kind of hysterical reaction to the bombing, some kind of post-traumatic stress disorder. I have a dreadful compulsion to read all about the bombings. In the mornings I pull on some clothes right after waking and go out and get the newspapers. When I open the downstairs door and step out into the street, there is that now-familiar burnt charcoal smell in the air. Across the river the fire is still burning.

My nocturnal yearnings for a hermaphrodite continue to baffle me. I find myself undressing for bed earlier and earlier. Last night I was under the covers at a quarter past nine. This time I imagine a hermaphrodite who is little more than a boy, a delicate cocoa boy with mochaccino skin, golden nappy hair and eyes the color of honey. His tiny cock, not much bigger than a praline in my mouth, tastes of cinnamon. I had three fingers in the slit below his caramel bon-bons. He was suckling gently at one nipple while with his nimble, wee fingers he pulled playfully at my snatch. The phone rang. I didn't want to leave him so I let the machine take it. The voice of Steve Nicholson, a painter and one of my dearest friends, floats out into the room. He has decided to move back to his family farm in Northern California. "My hands are always trembling," he said. "I'm too nervous to paint anymore. I sold my loft to Tony Bambini." I'm shocked, how will I cope without him? Now I jump up and grab the phone.

"Don't go," I say, "who will I complain to?" "I can't stay, I have to get out of here," he answers. "I'm terrified of more suicide bombers, toxic chemicals in the water supply, poison gas in the subway, anthrax. We can always talk on the phone, e-mail." He wants to come over and bring me a small lamp I have always admired. He had painted a two-headed moose and a pine tree on the lampshade. "I just don't want you to leave," I tell him, "and I'm already in bed. Why don't we meet at the Right Bank Bar tomorrow night? I'll buy you a farewell drink. If you change your mind I'll buy you two drinks." He says that he won't change his mind but he'll meet me at nine o'clock. When I go back to bed I find my little friend is still there waiting for me.

Steve is already sitting at the bar when I arrive. He looks like a lumberjack, a big guy who always wears plaid shirts and Levi's. The exquisite miniature landscapes he paints are a surprise. There is a brown box wrapped and tied with handles under his barstool which must be the lamp. His face just lights up when he sees me, there is a halo around his head. The air in the bar seems to be charged with electricity. I can hear it wizz around my head to the beat of "Jumpin' Jack Flash" on the juke box. The bottles behind the bar are covered with precious gems, rubies, emeralds, sapphires. The mirror is one solid sheet of diamonds. The sudden sense of heightened awareness, this pseudo-LSD glow is what Virginia, the bartender, calls the Twin Towers delirium tremens. She says everyone is getting them, they come and go.

"Well, if it's not Miss Dirty Stories of 2001," Steve calls out, his head doubling in size. I sit down on the barstool next to his. "Miss Dirty Stories doesn't have anything to write about, she's a fraud," I tell him. I met Steve, ten years ago, here at the bar. We got drunk on Wild Turkey and went off to his place to write a dirty story of our own. The geometry of his six-foot-five, 300-pound frame and my five-feet-tall frame did not compute. Skewered on his huge tool I felt like a tiny cock ring. I could not encompass him and kept sliding off. In the middle of what might have eventually been the act, he suddenly said, "Why beat a dead horse?"

We both got hysterical laughing. After we stopped, we decided to dress and go to Chinatown for a very, very early breakfast. Now we are great friends. We commiserate about the vicissitudes of our love affairs, our careers.

He pokes the box below his bar stool with his size-fourteen foot. "Every time you turn on this lamp, I hope you'll remember me," he says. "Yeah, I'll remember that when the going got tough, you ran away." The light goes out of his face and he looks sad. "Come on," he says, "give me a break, a lot of people are leaving. They don't want to raise their kids in the city." I stop him, "But you don't have kids." "I am a kid," he answers. "Anyway, weren't you going to buy me a farewell drink?" I motion over Virginia. She is wearing a low-cut, black leotard top to show off the tattoo of a butterfly on her chest. "Our usual, two Cuervo Margaritas, straight up, no salt, and make them extra strong. I have the tower tremens." "Who doesn't," she says, and then I say, "Can you believe this big oaf is leaving us?" "Yeah, I know, he told me," she answers. When she brings our drinks over along with the change from the twenty I put on the bar, she says, "The next one's on me."

Steve raises his glass and clinks it against mine. "To a better life," he says. "I hope so," I reply. "Besides it's gonzo crazy here," he goes on, then he tells me about a big loft party he went to on Saturday night. It was mobbed, everyone was making out, people couldn't keep their hands off each other. "It was like one long, extended daisy chain," he says. "People were screwing on the couches, in the bathtub. There was a woman on her knees in one corner giving men blowjobs. Can you imagine? There was a long line in front of her." I ask him, "Did you go stand on the line?" He doesn't answer, he hangs his head, maybe hoping I don't see that he is blushing. He changes the subject. "There was probably Viagra in the punch," he says. "Fear is a more powerful aphrodisiac," I state pompously, as if I'm an aphrodisiac expert. "You must be right," he says. "It's the end of the world, what else is there to do but have sex."

Then I tell him about my hermaphrodite dreams as we finish our drinks. Steve motions Virginia to bring another round. "Maybe you should go to the Eulenspiegel Society," he says, "Make your dreams become a reality. I'll be in town till the end of next week. I'll go with you."

"You look like a CIA agent or an übermensch cop," I tell him. "No one will come near us." "You're wrong," he says, "I'd be a big attraction, they'll be on me like flies on sugar, but right now, I have to see a princess about a frog, excuse me." He gets up and makes his way to the back of the room and the stairs that lead down to the bathrooms. I think about how I will miss him and suddenly feel like I'm going to cry. I pick up my drink and finish it in a great gulp. I make myself smile, I despise looking forlorn in public.

There are more people in the bar now. The tape is playing "Tumbling Tumbleweeds."

The couple on the other side of me gets up and leaves as a little crowd of five or six people come in. They occupy the newly vacated seats next to me and the others stand behind them. It is a group of Virginia's friends. They have tattoos, many visible piercings, shaved heads, long dreadlocks, blue hair, or Mohawks. One of the guys has silver studs shaped into a question mark on his cheek. They look like they are in some future-world punk band. Actually they go to school with Virginia at the Columbia University School of Economics. The guy sitting right next to me is slim and rangy. His sleeveless leather vest shows off his lean, muscular arms, which are covered with blue tribal tattoos. He has a clean-cut, handsome face, a young Henry Fonda in *Grapes of Wrath*. His dark hair is shaved close to his skull, and there is a Coptic cross tattooed in the center of his forehead. Virginia once introduced us. His name is Hook and we talked about how he is putting himself through school working for a silkscreen company. I wonder where Steve is and I look around. I see him at the back of the bar. A tall, elongated Giacometti woman with red hair to her waist is holding him by the arm and talking up at him. He looks over her head, catches my eye and smiles.

I turn my head and find Hook looking right at me. "Hi, aren't you the writer," he says. "Yeah," I answer, "I'm Simone de Beauvoir." He laughs. "I'm glad you left Sartre at home. Virginia showed me your poetry book," he says. "It's great, not gender-based, not that usual feminist glob that goes on and on about the glory of pussy. You're way beyond that." He is obviously a very smart guy. He wants to know when my next poetry book is coming out. I tell him I've been working on a book of erotic stories for a year, that the only poem I have written lately was about the disaster.

"How does it go?" he asks. I tell him the first line, it's all I can remember, *Bitter ashes of sunrise float down through the sky like dots in a comic*. "That's great. When do I get to hear the rest?" he asks, and I realize that he's coming on to me. At least he hasn't given me that terrible line, the one that will make me instantly reject him, he hasn't asked me if I like younger men. He offers to buy me another drink. I look back and see that Steve and the elongated redhead are kissing passionately in one of the booths. I accept the drink and start to flirt with him. We flirt through two more drinks and when he asks me to come home with him, I say yes.

Hook helps me on with my coat. I try to appear cool, nonchalant. I am breaking one of my own rules, one I have broken many times before; never go home with someone the first time they invite you. We walk down Bedford Avenue through a starless, cloudy night to Hook's apartment a few blocks away. I have forgotten the lamp but I don't care. Hook lives right above The Buzzards Nest Bar, a notorious hangout for the local cops. "At least the building is safe," he says, grinning at me as he unlocks the door. The music from downstairs is so loud it's deafening. Strains of Frank Sinatra singing, "New York, New York" float up though the floor. "That's all they play ever since it happened," he says. "It's driving me nuts." He ushers me in before him, shuts the door and switches on the light. In the stark glare of the single bulb, I see how thin he is, supple like a boy. His kitchen consists of an old stove and a table made out of a door and milk crates. On the wall above the table is a large blowup news photo of the second plane hitting the south tower. Underneath the image, the words END OF THE WORLD OR BEGINNING OF A NEW WORLD ORDER are printed on the photo in red Magic Marker in large block letters. Hook sees me looking at it. "I'm working on a silkscreen of that," he says. There are cardboard boxes filled with books everywhere. "My castle," he says depreciatingly. I tell him I like it.

We just fall on each other, start to kiss. Hungry, ravenous, we suck each other in. Still kissing me, he walks me backwards through the open door of his other room toward the bed. He puts his hands inside the waistbands of my skirt and tights and pulls them down to my ankles. I step out of them and out of my clogs. He unbuttons my cardigan sweater and slips it off down my arms. His lips keep me occupied, his mouth is a loving cup that I am drinking from. The bedroom window is open. I shiver in my bra and panties even though there is a fire building inside me. With one arm he shuts the window, with the other he pushes me down almost roughly on the bed. I watch him take off his boots, his jeans and his vest. I love his exotic markings, the blue wings on his back and on the top of his chest, the many tribal bracelets he wears burned into his arms. He is not wearing any underwear. His cock is very long and thin, not pink at all, a startling white. I notice that he has beautiful, large pink nipples. They look soft, fleshy, like the nipples on a woman's breast. I want to nurse there. He steps back, mumbles something I can barely hear, then I make it out. "This is going to be good, I know this is going to be good," is what he is repeating like a mantra. In an attempt to calm him and reach out to him, I ask him if he likes my underwear. I am wearing my favorite matched set, black satin covered with red roses. "Yeah," he says, barely glancing down. "What kind of flowers are those? Carnations?" he asks. "Sure, right, carnations," I say. I peel off my bra and panties and then I just grab his hand and pull him down on top of me. His body is so light on mine. The last time I found myself in bed with a man, he had a big belly like a sumo wrestler. Hook and I begin to kiss again but now he is more hesitant. We kiss for a long time. I'm getting wet, wetter, juice running down my legs, but I don't feel his steel pressing into my belly. I wonder if it's the extra ten pounds I'm wearing on my thighs but then he pulls his head up. He says, "You're so beautiful. I didn't think you would be so beautiful."

I realize he is terrified. I want him to ram his tongue so deep and hard into my mouth that my cervix opens up before it and he is tonguing my labia from the topside but instead he pulls away. He seems to be weeping.

"I'm very sorry," he says. "I can't do this, usually I'm hard right away." "O.K., don't feel bad, it's O.K.," I say. I put my arm around his shoulders. I pull him closer to me. He nuzzles my neck then rolls off me onto his back. We lie there beside each other like two beached fish at Coney Island. I wonder if this has happened because we are strangers or because we don't love each other. I wonder if the disaster has rendered him impotent or if it was the three beers he drank as he sat with me at the bar. I wonder if it's my old nemesis, tried and true, the luck of the draw.

I glance over at him. His eyes are closed. The wing tattoos on his chest start just above his sternum. It looks as if he is wearing a dainty scarf, a mantilla of blue lace. His large nipples are bubblegum pink. I want to touch them, chew them, suck all the sugar out. First I lean over and kiss him briefly, sweetly on the lips. Then I allow myself to suck at one nipple while I stroke his limp cock. I savor the taste of his nipple, while I learn the shape of his cock. I stretch it in my hands, then I tuck it between his legs. He starts to mumble something, perhaps a protest, but I shut him up by putting my mouth right over his. I push my tongue deep inside then I pull it out. I push in again, fucking him with it. Then I take his wonderful nipples between my fingers and I tug at them until the tip of each nipple pops out and hardens like a little clit. Finally, I put my mouth on his clit-nipple. The surrounding skin is soft and smooth like the skin inside my pussy. Hook must like what I'm doing because he is moving his body beneath me, rocking from side to side. I move my hands down below his hips squeezing his legs shut tight. He is pinned under me now, pinned with my mouth at his breast, pinned by my two hands below his hips. I take my hands off the sides of his legs and put them together in a V. I press down on his new vulva. I rub it, press it, caress it just the way I like to have my crotch rubbed before I spread my legs wide. Hook is moving under me with such frenetic force that he throws me off but I'm not angry. I have moved into my dreams. He is my hermaphrodite and he puts a hand out and touches my face. I kiss his wrist, his palm, the tops of his fingers and then he opens his legs. There it is, in all its splendor, pointing straight up to the skies, white, solid as marble.

As I rise and straddle him, I feel very happy. He is still touching my face. His prick fills me up to the top, hooks me into the center of life. He moves, thrusting higher and higher into me as I open wider and wider until we are at ground zero. From my position astride him I can see through the bedroom door the picture of the jet hitting the second tower. I hear a distant sound, a great explosion, like worlds colliding. The walls of the room are shaking, the edges of the ceiling beginning to break apart. Just as I am coming, he comes too. He explodes into me in a ball of fire and we are both propelled up through the crumbling roof, up, up into the black skies, our bodies disintegrating, mixing with the clouds like ashes.

all in a day's work

mistress morgana session notes

John

DOB: 5/9/42

10/25/01; 3 hrs; dungeon. Business suit and stilettos.

LIMITS: no nudity on my part; no strap-ons; no men in scene.

John asked to videotape our session during our initial phone conversation, classic executrix interrogation fantasy, sexy strong woman in business suit that shows just a little too much thigh, that sort of thing. I made it clear I would not appear in the tapes, but that I'd be happy to videotape his predicament. He came to the door with a huge case (not very discreet), and proceeded to set up two digital video cams and a digital audio recorder, which he immediately turned on, thinking I didn't notice. Had to remind him repeatedly that I would not allow him to record my participation in our session. In his fantasy, I was an Executive Director at the ACLU and John was my secretary who is secretly surveilled going through my in-office panty drawer. Heavy verbal interrogation about how I had caught him on tape and had irrefutable evidence of his misbehavior. Put him on the bondage rack in locking leather wrist, ankle, and thigh restraints, stretched to level 4, stuffed his mouth with the inflatable gag. Told him we had been working in secret with Castro for years on perfecting our interrogation techniques, and that if electro-genital torture was good enough for the Cuban government, it was good enough for us. CBT with electrodes and clamps; light cock whipping (he assured me he was masochist, but he can't take any real pain); sensual teasing; light breath play by smothering with breasts (inside blouse). Just lies there like a piece of plank wood, no energy exchange. When I went to turn the cameras on to begin filming him in bondage (surprise!) they were already rolling, so I had to take a moment to erase each tape before resuming filming (this took about 15 minutes, during which time the electro-unit was on level 28 balls and 34 cock, a bit too much for him but at this point I was so annoyed I didn't really care). No SR, only became visibly aroused when I repeated certain key words and phrases ("Surveillance" "Security" "teach the enemy a lesson"). Pushy, constantly tests boundaries, responsive as a tin of Spam, looks like every other client on earth.

Martha
DOB: 8/3/41
6/3/03; 1.5 hrs; boudoir. Sheer floral print slip dress, rubber apron.
LIMITS: no heavy pain, no lesbian rape role play

Gold Star client! Pretty middle-aged blonde with lots of great fantasies of the cathartic-release-without-pain variety. Wanted to work through her fear of inescapable captivity. Spread out a tarp on the boudoir floor, then sensually stripped her, laid her down and bound her wrists and ankles with latex Therabands. Used silk remnant from cross-dressing wardrobe as blindfold; drizzled chocolate sauce, honey, tapioca pudding and crème fraîche all over her body, mashing it around with my bare feet to create an emulsion while repeating "You're a very messy little girl!" while she moaned and giggled. Full-body cling wrap mummification over the big goopy mess we made, light tickle torture on soles of feet, GS over the cling wrap, keeping it off her face. After about 45 minutes, when she was warm to the touch but not too hot, cut her out of the cocoon and had her shower, then into the dungeon for toy show. Nipples the size of plums. Tipped twice the session fee, but I'd do her for free.

Larry
DOB: 11/19/33
9/30/98; 3 hrs; dungeon. Leather skirt and corset, open-toed stilettos
LIMITS: no heavy pain, blood, piercing, GS. No blindfolds.

Not terribly submissive or responsive, has the belittling habit of telling you what to do in the form of a question ("Don't you want to whip my ass? Don't you want to hit it harder? You want to piss in my mouth, don't you?") On the phone he asked for medium CBT; NT with fingers, clamps, and weights; spanking; strapping and caning. When he came in I decided we'd play mostly with gags. Resistant to any form of bondage, but I kept his suspenders in plain view and had to repeatedly threaten to tie his wrists if he didn't keep his grabby little hands to himself (note for future sessions: he's an ass grabber, don't see unless you have the energy to fight him off). Refused to use safewords but said "ow" and "stop it" a lot. Likes being positioned in front of mirrors so he can watch himself being tortured (and grabbing your ass). Rope and leather CBT, whipped clothespins off cock and tits, gagged him after 20 minutes and kept a steady rotation of gags in his mouth for the rest of the session (inflatable, ball, rubber bridle bit, stainless dental, o-ring). Finished him off on the floor under the toilet chair with a piss gag and funnel, ingested GS while SR. Don't see again for longer than one hour. Smelled like cheese.

Rick

DOB: 5/10/58

4/20/03; 1 hr; dungeon. Leopard mini-dress with furry ears and tail.

LIMITS: no religious iconography, no CD.

Goofball from PA by way of DC. High-energy session, heavy slut training and verbal fantasy. On the phone, he asked if I could wear a puppy costume or something like a football mascot outfit: I told him sexy kitten was the best I could do. No real bondage or torture, just lots of talking about all the cock he wanted to suck and all the different positions in which he'd be fucked by my über-macho gay male friends. He's a classic case of homosexual ideation that just can't translate into reality: he can't suck a dildo to save his life and could barely take my index finger, let alone a strap-on. Throughout the scene, he kept whimpering "If I don't do this well for you, Mistress, are you going to force me to serve your homosexual friends?" and "Homos have bigger penises, don't they, Mistress?" There was an uncomfortable 5 minutes in which he started talking about how he wanted to fellate my Rottweiler (didn't want to break his heart and tell him I own a Boston Terrier; then felt strangely protective of my dog). SR on his knees slobbering on my strap-on while shouting "I want to be your nasty homo slut bitch." Refuses to wear a condom. Nice enough guy with some serious repression issues, just needs to blow off steam.

Orrin

DOB: 3/22/34

1/26/02; 1 hr; parlor. Business suit over latex teddy.

LIMITS: none that I could find, nice heavy player.

Kind of stodgy older guy, cross-dressing role-play fantasy in which he was my secretary and I was his sexually harassing corporate lesbian boss. Put him in white Frederick's crotchless lace teddy (cheesy as hell, but it strangely suited him), white lace stockings, red stilettos (women's size 13), and the red and blue skirt and jacket combo. I called him into my office to let him know that his typing was not up to par, and that if he wanted to keep his job he would have to find a way to be more useful around the office. Lots of manhandling, face slapping, spitting. Had him crawl around under the desk looking for lost files while I repeatedly kicked his white flabby ass with the pointy toe of my leather pump. Takes a heavy spanking, strapping, caning, whipping, marks okay (pale, pasty skin, he marks easily). No limit to the amount of pain he can take on his tits, everything I did left him sweetly whimpering for more. After 30 minutes of smacking him around the office and berating him, I dragged him into the dungeon ("our corporate re-training center") and bent him over the bondage horse. I figured I'd do a little light strap-on play to teach him his real place on the corporate ladder, but much to my surprise he ended up taking my fist to within an inch of my elbow. Says he's been playing for about 30 years, has the distended nipples and anal flexibility to prove it. Thanked me profusely after the session, huge tip.

Trent
DOB: 10/9/41
12/2/02; 1.5 hrs; boudoir.
LIMITS: no marks

Average-looking middle-aged guy with a weird smile and a vague frat-boy quality, came in requesting traditional OTK role play. I was his young aunt, he was living with me while attending a prestigious Southern university. He disobeyed the house rules, and as a result had to submit himself to a thorough spanking or I would call the dean of his school and have him expelled. Started out as a fairly talented role player, but not great in the personal hygiene department. Had the annoying habit of grinding around on my lap while I spanked him: his masturbatory wiggling was so out of hand I finally incorporated it into the role play and told him he would receive the birch for his pelvic inappropriateness. At this point, he dropped to his knees and begged, "Please don't tell your big black boyfriend about this, please don't let your huge black lover come in here and punish me." After several minutes of this sort of ridiculous mumbling, I finally signed on and told him that my boyfriend wouldn't hesitate to take his big black hand to Trent's wormy little white bare bottom if he didn't do exactly as he was told. The rest of the session was spent trying administer discipline (wooden frat paddle, leather strap, cane) while listening to an increasingly sexual stream of negrophilic fantasies from a man who I can only suspect burns crosses in his free time. I made him SR while singing "We Shall Overcome." Creepy energy and nasty hidden racial agenda. Alert local hate crimes groups and don't invite him back.

Kofi
DOB: 4/8/38
12/10/01; 2 hrs; dungeon.
LIMITS: no military or other uniforms, no humiliation

K is quiet, very respectful. Classic "I've got too much responsibility in my daily life, everyone looks to me for leadership, and I just want to give it all up" scenario. Really nice energy; long slow meditative full-body rope bondage to St. Andrew's Cross; rhythmic flogging on back and butt (brought in his own music: Ravel's *Bolero*); medium to heavy OTK spanking (he can take a lot with a good warmup, lovely smooth skin, doesn't mark easily). Suspension sling and sensory deprivation hood (he got dizzy, we unzipped the eye vents); swung him around the room and let him feel weightless for a good half hour. Excellent Mistress' choice session, spent the last half of the session with him kneeling at my feet, stroking his neck and holding him while he had a nice long cry while telling me he just needed a place he could go to be safe and not have to make any decisions. Beautiful hands.

Glossary of SM Terms (from www.mistressmorgana.com)
CBT = cock and ball torture
CD = cross-dressing
GS = golden shower
OTK = over the knee spanking
NT = nipple torture
SO = strap-on play
SR = self-release (masturbation)
Toy show = masturbation show

the one you meet everywhere

by kola boof

People talked about her man like a damn dirty dog, and who was she, being such a lonely soul, to dispute them? But still, she longed for him every waking moment. In her mouth, on the I.R.T. going to work in the mornings, she could almost taste his flesh and would tense her throat muscles for up to half an hour so as not to lose his flavor by swallowing. She saw him from the back, his squared ego-worthy shoulders entering the World Trade Center (a building she'd never paid any attention to until terrorists…blew it and her man…to smithereens). And she tortured herself, imagining him from the front—his "*trust-in-me/In-God-We-Trust*" brown eyes lurking the corridors with a nutcracker's anticipation.

Waiting to see that pretty receptionist girl. Again.

Noelle had worked a job everday, not him.

"He was cheat'n on yoh ass," her mama told her while ironing clothes in the living room and watching *Young and the Restless* at the same time. "That's how he got kilt up in that World Trade Sin-ah. Uhn huh. No good Arab nigga—served his ass right. Prally was after you to marry him so he could get his citizenship. He ain't fooled me from day one. I told you to get you a black man."

"Don't no black man want me, Mama," was all Noelle managed to say through the pain of hearing her mother trash Hisham yet again, but right then, quick, her mother shouted back, "Don't tell me that mess! Y'all young black women today kill me. Good as you cook and clean house. Got a decent job mak'n a white girl's salary. Plenny of black men would want you!"

"O.K., then—I don't want *them*!"

She slammed the door behind her.

Dogs of Brooklyn barked in the background, but Noelle's heartbroken intellect reached for her loneliness and placed it—the loneliness—overtop her eardrums as though her ears had filled up with water or been muffled by some mountainous altitude. The blue sky hung over New York as though God had draped it there to tease rather than give inspiration, and Noelle realized that she wasn't going anywhere. She walked until the water blurred her vision, forcing her to come to a complete stop. Through the blindness of rage she saw a human figure moving toward her and instinctively thought to stretch forth her right arm in a pushing-away motion, but then, unable to make out the person, she was scared to do that. They might chop her damn arm off. Shit.

She came not only to a stop but a klutzy one, and rocked on the balls of her feet, leaning here and there, totally filled with the sudden fear that she and this blurry figure might be snatch-pitted by the bump of the universe, and then just as she almost keeled over the other way, her body sensing that they were about to collide, a hoarse voice admonished her, *"Don't you run yoh cry'n ass into me*!"

It was a man. An elderly black man, tall and wiry with a cane. He passed her muttering his complaints about having to have his "feel'ns hurt" by seeing a grown-ass nigra child crying on the damn sidewalk. "Don't brang yoh ass to my church!"

Noelle stood stock-still, swathing her eyes into a damp dryness and clearing her vision, but the clearer it became, the more dashing the thoughts in her head. Television images that danced into the coffins of memory cells as the sky in New York fell.

Her mother, Zapporah, back when the city had been clutched by pandemonium, had made a very concise observation that never left Noelle. It was in those first crowded, choking, pedestrian days when the burrows were without birds and white ash dimmed the sun. She had said, "Just think how lonely it must be for the people that are buried alive up underneaf all that shit. Having to keep on living—not knowing if somebody's coming to get them out or not. Now that's loneliness."

How do I get out?

Noelle stood there looking at the ground, because even after all this time, she still felt as though Hisham was buried underneath all that shit, guarding her heart for her, holding it. Still alive. Not knowing if she was coming to get it or not.

So she made herself walk. Inside her head she hummed one of the songs that she'd written during that long, lonely time before she knew Hisham. She sang to herself:

Once you said you love me…times my phone would ring
Come and get these memories
'cause
Children…oh, children
shouldn't play with dead things.

Federal authorities had shown up at Noelle's apartment a few days after the bombing. In fact, they were inside searching the premises one afternoon when she'd come back from getting groceries.

Agent Dick Vickers, a thin white rail of a man, asked her questions about Hisham's likes, dislikes, habits, his family, his way of screwing her.

"You're not thinking my boyfriend was a terrorist, are you?"

"Just how deep off into Islam would you say he was?"

"Not much, really. It was sort of like he had his own religion."

"What about you, Ms. Reason—were you interested in Islam?"

"Yes. I told him that I would become a Muslim, to be closer to him, of course."

"What did he ever say about Palestine?"

"Nothing."

"He ever mention Osama Bin Laden or the word *jihad*?"

"No."

"What did you two talk about most often?"

"Uhm—music. What we were gonna do when we had money."

"What proof do you have that he was in the World Trade Center when it was bombed?"

"None."

"Do you think he might still be walking around, then?"

"No. I take Braid Bitch's word…"

"Braid Bitch?"

"…ah, that's my best friend, Colleen, but no one's called her Colleen like since she was fourteen. She's a white girl who wears braids and hangs around black people all the time, she likes everybody to call her Braid Bitch, because she braids hair on the side. She saw him go in there. She used to work across the street and saw him go in there several times. He always went to something like an investment firm and talked to this girl at the receptionist desk. Braid Bitch called me at work and told me that she'd just seen him go in. And then fifteen minutes later, it was all over the TV that terrorists had crashed a plane into the main floor of the investment firm where Hisham always went to talk to that girl."

"Who did you vote for in the last presidential election?"

"President Clinton."

"Any particular reason?"

"Uhm, because he's cute and he plays the saxophone."

"What do you think about affirmative action, Ms. Reason?"

"I've heard that term before, but…what is it?"

"What did Hisham say about America?"

Hisham was the one who used to say it!

Marijuana smoke curled out of a cough.

Noelle nodded vigorously, lying in bed, staring at the ceiling, nearly pointing a finger in agreement with herself. It *was* him who said it.

New York is a good place to make love…if you want to make it like a memory.

And Noelle remembered asking him, "Why did you come up to me that day? Did I look cute to you?"

"I came up to you because you reminded me of the one you meet everywhere—God."

"I reminded you of God?"

"Yes. Because I never saw a girl like you. That's the thing about you black ones. Each of you looks so different. The colors, the shapes, the weird African hairdos, the accents. Of all the American women, it's you black ones that intrigue me the most. I don't know if you're supposed to be like that on purpose or if you're all fucked up. I never saw women like you before, not even Africans. African women are normal like whites. I saw a few African women back in Amman, they're just normal wives and mothers. But black

American girls…I don't get what your meaning is about. I always look at black girls and wonder—what do you mean in this country? Where do you belong? So I thought…she's the one you meet everywhere. She's God."

He could have been lying, but his bang was sore and warm inside her and the heat of his body felt like the sun.

"When I first saw you, Hisham, I thought you were a Latino or a Greek guy. I thought you were *soooo* handsome."

"Did you want me to kiss you?"

"Uhm…no, but," she laughed and laughed.

Between his fingers, he took two of her soft braids and rolled and squeezed them in the dark. He loved the way they smelled like a combination of fresh rain and coconut at the moment you crack it.

"Do you think I'm pretty?"

"Why do you always ask me that?"

"Why do you never answer me?"

"Because I don't think the word pretty does you justice, Noelle. You're like God. You're above beauty."

"You don't think God is beautiful?"

"Hell no. No one that is beautiful can remain beautiful forever—that's the whole lesson about beauty right there. Beauty is not a virtue. God made beauty for the same reason he made sex—to show us what hypocrites we are. I don't like beauty. Not the kind you're talking about. I like the kind of beauty like…have you ever seen two dogs stuck together after they've fucked?"

"Now yoh ass is sick!"

"I'm dead serious. Hey, look at me, I'm serious, Noelle. That's beautiful. That's real, that's God."

"Yeah. Tell me anything. You had me going until you said that, Hisham. Your ass is just too much for the report."

"My ass?" he asked with a straight face. "How come black girls talk like that?"

"Because…we're God."

He had kissed her, inserting his tongue, as an olive-colored hand squeezed her brown titties into oneness. He said, "New York is a good place to make love if you want to make it like a memory."

"Are we in love, Hisham?"

"I am."

* *

It tortured her now to think that whatever he had felt for the pretty receptionist at the World Trade Center had been strong enough to blow them up together and cast them, united in death, forever after, beyond the fervor of Noelle's longing. *It should have been us*...not you and her, thought Noelle. We were the ones in love. We should have been together on September 11th.

I had thawed out taco meat for dinner and everything, Hisham. I was finally gonna suck your dick. I had decided that our relationship had become serious enough for me to do that.

I even bought this head scarf. I was going to wear it that night so that you could see how I look with my hair covered up Muslim style.

Hisham, before I met you, it had never occurred to me that I could know any other men but the ones like my father.

I was invisible until you looked at me.

All I did, every day, was daydream.

On my copy of the *New York Observer*, the one that showed that the sky was falling, I took a blue ballpoint pen and wrote all over the color photograph: *Love is the drug. Love is the drug. Love is the drug*. I wanted to crawl beneath the World Trade Center and die with you.

Goodbye, Noelle.

The sight of Braid Bitch's white flesh and her long, beaded African rope braids was enough to make any black girl's daydreams dissipate. Noelle hugged her back, though.

"Hey girl."

A pair of brown eyes watched them from a studio sound booth.

The American flag took up the entire wall behind them. Red, white, and blue. White stars. Noelle had taken her braids loose and wore her hair in a soft springy Afro. It looked like a bush, a glorious tumbleweed.

The brown eyes sparkled—the stare owning the beauty before it as though the movement of the eye controlled them.

Noelle said, "Did you hear about that new disease over in China? SARS? It's killing people in Canada now."

"Population control," sniffed Braid Bitch. She waved her newly painted red, white, and blue acrylic fingernails for effect. "Girl, men made that shit in a lab, they already got the cure stashed away and everything. And you know damn well that Saddam Hussein's fat evil ass ain't dead. Bush just trying to front so we'll reelect him...or should I say...finally elect him in the first damn place. Me, personally, I want Clinton back. That nigga was foine."

"Won't he though?" They slapped hands.

Braid Bitch shook a Newport out of its green box, seeming to light it, puff it, and blow smoke all in one motion. She said, as though announcing a close friend's unexpected death, "I had a dream last night."

Her wild eyes, slate gray, commanded Noelle to look at her.

"I dreamt about that time when we were kids and we found that dead baby in the abandoned church behind the basketball court. Remember how rubbery it was? We almost thought it was a doll when we saw it. But it wasn't fake, it was a baby. A real baby."

Noelle's lips formed the words, but no sound came out as she nodded, "*I remember*."

"I dreamt we were in there again. The baby was barely alive, but she was breathing, and she wanted me to name her. She said that she couldn't be free from this world until somebody named her."

Noelle's mind flashed to a different memory. She and Braid Bitch, not yet pubescent, pulling down their panties and rubbing up against one another, kissing and groping one another in the trashy forbidden corridors of the dead boarded-up church.

Tears suddenly filled the brown eyes that watched them. Night and moonlight tears, shimmering bright as joy.

Braid Bitch said, "We come here to be named."

Noelle snapped at Braid Bitch, "Stop it! I don't want to remember that shit. There are some things that just shouldn't be remembered."

"I named her Euphoria," said Braid Bitch, defiantly. "I told her that she was soft and beautiful and that her name was Euphoria. I told her that she was the thing that made people cry with joy. And then I saw her spirit leave her body, but her eyes...she had the prettiest brown eyes...and they were watching me. Everywhere that I went, they followed me, watching over me."

Noelle's chest heaved as though about to vomit, but instead her eyes burst with a hot wet rage. She bowed her head and felt the unexpected might of her weeping contort her face and flood her throat.

Braid Bitch blew smoke and smiled as the brown eyes shut and let them go.

Noelle told her mother, "It's just that sometimes...I don't think he's dead. I think he's somewhere out there."

"I wouldn't be surprised if he was," smirked Zapporah, flipping pancakes. "Your Aunt Cookie's old man walked out the front door to get a pack of cigarettes and never came back. 'Course, he ain't have no World Trade Center to blame it on."

"No, he's dead," snapped Noelle. "Hisham's dead."

"Well, if he's dead, then why you always feel like somebody's watching you?"

"Because it's the government. They're watching everything I do now. I slept with an Arab. That makes me suspect, you know."

"Well, go fuck a few white men. Prove you're an American."

"Mama, I wish you would take me seriously."

"Look, girl, you need to go on with your life. Any woman obsessed over a dead man is wasting precious daylight. Youth is the only free wealth that a woman gets, Noelle. Say it with me—youth is the only free wealth that a woman gets. Now let his ass go!"

He had passed Noelle again that morning. His cane pressing the unkind numbness of his scrotum into the sidewalk. He had looked into her face, and this time without tears, she had looked back and known that it was him again, and he had seemed so black and arrogant, so anciently powerful that he must have been God. A real asshole with power as she had always considered the good lord might just be. For what else could explain the distance between herself and this white-haired chocolate deity whose marble-black eyes burned against her baby face as though surely she were the stone that had come out of his own bowels.

Who else but God could explain the loneliness that human beings feel even when surrounded by one another?

People—not insects, but people—had crashed their souls into buildings so that other souls would be snatched out of the killer's reality and ripped from the noontime of the ones who needed them. Noelle had seen the rage in his eyes as he passed her on the street. She had felt the arthritis in his withered hands and the gathering spit that rested just inside the pretty caterpillar shape of his pinkish lower lip. Her mother and a lot of people had those West African lips. Even some white people nowadays—the ones you meet everywhere.

But with his watching brown eyes he thought about artistic people like Noelle who crafted stories expressing their being lost, their being lonely, their lust and pride and despair. The living for the love of God people—the ones all over the world that you meet everywhere.

As though she could hear him, he spoke and said, "I'm going back to my used-to-be."

His feet moved across the gritty floor as a radiant sunny Brooklyn sidewalk awaited him outdoors. Then he heard her voice. Noelle's small, plaintive singing voice. It stopped him in his tracks, because by the sound of it, he could tell that he was no longer there. Her loneliness draping her like a favorite sweater as she sang:

Blow me a charge of your love.
Show me a picture...of your life.
Blow me a charge of God up above—
tell me every thang...
is gonna be alright

eight hundred pages

by elizabeth tallent

If, twenty-four years later, you're still bitterly wishing you'd never seen that person's face—I call that love.

He had that wounded, brooding, lost-soul thing going on, and my twentysomething self fell for him absolutely, with a light-hearted self-destructiveness that has since proved impossible to recapture. What was addictive was the no-holds-barred bliss of it and the meanwhile-secretly-knowing how wrong it would go. Why that should prove such an ecstatic combination, I have, now that I am disguised to myself as an adult, no real idea. Yesterday one of my students said, trying to describe that lightning-strike intoxication, "You know how it is when your heart's in your head." She didn't amend this to *when your heart's in your throat,* and probably wasn't aware she'd made any mistake, but the other students at the seminar table gazed at her with pleasure: a slip they could use, and so can I, for what is a teacher of writing but the secret student of her students?

He and I had spent nearly a week, that long-ago spring, at *our* seminar table, intent, with the other sort-of-luminaries, on deciding who among our heaped-up files of unsuspecting candidates should receive five years' serious beneficence. It is impossible to give away money with someone without learning the essence of their character: surely it rivals sharing a foxhole for naked mutual revealingness, and I can tell you he favored daring in women and convention in men, an aesthetic less uncommon among misogynists than you'd think. I had been set on daring myself for some years by then, but unlike him I didn't care who else I found it in, as long as I was sure it was alive in my own heart. He wouldn't have had doubts like mine, or needed to conduct the sort of blind Braille search of his own dark heart I continually practiced, because he'd already incarnated his daring, eight hundred pages' worth. A famous novel. For much of the last week he'd kept his baseball cap tugged down low over his forehead so his gaze had a shaded quality, and he seemed pretty deeply holed up in himself. When he spoke, he kept it brief, but brevity is the soul of charisma, and by the afternoon of our second day everyone had begun waiting for him to rouse himself and give the discussion a sardonic twist of dismissal, or the rare caress of his approval. A trick beautifully carried off, I thought, this watchful Zen ferocity, as if he were our conscience. But that was before I knew that roomfuls of people always designate a conscience. He had been a lieutenant and some disreputable trace of moral authority still haunted his bearing, even when he slouched low in his leather chair, swivelling childishly, tirelessly back and forth with that baseball cap shading his gaze down to an unreadable now-and-then gleam directed my way from across the table. Fuck you, I thought, gleaming at me because you're famous. You can't have me. I had worn a black rag tied around my arm for two years during Viet Nam, and fasted with other students on the cold stone steps of the dreary administration building until the police came and knocked some heads together. In the mad scramble as the handcuffed were parted from the vengeful un-arrested, I had called a blue-eyed boy cop *honey piggy* but he'd only laughed and tapped his nightstick happily on the tip of my nose and said, "You!" Since then I'd had bad dreams in which a dark figure cried out "You!" and I woke sweaty with self-loathing, my body having a tendency to treat guilt like the *hardest* hard work. But it wasn't all guilt, resistance to that war: there were wrenching little romances all over the place. On my left ankle under my black stocking was tattooed in typewriter-rickety letters the name of a boy who had failed to come back to our hometown. I had never even liked him before but we had lain out one night on a blanket thrown over the prickling stubble of a new-mown field after he knew he couldn't get out of going, and he'd kept his hand clasped around my naked ankle for the five hours we'd talked. I lay on my back with my arms flung over my head, afraid to move for fear he would never again have anyone to tell everything to, tracking the itches springing up at random down the length of my body, me so at ease, pinned to earth by the moonlight and his need, so *valuable, completely at one* with him if it hadn't been for these sudden match-strikes of itchiness and distant dogs barking in a haywire concert and my thinking that we had unconsciously arranged ourselves in a pose evocative of the saved and the damned. If you had seen us from above we would have looked like a drowning man refusing to relinquish his hold on the girl whose swift streamlined ascent would cause her, within seconds, to break the surface.

So while at that long-ago seminar table I believed myself politically and ethically insulated from his brooding, gleaming, casual assault, my body, far more easily seduced than my soul has ever been and dressed for the sake of the pretty lime-twist of perversity I believed I brought to the group in a tight little black dress, my foolish body was interested. His sadness was notorious, because nothing he had written—nothing in eight hundred pages against whose beauty even I couldn't argue—had caused it to loosen its hold. My sense of the relation between damage and art altered over the course of that week. He'd made beauty and was still ruined—this fractious, attractive person rousing himself to say ugly things about other writers who did not deserve the money he conceded they were going to get. He was good at funny, last-minute savaging: no one really needed to protest because the matter had really been decided before he spoke up, and his wit relieved the awfulness of having so many writers in one room intent on doing good. If he was clear-eyed and undeceived—if he called a hack a hack—our trance of politic acquiescence could safely deepen. He was our secret self. He could not be bought, and thus, it seemed, neither could we, despite appearances.

Also, I was jealous of him—-jealous of the duration of his readers' attention. My own readers, how well did they ever know me? You could know him far better—know him inside out, if you believed he was the boy. If, in prose too cool ever to be tainted with charity, the boy did terrible things, someone had to have done those things in real life, right? The boy had gone before his draft board to speak of his love of cocksucking, wearing on his well-muscled, clean-shaven legs a pair of his mother's stockings and borrowed heels that endowed him with a teetering grace, but it hadn't fooled anyone and the boy's father had shoved him against the wall of their kitchen, saying *You go where your country tells you or I never need to see your sly little face again.* The boy had traversed minefields while obsessively stroking a shamrock-green rabbit's foot a girl had given him. When this rabbit's foot at last was lost the boy had wept. The boy had killed a girl, a fourteen-year-old prostitute with a sly little face, with his bare hands. The boy had been sent home with shrapnel in his knee. *His* dishevelment—a rumpled, wary, sleeping-under-a-bridge unkemptness—was as pretty as if he were French. He had a seriously insomniac gaze, I thought. This turned out to be accurate: he could not sleep. I liked this because it fit with his war-sadness and rumored craziness. There was to be no second book, it seemed. Because the war book had been such a smash hit it was considered a kind of insanity that he did not have a second book well under way. Who but a crazy person would let fame slide out from under him? It needed holding on to, fame as burning-bright as his had been, and if the care and feeding of fame was proof of sanity, he'd failed a national test, and disenchantment was beginning, ever so faintly, to haze his name. But I liked that too.

On our collective last day he caught up with me as we left the room for lunch. I liked getting away from the others during lunch because if I could get away it meant an hour when I didn't have to think about writing or reading or anybody's brilliant future but my own. I liked keeping the little votive light of my future brightly lit and that needed at least a lunch hour's worth of sweetly uncompromised narcissism a day, so it worked out. But this time he caught me, and when I turned to him, he did a strange thing: he took hold of my wrist to turn my palm upward and then he lowered his face. Though later my slow-wittedness would strike me as yet another inexplicable thing about that day, I said "What are you doing?" If there had been a pearl in my palm his tongue could not have been more exquisite. I hadn't asked a question that needed an answer, so when he was done persuading my nerve-endings that to go through life without him was to exist in such a sorry state of deprivation it was as if one's entire body were blind, he held me in his wounded, dark-eyed regard—a thousand-yard stare that suddenly found *you*—and said, "Hey, we can go to my room."

"Hey, you don't even know my name."

"Sure I know your name."

There was a silence. He didn't know my name.

"Green my eyes and pretty my mouth, that would work. Stroke of luck, that could be your name. Or sanity. Conceivably your name is sanity."

"Wrong on that one. So wrong."

"I'm wrong and we've only just met."

"How long do you usually know someone before she tells you you're wrong?"

"Not long," he said modestly. "It's true. All sweetness and light, then *bam, smash,* the fall from grace. But I don't think we will go that way, you and I. I don't think we will turn out badly. I'd honestly like to go upstairs and do something with you."

In the elevator I said, "Amy."

"Amy," he said. "Absolutely. Amy."

Then after a longish pause of several floors' ascent he said, "Did you ever in your life see such beautiful chairs?" Meaning he loved the chair he'd been swivelling back and forth for the last week. Meaning that like the boy in the book he came from a town where there were no such chairs. He ran his fingers with an assessing kind of bashfulness along his own unshaven jaw. Humble simplicity was his style in elevators. I thought *I wonder what you're like without your baseball cap.* It crossed my mind to try something cute like stealing it from his head and settling it on my own but I didn't, though I was desperate to do or say something wrong and extricate myself. The Muzak was "Raindrops Keep Fallin' on My Head." I couldn't help wondering why my body in its tight little black dress persisted in believing something good could come of this hideous situation. He didn't turn to me or try harder to elicit some answer to the chair question. My stockings were the exact shade of black of my heels, a feat of hurried 8 A.M. self-assemblage, and my stance conveyed what I thought was a nice but not sluttish degree of carnal challenge. I remembered the boy wobbling toward the skeptical draft board in his heels and thought *at least I do this better than him.* The draft board would never have sent me anywhere.

"Great hotel, huh," he said.

Another floor up, and he sang a little of "Raindrops Keep Fallin' on My Head."

All at once I liked him for this willingness to sing something so stupid—for having ceased to be a gleaming, compelling person—and liked, in bed, the dark hair falling past his eyes, the rasp of his unshaven cheek against mine. Once the baseball cap was off, he'd seemed even less mysterious. He'd stroked the name tattooed on my ankle and said, "Someone you loved?" and I'd answered honestly, "Just someone," and he'd said, "Then why did you want his name if it wasn't love?" "I think *because* I didn't love him." He said, "Nobody has my name on their ankle that I know of, love me or not." With a fingertip he wrote his name under my left collarbone. "Here's a nice blank space for me," he said. Sex proved he wasn't in good shape, and before long his breath came raggedly. All at once he withdrew from me, sat up, rummaged through the litter on his bedside table, clasped an inhaler against his face, and began rocking, hunched over himself, the rocking delicate, constrained, out of sync with his raggedy, despairing inhalations. Me, I was breathing in time with these. I couldn't help it. I couldn't breathe unless he breathed. It wasn't love that had panicked my breath from any independent rhythm but ordinary sympathy. You can't help wanting someone beside you to figure out how to live. You yourself live through that going-wrong moment with a sureness, a *thereness* you hope the other person will catch. You just sit there and *live* as brilliantly as you can, as if telepathically to convey how it's done.

He did know how it was done. Because I had read his book I know he also knew how to stop someone from doing it: ways you could use your hands to prevent another person's taking that next breath. Because I had begun liking him I had stopped wanting to believe he had done this, but because of the book I knew he had. He had been nineteen years old. Who was I, this half-fucked girl at the far side of the rumpled bed, to begin to feel revulsion for that boy, alive for eight hundred beautiful pages, otherwise long gone? He was still rocking, rocking the bed with the ferocity of his need to breathe. I would have touched him except I feared startling him from his arduous communion with the inhaler. "Tell me what to do," I said, "because I can call the desk for a doctor," but with his back still to me, he shook his head. I felt reproached, unfairly, and startled that in the midst of panic a little blame should still sting so. I had scratched his back and now these scratches, with their hyped-up ardor, made me ashamed. In sex I was always self-conscious. I had wrecked his back for dramatic effect. He hadn't moved me much: all had remained clear and calm inside my head. The best moment was still what I had felt in the palm of my hand. But sitting up in that wrecked bed I was as lonely for him as if I'd known him since childhood and we were very near and dear to each other and he had just been struck this incapacitating blow that, if it wasn't his death, was like some kind of rigorous practice for death, a harsh run-through of the real brutal thing, the thing itself so hugely possible that I was light-headed in my immobilization, waiting for him to breathe his way through terror and back into this room, this bed, to me who didn't yet love him, though if I had known enough to say then you will be all right, there are no ghosts, I would like myself better now, and not mind so much that in his sleepless nights throughout the year we spent as lovers, I believed he deserved his ghosts. I thought I knew what ghosts were, then, despite having none of my own. I thought I could secretly point to him and say yes, you, you should be haunted. Now I know he must have read in my gaze that very willingness to accuse. Now I know who the ghost was, in that room, when my love couldn't breathe.

Now there is a different war but they don't believe they'll ever go—my students. As their secret student I fear they could all be wrong.

"So it wasn't love," he said a different time, reading my ankle.

"It's so my body remembers," I said. "Because that's the part of me that's willing to forget."

Eight hundred pages or an inscription on an ankle, try telling the body there's such a thing as death. It will look back at you with eyes that know better, the eyes of any student in this room.

the politics of destruction

i believe i'm in love with the government

by nasri hajjaj
translated by ibrahim muhawi

Using a kitchen knife with a sharp blade, I slew my three sons. Blood spurted from their tender necks and the drainpipe overflowed into the alleys of the neighborhood, sweeping along as it gushed forth stones and soil, their schoolbooks and the traces of their little feet and their innocent laughter, along with my soul.

Then I saw the blood colliding with the leftover sandbags, which had been used to repel the enemy, but it flowed over them and continued its rush to the sea, mixed with the blue water and changing it to a color I had never seen before.

As for my three daughters and their mother, I preferred to strangle them with my bare hands because I did not want to repeat the scene of blood. Also, I was anxious about being accused of terrorism and savagery. That might hurt my personal reputation and that of my homeland, which had not achieved such a high degree of esteem among other nations without huge effort and much sacrifice.

I put the bodies of my children and their mother in a large wooden box and nailed it firmly shut with steel nails; then with great difficulty I lifted the box up and placed it on a wooden cart which I use for selling vegetables. After that I sat on a small stool, leaned against the cart, and took a cigarette from the case I carry with me. I lit it and set to smoking with great gusto. From time to time some drops of blood dripped on my face and I wiped them with the palm of my right hand until it became red as the palm of a bride on her henna night.

After I finished smoking my cigarette I rose from the stool and started pushing the cart, with blood still dripping from the bodies of my children. The blood drew a red line along the street as though the city council was itself responsible for putting it there to organize the traffic on our miserable streets. As for flies and mosquitoes and other insects that live on blood, they were so thick that the city appeared in a dense fog, as if black clouds were threatening to rain down black soil.

And so, pushing the box in front of me and looking neither left nor right, I walked in my glorious procession in the shadow of insects and in the company of cats and dogs, with the bodies of my children and their mother in the wooden box that seemed like a howdah from a myth and headed for the Ministry of the Interior of our beloved country.

As if a hidden power from some unknown place had crept into my body, I spent several hours pushing the cart at a brisk pace yet felt no fatigue, although wandering around selling vegetables usually drained me. In an instant there rose, above the barking of the dogs and the meowing of the cats, the sounds of human beings and when I looked back I saw hundreds of men, women, and children who had penetrated the crowd of hungry animals and were prancing about in beautiful clothes, dancing and singing as they went, joyous at walking in my procession.

In the distance, I could make out the awesome building that housed the Ministry of the Interior. It was taller than all the other buildings, something like a Great Pyramid, with all that attaches to it of age, majesty, and sacred wonder. And here! I have arrived.

The crowd grew larger as the cart got closer to the building. We reached, first, the great courtyard in front of the Ministry with me pushing the cart and the people dancing behind me. On the balcony overlooking the courtyard stood the leader of the country, with the Prime Minister on his right and the Minister of the Interior on his left. Behind them was a group of high officials but I could not be certain who they were. I came forward, pushing my cart over a white carpet spread out in the center of the courtyard, and the people made a circle around me. I looked behind and was surprised to find that, as I came forward, the part of the carpet I had walked over was changing in color from white to deep red due to the blood of my slain children dripping on it. At that moment I understood why red carpets are laid out for leaders and kings.

Before we reached the great stairway the leader of the country signaled me to stop. I stopped and looked up at him with a feeling of honor and great reverence and realized from this close distance to what extent he is a magical person with the light that shines from his eyes and the kindness that his sacred presence evokes in the spaces of my soul. The leader of the country reached for the microphone. With his left hand he placed it in front of him and with his right pointed to me, and goose pimples immediately bristled over my body and tears welled up. I felt the huge desire to kowtow before him in an act of worship. Then he started addressing the crowd:

"As of today we shall give this courtyard the name of this ideal and simple citizen in appreciation of his creativity in helping to find a wonderful solution to the crisis of paper which has plagued our country since independence and which has made it impossible for us to grant passports to all our citizens. By getting rid of all the members of his family, of his own accord and without the government having to issue an order to that effect, this citizen has rendered the country a service that cannot be described or forgotten, for he has helped alleviate the burden of foreign debt and the loan that would be needed to buy paper for the printing of the passports. And today, on behalf of all of you, I declare this person an ideal citizen. A statue the size of the Ministry of the Interior shall be erected in his likeness in the center of the courtyard in which you are gathered to honor him. The government urges all its citizens to consider this one citizen an example of creativity and sacrifice to be imitated. Long life to you, and long live the homeland!"

The citizens applauded for a long time; meanwhile the sun, with its bright scorching rays, had settled in the middle of the sky. At that moment I turned around in the direction of the people and saw a forest of knives raised to the sky, shining with a blinding brightness that would melt steel and then falling on the necks of the children and slashing them until blood gushed out in a huge flood, while the throats that had been cut were letting out death rattles louder than any other sound could be except for the sound coming from our own throats as we called out long life to our leader, asking God to save our leader and our country.

An earlier version of this story was published in England in Banipal, No. 15/16, Autumn 2002/Spring 2003.

memo to our journalists

by mark lee

1. Keep track of your sat phone! This is a valuable piece of equipment and the company wasn't able to insure its use in Iraq. For staff reporters, the destruction of your sat phone will be charged against your salary. For stringers, the cost will be taken out of your bi-weekly payment check. Senior editors trying to prove that they've still "got the stuff" will not be charged for lost phones.
2. The most dangerous thing in combat is not the possible use of weapons of mass destruction that may, or may not, exist.
3. The most dangerous thing in combat is your own country's Air Force accidentally dropping bombs on you.
4. Reporters experiencing a mortar barrage or "friendly" fire should take cover immediately. (Note: this does not apply to staff photographers, who should take the picture first, then seek cover.) Road ditches are a good choice. Stay away from anything filled with gasoline. If the attack continues, repeat the following: "Dear God. Please, save me. I know I was an atheist in college. But, I believe. I really do believe. (pause for breath) Please, save me. Oh, God. I beg of you. If you save me I promise that I'll be really, really good for the rest of my life."
5. Spiritual promises made during these situations can be ignored and quickly forgotten.
6. Some of you may be "embedded" with American troops. Having written articles about elections, oil spills, and tax reform, you might assume that you will be objective about everything you see and experience. Discard this illusion. You will be partially compromised within three hours and completely compromised in a day. These young men and women are defending you. You will eat, sleep, and complain alongside them plus

they speak English and know the lyrics to the *Gilligan's Island* theme song. The civilians you'll see in the war zone won't speak English. They will either run away or try to kill you.

7. This is what soldiers talk about: Fuck this war. Fuck the President. Fuck the Captain. Goddamn, I'd really like a beer, a joint, a steak, a blow job *right now*. I hate this country. I hate these people. Look at the way they live. Shit. Watch out. They're firing at us. Watch out. Incoming. Kill them. Waste them. Yes. Damn. Blew the little fucker away. You see him? See that? You okay?
8. This is what you will write about: Lance Corporal (Perez, Jackson, Smith) really misses his (wife, girlfriend, parents, dog), but he/she feels that we need to defend America from (terrorism, Middle East dictators, vaguely perceived threats).
9. Anyone over the rank of colonel is lying to you.
10. If you and your embedded unit are lost in the countryside and searching for the main road, remember that every adult in the world lies about most things much of the time. Look for a smart, honest nine-year-old.
11. Things to bring: Cash. You can never have enough of it for bribes and souvenirs. Do *not* go to Abercrombie & Fitch before you leave and buy a khaki vest and/or safari jacket with lots of loops and pockets like the journalists you've seen on television. These journalists are probably better looking than you. They will be filing from the Ritz-Carlton Hotel in Qatar. You should bring one pair of pants. Two cotton shirts. One warm jacket. Shorts and flip-flop sandals for the outdoor shower at regimental headquarters. Bring a hat—definitely—but not a stupid-looking one.
12. Also pills. Lots of pills. Pills to go to sleep or to stay awake. Pills for amoebic dysentery and malaria. Eye drops for the dust. Deodorant for an interview with a general. A few condoms. (In a war, anything can happen.) You don't need to bring bandages. If someone is shot and the medic is missing, ask a female soldier for a few of her Kotex pads. They're sterile and absorb blood.
13. Re: blood. If someone is shot in front of you—especially in the head—blood will splatter in a wide area. Even though you've seen blood in the past, the brilliant red color is always surprising. As someone bleeds to death in front of you, you will be amazed how much blood is in the

human body (six quarts for a staff sergeant from Austin, Texas, who once proudly showed you a photograph of his fiancée wearing a bikini). If a piece of shrapnel the size of a dime hits someone in their carotid artery, they will die in a minute or so. Sometimes, it takes a little longer.

14. Chunks of bone rarely adhere to clothing. Not so for small particles of the human brain. Without bleach, it's difficult to completely remove blood from jeans or a cotton shirt. Best to just throw them away.
15. If you want to impress a current lover or possible future lover of either sex, an old college roommate, or your editor, use the sat phone to call them from the war zone. The proper tone is: matter-of-fact.
16. Do not ask the following questions in your articles: Why is the enemy fighting for Iraq? If the 9-11 terrorists were from Saudi Arabia, then why aren't we invading *that* country? How come we seized the oil fields first? Why the hell are we here anyway? These questions are for columnists and editorial writers, not for people directly experiencing war. (Please reread point #6 regarding objectivity.)
17. This is the secret about war: if you are lucky, it is exhilarating and fun. You get to drive around the countryside and watch things get blown up. For one of the first times in your life, you truly will be living in the moment. You do not have to worry about your Keogh fund, your thinning hair, or the rust on the underside of your car. You may even forget that you own a car. The stories that you send out will be published—not spiked—and people will praise you. When you finally come back to America, staff reporters may be promoted and stringers may become permanent hires with medical insurance (no promises!).
18. War stories, told casually, blow away all other stories at cocktail parties. Hey, perhaps you'll write a book.
19. This is the secret if you have a bad war: you will see things that will be impossible to forget. Three years later, you will burn something accidentally on your barbecue and the smell of burnt flesh will make you want to vomit. You will drink more alcohol when you come back. You may take more drugs. You will wake up at three o'clock in the morning with a dry mouth and a memory like a worm trying to eat its way out of your skull. You will walk into the bathroom and stare at yourself in the mirror. You will cry. Silently. For the rest of your life.
20. Good luck!

the shield

by f.s. yu

At night the world is a sandstorm. Like a light brown gauze over your face blocking the black velvet sky. We call it the edge, Anterim, Jordan, the Angor hotel. Here is where boats cross in the desert. Rusted buses bring troops and shields to the border of Mesopotamia, heading into Iraq two days after the fighting has already started. The vehicles make small crunching sounds over the terrain and creak with rust like boats crushed between glaciers, so that the desert sounds like a house about to collapse in the wind. These square dark hulls with their Argonauts, their windows cracked, their crazed cargo of idealists and warriors. A month ago the buses were clean, the engines smooth, British double-deckers, like the kind you tour London in. We watch them now and shake our heads, our feet heavy on the earth, our clothing soaked in dull clay. I can barely see the outline of the three South Africans standing off near the phone booth. If they go much farther they won't be able to find their way back.

Our boats pass the other way, westward toward Amman. Taxis with Iraqi license plates stop to pick us up. Flatbeds full of possessions but short on gas take passengers for American pocket change, minivans with international stickers, diplomat stamps, NGO labels stuck in bright yellow letters over the window or in blue tape on the roof. We're going back to wherever we came from: Pakistan, Russia, Australia. Some of us, like me, have already been inside the country, Human Shields for Saddam's Baghdad and the civilians there. Others never got over the border. The border's tightened since the war, but the border runs a thousand miles and is porous. If you want to get into Iraq, you'll get in. I'm going home, San Francisco, 7,500 miles away. But I might take a few more days. Just a couple more. I don't want to leave yet. I've gotten used to the smell of sulphur and gas as the retreating Iraqis light another oil well on fire or the Americans send more missiles into the lightly strafed western edge of the country.

"You know what's here?" I asked my girlfriend, Theresa, when I finally got through to her. C-130 troop transports were crossing the sky like claws. There are only supposed to be 2,000 American troops in Jordan for defense purposes, but they take off from secret airbases near Ar'ar. Miles south they say hundreds of tanks are rolling from Jordan toward Baghdad. I was hoping she would say something along the lines of Thank God you're alive. But she didn't. It was like I was calling from my own apartment a couple of blocks away from her, just with more static.

"What's there?" she asked. "What are you seeing?"

"Nothing," I told her, ignoring the swarm of warplanes, the helicopters like bees. The phone is a dark blue plastic contraption with a cracked mouthpiece. "There's a little village here and a hotel. It's a stopping point for people entering and leaving the country. There are more people in the air than on the ground. People are very drunk. They're drinking Arak. It's like Pernod, they drink it like milk. Nobody showers except the owner of the hotel."

"Are there any demonstrations?" she asked.

"Who would we demonstrate for, the camel? There can't be more than five hundred people here and half a dozen mules."

"Fifteen hundred people were arrested in San Francisco today," she said. I heard her cradle the phone between her shoulder and ear. I thought I heard another voice behind hers. "My affinity group blocked traffic from Powell to Polk."

"Affinity," I said. "Is another word for cheat."

"We broke the window of the Starbucks on Market and dragged newspaper bins into the street. Some of the protesters were putting the bins back, can you believe it? I mean, whose side are you on?"

The phone is twenty feet from the hotel and away from any shade. I felt myself getting very thirsty. "So how is Sherman what's-his-name? Hello?" She hung up on me. I was calling her from the desert less than a hundred miles from the war she was so busy protesting, and she hung up on me.

Theresa's body is like a statue, thin and hard from training and long rides to Yosemite National Park. She swims with the Berkeley team, and the girls on that team are ten years younger. Her skin is thick and tight from time in the sun without protection. She doesn't disinfect, she doesn't use soap. Instead she wipes things down all of the time. Instead of deodorant she sprays salt under her arms. She's taller than me, and German, and she smells like a man. When she sleeps behind me, when she used to, when I was in San Francisco with her, and if she was feeling protective, she would wrap her arms tightly around me and I would curl up like I was her baby. And she would squeeze me so tight I thought she would break a rib.

I've been at this lonely outpost ten days now. Two days ago the missiles started falling on their "targets of opportunity." There are no newspapers here. We get our news from alJazeera, which is just a series of pictures to me as I don't speak Arabic. The pictures of the war are spliced with white houses along hilltops surrounding Hebron and then Arafat and the incoming prime minister, Mahmoud Abbas.

"There's 80,000 protestors in the street yesterday in Athens," Mahfouz says. Mahfouz runs the coffee shop here. We play chess together. We're about evenly matched. I've caught him cheating twice. He's so thin it's painful. "Cairo, Islamabad, of course. You know how many protestors in your own country? A thousand in Chicago, two thousand, three thousand in New York. Nothing. Not even in San Francisco where you say you're from."

Mahfouz' daughter places another cup of mint tea near my fingers and I shear her off 800 fils from my small stack of fils and dinars without taking my eyes from the board.

"That's because Americans are apathetic," I say. "Even during war. The Republicans are pumping horse tranquilizers into our water supply. *Joe Millionaire* does the rest." I mean it as a joke. But when Mahfouz looks at me with a strange smile I think for a second it could be true.

Ten days ago they kicked me out of Iraq. I had been sleeping in a power plant on the southern edge of Baghdad. The power plant was destroyed during the first Gulf War and was expected to be destroyed again. Either they decided I was a spy or they worried that my death would only cause them more trouble when the war was over. When I get home Ashcroft may try me as a traitor, but probably not. Still, I'm not ready to go yet.

My girlfriend is a real revolutionary. She belongs to a small affinity group known as the Red Razors. For as long as we've been together she's been preaching violent revolution, and I've been ignoring her, because she teaches at Berkeley and everybody at Berkeley talks that way.

"Take your violence out on me," I'd say, when times were good, tucking my hands beneath the pillow. And she would reach for the pile of rope and pocketknife she kept on top of her dresser and say something smart like, "Maybe I will."

All of that ended when the clouds of war settled down to stay. Affinity groups are cells of three to twenty friends, ready for direct action. They exist in every city. She started going out with her affinity group every night, planning their uprising for after the war broke out. She'd come home manic and stinking of whiskey and sex, furious over something she'd heard John Ashcroft or Donald Rumsfeld say. As if they were talking to her. And if I tried to get some affection from her, if I tried to say something cute like, "Who's my Old European?" she'd ask me if I knew how many people were going to die on the first day of war. I said I didn't and she didn't either. I said it was all speculation. I said we won't know who's right and wrong until after the war and she should stop cheating on me. She said, "Fuck you and your speculation. You're a coward." So I signed up to be a Human Shield, to prove my love.

"So," Mahfouz says, slipping my bishop beneath his index finger. Our game is going to end soon. "So, so, so." He pulls a small silver flask from his cabinet and pours us each a measure. "You came out here to swallow a missile launched by your own country. When you come back the Kurds will have Holiday Inns presuming the Turks haven't killed them all."

The liquor burns in a good way. I didn't intend on drinking here. I didn't know the alcohol would be so plentiful.

When I first arrived, I came in through Syria. There were journalists waiting for passports but we were given slips immediately and driven over the border at night. The little children in the schools near the power plant were Christian and Muslim. They played soccer in the streets and were taught to chant, Down Down America. They'll all be dead soon.

"I'm no different from any other civilian that dies in a war," I say.

"When you make a choice, you are different. Don't fool yourself. I believe you're in check." I slide my remaining knight in front of the beam cast by his queen. I see perpetual check. He's staring at the board, his brow creased together. Back across the desert, fourteen hours by bus, there are still Human Shields at the Daura Power Plant, their minders squirreled away in a bomb shelter somewhere. Perpetual check is a draw. He should have won this one.

"To tell you the truth, I came out here to impress a girl."

Mahfouz smiles slightly, still perplexed by the board. If he moves his rook I go king two. If he moves his queen I go bishop three. It never ends.

"So you came out here for a girl and she is of course back home with someone else." He rubs his finger over his own thick stubble. His wife passed away six years ago. It was one of the first things he told me about himself. "Then you are crazier than I thought. You are as crazy as your own president."

"No," I say, tapping the glass rim. "I'm an atheist and I drink. I don't have his conviction and I haven't harmed anybody."

An orange flash of light and a bang sounds off in the distance. From here, it's like fireworks. But still, it shouldn't be this close to the Jordanian border.

"They weren't supposed to go from Jordan." He rests his fingers on the board's edge. Theresa will never know war, only protest, and when I get home she'll never take me back. A missile falls so close the hotel shakes. "There will be a lot of bombing tonight." Mahfouz sweeps the pieces into his satchel and tightens it with the strings. "We can play again in the morning."

THE VAMPIRES OF DRACONIAN HILL

"You show me a capitalist, and I'll show you a bloodsucker."
— Malcolm X

written by brian gage • illustrations by von do

The children who live in Draconian Ville
Are ruled by the dead on Draconian Hill
A castle of ivory perched high in the sky
Is watching their village with bloodsuckers' eye.
The children snack blithely on cupcakes and sweets —
They're plump from their heads to the balls of their feet.
Their gluttonous, carefree, and ignorant bliss
Spawns from the care of the vampire's kiss.

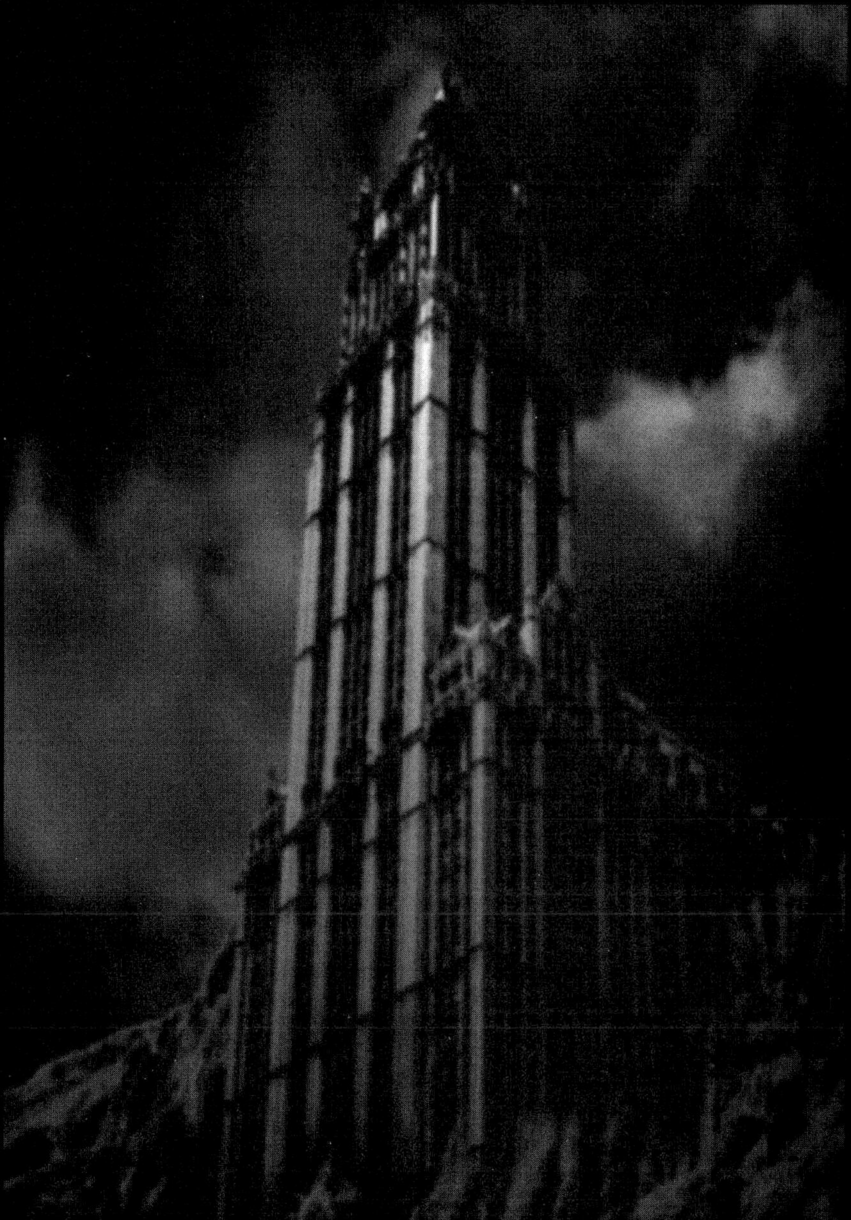

The yearlings sleep soundly in plush, velvet beds;
Not fearing the dead will soon come for their heads.
The vampires need them when day smothers dark —
They fear for the wood that is aimed at their heart.
The children tend duly to high granite walls
That keep the outsiders from storming their halls.
For outside the village and stretched 'cross the land
Are others with razor sharp stakes in their hand.
They'd storm the white castle when night turns to day
If not for the ramparts to keep them at bay.

The vampires surface, but only at night
To torment outsiders with clamorous might.
They transform to bats and fly from the spire
To search for fresh cruor with flagitious ire.
They suck dry the blood from the field-tanned napes,
And steal all their treasures and trinkets and drapes.
They swoop upon villages useless and weak,
And prey on the ill and the limp and the meek.
Murder: their cannon; Oppression: their creed.
Driven by blood thirst and vengeance and greed.
The vampires ravage each village and town —
No soul is spared till the moon has gone down.

The sun could destroy vampires roaming the night —
A sun that is hidden from toddlers' sight.
Instead they stare blankly at glowing blue globes —
A gift from the dead that is placed in their homes.
Its beauty transfixed upon all those who stare —
It lulls them with hypnotic, somnolent fare.
When they look to it, they see not the dead,
But charming old statesmen — no fangs in their head.
"Believe in the globe," vampires implore.
"Pay you no mind to our hands bathed in gore."
"Pay you no mind to the bones in our bins,
Nor deep crimson blood dripping fresh from our chins."
"We are your protectors, providers, and clan.
We bath you in goodies and rubies and flan.
Eat up, good children. Sleep tight in your sacks,
And keep strong our walls from outsiders' attacks."

The vampires live on Draconian Hill —
Feel nothing for women they callously kill.
Feel nothing for elderly sick in their beds,
Feel nothing when sucking the blood from their heads.
And yet the small children who sleep in their town
Feel nothing but glee for the vampire's crown.
The globes they stare into infect them with lies
They hear not the outlander's harrowing cries.
They see not the foreigners' ripe, mangled necks —
Think not of their lives as the vampire's hex.

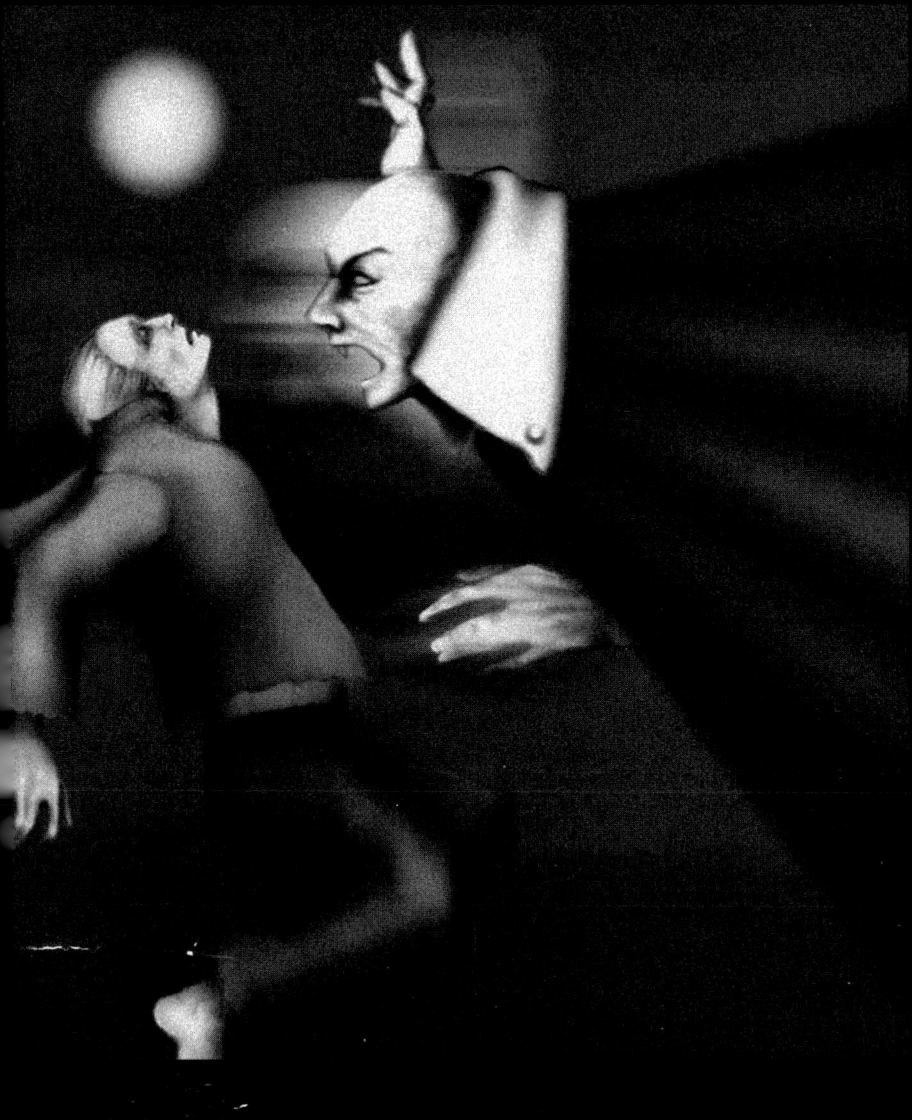

A day is soon coming when bloodstock runs dry

The dead will not find it at night when they fly.

The countryside once so abundant and flush

Will yield no jugulars plump for the gush.

The hunger inside them will grow when they sleep,

The moon when it rises will shine on the sheep —

The ignorant children so plump and benign.

The blood in their veins like sweet, sapid wine.

The dead will then wake on Draconian Hill,

And feast on the children asleep in the Ville.

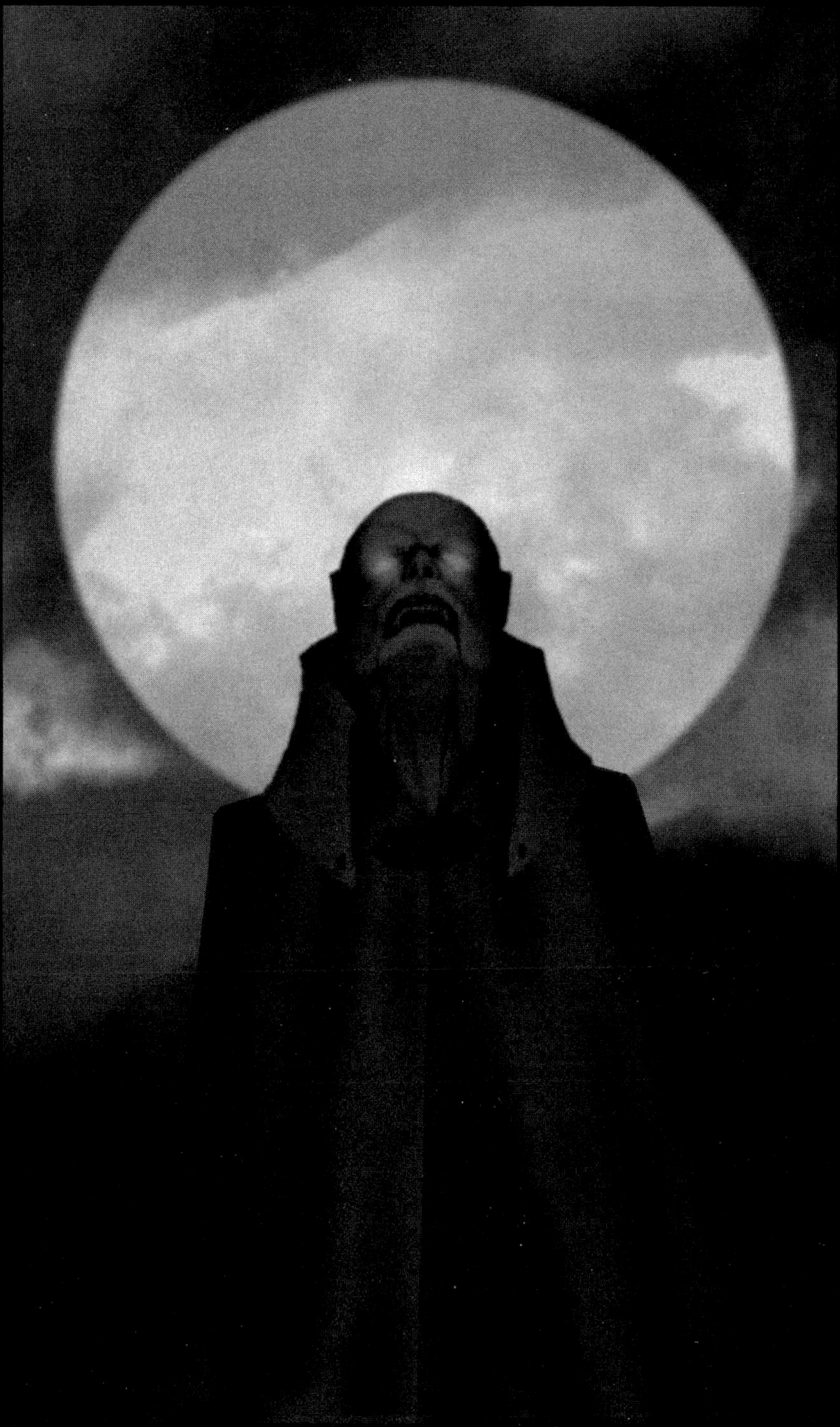

i am a CBU-87/B combined effects munition (CEM)

by david rees

It's so weird—usually when I walk down the street, I am who I usually am: A thirty-year-old man whose leanness has been compromised. By beer. Also, distracted. Disheveled. I think those are synonyms. Maybe you can say "to be distracted is to experience dishevelment on the mental stage." That's fine. If that statement is true, it becomes even more accurate vis-à-vis my little life I've got going here. And I can live with that. That's not the weird part. The weird part is when I walk down the street and suddenly I am a cluster bomb.

I don't mean I'm a cluster bomb in a metaphorical way. It's not like I walk down the street and suddenly I am "as angry as" a cluster bomb, or "as filled with the potential for ass-kickin' as" a cluster bomb. I mean: sometimes I walk down the street (or get up to change the channel; or bend to water the plants; or roll my eyes because I have to scrape oatmeal out of the pan) and I become in a TOTALLY LITERAL WAY a cluster bomb.

Here is a critical point to make, as clearly as possible: I am not a suicide bomber. I'm not saying I become "in a TOTALLY LITERAL WAY a cluster bomb" because I'm too much of a pussy to simply say, "I am a suicide bomber; my whole thing is to make a bomb of myself." No. It's not that I make myself the human analogue of a cluster bomb by strapping explosives to my chest and then detonating on a street corner, with my weaponized body parts exploding in a bloody tornado, wrecking the awnings with hemoglobin and filth.

When I am a cluster bomb there is no human form involved. I become a fuckin' CLUSTER BOMB, man. If you look at me you won't see my smiling face, my feet, my elbows, or whatever random part of my body your eyes perceive while taking me in. You will see a big, metal cylinder lying in the street looking goddamn *inert*.

In fact, when I am a cluster bomb, I barely have a consciousness. That's how metal it is.

I can prove this point about how literal my occasionally being a cluster bomb is by telling you specifically which type of cluster bomb on earth I become.

OK, so I am a CBU-87/B Combined Effects Munition (CEM) manufactured by Alliant Techsystems. You might know them as Honeywell. (As in, "Thanks for lunch, Honey. Well, I better get back to the business of making bombs!")

But enough about that fictional couple; more info about me, so you know which bomb I am. I'm seven feet, eight inches long. I weigh 950 pounds. Would you like to know my diameter? (Heh, heh! Oh my God, don't go there!) Seriously, my diameter as a CEM is 15.6 inches.

Do I have a guidance system? NOPE! Do I have an autopilot? Again, the answer is NOPE! "OK, smart guy—do you have a propulsion system?" My answer is, "Uh, let's see. The last time I checked, objects dropped from a B-52 Stratofortress didn't exactly need additional propulsion!!!" OK, I had to top it off with a little triple exclamation point action (my trademark)!

When I'm in CEM state, I only barely know what I am. If I'm able to exert a moment of thought in my cluster bomb mind, it kind of just floats down and down, descending like a falling leaf of great delicacy. I can't really tell it where to go, or what to consider while it's falling. It's not robust and beholden to the inside of my self, where for instance all these thoughts are anchored, as I type this personal essay.

For instance, my human name is David Rees. This is something I'm always aware of—intensely aware of—so long as I am not a CBU-87/B CEM. If someone screams "David Rees!!!" on the street, and I am not a cluster bomb at the time, *I will totally and without reservation turn to look at them and see what the fuss is about.* But when I'm a cluster bomb, I lose sight of that name.

How little of myself can I carry along before it's not my me there? That is the great question for people who sometimes turn into cluster bombs. Who is the "I" in "I am a cluster bomb"? That is my question.

Anyway, let's get real. Who is to drop me? Because if you are a cluster bomb, sooner or later someone is going to get it in their head to drop you from a great height and thereby to bomb the hell out of something, since that's the whole reason you exist in the first place. Who'll drop me? My research leads me to this answer:

Some big-ass plane, probably gray, enjoying a very severe elegance.

Hello, plane, are you ready to enshadow some foreign landscape beneath your wings? I am with you, underneath you. Just drop me and let me fall, fall, and more fall, descending in the air unto that earth—to give it a wallop and an immediate bright star of strength.

Actually, what the heck am I saying? I don't make one big "immediate bright star of strength" (whatever the poetic hell that means). I'm not a nuclear bomb; I'm a cluster bomb! What I make is, or *are*: multiple little stars of strength, or scores of shining, ordered constellations of strength. I have a payload of 202 bomblets and I'm assuming the average amount of stars in a constellation is seven. Two hundred two divided by seven equals "scores." (Perhaps you'd say, "the astronomy of munitions is star-studded with action!")

OK, plane, we're back from stargazing and we want to know more about you, you who births these mighty stars I am: Who are you? Or who did you used to be, until a few moments ago when you entered B-52 Stratofortress state and took leave of some base and started flying with mechanical finality?

What if you turn back into a human in the middle of our journey, plane? Will the mission end with me-as-cluster-bomb lying inside your stomach as we plummet? I wonder if I would rip through your bowels and chest cavity and continue my mission, or if we would turn back into humans simultaneously? Would I turn into a fetus inside you? Would we have an orgasm if that happened?

I have another question, which is about exploding. I know that if this keeps up long enough, there's going to be some exploding, courtesy of me. Once my proximity sensor has deemed it "exploding time," will I feel myself open up, airborne, to release bomblets, and then will I feel each individual bomblet explode? Will I blossom into 202 separate identities from one single big-ass identity, and then have 202 separate identical deaths? Or will my identity remain tethered to the emptied shell?

Actually, if I had a big-ass identity as a cluster bomb, things might be easier. I might know how to morally interpret all this shit. As it is, as the

CEM, I'm just a big enormous dumb object, whose consciousness is just barely scraping by, feebly clawing its way to continuity. Let me now claw forcefully, while I can, and ask: I probably don't have enough agency to be evil, right?

If there was a six-foot-tall robot with six arms, and each arm had six hands with six fingers each, and each finger was a spinning rotary saw blade, and the robot just rolled around on dirtbike wheels and spun its arms with frenzy whenever something got in the way of its infrared laser eyes—and so when it rolled down the street it just tore through hundreds of pedestrians—that robot, would it be evil? No, because it's just a machine. It can't feel sad or happy! If it felt happy, it would be evil. Its revelry would be an index of its evilness.

So if I turn off my emotions, does that catapult me beyond the jurisdiction of evil? God. Please God let that be true. And isn't that just what happens when I'm a cluster bomb? Yeah, I think it is. I can't be evil when I'm the cluster bomb.

But I can be evil *before* I'm the cluster bomb. Damnit! And surely I can control how perfectly I become the cluster bomb. For instance—why not just say it?—I could jump out a window as a human. And then the next time I entered CEM state, I would reveal a harmless damaged weapon extrapolated from my heroic damaged body.

I will undertake a simple experiment.

Hold on.

OK, I just cut my cheek. It's bleeding a lot. Can you guess what my plan is?

Now it's two weeks later. I have a big scar on my right cheek. I haven't yet gone into CEM state, but when I do, I will ask my friend to take a picture of the cluster bomb—and we'll examine it to see if there's some sort of scar on the cluster bomb. That would mean I can control the CEM's fitness.

Well, now it's one week later. I went into CEM state on Sunday evening. My friend said there was a slight discoloration near the tip of the CEM! He showed me the photo. Awesome! I am now officially in control of my destiny.

Now, if "scar" in human form = "slight discoloration" in CEM state, what would I have to do to myself in human form in order reduce my lethality in CEM state? Also, it would be nice if I could still be alive as a human once I've finished my mystery preemptive decommissioning! That's why I'm not going to jump out the window.

Maybe if I go into CEM state when I'm on drugs, I would be so high that I could have more consciousness in CEM state. Maybe I could deliberately shut down some mechanical elements within the bomb. Maybe I could pacify all the explosives through a blood-curdling bad trip scream into myself. All the violence I birth would be stillborn. I'd be emptied of it. Then I would just be a benign huge freakin' useless weapon with ornamental purpose and the only way I would be responsible for someone's death would be if they tripped over me and landed on their head and died of their own unhappy accident. And the probability of that happening is very low!

When I'm in CEM state, I would feel relaxed if also on drugs. Hopefully this is true and it would lead to a deeper understanding of myself.

As you can tell, I'm trying to maintain a can-do attitude and focus on my future but I keep thinking: *I will be dropped.* The dropping is my deadline. Once I'm dropped, my quest for personal understanding will end as I plummet toward the target area and release my bomblets. And most of me will hit the earth and flash apart forever, while some of me will lie in scattered wait, until moved to self-negating action by an ignorant civilian's curiosity.

What will happen when that undetonated bomblet of me is roused? Maybe some kid will handle it while she's hunting for scrap metal to sell, and the reward for her industry is: I'll simply erupt in her hand. I'll undignify her body into an incoherent swirl of opened organs. Or maybe just a local part of her—some of her fingers will fly apart like trinkets that bend uselessly. Pretend this personal essay is the girl's body. It would be like if some of the words on this page splintered into little broken spiders that no longer communicated with you.

Actually, this is easier—don't pretend this essay is the girl, pretend this book is *me*. You're holding me. Fuck it, I explode.

OK—

What happened to your hands? Are they on you? What happened to your arms? Are they on you? Are you blind and you can't finish reading my personal essay? That's what will happen to that girl, I guess.

A corrupting flash! Her wholeness is ruptured and bloodily turned to meal. Gross! Jesus, what did I do? I need to go lie down.

Now it's three weeks later. Some things happened. It turns out I didn't need all those drugs I mentioned. I achieved a deeper understanding of myself while cutting myself. But it's like the more I understood of myself, the less of myself was still there—like a shadow shortening as noon approaches. I'm pretty cut up. I used to love noon. And all the times of a peaceful day. And I used to have my energy ever-replenished in my dreams. But after this personal war, and the toll it took on me, I'm content to dreamlessly sleep as much as possible every day and only get out of bed when I really, really have to. My sheets almost seem to have decayed into a film, like a shed skin. Some evenings I can't even tell if they're touching me at all. Maybe they're floating above my body, like I just exploded and we're caught in the moment when the expulsion of air and guts is just beginning to shoot my sheets unto heaven.

Unto heaven! Where I long to be.

Holding me.

the politics of war

lamentation over the destruction of ur

by paul lafarge

Jane and I were in bed when the war started. People drove by our house, leaning out the windows of their car, calling, "It's wartime! It's wartime!" through the leafless trees. The last time they came by, the Commonstock High girls' basketball team had won a place in the northeast regionals, where they were defeated, I think.

"I guess we should go look," said Jane.

I was disappointed. After a winter of hesitation, Jane had finally agreed to try on the costume I bought for her birthday, and we were just beginning the game that went along with it. But war was war, and we had to watch it, even if watching wouldn't do any good. We trooped downstairs and settled on the leather sofa. The newscaster was pointing to a map of a country that looked like New York State. "Our forces have entered the port city of New York," he said. He explained that the city was not actually New York, but the military was referring to it as New York because the real name was too hard to remember. "Resistance has been lighter than expected," said the newscaster. Our rockets and missiles lit up the sky over a dark city. "A scene of total chaos," said the war correspondent. "People are moving in all directions."

"Of course they're moving." Jane hooked her finger in the bust of her corset. "We're shooting at them."

"Anyone with any sense is at home right now," the war correspondent said. For some reason it reminded me of when I was a child in the real New York City. One night I snuck out of my parents' apartment in the middle of the night and walked down Broadway as far as the old Woolworth's. The streets were full of people I would have been afraid to meet by day, but when I saw them at night there didn't seem to be anything dangerous about them. They were just people, who lived in the city much the same way as I did. We had an unspoken understanding that we would leave each other alone. I don't think I was happy at the time—would I have been walking around in the middle of the night if I were happy?—but in retrospect it seemed like a happy memory.

"Ladies and gentlemen, the Secretary is going to speak to you now," said the newscaster. The Secretary appeared. He was short and menacing. "Let me make one thing clear," he said. "We are going to fight this war as if it was a war."

"As if it *were* a war," I corrected.

"Ssh," said Jane.

"We are going to be warlike in our demeanor," the Secretary said. "We are going to act warfully."

"That's not a word!"

"Will you be quiet?"

"And we will not stop," the Secretary said. "Are there any questions?"

I raised my hand. "Do you speak English?"

"The Secretary isn't listening to you," Jane said.

The television thought we might want to see more rockets and bombs, so it showed us rockets and bombs. You couldn't see the city any more, only the streaks of light across the sky and the explosions.

"I wonder who's down there," I said.

"The war correspondent said everyone had gone home."

"Those are their homes."

"Not anymore," Jane observed.

I put my hand on the small of her back, below the giant bat wings. "You can be so matter-of-fact."

"Is there anything wrong with that?"

"Maybe not."

"I'm going to bed," Jane said.

"To bed, or to sleep?"

"To sleep."

"Then I'll stay down here."

"Suit yourself." Jane went upstairs. The ceiling shook a little as one of her boots came off, then the other boot. I lay on the sofa and watched the bombs fall. I must have dozed off, because suddenly it looked to me like they were bombing New York, not the modern New York, but the grubby, dark city I remembered from my childhood. It was as though our satellite-guided missiles and cluster bombs had the power to reach into my memory and to destroy things that didn't even exist anymore. I cried, or maybe I only dreamed that I was crying. When I woke up the sun shone through the blinds and the television was still on. "We're talking with an expert on rubble," said the morning newscaster. "Tell me, what are some common mistakes people make when handling rubble?" I rubbed sleep from my eyes and felt my cheek, where the sofa's seam had left a deep indentation, like a scar.

I am a teacher of English. For years I wanted to be a university professor, and in fact I did most of the training one does to become a professor, but at the last minute I felt that it would be wrong for me to teach at a university. A university professor, I thought, was like a preacher at a revival meeting; he had to be able to get up in the middle of the circle of the faithful and assert in a big voice that what he was saying was absolutely the truth. Whenever I imagined myself trying to do this, the circle of the faithful grew wider and wider around me until I was effectively alone in the middle of a field, with my small voice that would not reach the faithful, my small precise voice that did not have faith even in itself. So I left graduate school and became a teacher of various English classes: Power Vocabulary for high-schoolers preparing to take the SAT, Language Fundamentals for young kids, Copyediting for Professionals, and American Conversation for advanced foreign students, which was my favorite. My students had been living in this country a long time, in some cases all their lives, but they still didn't feel at home here; together we conducted role-playing activities that would give them the sense that they belonged—in our class, at least, if not in the nation as a whole. The pay for all the classes put together was considerably less than what a university professor makes, but Jane had a good job at the cemetery and that kept us going.

We had American Conversation the first day after the war started. As I had planned, I proposed to the class that we play cowboys and Indians, a game that has its roots deep in American history. My students would have none of it. They wanted to play soldiers, and in fact they had already divided themselves into teams. Mrs. Starodoubtseva the optometrist would lead the invading army, which consisted of her, Mrs. Dayal, and Lisa Michaels, a pretty girl who worked at the paper mill. On the other side would be Mrs. Singh, Ms. Barabanovic, and George Pouliadis the landscaper, who I suspected was only taking the class because of his as-yet-unrequited passion for Mrs. Starodoubtseva.

"We are going to pound you into submission," Mrs. Starodoubtseva said. She was a looker, I have to admit, in a tough, upholstered kind of way.

"Never," George Pouliadis snarled.

"You'll see if we do!" said Mrs. Dayal.

"See if we *don't,*" I emended.

I instructed the invading army to wait in the hall. The others, the invadees, I had take up defensive positions behind their desks. We used a classroom at the junior high school, with small desks bolted to the floor. They would be just right to stand for bunkers, or low buildings of the kind I thought the enemy probably had. "All right, ladies," I called, "invade!"

The door flew open but for a moment no one came in. We heard Mrs. Starodoubtseva cry, "The bombing is begun."

"Has begun," I corrected.

"Boom!" said Lisa Michaels. "Pow!"

Mrs. Starodoubtseva came in. "I am armored column," she informed the defenders. "You may shoot at me, but it will be vain."

"*In* vain."

"Pow!" said George Pouliadis.

"George, you are already dead. You were killed by the bombs."

"Do I look dead to you?"

"It does not matter how you look. This is simulation."

"Simulated," I said, "or *a* simulation."

Mrs. Dayal came in. "Marines!" she cried.

"Infantry," said Lisa Michaels, just behind her.

"Sniper!" said Ms. Barabanovic. "Infantry is dead."

"Are dead."

"Not all of me," said Lisa. "One sniper can't do that."

"George, lie *down.*"

"Long live the revolution!"

"Really," said Mrs. Singh, "I must surrender. This is too silly."

The game went on. As my students bombed and shot each other, it became clear that they would have to find some system to indicate who was dead and who was still living. "Why don't you take off your shoes when you're killed," I suggested. "And those of you who are killed again can take off your socks." The students agreed to this and in no time the defenders' feet were naked, as were Lisa Michaels' feet, her lovely, white feet. Only Mrs. Starodoubtseva kept her shoes on, claiming invulnerability; Mrs. Dayal hopped on one black tennis sneaker, shouting "Put them up! Put them up!" despite my repeated correction.

George Pouliadis crawled toward Mrs. Starodoubtseva. "I am your prisoner," he said.

Mrs. Singh sat at the back of the room with her arms folded on her chest. "Please do not tell me that I am going to be forced to crawl."

"Everyone crawls," said George. "That's what war is about. When I was in Vietnam, we crawled everywhere." He was almost in range of Mrs. Starodoubtseva's knees.

"The floor is cold," Lisa Michaels complained. "How long is this war going to last?"

At six o'clock the players agreed to a negotiated truce: everyone would get their shoes back, and the invaders would buy pizza for the class the following Thursday. "It is your duty as occupying power," Ms. Barabanovic said.

"*The* occupying power, Nadia," said Mrs. Starodoubtseva.

"Don't tell me how to talk," said Ms. Barabanovic.

I hurried them out of the classroom before the fighting could begin again. When they were gone I sat at my desk, the teacher's desk, and wondered if I had done my students a disservice by allowing them to play this game. But no, I thought, as long as it helps them to feel American it's all right, and didn't they seem at ease in their new roles? I thought of Mrs. Dayal hopping around, and of Lisa Michaels on the floor, her bare feet, the coral nails of her delicate little toes.

I went home and tried to take a nap. There was a sound, dink, dink, from the yard so I went out to see what it was. My neighbor Gruber was in his back yard, digging.

"Whatcha doing, Gruber?"

"Just digging." He had marked off sections of the yard with stakes and lengths of string.

"Looks like something big."

"This is just the beginning," said Gruber. "Actually, it's not even the beginning. This is the part before the beginning."

"What's it going to be?"

"You'll see."

"Fine, but can you keep it quiet? That's my bedroom up there." I pointed.

Gruber agreed to dig as quietly as he could and I went back upstairs. But he had made me nervous. Was there something I ought to be doing, now that we were at war? I went downstairs and turned on the television. The Secretary was there, as though he had been waiting for me. "Our forces are implementing a policy of contained containment," he said. A reporter raised her hand and asked how that was different from regular containment? The Secretary made no effort to conceal his irritation. "Contained containment is a kind of containment which is itself contained," he said. I was still watching television when Jane came home. She flopped down on the couch and took off the big orthopedic shoes that she has been wearing lately. "I've been running around all day," she said, rubbing her feet.

"Let me do that," I said.

Jane is not the most beautiful of wives. She is large and soft; there is too much of her, particularly of her upper arms and chin, and her eyebrows are very light, which makes her look like a baby or an extraterrestrial. What I love about her, what first drew me to her, is her straightforwardness. She may not be exactly what I want, but I know exactly what she is, or at least I think I know.

"Mm." She closed her eyes.

"Rough day?"

"Do you remember Mrs. Allsop?"

"The garden-supply lady. Did she die?"

"Crashed on Route 18."

"My god. What a time to die."

"What do you mean?"

"With the war just starting, I mean."

"People don't stop dying because there's a war."

"I know that." But I couldn't explain what I meant. "What do you want for dinner?"

"Something serious," Jane said. "I'm starving."

"Chinese?"

"Fine. As long as it's easy to explain."

Jane accuses me of trying to surprise her too much. Once I ordered Lover's Nest, a basket of fried noodles with shrimp and chicken inside, and she refused to eat it; in the first place that was a ridiculous name for a dish, and in the second place she wanted to see what she was getting up front. Dumplings are out; so is anything that you have to roll in a pancake; to her, pancakes speak of culinary cloak-and-dagger work. "Those moo shoo things *skulk*," she says. "No wonder you like them." When I met Jane, I hadn't decided yet to give up my university career. When I went into private teaching, after we were married, she may have been upset. If so she got over it quickly. She is the administrative director of the Commonstock Cemetery; the living and the dead are in her hands. She has nothing to complain about.

I ordered vegetable stir-fry and chicken with cashews.

"Do you think the war is going to be good for business?" I asked.

Jane shrugged. "Our guys go to Washington. I don't think we bury their guys."

"But insofar as it calls attention to the idea of death."

"You don't have to call attention to death," Jane said. "That's the great thing about it."

"Gruber is digging a hole," I said.

"Gruber is always doing something stupid," said Jane. "You remember the basketball court?"

"You're right."

"What a disaster."

"*Fiasco* is the word for it."

The food came and we ate in front of the television. "Our troops are outside the strategic western city of Watertown," said the newscaster. He didn't need to tell us that it wasn't really Watertown, that the city had another name. By then we had learned the language of the war.

The next morning I went to the Commonstock PathMark to buy some props for my Power Vocabulary class. Mrs. Singh was in the toy area, looking at a green plastic submachine gun. She wished me a good morning and asked if I thought spark guns would be helpful.

"Helpful for what?"

"To defend ourselves."

I tried to remember if anyone on television had told us to buy spark guns. But the television had told us to buy so many things, I couldn't keep track.

"These are just toys," I told Mrs. Singh.

"Of course they are toys. You do not want me to purchase a real weapon?"

"Hold on. Are these for our class?"

"Mrs. Dayal has a Super Soaker with fifty-yard range." She put the submachine gun back and selected a pair of orange water pistols. "I am not saying she will use it, but we must be prepared."

"Please don't bring those to class," I said. "And please tell Mrs. Dayal not to bring hers, either."

Mrs. Singh sniffed. "It is not only her. All of them are armed."

All of them? "You won't need the guns in class. I'm going to give you a different exercise."

"Fine," said Mrs. Singh. She carried the guns to the checkout counter. I followed with my plastic barnyard set.

"You won't need the guns," I said again.

"But it is good to have, don't you think? See you Thursday!" She waved the pistols at me and went out to her car. I paid for my barnyard set and tried not to imagine what was going to happen when our class met again. As it happened, though, I couldn't put the game out of my mind for that long. My vocabulary students had heard about it and they wanted to play war also. I told them that war wouldn't be of any use to them on the SAT verbal test, and I began to set up the animals with which I wanted to illustrate some new words. The class would not be dissuaded. "War! War! War!" they shouted, and strained against their bolted-down desks. I was alarmed by their enthusiasm. Most of them were in the class because their parents made them go; I had never seen them want anything on their own account before. Finally I agreed that they could play war, but with one proviso: instead of shouting *bang* or *boom* they would attack with words from our weekly word list; and the defenders would reply with definitions, if they knew the definitions. They agreed to my terms and half the class left the room, then came back in, shouting, "Peripatetic! Enervate! Indemnity!" and other words from our list. At first the defenders shouted definitions, but because the definitions were so much longer than the words, the attackers had a murderous advantage. The defense fell back on shorter phrases: "Never!" and "Die, pig!" Soon the attackers were shouting *boom* and *pow.*

"Words!" I said. "Use words!"

It was too late. The defenders counterattacked; the invaders were driven into the hall; someone threw chalk at someone else and they were all running, running down the halls of the junior high school, dispersing into the courtyard, shouting words of one syllable on which they would never be tested. I didn't know who had won their game but I had surely lost. I drove home and took off my shoes and lay on the leather sofa. The television was on—one of us must have forgotten to turn it off; or else it had been authorized to switch itself on by some act of Congress passed in secret. "Our troops are at the gates of Syracuse," said the war correspondent. I had cousins in Syracuse, my grandmother's sister and her children and grandchildren. We went to visit them one summer before my father moved to Texas. I remember playing in the yard with my cousins, who had an almost complete collection of *Star Wars* figures. My parents were fighting on the porch. With a little effort, I discovered that I could transform the sounds they made into something completely unintelligible, although I couldn't pretend that they weren't fighting. I kept playing; my tiny plastic person chased other tiny plastic people across the grass. My cousins looked back at my parents, who had raised their voices. "They do this all the time," I said, although in fact they had never done it before. We kept playing. At the end of the summer my father went to Texas, to work on the big particle accelerator they were building in the middle of an even larger field. I heard later that the project was canceled, that they never got further than digging a ditch for it, but my father didn't come back. I turned off the television and closed my eyes. I could hear Gruber's shovel dink, dinking quietly in his yard. It seemed to me that my life was going in the wrong direction. After my father left, New York was an unhappy place, so I went to college and graduate school in New Jersey. Then graduate school was an unhappy place, so I moved with Jane to Commonstock and taught my private classes. Each time I made a decision, it seemed that there was a good alternative and a bad alternative, and I had always chosen the good alternative. How was it that everything had turned out so badly? "We are waiting breathlessly," said the war correspondent; then I turned the television off.

Jane found me sprawled on the sofa. She gave me a dark look—usually *she* was the one who lay down at the end of the day—and sat in the green armchair that we called the Uneasy Chair. "God, I'm tired," she said. "Did you pick up anything for dinner?"

"No," I said. "Did you?"

Jane bit her lip as she does when she is thinking. It's a good tactic: it gives you the impression that she is keeping some terrible utterance in check. "I was at work *all day,*" she said. "I work *all day.*"

"So?"

"You're the one who has time. Didn't you go to the PathMark?"

"They were buying guns at the PathMark," I said.

"Who was?"

"All of them, I think."

Jane turned on the television.

"Don't do that," I said.

"Don't tell me what to do." She turned the television off.

"Anyway," I said, "you eat too much. Look at you, even your arms are getting big."

Jane's eyebrowless forehead wrinkled and her gray eyes grew large. A moment later I heard her car grumble away. Her orthopedic shoes remained where they were, in front of the Uneasy Chair.

Jane came back half an hour later with a roasted chicken. She didn't bother to put it on a plate; she just sat at the kitchen table and tore parts of the bird up and put them in her mouth. I watched her eat. "Did you get me anything?"

"Nn." The black plastic container the bird had come in held little more than a skeleton.

I drove north on Route 18 to the White Kill Outlet Center, where they have a Waldenbooks that's open until nine o'clock. I walked up and down the aisles, looking for a book that would allow me to believe that some things were not lost, if only for a couple of hours. But their fiction department seemed to have only books about pets and single women in New York; the rest of the store was divided among guides for pet owners and single women and books about your garden and other people's gardens. On the remainder table I found a photographic guide to the wonders of Ancient

Mesopotamia. Of course, none of the wonders existed anymore; the pictures were of stony ravines, rolling hills and fields where the ancient cities and gardens had been. The accompanying text described the things the Sumerians and Akkadians and Babylonians had built: the ziggurats that rose up to heaven; the mechanical warriors whose bronze swords shone in the sun; the water clocks that told the phase of the moon and did not have to be adjusted for a hundred years; the silver mechanical birds that sang in the gardens at night. "The techniques by which these wonders were manufactured have since been lost," the book said. "Lost, lost, lost." The catalog went on and on. "Lost, lost, lost!" I put it back and in the end I bought a desk calendar with pictures of the Earth as it would look from other places in the solar system.

On the way home I stopped at an all-night diner and ordered a cheese and bacon omelet. George Pouliadis was sitting at the counter, drinking coffee and watching a basketball game on television.

"Welcome to my hideout," George said.

"Thanks."

"How are things at home?"

"What do you mean?"

"You're hiding, right?"

"*Hiding* is a strong word for it," I said.

"You should know," said George.

As a rule I don't talk to my students about personal matters, but George looked like he knew everything already, as though he had the power to read my heart. I told him about my fight with Jane, if you could call it a fight. It was impossible for me to explain what had happened without telling him the whole story, so, as my omelet cooled, I told him how I had left graduate school, and how nothing since then had been right. Maybe I should have listened to my advisor, Dr. Gloss, a dwarf with fantastic gray eyebrows, who told me to be careful of false scents, but how was I supposed to know which scents were false, and which ones were true?

"Whoa," George interrupted. "When was the last time you had sex?"

"We were about to, when the war started."

"There's your problem."

"You think so?" The omelet had hardened into an undifferentiated, patently inedible mass. I prodded it with my fork.

"Sex," George said, as though unveiling one of the great secrets of life, "sex leads to children."

I asked George if it was true that he was in love with Mrs. Starodoubtseva.

He held the mug of coffee to his lips. "*Love* is a strong word," he said.

I thanked him for the advice, paid for my uneaten dinner, and drove home. Jane was in bed. I touched her shoulder and asked if she wanted to make love? We could be ourselves tonight, just ourselves. But she was sound asleep; she lay like a lifeless person with her face to the clock that was set to go off in the morning and bring us to our feet again.

In the days that followed Jane and I tiptoed around each other like two invalids, upstairs, downstairs, as Syracuse fell and our armies advanced on Rome and Troy. I taught my pre-K class and my copyediting class for professionals. No one wanted to play war, nor would I have allowed them to if they did. I had learned my lesson. Although in fact there were disturbing signs that my lesson, if it was a lesson, wasn't over yet. One afternoon I stopped at the garden-supply store to pay my respects to Mrs. Allsop's children. I hadn't exactly known Mrs. Allsop, apart from my annual visit to buy seeds with which to ornament the patch of dirt behind our house, which, despite all my efforts, remained a patch of dirt. Still I thought it would be seemly to say something to the children. These were difficult times, and we ought to stay close together, I thought. We ought to make gestures, to let each other know that we were loved, that we were still loved. The garden-supply store was closed. As I walked back to my car, I passed Mrs. Starodoubtseva, who stood in the doorway of her eyeglasses concern, waving what I hoped was a toy pistol. The front of her white smock was splashed with red paint. "You bitch!" she shouted. "I'll slaughter you!" She pronounced *slaughter* to rhyme with *laughter.*

"Slaughter," I said. "What's going on?"

"What do you think? It's war."

Mrs. Starodoubtseva retreated into her shop and turned the sign on the door to read CLOSED. A number of stores in Commonstock were closed that afternoon. Where had their owners gone? I saw three boys from my SAT class kneeling outside the Blockbuster, their feet bare. I didn't stop to ask what they were doing.

When I came home, Jane was on the sofa, covering her eyes with her forearm. "Everyone has gone mad," she said.

Apparently a dozen people had gone to the cemetery and lay in the office parking lot. They claimed to be dead and wouldn't move. Traffic couldn't get through, and two funerals had been postponed.

"Did they have shoes on?" I asked.

"Do you know about this?"

"My students were talking about it," I lied.

"It's insulting to the whole idea of death," Jane said. "Not to mention the people who have real grieving to do."

"Maybe they have real grieving to do."

Jane shuddered. I touched her arm. "I'm sorry."

"I feel like I don't understand anything now."

"Me neither."

"Yes, but you're used to that."

I didn't know how to answer her, so I went upstairs and lay on our bed. I could hear Gruber working in his backyard. I didn't see what he was doing. I lay on my back and looked at the sunlight on the ceiling, and the shadows of the branches with their little buds. Maybe this was the way to live, I thought: not moving, just guessing what was happening outside by the sound and the light it made. Of course there was the problem of food, but maybe if you lay still for long enough you could learn to live without it.

Thursday came, and with it came American Conversation. I arrived at the junior high school at four o'clock and waited for my students. No one came. At a quarter to six, a stranger in a red jumpsuit knocked on the door, and asked if I had ordered a pizza? I paid for it and left the box on the teacher's desk. Maybe my students would show up later, or maybe someone else would find it, if there was anyone left in the school.

By a clump of bushes behind the parking lot, Mrs. Singh and Ms. Barabanovic were sitting on Lisa Michaels' back. "Take off your shoes," Mrs. Singh said, swatting Lisa with a leafy branch. "You are dead! Nadia, take them off!" Ms. Barabanovic took off Lisa's running shoes and the two women stood up.

"We killed her," said Mrs. Singh. She held one of her orange water pistols.

Lisa got up and brushed mulch from the front of her suit. Her face was dirty and wet with tears. "What do I do now?" She looked at me.

"What does it matter what dead people do," said Mrs. Singh. "Do whatever you like."

"Can I h-have my shoes back?"

"Absolutely not."

"Please," said Lisa.

Mrs. Singh tucked the shoes under her arm. "Come, Nadia. We have won a battle only."

Ms. Barabanovic looked over her shoulder at Lisa. "Crawl," she hissed.

Lisa looked at her grubby suit, her soiled blouse. She got down on her hands and knees and crawled away from us. I didn't know what to say. Had she made a mistake? Should I correct her? The removal of the shoes had been my idea, after all. "Lisa," I said, "do you want some pizza?" She didn't answer. I have to admit I watched until she was all the way out of sight.

The war had gone too far. Maybe if I made an announcement, I thought, if I took responsibility for the whole thing and begged people to put their shoes back on and open up their shops, maybe it would end. At the very least, the people who were now slaughtering each other would be encouraged to unite against a common enemy, me, a man with only two feet, who could be killed only twice, like all the other players in the game. They would kill me and it would be over. As I walked across town—it seemed appropriate for me to walk, even though the junior high school was almost a mile from the center of Commonstock—it occurred to me that every decision I had made in my life, good or bad, had led me to this moment, and that no matter what I did at any point before this, I would not have been able to escape being here. I squared my shoulders and strode past the shuttered windows of the optometrist's, past the hardware store and the gift shop that sold dolls and clothing for animals. Everything was closed. The historical society, the public library, even the First Republic Bank. It occurred to me that even if I could have chosen to be another person, I would still have chosen this, the one thing I could do that no one else could. I stepped into the little square, bounded by the Presbyterian church and the town hall and the bank. Twenty or thirty people were kneeling in front of the town hall. A surprising number of policemen ringed the crowd, some of them wearing helmets. One of the policemen spoke to the kneeling people through a megaphone. "This is an order to disperse," he said. "Please disperse immediately."

"We can't," someone called from the crowd. "We're dead!"

The policeman was silent.

"Listen," I called. "This is absurd!" A few people turned to look at me. "Your game is officially over! Those of you who study with me can come to your classes and we'll figure out who won in a rational manner." The ones who had been looking turned away. "Listen to me!" I shouted. But it was just as I had feared: the more I spoke, the farther away the crowd seemed. Eventually a policeman approached me. "Sir, we'll handle this."

"I just wanted to tell them..."

"Please, sir. This is our job."

My throat had closed up and I was afraid of what would come out if I tried to speak. I left the square and walked up Elm Street. Behind me, people were shouting. There was a sharp *crack!* and a puff of greenish smoke rose into the sky. I didn't know what had happened, and I would never find out. Even the *Commonstock Gazette* had nothing to say about the incident; it was as though the square and everyone in it had been pushed out of sight, replaced, if I remember correctly, by a rose show in the neighboring town of Eastwood, and a two-page feature on the new global coolness.

I went home and turned on the television. The news showed us pictures of a town in New York State, because the other place, the one we were really invading, had become too horrible to watch. People stood in front of their houses, waving American flags. A blond boy did a cartwheel for the camera. His bare feet flashed in the sunlight. "Dennis!" his father called. "Come here, Dennis!" "As you can see," the war correspondent said, "everything is under control." There was a report of a disturbance in New York City; the television showed us soldiers in camouflage guarding a mound of shoes. The Secretary spoke to the press, to tell them not to worry. "We are confiscating the enemy's footgear," he said. "In this way we will deprive them of vertical capabilities." I couldn't stand the way he spoke. Why did he have to say *footgear* when he meant *shoes*? And *vertical capabilities* when he meant *walking*? People were kneeling in midtown Manhattan. "Right now we have them on their knees," the Secretary said, "but we won't stop until they're on their hands and knees." I wanted Jane to come home so I could tell her what the

Secretary had said. Maybe we could find some common ground in our dislike for the Secretary. Evening came, then night. I went into the yard. Gruber was working by electric light. He had finished digging; now he was making bricks out of mud and straw.

"Hey, Gruber," I called. I leaned on the chain-link fence that separated our properties. "You haven't seen my wife?"

"Haven't seen her."

"You're making bricks."

"That's right."

There was a pile of bricks by the fence. I picked one up and examined it. GRUBER was stamped on its face. "Hey, this brick has your name on it."

"They all do."

"Really?"

"Uh-huh. Took a lot of doing."

"What's that for?"

Gruber seemed reluctant to talk about it. "I want people to know who I am," he said.

"That's smart," I said. "Listen, if my wife comes home, can you tell her I'm looking for her?"

"Can do."

"Gruber, what are you making?"

"You'll see," Gruber said.

And I would, my god, I would.

I went to look for Jane. Commonstock was deserted; the square was empty, although a few shoes lay by the fountain. I looked for her in the PathMark and the CVS, in the White Kill mall and in the diner where George Pouliadis hid. I drove to the cemetery to see if she was still at work. The office was dark but her car was in the lot. I parked mine next to it and got out. "Jane!" I called. I knocked on the office door. "Jane!" I walked a little way into the cemetery itself. "Jane!" It was a lovely night; the trees in the cemetery were blossoming and the air smelled of flowers and pollen. My shoes scraped on the gravel path. It felt good to be walking, so I walked. I wondered if my mistake had been staying so close to New York—Commonstock was only an hour and a half from the city by car. My life might have been better if I went to Montana, or to Oregon, some place where nature still had some say in how the world worked. "Jane!" But there was no point in thinking about it now. I had chosen what I had chosen; I could choose again later if I had to. "Jane!"

"Over here!" she called.

She was lying on a strip of grass between two graves, looking at the sky.

"It's a nice night, isn't it?" I said.

"Peaceful," Jane agreed.

I lay down beside her.

"I couldn't go home," Jane said. "I'm sorry."

"That's all right. I couldn't go home either."

"What are we going to do?"

"George Pouliadis thinks we should have children."

"George Pouliadis is a scoundrel," Jane said. "Do you remember how he painted the leaves, to trick those tourists into thinking it was fall?"

"You're right," I said.

"I could just stay here," Jane said.

"Me, too."

"What are we going to do?"

"I don't know." I thought of all the people I knew, and all the things they were doing, of my students chasing each other through the streets with toy guns, and Gruber making bricks, and Dr. Gloss giving lectures, and my father working on a vast machine that would never be built, and my mother in an apartment by herself, talking to women on the telephone, and Mrs. Allsop who had worked in the garden-supply business all her life and was now buried not far from where we lay, and it seemed to me that we were free, even if we had not always been free, even if there would come a time when we were not free again. "I don't think we have to do anything." I put my arm around Jane's shoulders.

"Mm," she said.

We did nothing. The night continued. Far away, in the trees at the edge of the cemetery, I heard the piping of one of the silver mechanical birds that we had not seen yet, but which we would see more and more of as that last year passed.

freedom oil

by anthony swofford

I.

Oil is the Lord of the east and the Lord of the west, and all that lies between and above and below. If as a young man you live in Texas and you have sense, you know this about oil.

As a young boy and then as a young man returned alive from the Korean War, Daddy Freedom had been known as Daryl "Dinky" Freeler. Private Freeler had committed horrible acts in Korea. He'd advanced in rank with speed and violence and honor and at the end of the war he held sergeant stripes until the night, in a beer house in Pusan, he beat a captain close to death first with his fists and then a full bottle of *soju*. Daddy Freedom recalls beating the captain because of a series of remarks the captain made in favor of communism, but witnesses claimed the two men fought over the attention of a Korean prostitute named Sheila.

After the war and a short stay in the Camp Pendleton brig Dinky returned home to Texas. He spent a few months sitting around his parents' house drinking beer and then found a job.

He started in the mail room at XS Oil, sorting the incoming and ensuring the outgoing had sufficient postage affixed. It was summer, and his two temporary co-workers were girls from the high school. Dinky liked the look of the girls, their bird legs, their breasts like small fists, and the girls liked the look of Dinky because they had never known a man who'd come home from war.

Dinky had been a virgin when he went off to fight the commies. But the

U.S. took seriously the issue of troop morale, and once in country he'd had ample opportunity to purchase sex, and he also participated in a number of gang-rapes of village girls, and the gang-rapes were always free.

Dinky began dating the sixteen-year-old from the mail room, Mary Sapp. Mary Sapp's father owned XS Oil, and while the oil world had been plagued by post–World War II price control, Sapp was still a famous and rich man. Mr. Sapp enjoyed hearing Dinky's war stories. He'd become especially moved when Dinky explained the reason he'd left the service only a private, his beating of the communist Marine. Stan Sapp hated injustice, and he knew injustice when he heard it. He was convinced that his mail room boy had been served rotten by the Marines. He liked the boy and gradually promoted him, even though no one could claim that Dinky had mastered his duties in the basement, as mail continually flowed back to the company postage due, and numerous important parcels en route to Mr. Sapp's office never arrived.

Mary and Dinky's courtship progressed with ease. They had long conversations about the importance of profitability, whether the venture be in love or oil or beef. Mary admitted that during the Korean War she'd written coy letters to a few local boys who never made it home. These were boys Dinky had known, and he was happy that they'd died and he'd lived—back from the war to claim a pretty local girl, heir to a fortune in oil after the dead boys had accomplished the work and waste of writing letters during combat.

During the lunch hour Dinky and Mary had sex in her father's office. They especially enjoyed using his leather-topped desk for their noontime flesh flings. Dinky made love to her tenderly, and she was impressed with the ease with which he brought her to come. She had never come before Dinky. A few boys had shoved themselves inside her, under the basketball bleachers or in a distant barn, beer in their bellies and the whiskey thick on their shirt collars, but she could never go back to a boy. What did the fake polish of the basketball court offer when compared with the Frozen Chosin, the great fighting withdrawal? What could a goosed-up Chevy and a six-pack offer a girl that harsh memories of tanks and artillery couldn't literally blow away? Mary would never know that Dinky had learned to fuck so well by low-balling prostitutes and gang-raping village girls in Korea. He'd turned his intimate knowledge of savage wartime acts into an inversely tender love-making strategy.

But Dinky didn't just make love to Mary. He made love to the earth, to those wells thirty thousand and farther feet deep in the earth. When inside of Mary, he thought of his dick as an oil drill, and he couldn't stop counting his future wealth. This is partly why he lasted so long, and the reason that he'd yell, I'm bursting! when he came.

Mr. Sapp promised to spend the initial cost of one oil well on the wedding, and he did. Society people from Fort Worth and Dallas, ranchers and oil men and their long lists of prolific kin, filled the church. Also, Dinky's family, his parents and siblings and a few aged aunts and uncles come in from Temple and Mineral Wells.

The minister was Presbyterian, and he spoke of the great sacrifices women and men must make for one another in wedlock, that the institution is not for the weak or slovenly, that day to day the life of the married is work and work and more of the same. He instructed Mary and Dinky to love each other and each other only and to not let even their minds wander through the devil's pastures of sin.

In the long receiving line, Dinky shook hands with men he did not know, but whose names he knew by heart: Brown Oil Reserves; Andersen Oil East/West; Smith Bros. Petrol; Mathers & Sons Fuel & Futures.

In the reception ballroom, except for the bow ties and shoes of the men, the colors were white and pink. Ten wedding cakes five layers each rested on a table. A chamber group played Berg and Stravinsky and Bach. Dinky and Mary danced the first dance as Mr. and Mrs. Daryl Dinky Freeler. Mr. Sapp cut in and the floor filled with old couples and children grasping the pants legs of fathers, near-blind grandmothers forcing teenage grandsons to clumsily lead.

Dinky danced with his mother. She whispered, "I don't know what you have gotten yourself into. Oh, dear son, please don't falter."

"Mama," Dinky said, "Mama, I won't falter you. I'll do us all proud. I'll work hard and honest. I'll always be your Dinky."

Dinky's father cut in and rubbed his son's back. In an extreme breech of etiquette, the two men danced together. His father was a sad man, preoccupied with shoes and the fixing of them. The guests pretended not to notice the groom's father weeping on the groom's shoulder as the two men danced.

Dinky and Mary never retired to the honeymoon suite that first night, but they napped occasionally in chairs while not being bothered by the good wishes of strangers. Some of the old oil and beef men whispered good luck in Mary's ear and shoved large bills into the soft folds of her breasty dress.

The party carried on. On the afternoon of the second day, the chamber players were replaced by a local country music band. The men of the party changed into jeans and boots and their wives wore casual dresses. The children were sent home to be cared for by servants while their parents continued the nuptial festival. The celebration ended at different times for different folks, as some had work to tend to Monday morning but others were able to stretch their time off into midweek.

The Freeler/Sapp wedding is remembered as one of the finest Fort Worth has ever seen. The final bill totaled just below three hundred thousand dollars. The party consumed 292 hams, 249 whole turkeys, 243 whole chickens, 147 sides of beef, 740 pounds of potatoes, 500 pounds of miscellaneous vegetables, 230 loaves of bread, 240 kegs of beer, 195 cases of champagne, and 300 cases of whiskey. Over the six days of celebration, seventeen attendees were arrested for public nudity and drunkenness and the total cost of their bail, charged to XS Oil, was seventeen thousand dollars.

When Old Man Sapp died and Dinky assumed control of the company, holdings both foreign and domestic, Dinky changed his last name to Freedom, and he insisted that everyone call him Daddy. XS Oil became Freedom Oil.

Linda Freedom was ten years old when her daddy gave her her first oil well. "Some girls get ponies," he said. "But you are not some girls. You are Daddy Freedom's girl. All ponies do is sleep and eat and shit and tromp around. Ponies do nothing but take. Oil wells give. What are you gonna name your well?"

"Daddy," she said. "I wanna name it Pony."

II.

The Persian Gulf conflict is in its early days, and Daddy Freedom hasn't left his office or turned off the television since August second. Daddy Freedom is absorbed by the Standoff in the Sand, as the cable news people are calling the Iraqi occupation of Kuwait. If Saddam Hussein fires up his tanks and rides into Saudi Arabia and if in doing so he accomplishes the unimaginable and gains control of two-thirds of the world's oil supply, Daddy will make out OK, he thinks, as the price for crude will climb, and the available free-market Million Barrels Per Day will diminish. If the United States and Saudi Arabia drive Hussein out of Kuwait and proceed to establish a permanent American military presence in the Gulf, Daddy will be comfortable giving the go-ahead on an offshore drilling site near Oman that he's been waiting to drink from for two decades. All ways out, Daddy is a winner. Goddamn oil, he thinks, all you got to do is ride the bitch.

"War is splendid," Daddy says to his Scotch, as the satellite link to Baghdad goes down.

Watching the troops preparing to leave and thinking of his own heroic military days, the sad departures and glorious returns, the misery between, the doubts and insecurities—Why am I fighting, What am I fighting for, Where am I, Where are the whores and whiskey—Daddy Freedom has an idea. He calls his daughter Linda, head of Freedom Oil Public Relations.

"Sissy," Daddy says, "what if we put together our own USO? I mean a damn drum-beating, whiskey-swilling, good time-having troupe of crazy patriots, flying from airport to airport where the servicemen are waiting to be deployed, dropping into the bars and showing support. Not this goddamn pansy Bob Hope and Lawrence Welk bullshit."

"What kind of support and who?"

"Support for America, support for freedom! Just show the boys a good time. You're on a stopover, on your way to a company party. Between flights you hit an airport bar for drinks with some of your people and you run into the young fellas about to go off and fight. You support America's defense. You buy their drinks. Maybe you offer other favors. You give them some money. You give them some sex."

"And who is the you?"

"The you is however many people you think you need to accomplish the mission. Open it to all current Freedom employees. It'll be a traveling party. Covert PR for the war and the oil business. We'll write the goddamn thing off! Take the jet! Unlimited budget! The project starts ASAP and doesn't stop until the war is over."

"Are you pimping me, Daddy?"

"Hell no, girl. I'm giving you the mandate and the resources to pimp others."

"I'll start work immediately."

"I want the goddamn plane in the air in three days."

III.

The two Marines find the USO and cash their boot camp checks. They graduated from the Marine Corps Recruit Depot, San Diego earlier this morning. For the fourteen weeks of their lives they've just given to the U.S. Marine Corps, they each received ten days of leave and fifteen hundred dollars, and subsequent orders to the Fleet Marine Force. Once in the FMF, also known as the Fighting Mother Fuckers, they'll join an infantry battalion and head to Saudi Arabia for war. They consider the next ten days the rest of their lives. Their plane boards in an hour. The Marine named Washington is going home on leave with the Marine named Plug.

Jarheads and squids are in every corner of the airport, arriving, departing, drowning in family hugs. Crepe paper yellow ribbons are stapled to walls and columns and plastic Marine Corps, Navy, and U.S. flags hang from every free space that isn't yellow—the regalia ruffles and waves with the rush of arriving and departing passengers. Plug feels like he's been dropped head-first into a parade, the swirl of colors, the cheap pomp of easy pride. The two Marines duck into a pub called Amelia's Island and buy each other a whiskey.

Because they are now done with boot camp, they laugh about it. They laugh about the Filipino guy, Cortes, who laughed when someone farted during rifle drill. Cortes was thrashed with sit-ups for so long that his body cramped into a ball, he looked just like a pill bug as the DIs carried him to sick call. They laugh about the time Washington got beat over the head with the flashlight he was using in the middle of the night to read a letter from his mother. They laugh about Plug's request for a weekend off. Now that they have war to look forward to, it's easy, and even comforting, to laugh about petty boot camp violence.

An arrival at a nearby gate prompts the small pub to fill with businesspeople from somewhere south, en route to San Francisco for a company-funded debauch. The businesspeople are mostly businesswomen. Their Southern drawls are impeded by early, airborne drink, and it sounds as if their mouths are full of cotton. They cheer one another, cheer the company's performance on the stock exchange, cheer the new benefits package, toast each other's spouses and children. Two men in dark suits stand at either side of the entrance to the pub, as though they are sentries.

Plug and Washington retreat to a corner of the pub, but a woman from the group spots the Marines and drops into their position like a warrior into a friendly bunker after a fierce fighting withdrawal. She's wearing a black business suit and European sunglasses, and her hair is platinum blonde. She looks, to Plug, like she might be famous.

"Let me buy you Marines a drink. What are you having?"

Washington answers whiskey and she moves promptly to the bar, elbowing away younger, softer co-workers, less thirsty co-workers. A man in a pinstripe suit feeds the jukebox and the sound of Seventies funk fills the pub.

Linda Freedom deposits three tumblers full with double shots of whiskey onto the table and her small butt onto Plug's lap. She smells like a long morning of tequila and orange juice. She grabs Plug's chin with one hand and Washington's with the other.

"Aren't you beautiful. Double the defense budget!"

The crowd roars approval from the four-deep bar.

Linda says, "Are you boys going over to fight, are you gonna go get Saddam?"

Washington says, "We're just out of boot camp, ma'am. We got some leave and then we're going."

"I hope you go kick his little brown ass. I hope you kick his little brown ass all over that desert."

She nearly falls out of Plug's lap as she turns to ask someone what time their flight departs. For balance she reaches between his legs, into his crotch, and kicks her feet up, and one of her shoes launches into the crowd. Washington goes after her pump. Plug notices that her chest is flat. Her yellow bra is peeled back from the flatness, exposing a tan, freckled bone desert. Washington slides her shoe on and she thanks him.

She says to Plug, "You look uncomfortable. Stiff. Are you afraid of a woman? Haven't seen one for a few months, have you?"

He says, "I'm not afraid of you, ma'am. I don't understand your world. Business trips and free drinks. This is not my world."

Washington gets up to talk with a blonde woman at the bar who has called him over by licking her lips and mouthing, I want you.

Linda says, "Is fucking contrary to your mission? Is taking me into the bathroom and bending me over the shitter contrary to your mission? Lighten up, jarhead. It's only a motherfucking war. I know how to talk like you. Fuck fuck fuck. Clusterfuck. Cocksucker. Piss-ant. Pussy pussy pussy. My daddy was a jarhead. My sweet papa. You think I don't know how to talk your jarhead games?"

"I think you can talk any game you want."

"You're right I can. You see these people, this bar full of people? I own them. I own them because my daddy owns them. I can do whatever I want. I'm buying their drinks and my daddy has them by the balls, he's paying their mortgages and car payments and financing their long-term savings plans. He's sending their ignorant children to third-tier colleges and paying for spring break in Veracruz."

Her hand is still in Plug's crotch and she grabs tighter.

He says, "Your daddy doesn't own me. I don't know who you are, lady."

"I'm almost old enough to be your mother. I'm thirty-five and I want to fuck Marines who are about to go get their heads blown off. That's who I am."

Two women, one in a pink business suit, one in dark blue, dance with each other on the bar. The bartender yells that they are scarring his lacquer finish, and with quick snaps of their thick ankles they launch their shoes into the terminal. Both of the ladies are overweight and not at all attractive, yet their co-workers cheer them on. Plug checks the bar clock, as the pitch of the party is so high it runs contrary to a time check of 1300. But it is 1300! And two grown women are acting like college girls grinding on each other halfway into a night of whiskey specials. Plug saw this act many times before dropping out of college. The career women are no more or less exciting than awkward college sophomores. The woman in the pink suit falls into the crowd and two men catch her and hold her afloat, continuing her heavy sway. She looks like a disabled tanker in a rough sea. The other woman does not stop her grind, knocking over drinks and nearly tripping into the barback as she loves herself to Curtis Mayfield.

The woman Washington had been kissing pushes him toward a mirrored corner of the pub and attempts to camouflage her intentions by hiding behind a large plastic plant. She kneels in front of him.

Linda says to Plug, "This is what you fight for, jarhead. This is what my daddy fought for at Pusan in 1951. This is freedom. Freedom to do as you wish. These people work hard. This is their reward, total stupidity in a city not their own. The old bartender, I'll give him a good tip, and he'll fuck his wife tonight for the first time in months, thinking about two women dry-humping on his bar. He'll buy his grandkids toys with the tip money, new toys, not the usual from Goodwill. The woman on the bar, she's my secretary. Her husband is a drunk and he beats her and calls her a fat whore. But today she's not a whore, today she's sexy and someone nice wants her, the new mail boy from Bullock. The woman giving your friend head, I've known her since college. She loves giving head to strangers. She's sucked more than five thousand dicks. What's wrong with that? The man with the yellow tie, he's gay. His wife doesn't know, but I do. I'll be paying him to have good gay sex. I'll drag him kicking and screaming out of the queer biker bar on Folsom Street in San Francisco. Me, I've got a husband at home. We love each other and we have great sex every night in our big expensive house. You, young man, at your peak, you can't even do me as good as he does. But I'll let you try. This is what you fight for. This is freedom, jarhead. We are here to reward you."

The bar crowd sings along to the music and continues at their deep drinks. Citizens peer in as they walk to and from their gates, unable to recognize what they are seeing, but wanting in, knowing they won't be allowed.

Linda leads Plug to the men's bathroom, across the corridor from the pub, and hurries to the far stall, the handicapped stall. Men turn from mirrors and stare; they stop brushing their teeth or straightening their ties. Linda locks the door and peels off her skirt and hangs it on the coat hook. Her tights, bunched at her ankles, look like thick rubber bands.

"I have no tits, so I'll keep my blouse on. No use in you trying to convince me that I do. My husband quit years ago. Why try to convince someone of something that doesn't exist?"

She takes Plug out and they kiss and fondle and she sucks him off before bending over and guiding him inside of her from behind. He has never felt anything better. Twenty minutes prior he'd been bored by the drab plastic patriotism, the stapled gestures of easy faith hanging from the dirty airport walls, and here now Linda Freedom is giving him flesh, the purest faith one person can have in another. To drown out their noise she flushes the toilet and holds down the handle. Her other hand, fingers splayed, is palm-flat against the wall. Plug thinks of tossing knives between her fingers, from twenty feet behind. He sees himself from those twenty feet back, the knife thrower, witness to a man inside of a woman inside of a bathroom stall. The showman's apprentice, this morning he'd been first out of the bent mirror funny house of boot camp and this is his prize, lavatory lay, flesh patriotics. He grabs her platinum hair with his hands, and in his mind he doesn't know if he's inside of her because he wants to be or because he must be. She reaches back with both hands and grabs his hips, her back arched deeply, driving him into her, fingernails tearing at the flesh of his buttocks, breaking skin, he feels the blood. Her head knocks hard against the wall. They come together. He pulls out of her and watches her get dressed. She takes him in her mouth one more time, then smiles and says, "Clean up." She yanks his trousers to his waist and says, "Goddamn, boy, let's go. We could get arrested for this." He follows her. The same men who stood at the washbasins when they entered are still, their eyes fixed on the sex stall.

As Linda Freedom and Plug enter the pub the sentries hand them each a fresh drink, and at the bar Washington kisses the blonde woman. Plug feels as though he's lived through an ambush.

Linda stands on a bar stool and announces to her charges that she's soliciting collections for the two young Marines preparing to warmonger in foreign lands. She wants to ensure that they enjoy their leave, that they eat and drink well before "taking rifle to shoulder in the name of my father, the Stars and Stripes, and the rich oil fields of the Arabian Gulf." The crowd yelps and cries, shoving their drinks high in the air, liquor and beer sloshing from glasses—a short woman with long black tresses catches most of her neighbor's screwdriver on her head, thick pulp and a cherry spoiling her pretty hair, and the gay man wearing the yellow tie, in midair twice clicks the heels of his brown, tasseled loafers. Plug and Washington protest the alms, but the mad rush and call, the insane clobber of the donating herd drowns out their voices. The Freedom Oil people generously open their wallets and purses, stuffing four pint glasses full with bills, the dancing woman in blue still teetering on the bar, bent over now, writing a check against her plump left knee.

She says loudly, to no one in particular, "Who should I write this out to? Fuck it all, I'll just leave it blank."

A San Francisco flight is called and the deranged herd grabs their carry-on bags, swilling the last suck from the cold corners of their drinks. The woman bounds from Washington's lap toward the door, blowing him kisses the entire short way. Linda Freedom settles her tab with the weary-looking bartender, his face brightened as though with Brasso by the total she pens in.

Linda hands Plug a pen and her bar tab and tells him to write down his name, rank, and serial number.

He looks at her and begins to speak but she hushes him with a finger to her thin pink lips. She hands him her card and says, "Call me when you get back," and runs toward her gate.

Her red, white, and blue striped card is in the shape of the state of Texas, and reads:

LINDA FREEDOM
FREEDOM OIL
TEXAS AND THE ARABIAN GULF
WE MEET YOUR FUEL AND LUBRICATION NEEDS
1-800-FREEDOM

Broken glass covers the floor of the pub, and a few tables are turned on their sides, one chair broken to splinters. Washington removes bills from the pint glasses and peels the wet check from the bar. The bus boys scurry from mess to mess, cleaning the place for the next rush. Two airport security guards and the Marine USO Liaison run into the men's bathroom. The final boarding call for Plug and Washington's flight is announced over the PA, and they double-time to make their gate.

Safe in their seats, ascending for the short flight, Washington pulls out the cash. All of the bills are hundreds, forty-one of them. Washington says the only other time he's held that much money in his hands is after doing something illegal, and he isn't entirely sure that they weren't just breaking some kind of law.

He says, "What do you think that was about? It was like we sat down in someone else's dream, and the thing rolled over us."

"I don't know what it was. Jarhead heaven? They're from an oil company. It's some kind of scam."

"I asked her, 'Why are you doing this' and she wouldn't answer, she just smiled. She kept smiling and sucking my dick. What about you?"

"I didn't ask any questions. I don't think I want to know."

"What are we gonna do with this money?"

"Spend it. Fast."

The sex-and-booze party rings in Plug's ears. Is Linda Freedom his Mephistopheles, or a modern Betsy Ross (thimble, thread, how long did she sew)?

He pulls out her card and studies it, looking for a sign. Freedom. Oil. Patriotism. *Poilon*. Poison.

The poison is what we seek, its soft drip and easy drop into the mainline. Alcohol, promiscuity, drugs, prostitution, racism, sexism, xenophobia, obliteration, profits, contradiction, subornation. Poison, it must be had, Plug thinks. For I am probably a better man without it, but I'd rather be much worse. I need the poison for my living. I am out of breath and I am burning tons of fuel. I am ready for this war.

the smell of despair

by nick taylor

My father kept two llamas when I was a boy. In those days, the suburbs of Lima melted into the rural Andean highlands, so it was not uncommon for a Peruvian family to keep a couple of llamas or alpacas around as pets.

Tell me, how much do you really know about your family dog? About his hopes and dreams and so forth? More important, what do you know about your dog's political inclinations?

I asked myself these questions the morning of March 20, when I heard about the incident in Upper Huallaga Valley. The night before, a herd of llamas had seized control of a farm near the town of Tres Luces. They'd taken the owners of the farm and all of its employees hostage and were making demands of the Peruvian government.

I work as a correspondent for a newspaper in Lima. At the risk of immodesty, I should properly say that I am considered one of the preeminent political reporters in Peru. I have won many awards, especially for my work on United States intervention in Latin American politics. I tell you this not to make an impression, but rather to explain why the llamas chose to contact me.

But I'm getting ahead of myself. When I switched on the television the morning of March 20, I had no idea that my involvement with the llamas would go beyond a few paragraphs of reporting in the evening edition. I fixed my coffee and called the paper to arrange credentials for the press conference that afternoon. The leader of the llama group was going to address the nation.

Truth be told, I was less than excited by the whole thing at first. I felt sure, just by intuition, that the llamas were probably just another arm of the *Sendero Luminoso*—the Shining Path. This is the militant Maoist group—

you've probably heard of them—whose stated goal is to demolish the Peruvian national government and replace it with a grassroots communist regime. "Peru for the Peruvians," and so forth. When I learned that the hostages had been taken in the Upper Huallaga—the *Sendero*'s seat of power—I was even more certain. The Shining Path is brutal, I grant you that, but they are not at all unpredictable.

The press conference was held in the Tres Luces social hall, a converted barn at the end of a long dirt road. The hall still smelled of earth, and of wet llama wool. A traditional Peruvian peasant tapestry—a wide mat of woven multicolored cotton—hung behind the podium. In retrospect, I feel certain that every detail of this presentation was contrived by the llama leadership. They are quite sophisticated animals, as you'll see, and I know they would have been just as comfortable in a sleek, modern television studio as in this barn.

At precisely the time that the conference was scheduled to start—llamas are unerringly prompt—an enormous bull took the stage, front hoofs propped up on the base of the podium.

"We have fifteen hostages," he said, his split lip quivering as he spoke. He stared intently into the camera. He was a majestic animal, well over two meters high at the ears. His eyes gleamed like two glassy brown billiards.

The national media had turned out in full force. At least a dozen camera crews jostled for position beneath the podium.

A young man in the front asked how long the llamas intended to keep the hostages.

"As long as it takes," the llama said. He reared his head back, swiveling his long muscular neck into an S-curve. His eyelids drooped and he glared at the reporter.

The reported adjusted his glasses. "I see," he said. "Well, let me ask you this. Are you and your ah…" The reporter chuckled and beamed knowingly around the room, like a stand-up comedian milking the punch line. "What I mean is, are you and the herd scared at all? I'm sure you realize that the Peruvian government will do whatever it takes to suppress your rebellion."

The llama brayed defiantly and cocked his jaw to spit. The press corps sat still. This would be the last time a llama's head-tilt would be treated with such nonchalance. The llama brayed again, and then promptly knocked the reporter's glasses off his face with a stream of watery cud. The humiliated reporter groped for his glasses on the dirt floor. The llama stood erect behind the podium, patient and expressionless. Green spittle flecked his lips.

"Next question," he barked.

Someone rushed in with towels.

When I returned to Lima that evening, I remembered something my father told me the first time our llama spit in my face. I was ten. I cried for hours, humiliated and determined to beat the llama into submission the first chance I got. I suppose I would have, too, if my father hadn't calmed me down.

"Alfredo," he said, "most of the time a llama doesn't care that you can't understand him."

He sat on the end of my bed, stroking his bare chin, waxing pastoral.

"But when he spits—whoa *mijo*! When he spits, you better listen, because he's got something to say!"

My father was neither a farmer nor an animal psychologist—he was a dentist, in fact—but for some reason I trusted his advice. I spared our llama the club that day, and until he died six years later I made every effort to pay attention when I saw him rearing back for a cud shot.

The next morning, I got the call. It was a low, wavering voice I did not recognize.

"Alfredo Echeverria?"

"Speaking," I said. "Who is this?"

I heard labored breathing.

"I don't have a Spanish name," the voice said.

I heard more breathing, and then a flapping noise like a horse blowing air through its lips.

"What is this about?" I demanded. "Tell me immediately, or I will hang up the phone right now." After thirty years of asking difficult questions, I am quite comfortable being firm when necessary.

"Please," the voice said. "I have some information that I believe—" He paused. I heard a rustle, and then more shallow breathing. "I believe what I have to say will interest you a great deal."

"Who is this?" I repeated.

"I must see you," the caller said. "I will tell you what I know in person. Do you have a pencil?"

He gave me an address, the intersection of two rural routes across the mountains from Lima, several hours away by car.

"I will see you there at exactly twenty minutes before sunset tomorrow," he said. "Don't be late."

The following day I took my car out of the garage and drove east from Lima. According to my map, the intersection was just a few kilometers from Tres Luces, the farm where the hostages were being held. For this reason, I chose a roundabout route over the mountains, approaching the area from the south to avoid checkpoints and whatever other obstacles the *policía* might have created to keep curious citizens away from the scene of the revolt.

As it turned out, the only obstacles I encountered were the Andes themselves. My little Volkswagen chugged up one incline after another, cooling its engine with fresh mountain air on the down hills. I saw peasant women in brightly colored tunics, working the tiny potato fields that are tucked like swallows' nests into the nooks and crannies between peaks. The soil in these mountains is rich, but there's not much of it; no cubic centimeter goes uncultivated.

I arrived at the rendezvous just as the sun touched the highest peak in the west. The splintered signpost and an ancient rock wall along the side of the road were the only signs of human life. A long green field—easily a hundred hectares—stretched out before me. The mountains rose beyond that. Tiny dots in the distance suggested a flock of sheep. Or llamas—they were so far away I could not tell for sure.

I returned to my car and opened a book, *The Llama: Our Native Camel*, by Pedro Ruíz de Cuzco. I had used my privileges at the library of the National University in Lima to snatch up this suddenly valuable reference. Already four junior reporters at the paper had called to ask when I might be finished with it. In my trade, the perks of seniority are few, but I use them as often as I can.

I sat down in the passenger's seat of the Volkswagen. "Llamas are territorial animals," Ruiz de Cuzco wrote. "This is because of the austerity of the Andes and the scarcity of good land there." I considered my observation of the potato workers. This could just as easily be a text about Peruvian peasants, I thought.

I heard a rustle behind me and then that same flapping noise I'd heard on the phone. I turned and saw that a llama had suddenly appeared at the wall. The animal's jaws mashed mechanically, while its two brown eyes stared at my car. I returned to my book.

"Echeverria?"

I turned back quickly. The llama's eyes were focused on me now. The chewing had stopped.

"Thank you for coming," the llama said. He spoke in even, measured Spanish. "I cannot stay long, so let us begin."

Speechless, I rose and approached the wall.

"I chose to contact you because of your work on American intervention." He mentioned the name of my newspaper. "I have read your columns, and I believe you should hear what I have to say."

The llama craned his thick neck around to make sure we were alone. I saw frozen drops of mist glistening on his wool.

"At a press conference tonight," he said, "the *junta* is going to demand a meeting with the American diplomatic delegation in Lima. If the ambassador won't negotiate—or if he can't—they're going to appeal directly to Washington."

The llama stared at me intently. His ears flopped forward, lips quivering.

"Who are you?" I asked.

The llama blew air through his lips, then began to chew. We held silent eye contact for a few seconds.

"So this *junta*," I said, moving on with my questions. "How do you know what they are going to do?"

"We all know." He lowered his voice. "This has been years in the making." He curled his lips into the same incredulous snarl I'd seen at the press conference. "You didn't know about this?"

"No—"

"Interesting," he said. "I thought for sure that you—well, no matter. I'm telling you now, then." He paused a beat, then continued, "So you didn't know about—" He rattled off the names of half a dozen legendary Incan rulers. "You honestly didn't know about that? About us and them?"

I shook my head.

"Well," he said, "I guess the revolution works in mysterious ways. Consider yourself informed."

"So you're with the *Sendero*?" I said.

The llama brayed again, then laughed. "Are you kidding?"

I shook my head.

"This is terrifying," he said flatly. "To think that one of the leading political voices in Peru would be so ignorant as to associate us with those fools! It blows the mind."

I heard a gurgle in the llama's throat, and he resumed chewing.

I stammered, "But why me? Isn't there some risk in telling me all this?"

"Tremendous risk," he said. "I could be trampled to death if they knew."

"So why take the risk?"

"You know why," the llama said. He batted his long eyelashes. "I smelled your reaction when I mentioned the appeal to Washington."

I had been alarmed, of course. This was my area of expertise after all, the subject of many years' research and countless column inches of original reporting. No one knows better than I what happens when a terrorist group makes an appeal to Washington. But had I given any outward signs?

"I smelled your reaction."

On one hand I felt violated, but on the other strangely glad that he knew how I felt. Sometimes the most difficult part of reporting is finding witnesses who will trust you to relay their version of the story. Witnesses are often suspicious of your motives. With the llama I had nothing to hide. I knew that I had that trust.

"You say you've read my work?" I said.

"I have," the llama replied. "We all have. Some of us give it more credence than others."

"I see."

Behind the llama's head, the sun dropped below the ridgeline.

The light on the field dimmed noticeably.

"I have to go," the llama said. He turned and galloped to rejoin the herd.

As the last wedge of sun slipped behind the horizon, the entire congregation—fifty head of llama or so—turned in unison and faced the sunset.

Later that night, at home in Lima, I read in Ruiz de Cuzco that the llama faces the sun by instinct twice a day—once at dawn and again at sunset. This observation led the Incas to associate the llama with the sun god.

I let the book fall on my chest. I had witnessed a mass prayer.

It would be suicide to call Washington.

Predictably, the Peruvian government refused the llamas' demands. Among the more attainable of these was the release of political prisoners captured during an uprising several years ago in the Upper Huallaga. It made sense for the government to refuse—they must have realized that if they freed these prisoners, then radical groups all over the country would grab hostages and demand the same for their captured leaders. This is the logic behind the United States' stock response to this type of thing: *The United States does not negotiate with terrorists.*

My editorial about the llamas was published, coincidentally, in the same edition of the paper that reported the dispatch of a fresh diplomatic team from Washington to Lima. The American administration had been hesitant at first to respond to the llamas' demand for negotiations, and they had only agreed when the Peruvian government agreed to act as an intermediary. Under this arrangement, the American delegation would meet with the government of Peru, period. The Peruvians would handle the llamas.

My column outlined the reasons why I felt that Peru should resolve the llama standoff as quickly as possible—or else face disastrous consequences from outside its borders. I did not mention the United States by name, but it would have been obvious to any reader with a hare's knowledge of geopolitics where I saw the threat. Upstaged as it was by the front-page news, I was certain that no one read my piece that morning, but as you'll see, one can never be sure of that.

The last line of my editorial read as follows: "Our prediction is that no party will make any significant gains from this standoff—not the llamas, nor the Peruvian government, nor any foreign powers that may choose to become involved. But among these, the llamas will be the big losers. God willing it would be otherwise, but unfortunately this is not a matter of faith."

I went back and forth on whether to include this line. Part of me felt that it was too overbearing—false omniscience. But then again, what is an editorial but false omniscience? I left the line in the final draft.

That night, I received another call from the llama.

"The *junta* is very upset," he began. "They read your editorial. They feel that you've misrepresented our cause."

"I'm sorry," I said. "I thought it was what you wanted me to do."

"Humans are so indelicate," he said. "So blunt. You can hardly greet each other successfully, let alone persuade one another in print."

He flapped his lips. I heard chewing.

Suddenly, I remembered a passage from Ruíz de Cuzco that explained how that flapping noise—the blowing of air through the lips—is actually a llama greeting, the subtleties of which apparently still elude human science.

Pride gripped my throat. I decided to show the llama how indelicate this human could be. I took a deep breath and exhaled heavily, flapping my lips as best I could. Unsatisfied with the results, I repeated the gesture twice more. I nearly hyperventilated.

The llama brayed so loudly in response that the tiny telephone earpiece crackled like a CB radio.

"I'm sorry," I whispered. "I did what I felt I had to do."

"We'll see," the llama said. "I won't call again. This line will be monitored."

"When will I hear from you?" I asked.

"Meet me at the same place tomorrow," he said. "Same time."

I hung up the phone, embarrassed by my attempt to speak llama. It is not something I would normally do, but his accusation—that we cannot even greet one another—affected me deeply. As an editorial writer, I'm comfortable with my failure to persuade in print, but I thought I had "hello" down pat.

Early the next morning I stepped onto the landing outside my apartment to get the paper. Bending down, my eye came level with the banister, where I saw a llama's wooly head, roughly severed, impaled on the end post. The blood at the base of the railing was brown and covered in a thin dull crust—evidence of several hours elapsed. The llama's eyes were open, bulging, but the gloss was gone. The split lips hung thick like chicken breasts, stiff and motionless.

I immediately suspected the leadership of the llama rebels, that they had found my contact—plugged the leak.

But was this my llama? I chastised myself for not remembering any distinguishing traits—scars or other imperfections—that might help me identify him. I heard the llama's voice in my head: *So we all look the same to you, Echeverria? Even you*, the voice said. *Even you!*

Driving out into the country the second time was a completely different experience. Since the arrival of the American diplomats, the entire country had gone into lockdown. I was stopped at a roadblock an hour out of Lima by two uniformed policemen.

"Out for a drive, sir?" the taller one asked when I got to the head of the line.

"I am," I said. "Beautiful day."

The policeman stuck his head inside the car. His eyes caught the pile of books on the passenger seat.

"Interested in llamas?" he said, noticing the titles on the spines.

"I'm a reporter," I said. I mentioned the name of my newspaper in Lima.

"Please pull to the side." He gestured toward his partner, who was patting down a truck driver.

I'd been in situations like this before—in Colombia in '88, Bolivia in '73. These country *policía* could be trouble if they got the feeling you were trying to manipulate them. The best strategy is to play along and say as little as possible.

I pulled over and stepped out of the Volkswagen.

"Please remain in your vehicle, sir," the partner called out. I saw his face soften a little when he noticed that he was yelling at an old man. Say what you will about press credentials and letters of transit—in my experience, nothing greases the wheel like a head of white hair.

The two policemen conferred and then approached my car. The taller one asked me to step out. He patted me down nervously, more embarrassed than scared. *Strip-searched* mi abuelo *today,* he'd tell his wife over dinner. She'd roll her eyes, heaping steamed quinoa onto his plate. *We found some books,* he'd say. *You can't be too careful these days.*

* *

The policemen let me pass. The taller one copied down the author and title of each volume in the front seat, carefully checking and rechecking the scrawled lettering in his notebook. I showed my press credentials, but as I said, I think my age was all the identification they needed to see.

My llama was waiting at the stone wall when I arrived. I breathed a sigh of relief.

"You're late," he said.

"I apologize. The *policía* stopped me, and—"

The llama brayed and scraped at the ground with his hoof.

"Forget it," he said. "I'm sure you know that the talks have broken down."

I nodded. I'd heard reports in the car on my way out of Lima. That morning, I'd watched the arrival of the American delegation on CNN. Two American military officers stepped down from the government 747 onto the tarmac. They paused at the foot of the steps, waving to the cameras. The harsh Andean sun lit the colors on their chests. The generals were followed, almost as an afterthought, by a pair of diplomats in navy blue suits. A Peruvian military detachment escorted the Americans to an armored Chevy Suburban.

"The generals and the diplomats sat at opposite ends of the table," the llama said. "They joked with the Peruvians, small talk mostly. They probably said more to the waiters than to our delegation."

His eyes were wet, enormous dark pupils fully dilated. I saw that his lashes were encrusted with spit. Apparently things had taken a nasty turn in the llama camp.

"After the dishes were cleared away," he continued, "one of the American generals stood up. He announced that they were sorry we'd been unable to reach an agreement. Our leader rose from the table and asked how he could say this when we hadn't even started talking. The general smiled at his colleagues, then winked at his Peruvian handler. 'I will relay your concern to the Secretary of State,' he said."

The llama bucked and scraped the earth as he told the story.

"We hadn't even started talking, and already they were pulling out! Our leader lost control of himself and spit at the general. As you can imagine, that sealed it. The *policía* escorted the Americans back to their plane, and they're probably halfway to Washington by now."

This all seemed eerily familiar to me. I had heard almost exactly this same account from dozens of Latin American diplomats over the years.

"We don't know what will happen next," he said. "The herd is terrified."

I nodded my head. The llama's nostrils curled around his breath, and we sat silent. Fifty years ago, I sometimes shared these moments with my family's pets. Then, it was a furrowed brow that asked if little Lupe would ever stop crying. Or: *The breeze on my back feels good. Do you feel it?*

Now I knew there was no need to speak or even to raise a brow. How would you describe the smell of despair?

I'd been right in my editorial when I said that the llamas would fail. However, that wasn't their objection. What upset them was the way I discredited what they considered an honest appeal for justice to a world power that prides itself on freedom. Llamas are literalists—men (bulls) of their word—and for all their extrasensory prowess, they will never comprehend the deceit that underlies human interactions. As I said in the editorial, God willing it would be different. But foreign relations is never a matter of faith.

When the sun touched the horizon, the llama galloped off to join his comrades in the field. The herd assumed the position, saluting the sunset just as their ancestors had done for thousands of years before them. I might have been Francisco Pizarro, standing there with the mountains behind me and the pure Andean plain glistening as far as I could see.

I was sitting in the Volkswagen, having trouble with the ignition, when I heard the first American warplanes roar overhead.

the designated marksman

by otis haschemeyer

In my fingers I had this one cigarette and a matchbook of three matches wrapped in cellophane. I'd found them in an MRE when I was in the desert, which is just one of those crazy things that happen, an old MRE mixed up with the new ones, or maybe a joke by a Storekeeper somewhere. I figured this was the perfect time to smoke it, in the canteen, now that our job was over. We were drinking beer and a good quantity of Canadian Club. A huge guy from another outfit came over. There's a lot of guys with a chip on their shoulder, and a lot of guys with something inside them that they are trying to get out, but they don't know how. This guy walked up and pushed my shoulder. It doesn't matter with me, but with the SEALs sitting around me that is a bad career decision.

Tee stood up. "Touch him again, and I promise you, I'll stuff you and all your buddies into a knot hole."

The guy said something like, why, who's the old man?

"It doesn't matter to you who he is," Tee said. Some of the other guys were there. Belmont and Hector and L'Heureux. I'm not exactly sure. I was getting pretty obliterated. But they didn't get up. They would have gladly watched Tee dismantle the guy and all his buddies, and probably figured that Tee deserved a little fun since he'd been saddled with me for the last ten days. Wisely, the guy did not accept Tee's invitation. He did not touch me again, and he backed away.

The next day, the team met in a trailer and had our debriefing. I was highly hungover. The SEALs seemed fine. A high-ranking officer was there. He wore a trident. He said, "Everyone enjoy your outing?"

We responded together, "It's a fine Navy Day, and we're proud to be here." In the Navy that's something you sometimes say sarcastically, but today we meant it.

For the most part I stayed out of the debriefing. I thought it might be possible I'd be called down. I wasn't. I heard them saying something. I can't remember what—something, something, and my call sign—sandman. In general, when I heard that word, it meant someone was .8 to 1.6 seconds away from dying. I also heard just enough to realize how little I knew.

You see, during my time in country, behind the lines and moving along with the SEAL team, I knew nothing—nothing. I was totally in the dark.

And if you spend time in the dark, like I have, you learn something very important, that the brain is a very active muscle and a hungry one. Deprived, it will make the most out of what it gets. So it was with me.

Tactically, I didn't need Cyclops NVDs—night vision device. I had my thermal detector and light enhancement on my scope. That's all I needed because that was all I was going to be used for. Before we left, the CO said I was like an expensive piece of equipment, and they would look after me as if that was what I was. I don't fault them anything. They got me out of there alive.

And I didn't need information either. I didn't have the training those guys had. I didn't know how to respond if we were captured. For the safety of the team and the mission and the larger world—because we were responsible for that too—I knew nothing. I was just a tool, and I had only one purpose.

Still, a man is not a tool. So if I say that maybe I was a little crazy, and that I thought we were somewhere when we weren't, or that I had a special purpose when really I didn't, I hope you will understand. Walk in the desert in the dark, day after day as I did. Follow shadows in the dark.

After the debriefing, I meet with a shrink, and I would not tell him what I knew, the small piece of knowledge that my hungry brain *had* gleaned, because that shrink had only one purpose too—he wanted to take it away from me. He was a sharp little man and we sat in straight-backed metal chairs. He slouched and leaned back in a way that he must have learned in shrink school.

"So tell me about your experiences," he said.

I looked out the window and calculated the distance to the next trailer, and then I looked off farther and calculated the distance of the next trailer and I did that until I reached the hills, where I saw something just about half a centimeter high, which would be the size of a man at 500 meters.

In country I'd only paid attention to longer distances, leaving the work of appreciating the immediate distances to the SEALs, and this was the case when we were leaving Mosul, where we actually were and not Baghdad at all as I'd thought. We'd been in town for the bombing the night before, and at predawn, with the bombing over, we were on the move.

I was the first one to see the machine gun barrel emerge from a side street even though I was near the flank. The man carrying it was followed along by a group of children and what looked to be several women. The women wore headscarves, were round and formless. I turned to Tee and pointed and then I was high-tailing to good cover even before Tee could grab my shoulder. As I darted out of the sight line I saw the man taking position at the corner. That position pinned the SEALs at point into doorways some two hundred yards from the man, but the man hadn't seen them. The children didn't seem to be there for any purpose other than that they were interested in guns, like children are, but they served another purpose just then—they stopped the SEALs from moving in and wasting everyone.

Tee was listening to the headset. "Can you take a shot?" he asked me. I held my rifle out of view and looked around the corner. I could only see the children.

"Not from here," I said.

"Then from where, Christ sake. I'll get you there."

I looked around. Across the street was a low flat building no higher than ten feet or so. That might be good enough.

I pointed and we went.

"We should go around," I said, meaning we could go around the block and cross the street farther down. We were already about four or five hundred yards away. Another hundred and the man would never make us out.

"We are not separating from the team," Tee said. "If we have to fight our way out of here, we have to be together."

We got down on our bellies and crawled across the street. I matched Tee's speed, which was slow.

On the other side of the street, behind the building, Tee gave me a leg up. I crawled over the side of the building and onto the roof. I looked back over and Tee handed up the rifle. "This is your signal." Tee held two fingers together then he spread them. "Open up," he said. "Got it?" I gave an OK sign.

I set the bipod down on the other side of the roof facing down the street. The women and children were still around the man. He was now down even lower and finding his position behind the weapon. I wasn't high enough to get an unobstructed shot. I looked over my shoulder. I could only see Tee's hand above the edge of the roof. His fingers were spread. "Open up," was the order. But I didn't have a shot. Moving to tell Tee that might mean losing an opportunity. I looked down the scope again. The man settled himself down, cross-legged behind the machine gun. A woman next to him was there to feed the ammunition belt into the machine gun. I placed the crosshairs on the man's cap and calculated my elevation. I was below my zero and had a drop. My scope was fixed and didn't adjust by way of clicks. From elevation, and at that distance, just under 500 meters, my arc would flatten and I had to put the crosshairs even lower. I couldn't bear to look at the sight picture that way, though I knew the truth of the bullet's trajectory was not what I saw. Still I saw the crosshairs fixed into the backs of these children.

This might be something the SEALs wouldn't understand, but the rationalist shooter in me would argue, if I had the time, that confidence was the greatest gift of the marksman, and that analysis of this shot would preclude shooting. I didn't feel confident looking into the backs of these children, their dirty necks, their black hair strung thick with dirt like my own, no bigger than my own children, thin arms swinging like sticks from soiled T-shirts. Nothing, nothing, could be worse than a parent surviving his child. I remember when Buzz slipped in the tub—and it had been my fault—and my fear and the grief even though he had only broken his orbit. If there was a benefit to having the children there for me, it was this: I hated the machine gunner for bringing children into a field of fire and figured the world would be a better place without him. In fact, I relished the idea of killing him just for this reason.

I looked over my shoulder. Tee's hand jerked urgently.

I looked back through the scope, and the man did something that endeared him to me. He had a very square head, and he waved a hand at the children, first kindly, and when they didn't respond, with more anger and his mouth grew wide and his brow narrowed. He wasn't furious, but he wanted to get his point across. Sometimes it is necessary to put a little fear into a child to get her to move, to realize the gravity of a situation. I yelled at Patsy that day Buzz fell because I needed her to look after the baby. I had to run with Buzz to the hospital. Patsy started to cry. I yanked her by the arm and said, "Do it now." So the machine-gunner crouched down and swatted the shoulder of the boy in my crosshairs, a heavy thump that moved the boy's shoulder. I thought that was all right. And the children moved down the street from where they'd come. Now the machine gun was manned by him and the woman to feed ammunition—maybe you'd call her a girl. I guess that would depend on who you were. I couldn't really tell, she was so wrapped up.

She blocked my shot too, but then the man jerked his head. He'd heard something down the street. The SEALs who were pinned might even have planned it that way. When he heard whatever it was, he stood up to get a better look. I had no time to hesitate. That's my shot. I squeezed the trigger.

When I shoot nothing is left to chance. I calculate all aspects of a shot, meteorological conditions, windage, and elevation. I know fine points of target acquisition, psychology, and body language. I know the nuances of internal, external, and terminal ballistics, though with the .50 caliber bullet I was working with, nuance might not be the right word. The .50 caliber, designed for hard target interdiction, destroys people.

With the shrink, I said, "I'm not sure what to tell you, doc. We went in and did our job."

I had a furlough in London for a week on my way back to the States. Everything was arranged ahead of time. I had nothing to do but show up. I wore civilian clothes as a security measure—a blue suit that I'd bought when I worked for Pinky—and I took a troop transport C-141 to Ankara and transferred onto a commercial airliner to Germany and then on to London. By the time I arrived, I was too drunk to do much more than push the papers I carried at the taxi driver. I lay back, my shirt pulling from my trousers, but I didn't care. Sometime during the ride I became aware that the driver was dark-skinned.

"We're really whipping your fucking ass over there," I said. "You know that?" The driver seemed not to hear. He looked straight ahead and moved into a rotary. If he was any man at all, he'd throw me out of the car and hammer me into the sidewalk. Kick my teeth in. I resented him for not being more of a man, and involuntarily I swung my fist around and hit the back seat. The driver glanced in the rearview mirror then. I reached for a cigarette, found one in my front pocket. On the dashboard there was a clear sign that said *No Smoking*, but I ignored it. I slapped around for a few moments looking for matches, checking my front pocket and slapping my pants pockets again and again. Finally I just seemed to lose steam. I laid my head down.

When we arrived at the hotel the bellman put my duffle on a brass cart and the driver came around and opened my door and pulled me out. I felt myself passed to the bellman, a large thick man in a red overcoat. The bellman pinched my arm, just above the elbow. That straightened me up, and we walked together through two large brass doors.

"This way, sir," the bellman said,

"I work for a living," I said. I seemed to slide along the polished marble floor and through the singsong modulations of English chatter. To my right was a large red velvet settee and around it small marble tables on spindly iron legs. A few couples sat and drank tea or had highball glasses in their hands. One young woman was dressed in a navy blue cape with two large black buttons. Her hair was pinned back and a long curl of brown hair hung over one shoulder. She walked rather swiftly toward a blond child who was wandering into a dark oaken restaurant. Where was I? I felt somehow that they were putting on a show for me, that this couldn't possibly be serious.

"The buffet is excellent, sir. Service begins at seven." The bellman released my elbow and left me facing the concierge, who had been tending to a pair of overweight Americans, a man and woman with identical flattop haircuts and pastel polo shirts. The man had a small towel around his neck and was flushed. The concierge wore a nametag and had a funny name, Mr. Turnbull. He turned away from the Americans and faced me, his upper lip folded over the lower. I handed over my papers. Mr. Turnbull looked over the papers, and I felt a tap on my shoulder. For a nanosecond, I thought I'd been taken. I looked over at the American man who had touched me.

The man said something. I watched his mouth move, and the large face swell, the teeth extend and the lips widen. I was moving far away, and the man's face was still there, a full view, at least a half-meter in all directions, a perfect circle. I don't know how he knew I was military except that's a bearing you have and you can tell.

"Yes, sir," I said. "Thank you, sir."

"It's not like we see it on TV, is it son?" he asked.

"I don't know, sir," I said.

And then the two of them, the man and the woman, stood side by side, he in teal and she in peach. They drew themselves up to their full heights, he at about 5'8", and she at 5'6", stiffened, and brought sharp hands to their foreheads. Then the woman said something about marching her husband off. They smiled and waved so long. I turned back and stared at Mr. Turnbull.

"Mr. Stacey, sir?"

An incredible weight developed like a load inside my forehead and pushed against my eyes. I was doing everything I could do to hold it back. "Mr. Stacey?" Mr. Turnbull asked again.

The weight was enormous. I felt my face pinched up tight. "Sandman," I whispered.

"Pardon me, sir?" Mr. Turnbull said.

I was going to reach out and grab hold of Mr. Turnbull's larynx in just about two seconds and shake him like a chicken. The fingers of my right hand were already crooked for the purpose. "Just give me the fucking key," I said.

That night, I ordered room service. I forced myself to eat the prime rib—always eat, was our motto in the field. Later I threw up and lay with my head resting against the cold porcelain of the toilet for a long time as tears wet my face. The first time I shit, I shit deep and ugly things and the water blushed with the color of my blood. I tried watching the television but it enraged me and I was afraid I would kick the tube in. I didn't even know for sure what was bothering me. Outside of Mosul, when the team gathered for a moment, the CO must have seen something in my look. He yelled at me, his breath hot on my face, "Get over it. It happens." OK, that's true. But often in the hotel room, I felt unmanly and would have to hold myself in check. Just deal with it. Then my mind would start to slip, free-associate itself into recollection, and what I recollected gave me peace, the sanity of calculation, the adjustment of elevation, the consideration of wind speed and humidity, the calm breaths, the smooth trigger pull.

Tactically I'd never made a mistake unless you count the one time I had to take two shots in a row and had forgotten to breathe. That time the pressure blowback from the muzzle-break burst the blood vessels in my eyes. Still, I'd killed both targets, a radioman and a driver, and with the driver the bullet continued through the engine block and disabled the vehicle he was driving. Or if you count the last shot—but that wasn't a tactical mistake. Maybe I should have used the IR to calculate the distance—but I never used the IR. Or maybe I should have taken a head shot—but I never took head shots. Why do it with the .50, when the .50 destroys people? A marksman is pragmatic. My job is to kill with one shot. Nothing fancy. I have nothing to prove. The chest is twice the size of the head.

I looked around the room, at the heavy flowered drapes. The two ashtrays overflowed with butts. I wouldn't let the staff clean the room because I didn't want them in there with me. That probably suited them fine too. There was a mirror. I stripped down in front of it. I was emaciated, my ribs sticking close to the skin, my hipbones pointy, but also I looked strong, every muscle lean and taut: my arms now in comparison to the thinness at my waist—I looked like a welterweight, my legs thin and as strong as steel cables. My hands and face were dark red like a mask and gloves on my pale body. I drank Scotch and looked at the flex of my arm as I did so. I could see the split muscle of the bicep and the ripple of muscles in my forearm. I cupped two hands as if holding an infant, flexed my abdominal muscles.

I knew that I was naked but it wasn't the lack of my clothing, it was the lack of a load-bearing harness, my equipment, and the .50 caliber rifle I carried, a rifle as heavy as Buzz when I carried him soaking wet from the tub and had to get to the hospital.

I raised my hands up as if I were shooting a rifle off-hand, like my buddy Johnson had to do that one day in school, and imagined how the .50 would have flattened me if I'd ever shot it that way, while the bullet—the bullet would pass through the wall and into the next room and through the next wall and room, however many there were, and through the exterior of the building, concrete and brick notwithstanding, and into the building across the street.

I laughed and noticed my glass was empty. I looked for the bottle of Scotch. It too was empty. I called down to room service. The woman's voice was very polite. Twenty long minutes later I heard a knock at the door. I slid a tip under the door and said leave it there. I waited a minute or two and then opened the door. I took the bottle and closed the door again. I didn't know for sure whose idea this furlough was, but certainly it was a potent version of hell. And at the same time my only real fear was that it would end.

Two day later there was a knock at the door. I don't know how long it might have been going on before I heard it.

"Just leave it there," I said. That was all I ever said and I didn't even know if I'd ordered something or not.

The knock came again, harder this time, and I panicked and tried to remember the date and how long I'd been there. I thought I'd overstayed and they were kicking me out. "Come back later," I yelled. I was having trouble standing straight and pitched around the room as I walked to the door. I leaned against it. The knock came again, and now I was sure that the knocking was a hallucination. Ridiculously, I said, "There's no one here."

"There's a friend of mine in there," I heard through the door.

I yelled at the door, "Go away." And then I thought about what the voice had said. Who would say something like that? I had no idea. I opened the door. It had a safety lock on it still, so I only opened it a crack.

Outside was a big guy in civilian clothes. When he turned to face me it took me a second to recognize him, it was so crazy that he should be there. It was Mac, an old friend of mine from the San Diego ICP. "I'm here to bring you home, buddy," he said.

I shut the door and took off the safety latch and opened the door again. There were probably a lot of things I wanted to say to him, ask him why he was there and such, but I didn't say anything. I was in shock. I was standing there naked for one thing and didn't notice it. He came in, looked at me up and down, and didn't say anything though his face told me plenty. I must have looked like death warmed over.

Then he took me in his arms and held me. He was sturdy and fat and I didn't realize I'd been cold, but he was warm. I thought that this was a good time to let something out, but I thought about it just like that and there was nothing. And then I thought about Mac, holding me like that, wanting to achieve something and failing, and I thought that he was truly a strong man and a great one.

Then he let me go and scanned the room. He went to the bathroom and turned on the shower. "Get in there," he said. "And then put some fucking clothes on."

As the hot water pounded my head, I heard Mac's low muffled voice on the phone. I stayed in the shower, not because it felt good, but because I knew that when I came out, I'd have to talk and I had nothing to say.

When I turned off the water, Mac handed my blue suit in to me. I put on the trousers and a T-shirt. Mac had the bed I'd been sleeping in made—more or less—and the bottles and garbage moved around so that most of it was on the table and the long dresser in front of the mirror.

Two room service guys came up and Mac met them at the door. Mac brought in the coffee tray, tossed the plastic bag on the floor and set an ironing board up against the wall. Then he closed the door and held an iron.

"What's that for?" I asked him.

"For your whites," he said. He set the iron on the table. "We'll drink coffee first and then we're going to clean up this mess."

"I don't need whites," I said.

"You will."

We drank our coffee in silence. "I appreciated you calling me," I said. It was a horrible effort to refer to it. I meant an incredible phone call I'd gotten while I was in the field. He'd done that, so I didn't even bother asking him how he knew I was here.

"I had good intelligence I thought you needed to have," he said.

"Yes, I needed to have it, Mac," I said. I couldn't talk about it another moment. Not another fucking moment. I stared into the coffee. I didn't know what to do.

"You got out all right?"

"Yes," I said. "We walked through a killing field at the end, Mac. A whole battalion of dead. Those stories are true."

"I know they are," he said.

Mac poured me another cup of coffee and another for himself. Then he went to the phone and got room service again. When he got off the phone, he said, "Assholes."

"They were all dry and wasted and they were trying to get away. They were all moving in the same direction," I said.

"You don't have to tell me about it," he said.

Mac thought I was telling him the worst of it. I wasn't. I was telling him the best. Mac was very kind to me and didn't press and after we'd drunk some more coffee, he got me out of my chair and told me to iron my whites. After, we were going out. I was in no mood to go out.

"Still you're going," he said. Then he went to my duffle and pulled out my white uniform—this came from a pack that I'd put together before I'd left that miraculously found its way from Coronado and onto the C-141 and into the cab and into the hotel. When I'd packed that uniform, I'd thought I would be buried in it. He threw the whites on the bed. Then he took the garbage bag and started to throw the empty bottles and old food that was still lying around and everything else he could find into it. There was nothing for me to do, so I picked up the shirt and looked at it. Then I opened the ironing board and began to iron, working the hot metal over the dense white cloth, and watched as the wrinkles disappeared.

"I think I'd like a haircut," I said.

"In short order," Mac said.

The hotel had a barbershop and Mac called for an appointment. We drank another cup of coffee and took the elevator to the lobby. If you have ever sat in a barber chair after a war, you will know what I'm talking about. I don't know how I got through it exactly, but afterwards I felt the kind of relief you feel after a terrifying ride is over. And as the barber used a mirror to show me the back of my head, I looked at myself, the hair shaved around the side and slicked down at the top, the slick skin of my cheeks and chin gleaming with aftershave, the red face and the eyes, the dark sockets and burst vessels.

Mac and I ate at the buffet. Mac had the prime rib and I had fish. We drank beer. The next day we caught a flight back to the States.

Mac flew with me all the way to Dallas. We mostly didn't talk, but somewhere in there he brought up the girl from what seemed like so long ago back in Coronado, the one he was going to fix me up with. I'd met her once. Her name was Sarah.

"She's still interested, you know," Mac said.

"Maybe, sometime," I said, but I knew I was lying. I'd never see her. I'd done a strange thing as I marched along in the dark and she was part of it. She was important to me. I'd fantasized about her as I walked. Nothing sexual, just simple things like sitting in church together. I knew I'd never want to see her.

In the Dallas airport, Mac handed me my bag, which he'd been carrying. He told me to go into the bathroom and put the whites on.

"I don't think I want to do that," I said.

"That's why I didn't ask you," he said.

"It's an order, then?"

"If it has to be," he said.

I went in and stripped down and put on the whites I'd folded so carefully. Then I came back out. Mac walked with me to the gate where I had to catch a bus for my connecting flight. Mac took my shoulders in his two hands. "This is it, buddy," he said.

"Yes," I said.

On the little plane I took to Fort Smith, I had too much time to think. Even a second is too long. A second is how much time it takes a .50 caliber bullet to travel 600 meters, and what a lot of people don't know is that as that bullet passes the focal plane there is a momentary ghost image as the bullet disrupts the air above the target. That's just science, but I could see it through the scope and it looks like a soul, a soul that departs the body before the bullet strikes.

I got in the habit of not using the IR because IR can be detected. I'd never needed IR before. With the man and the woman kneeling there with the machine gun, I couldn't see anything straight to set the split image on. She was so lumpy. Still, I used the split image. But what did it matter? I was going to shoot the man in the chest. I'd gotten in the habit of shooting men in the chest. If the .50 takes a shoulder, the man still dies from the shock. A .50 caliber bullet is more powerful at 600 meters than a .460 Weatherby Magnum is at the muzzle. The Weatherby is an elephant gun. The .50 caliber blows men apart.

When I got off the plane there was a crowd waiting for departing passengers and when they saw me in my dress whites come down they parted and I walked through. No one knew what I'd done. They were showing respect for the uniform. Then I felt a hand on my shoulder. I started and drew back a fist. It was my father.

"Son," he said. He must have seen the tears wetting my eyes. "Let's get you home," he said.

The familiar streets we drove down looked bizarre, like places I'd known in a dream. My father drove his new car—a Japanese car that must have really set everyone to talking. "What did they have you on to over there?" he asked.

I probably shouldn't have said, but I remembered a time a long time ago. This was after I'd come back with Buzz from the hospital in Dallas where we needed a special plastic surgeon, and after Pinky had let me go. My father called me one day and said he had a problem with his plumbing. He met me outside his house. He took the grate from the side of the house and climbed into the crawl space. I handed through the toolbox and followed. We crawled along, ducking the girders and the joists. He led with the flashlight. I brought along the tools. I noticed we were passing the bathroom, but I only got suspicious when we passed the kitchen at the north end of the house. Finally he got down into the far corner and rolled onto one elbow.

I said, "Dad, why are we here? We're not here to fix the plumbing, are we?"

"Son, what are you going to do?"

"About what?" I asked. I really didn't know what he was talking about.

He said, "About your life."

He laid the flashlight down and its light faded off into the dark corner of the house, and all at once I saw that he was exactly right.

He said, "I've already talked to your mother, and we would be willing to take the kids."

He'd been in the Navy and he recommended ships.

So as we were driving, I looked out the window and it wasn't as if I couldn't tell him. The road was flat and straight and we were passing barren fields. "They had me on to killing people," I said. He turned the car, passing a stop sign that had for so many years of my childhood been the boundary of my experience—the end of our street.

We were getting close to home and he slowed the car. "I'm sure you done us proud," he said.

"Yes, I think so," I said.

We pulled into the driveway and up to the closed garage door. My father made no move to open the door. I didn't either. We stared at the yellow garage door.

"Your mother's not going to want to know that," he said.

"Yes, sir. I know."

"I'll tell her something. Don't you worry about it."

"Yes, sir," I said. We stepped out of the car and walked to the door. My mother's face showed in the window for a second, and then I knew she was moving toward the door.

No one knows how long a second is better than I do. A lot can happen in a second. A .50 caliber bullet can travel 600 meters. My mother can stand up and look out the window. A woman can stand up. I was a student of psychology. I had to be able to anticipate movements. What will the target do? I need to deal with that second, you see, as the bullet speeds toward its target at 3,000 feet per second, carrying with it over 5,000 foot-pounds of energy concentrated on a single point. When the machine-gunner heard the sound down the street, the SEALs pinned in the doorways, he did something great, just what he needed to do, he stood up to get a better look. That makes total sense even though it ended up being really stupid for him. I don't hesitate. He stood up, and I was happy he did. I had a job to do.

And in the time it takes to be smashed by the recoil and realign optical relief, a woman can stand up, a girl who was only lumpy before, and just as the bullet disrupts the air in the focal plane above her, I see her face.

I had every tactical imperative to look through that scope. Tactically, there was no good reason for her to stand up. That's a lack of training. She had no reason to stand up. I don't think there was a reason.

Then I heard the locks on the door. If you want to talk about a situation in which I didn't know what would happen next, this was it. It was like dying might be—that's all I can think of. You don't have a choice. The soul leaves the body, and you just do it. You just walk on and through the door and see your family there, sitting around waiting for you to get there, Buzz who I let fall getting up and standing at attention like my father told him to do that, but holding his ground, and Patsy who I'd yelled at looking over, looking so much like my ex-wife, Delia, and put off maybe because I'm getting the attention and wondering what the big deal is, and Ruby, my baby, she's so big—so big already. My mother smoothes my shoulder and says, "Well, don't you just look fine." I can't look at her. And aside from her, no one coming close. My children keeping their distance.

"Well, leave him alone then," my father says. "He's awfully tired and would like to get cleaned up some." And then he turns. "Buzz," he orders.

Buzz comes out from behind the couch and stands front and center to me, his left eyelid sagging where the scar tissue restricts the movement of the lid, that one eye hanging more open than the other as he looks up at me. He says, "Welcome home, sir."

contributors

Charles Baxter

Charles Baxter is the author of four novels, most recently *Saul and Patsy*, four books of stories, a volume of poetry, and one of criticism, *Burning Down the House*. He lives in Minneapolis and teaches at the University of Minnesota.

Kola Boof

Born in Omdurman, Sudan, to an Arab Egyptian father and a blue-black Gisi-Waaq mother, Kola Boof was orphaned at the age of eight when her parents were murdered in her presence for the crime of speaking out against slavery in Sudan. With the help of UNICEF North Africa, Boof was eventually placed for adoption with a Black American family in Washington, D.C., and raised thereafter in the United States.

As an adult, Kola Boof returned to North Africa and began her career as a writer and anti-slavery activist, publishing the 1997 poetry collection *Every Little Bit Hurts* in North Africa and Europe. Immediately, Boof received death threats from such notable world figures as Hasan al Turabi, Osama Bin Laden and Gamal Ibrahim, all of whom complained about the strong anti-Arab, anti-Muslim sentiments in her work. These threats escalated for years, culminating in the January 2003 firebombing of Boof's publisher in Morocco, which forced her books out of print altogether. In spring 2003, a report on the floor of the United Nations confirmed that a fatwa death sentence had been issued against Boof's life by a sharia court in her native Sudan. In 2004, Boof will release her memoirs, *Diary of a Lost Girl*, in the United States, Japan, Germany, Belgium, and the UK. Boof is the mother of two sons and was pregnant with a third child as this book went to press.

"One thing I wanted to do was dispel the notion that I hate Arab people. People forget that I myself am half-Arab. So the idea of a lonely, young black woman artist, finding her muse in a hungry, young Arab immigrant who seems to genuinely love her, although she can't be sure, was exciting to me.

It's partly the story of my own real-life love affair with a white Jewish businessman in the 1990s and then it's partly my attempt to show how social loneliness and feelings of powerlessness can move us to create our own Gods...a God, who in Noelle's case causes her to dream up the perfect idol...and Gods, who in the case of the 9-11 attackers cause us to crash planes into buildings. I have always suspected that love is the drug that causes humanity to create a God in the first place, and this story allowed me to make an attempt at touching on that.

While I finished the story thinking it was about humanity's loneliness, my agent read it and claimed that it was about the inability of humans to control love, and then still, my brother says it's a story about spiritual greed. So at least I know it's a scat melody...meaning different things to different people."

K. Kvashay-Boyle

K. Kvashay-Boyle is a student at the Iowa Writers' Workshop. Her work appears in *McSweeney's*, *Best of McSweeney's*, and *Best American Non-Required Reading, 2003*.

Von Do

Von Do is an artist with a very specific agenda who manages to stumble into everything that he has been involved in. Von studied design at The Fashion Institute of Design and Merchandising in Los Angeles, but soon after decided that there was more meaning for him in the fine arts. He began painting in 1991 and has been ever since. Von believes passionately in balancing work and play, the importance of history, and the understanding of self. He lives in Los Angeles and spends far too much time restoring his car, motorcycle, and truck. http://von.fumanchu.com

Doug Dorst

Doug Dorst is a lecturer in creative writing at Stanford University. He holds an MFA from the Iowa Writers' Workshop and a JD from UC Berkeley. His short fiction has appeared in *Ploughshares*, *The Atlantic*

Unbound, *McSweeney's #9* and *#11*, *Epoch*, and other journals. His first novel, *Alive in Necropolis*, is forthcoming from Nan A. Talese/Doubleday.

"Many people have written eloquently about the dangers of giving in to helplessness. Helplessness begets hopelessness and apathy, which invite the people who've made you feel helpless in the first place to keep doing what they're doing. I have nevertheless *felt* helpless from time to time as the events of the last two years have unfolded. I wanted to explore that feeling in a story, and 'Jumping Jacks' is the result."

Marcel Dzama

Marcel Dzama is a twenty-nine-year-old artist from Winnipeg, Canada. His work can be seen in various McSweeney's publications and through the David Zwirner Gallery.

Alicia Erian

Alicia Erian's first collection of short stories, *The Brutal Language of Love*, is out in paperback from Random House. Her first novel, *Welcome to the Moral Universe*, will be published by Simon & Schuster in 2004. Her stories have appeared most recently in *Zoetrope: All Story*, *Playboy*, *The Sun*, *The Iowa Review*, *Nerve*, and *Index*. She lives in Brooklyn.

"I had previously written a failed story using the character of Mr. Roback, and decided to resuscitate him for this piece. I hate to waste a character. So that was part of my inspiration, along with the final year of my marriage, and the protests my husband and I attended during that time. He was a much better protester than I was. He went more regularly, had more fervor, made great signs.

I always think it's interesting, the conflict of opinion that often exists between those who have served in the military and those who haven't. One time I had this vet cab driver, and he pointed out the window and said, 'Look at that kid. He's protesting the war.' I could've said, 'Hey, I protested the war, too,' but I didn't. A vet can always shut a protester up. This was another part of my inspiration."

Brian Gage

Brian Gage was born and raised in Youngstown, Ohio. His degree in business from Ohio State was the catalyst for his political satire writings, as it opened his eyes to the policies and tactics used by corporations to interfere with markets, rape the Third World, rip off the Pentagon system, and keep U.S. citizens ignorant to all of the above. Today, Brian lives in Hollywood, writing and studying U.S. foreign policy. He is also author of *Snark Inc.—A Corporate Fable*, *The Amazing Snox Box*, and *The Saddest Little Robot*.

"The text portion of the story was inspired by the Malcolm X quote, 'You show me a capitalist and I'll show you a blood sucker.' The rest spawned from the Iraq invasion and the media's stranglehold on the information coming back from the war. During which I was amazed at how ignorant the American public was about the truth of the U.S. actions, and found it hard to believe they could celebrate and approve of the Bush administration's murderous agenda—must be the glowing blue globes they're staring into...I consider the story to be a cautionary tale, as once the plutocracy in this country realizes they've used all the other people and resources of the world, there will only be one place left to feast—the ignorant people within their own borders."

Ben Greenman

Ben Greenman is an editor at *The New Yorker* and the author of *Superbad* and *Superworse*. His fiction has appeared in *The Mississippi Review* and *The Paris Review*. He lives in Brooklyn.

"I can't say that I have a huge interest in Superman and the villains who tried to kill/embarrass him, but I have an ongoing moderate interest, same as any other American man. Mr. Mxyztplk was always the strangest villain, in that his misdeeds weren't particularly violent or aggressive—they were more subversive—and in that they were reversible. This seemed like a good prism through which to view the events of the last few years, partly as a way of counterweighting their horror, and partly as a way of foregrounding it. Also, it let me settle some old romantic scores."

Nasri Hajjaj

Nasri Hajjaj is a poet and writer, born in Ain el-Hilwe, a Palestinian refugee camp. He holds a BA in philosophy and psychology from Beirut Arab University and an MA from Middlesex Polytechnic, UK. He has worked as a journalist in Beirut, London, Cyprus, and Tunis.

Otis Haschemeyer

Otis Haschemeyer has an MFA from the University of Arkansas and was the recipient of a Stegner Fellowship from Stanford University. His work has appeared in numerous journals and been anthologized in the *Best New American Voices 2003*. He is at work on a novel.

Keith Knight

Keith Knight is a cartoonist and rapper living in San Francisco. His two comic strips, *the K Chronicles* and *(th)ink*, can be found in better publications across the nation. His semi-conscious hip-hop band, the Marginal Prophets, will kick your ass. www.kchronicles.com

Paul LaFarge

Paul LaFarge is the author of *Haussman, or The Distinction: a Novel* and *The Artist of the Missing*. He lives in Brooklyn.

Mark Lee

Mark Lee's critically acclaimed novel *The Canal House* was published in May 2003 by Algonquin Books. A former correspondent for the *London Telegraph*, he currently writes on international issues for *The Atlantic Monthly* and the *Los Angeles Times*. Mr. Lee's first novel, *The Lost Tribe*, was published by Picador USA. His play, *California Dog Fight*, premiered at the Manhattan Theater Club and the Bush Theater in London. He serves as a delegate to International PEN's Writers in Prison Committee.

Tsaurah Litzky

Tsaurah Litzky is a frequent contributor to the *Best American Erotica* series. A former newspaper columnist, she is also a fiction writer and poet. *Baby on the Water—New and Selected Poems* was recently published by Long Shot Press. Her novella *The Motion of the Ocean* is due out in June 2004 from Simon & Schuster as part of a series of novellas edited by Susie Bright. Tsaurah teaches erotic writing and erotic literature at the New School. She can see the Statue of Liberty from every window of her apartment on the Brooklyn waterfront.

"I used to also be able to see the World Trade Center from the windows of my apartment. I was away when the tragedy happened, came back two days later to a sky of smoldering fires, metallic ashes, and black clouds. That weekend the parties started. Ex-smokers started smoking again. People couldn't stop drinking and holding each other.

The erotic writing class I teach began for the fall term. For the first time in years it was filled up. During introductions almost everyone said they just wanted to have some fun. The beginning of this story was part of an in-class writing exercise. At home I thought I would expand it to a story about lubrication tentatively titled "Luberama," but then the hermaphrodites showed up. "End-of-the-World Sex" pretty accurately reflects my feelings and my perceptions of the world around me at that time."

Mistress Morgana

Mistress Morgana is a professional dominatrix and sex educator in San Francisco. More information is available on her website, www.mistressmorgana.com.

"Somewhere between the reality of my life as a professional dominatrix (I am a safe, sane, and consensual player who approaches SM from a place of health and respect) and the fantasy of the potential of my job (I'd love to beat the crap out of John Aschroft) lies the inspiration for "All in a Day's Work."

"While I am bound by the ethics of my profession to maintain strict confidence for my clientele, in a fiction anthology I wanted to create an all-star client database filled with the kinky exploits of news and policymakers.

"The format of my piece is real; professional dominants keep notes on our clientele to assist us in session planning, and it is a standard convention that these notes are filed by the first name and birthday of the client to protect his or her privacy and to help create a level of distinction among all the Johns, Steves, and Ricks that come through our door. The tenor and tone of the session notes are authentic, as is the language used to describe the content of an SM scene (a glossary is provided at the end of the article to help clear up any confusion about acronyms)."

Andrew Nielsen

Andrew Nielsen is an English major at Stanford University who draws a political comic strip *27th Street* for the campus newspaper, the *Stanford Daily*. When he's not inventing new characters or chuckling at his own bizarre jokes, he moonlights as a rapper who goes by the name MC Lars Horris. Andrew was honored to collaborate with Sparrow on "Duct Soup" for this anthology.

Stewart O'Nan

Stewart O'Nan was born in Pittsburgh, educated in Boston, worked on Long Island as an engineer, and then went back to Cornell to write. He taught for a while, but now is just writing. If you've never read anything by him, try his first novel, *Snow Angels*.

"One summer morning while I was walking on the beach in Rhode Island, I imagined what it must be like for Salman Rushdie to deal with the fatwah, and then, imagining him walking on the beach like me, I imagined the uncelebrated man who was charged with watching him, and I thought: well, isn't that kind of like Gatsby? I ran back to the cottage and wrote a draft of the story in one long sitting."

ZZ Packer

ZZ Packer is the author of *Drinking Coffee Elsewhere*. Her stories have appeared in *Harper's, The New Yorker, The Paris Review, Ploughshares,* and *Zoetrope: All-Story* and have been anthologized in *Best American Stories* and *Best American Non-Required Reading*.

David Rees

David Rees is the author of *Get Your War On* (www.getyourwaron.com), *My New Fighting Technique Is Unstoppable*, and *My New Filing Technique Is Unstoppable*. He lives in New York with his wife.

Peter Rock

Peter Rock was born and grew up in Salt Lake City, Utah. He is the author of the novels *The Ambidextrist*, *Carnival Wolves*, and *This Is the Place*. New projects are under way and may or may not become visible.

Jim Shepard

Jim Shepard is the author of the forthcoming novel *Project X* (Knopf, 2004) and story collection *Love and Hydrogen* (Vintage, 2004). He teaches at Williams College and in the Warren Wilson MFA program, and lives in

Williamstown with his wife, two sons, and tiny tiny daughter.

"'Dade County, November 2000' was the product of a longstanding literary fascination and a sudden need to vent about this great country of ours. The longstanding fascination was with the emotional and thematic premise of Conrad's *Lord Jim*: the idea of having to live for the rest of one's life with the knowledge of having devastatingly exposed one's self—dismantled one's self, really—by a single act resulting from a loss of nerve. I needed to vent because of my helpless rage at the timorousness of the Democrats and most of the media in the face of the Florida grotesqueries surrounding the election of 2000: from the butterfly ballots to the *Wall Street Journal*'s 'bourgeois riot' to the Supreme Court's principled decision. The Lord Jim parallel—all of us standing there at the moment of truth, and not answering the bell, and having to pay for it with shame and mortification for the rest of our lives—seemed, at that point, surprisingly and dismally appropriate."

Sparrow

Sparrow lives in Phoenicia, a hamlet in the Catskill Mountains. He studies French once a week with a Swiss woman named Claude. His daughter, Sylvia, is an actress, poet, and eleven-year-old. His wife, Violet Snow, is a photographer. *Yes, You ARE a Revolutionary!*, his recent self-help book, is at www.softskull.com.

"I was lying in bed one morning in March, and thought of the phrase 'Duct Soup.' Some writer has already used this pun, and parodied the Marx Brothers engaged in duct tape-plastic sheet hysteria, I decided. Then I wrote the dialogue anyway—because I heard Chico's 'Italian' accent in my mind, and Groucho's tart, oblique replies."

Anthony Swofford

Anthony Swofford is the author of *Jarhead: A Marine's Chronicle of the Gulf War and Other Battles* (Scribner, 2003). He teaches in the MFA program at Saint Mary's College in Moraga, California, and lives in Oakland. He's at work on a novel.

Elizabeth Tallent

Elizabeth Tallent is a professor in the creative writing program at Stanford University. Previously, she taught at the Iowa Writers' Workshop and the University of California, Davis. She is the author of a novel, *Museum Pieces*, and three short-story collections, *In Constant Flight*, *Time with Children*, and *Honey*, as well as a study of John Updike's fiction, *Married Men and Magic Tricks*. Her work has appeared in various publications and anthologies including *The New Yorker, Harper's, The Paris Review*, and *The Best American Short Stories*.

Nick Taylor

Nick Taylor is the recipient of a Dean's Fellowship for Excellence from the Creative Writing Program at the University of Virginia. He lives in Charlottesville with his wife and daughter.

Michelle Tea

Michelle Tea is the author of *The Passionate Mistakes and Intricate Corruption of One Girl in America* (Semiotext(e), 1998), the Lambda Award-winning novel *Valencia* (Seal Press, 2000), and the recent memoir *The Chelsea Whistle*, which was selected by the *San Francisco Chronicle* as one of the top 100 books of 2002. 2004 will see the publication of her collected poetry, *The Beautiful* (Manic D Press), an edited anthology of writings documenting the female experience of growing up poor, *Without a Net* (Seal Press), and *Thrills Pills Chills and Heartache*, a collection of edgy first-person narratives co-edited with Clint Catalyst (Alyson Press).

"Stephen Elliott asked me to be part of a special reading, partly in honor of Lydia Lunch coming through town, partly to document, as writers, the shitty events of our world since September 11th. Being a writer who traffics exclusively in my own personal dramas, it took me a minute to get my head around writing about all the death and destruction happening so far away from my little world, in a landscape I'd probably never see—I couldn't fathom it. I couldn't speak to it. But I could talk about how Los Angeles responded to the attacks on the twin towers. Los Angeles was where I was living at the time and it's absurd on the dullest day, so the response to everything was trumped up and crazed, and delightful to document, especially against the backdrop of my own miserable existence in that worst of American cities."

Anne Ursu

Anne Ursu is the author of the novels *Spilling Clarence* and *The Disapparation of James*. Her books have both been Booksense 76 picks, and she has been nominated for a Bay Area Book Reviewers Award and has won a Minnesota Book Award. She and her husband live in Mountain View, California, and Minneapolis, Minnesota.

Amanda Eyre Ward

Amanda Eyre Ward was born in New York City and graduated from Williams College and the University of Montana. Her first novel, *Sleep Toward Heaven*, was published by MacAdam/Cage in 2003.

Joan Wilking

Joan Wilking's short fiction has appeared in *The Atlantic*, *The Mississippi Review*, *Other Voices*, *The MacGuffin*, *Pindeldyboz*, *Parting Gifts*, *The Barcelona Review,* and many other publications. Two of her stories have been finalists in *Glimmertrain*'s Very Short Fiction Contest. She lives in Ipswich, Massachusetts.

"In the fall of 2002 my thirteen-year-old daughter was asked to perform *My Short Skirt* in a production of Eve Ensler's *Vagina Monologues*. I had never seen Ensler's show before. Most of the monologues had some humor in them with the exception of the one dedicated to the women of Afghanistan. Throughout, an anonymous figure stood motionless draped in a burqa.

The same week my daughter performed in Ensler's play she started complaining about how much she disliked being in her school's Extended Learning Program. She didn't like the teacher who she said spent too much time making them do what she considered to be silly brainteasers. That set me to wondering—What if? And the result was 'Proper Dress.'"

F.S. Yu

F.S. Yu lives in San Francisco.

editors

Stephen Elliott

Stephen Elliott is the author of *Jones Inn*, *A Life Without Consequences*, and *What It Means to Love You*. His fourth novel, *The Night Face Up*, will be co-published by McSweeney's and MacAdam/Cage in February 2004. He lives in San Francisco and lectures at Stanford University.

Gabriel Kram

Gabriel Kram is a writer living in San Francisco.

Lizzy Brooks

Lizzy Brooks is from Baltimore and pronounces it without the t. If the opportunity arose, she would found the United Alliance of Strong Female Pirates, a band of women who pillage their lives for stories and curse like sailors. She would sail across the world and hoard experience as loot. Lizzy thanks the writers in the anthology for watching the news and the culture with critical compassion. She thinks that good fiction is what keeps our feet planted when the world turns upside down.

Harriet Clark

Harriet is from New York City. After five years out West, she now loves California but still wishes people out here understood sarcasm. She is grateful to Stephen Elliott for this opportunity to involve herself in politics and activism. She also thanks her mom, who's written her a letter a week for the last eighteen years and has taught her everything she knows about what words can do.

Anna Rimoch

Anna Rimoch is from Mexico City. She likes frozen mangoes and the word "warfully" in Paul Lafarge's story. Anna would like to thank the Association for the Preservation of Jellyfish, all of the Muñuñus (especially the three Muñus and the Mu), the Society for the Emancipation of Trees, the white Eminem for affording this opportunity, and finally, her right hand and all those who have held it.

Jenny Zhang

Jenny routinely brags about the time she wrote a story about a naughty rooster in second grade and the principal read it over the school's loudspeaker for its superb moral content. But after having read the stories in this anthology, she is considering shelving that pride of hers for good.

acknowledgments

Thanks to the editors and the writers who put us in touch with the writers in this collection. They include Andrew Snee at *The Sun*, Padma Viswanathan, Cathi Hanauer, Daniel Jones, Katharine Weber, Chris Raymond at *GQ*, Paul Reidinger at *The San Francisco Bay Guardian*, Charles Baxter, Susie Bright editor of *The Best American Erotica*, Eli Horowitz and Dave Eggers at McSweeney's. Also David Poindexter for agreeing to publish this anthology at great cost and great risk and Anika Streitfeld and Kate Nitze, the editors at MacAdam/Cage responsible for shepherding this project through to completion.